Be sure to read Shari Shatt

Cally Wilde novel from Pocket Books

LOADED

"Exploding like a string of firecrackers let loose beneath one's feet, Shattuck's debut novel keeps the reader deliciously on edge. Raw action collides with secrets and family conflicts as one of the most vivid heroines to hit the shelves recently tries to discover who wants her dead. . . . Cally's voice spins a siren's call that, combined with Shattuck's electric pacing, will keep readers glued to this novel."

—*Publishers Weekly*

"*Loaded* is just that—loaded with emotion, sexual tension, greed, familial rivalry, and jealousy that all add up to a suspenseful, sexy tale."

—Thebestreviews.com

"I didn't want to stop reading and it kept me guessing. . . . There's enough sexual tension between [Cally and Detective Evan Paley] to heat Cally's expansive home, with some wattage left over to take care of the swimming pool."

—mysteryreader.com

"Crackling with repressed sexual desire, so much so that one should use potholders while reading this book. There are so many suspects with viable motives that readers will go crazy trying to figure out who the perpetrator is. . . . [This] has the making of a great series."

—allreaders.com

Lethal is also available as an eBook

Also by Shari Shattuck:

Loaded

Lethal

Shari Shattuck

New York London Toronto Sydney

An *Original* Publication of POCKET BOOKS

DOWNTOWN PRESS, published by Pocket Books
1230 Avenue of the Americas
New York, NY 10020

ISBN: 978-0-7434-6385-0   ISBN: 0-7434-6385-4

First Downtown Press trade paperback edition June 2005

10 9 8 7 6 5 4 3 2 1

DOWNTOWN PRESS and colophon are trademarks of Simon & Schuster, Inc.

Manufactured in the United States of America

Designed by Jaime Putorti

For information regarding special discounts for bulk purchases, please contact Simon & Schuster Special Sales at 1-800-456-6798 or business@simonandschuster.com

Acknowledgments

Thank you, Amy, for being a huge part of this book and my work. Thank you, Paul, for always encouraging me in such a positive way. Thank you, Joseph, for your constant love and support. And thank you, Caleb and Creason, for your many interruptions that balance work with a wonderful life. Finally, thanks to the many hardworking people at Simon and Schuster who made the book happen. I've never met you but I know you're out there!

For my dad, who said,
"No matter what you choose to do,
you'll do it well,"
and made me believe it.

Lethal

Chapter 1

Through the silver rain dripping from the rim of my umbrella our eyes connected with a sharp magnetic click.

Boom.

I couldn't look away, didn't want to. He was gorgeously Japanese, tall and slim, about forty, dressed in a flawless black suit with a long overcoat. His straight dark hair had a deep glossiness that women would kill for, cut so that the front was long, meeting the shorter hair in the back, and moved over his brow in a sexy sweep as he walked with a smooth, sure, long-legged gait, with his black flashers fixed on my blue ones.

Ooh baby.

I entertained an arousing picture of him moving underneath me with that same grace, his hands firmly on my hips, mine pressed against his smooth bare chest, or sunk in that thick luxurious mane to give me a handhold, traction. If I hadn't been walking, I would have crossed my legs.

We were fifteen paces away and about to pass each other. Still his eyes held me, smiling a secret between us, and I felt that thrilling hook of a sexual jolt that I love so much, but that happens so rarely. I returned the smile knowingly and then continued past him and on into the open doorway of the bookstore, where I lowered my umbrella and shook off the rain.

I thought, He's watching me, waiting for me to turn. Arching my back just enough to accentuate my curves and opening my raincoat to reveal them, I turned flirtatiously and looked up.

But he was gone. Nasty little shock to my ego. Most likely he'd disappeared into one of the second-floor restaurants in the Little Tokyo Plaza in downtown L.A. Damn. Oh well. My dark green umbrella stood out from the several common black ones when I leaned it next to the door and turned to search for treasure in the Japanese-American bookstore.

I browsed in and out of the aisles for at least thirty minutes, picking out the biggest, most expensive picture books as well as some sexy paperback comics, selecting one with a sharp-eyed, dark-haired hero that reminded me of Evan. I flipped through a few pages and admired the artwork—the hero with a gun, the hero with a sexy half-naked blonde. Smiling to myself, I thought, It *is* us, and I anticipated showing it to him that evening. Turning another page I saw an illustration where the heroine stood over the body of a bad guy with a smoking gun, and I thought of how I had met Evan that way. Except I had been the one with the smoking gun.

But a glance at my watch told me that if I was going to make it back to the courthouse on time I had to get going, so I handed over six hundred–odd dollars in cash and was bowed out of the store by the happy manager. The package, wrapped with twine, was heavy. He offered to help me carry it to my car, but I responded with one of my usual smart-ass replies that I was still young and strong and heaved it up. Trying to look as though it were easy to handle, I went outside. To my left, under the same awning was a jewelry store with a smart Bulgari watch in the window. I went in and inquired about it. Stainless steel, black face, diamonds. The first thing the shopgirl did was to tell me the price.

I hate that.

Turning away from the counter dismissively I perused a display case by the window. I glanced up over it, and through the rain-speckled glass of the storefront I saw the handsome man again. He was listening with polite attention to the female half of a wealthy-looking couple. The way he held his body spoke of elegant well-earned confidence and subtle sensuality. He knew I was there because as he bowed his good-byes to the departing couple, his eyes pierced the glass and space between us, and he stood for a moment with that same heated smile. I regarded him with an intimate gaze, an unspoken acknowledgment of our mutual attraction, and then he bowed and moved away.

I sighed, thought of Evan, wondered if I could ever really give up hunting, and then I went back to the shopgirl, who had made the mistaken assumption that I could not afford the watch I had asked about. I made an obvious motion of pushing back my hair so that my sleeve would fall down and reveal the Patek Philippe watch I was wearing, a little twenty-thousand-dollar birthday bauble from Evan. As her eyes spotted it, I watched her whole attitude change from contempt to one of simpering attendance.

I hate that too.

"Would you like to see the Bulgari?" she asked, all smiles and sweetness.

"Sure," I said, disinterested now. I tried it on, watching her eye the Patek when I put it on the counter. She was checking to see if it was real. It was. "How much did you say this was again?" I asked, ribbing her now.

"Five thousand, seven hundred dollars." A look of avid expectiation on her face.

"Mmm." I took it off, wrinkled my nose a little distastefully, and said, "Is that all?" Then I smiled brightly at her surprised look and turned to go. I would buy the watch from someone who respected me.

I regretted my flippancy at not accepting help carrying the books as soon as the weight of the awkward bundle bit into my palm where I grasped the rough cord. I was wondering how I was going to handle the books with one hand while holding the umbrella with the other as I retrieved the latter from the damp bin outside the door. I set the package down on the last bit of dry ground under the awning, and holding the umbrella by the handle, I pressed my thumb on the button. It opened like a tiny parachute. Though the umbrella unfolded, the note that was in it did not. It fell to the white tile at my feet.

Trying not to look too obvious, I scanned around for a sign of whoever might have secreted a note but saw no one. Maybe it was just a receipt, dropped by mistake, and then again . . . I picked up the curiosity and placed it casually in the pocket of my Burberry mackintosh, lifted the books again, and headed out into the rain.

Back on the street I continued on through the clean, sparsely populated shopping area. I wondered if it was the rain that made the place feel so deserted. As I crossed a concrete bridge over a subterranean shopping level, I leaned out a bit to try to see what was down there.

What was down there was a girl, a man, and an ugly confrontation.

A large man, in an ill-fitting suit and a baggy overcoat, had backed a pretty Asian girl up against a wall in an awkward niche behind the curved stairs. No one on the same level with them could have seen the two, hidden as they were by the wall.

The girl was turning her head away from the man as he pressed against her, talking to her fast and angrily. I froze and looked all around me. Nobody. I backed up a few steps to the top of the stairway, keeping my eyes on what was happening below me. Neither of them had seen me. The stairway curved slightly, and I would be out of sight for a few seconds. I started down the stairs as noisily as possible. Hoping that it would scare the man away.

I coughed. I cleared my throat. I stamped down the stairs with purpose. Instead of going the obvious, straight way into the shopping tunnel I turned right into the little nook, which reeked of urine, and coughed loudly again. But even a few feet away the man seemed oblivious. He was so focused on the girl and spewing his anger at her that he didn't even seem to hear me. The girl's eyes, however, shot to me, and there was a plea in them. *Don't leave me,* they begged. Her face was pale with fear, and her features distorted, like a confused, trapped animal, but even so, she was stunningly beautiful.

The man noticed her glance and followed her gaze.

"Just keep going, it's none of your business," he snarled at me.

"See, it looks more like personal than business to me," I said. It was all I could think of.

"Keep walking, we're fine." He tried to smile. "Just a little disagreement, that's all. Isn't that right, sweetheart?" He shook the girl a little, prompting her to answer.

But I could see her answer as her eyes looked down between the two of them and then back up at me.

I was sweating now. The tension was palatable and getting more grotesque by the second. I couldn't walk away. I wanted to scream at him, shout what a disgusting piece of vomit he was. I hated him for thinking that his power was superior to mine, and for thinking he had the strength to overpower her.

Instead I stepped in, almost casually, and smiled in what I hoped was a disarming and polite way.

"How about it 'sweetheart'?" I directed at the girl. "You think you two can work this out without counseling?" I took one more step forward, and he released her arm. He was still blocking her in with his body.

She tried to speak, to buy some time, to keep me there.

"I don't know, I guess so." There was still terror in her eyes.

"My professional opinion," I ad-libbed, "would be that you need at least a weekend seminar. Possibly a seven-day retreat with some serious trust-building exercises." One more step, and I saw the gun in his oversized hand.

"Take a fucking hike!" the man growled at me, raising the gun toward me, to scare me. It worked. The girl saw him aim at me, and with a scream, she grabbed at the weapon; I knew that was a mistake. With the umbrella in my left hand I swung down even as his arm came up, trying to point the gun and both their hands toward the ground, knowing it was hopeless, that his arm was far stronger than the flimsy aluminum and nylon. The man grabbed the girl by the hair with his other hand and threw her toward me. I heard the gun go off, felt a pressure against my stomach as the girl screamed and hit me, shoving me—books, umbrella, and all—to the ground. My left hand flew up, and the back of it smashed against the concrete wall. In my abdomen I felt a sharp, stabbing pain. I've been hit, I thought. Oh God, I've been shot. I got a quick view of the man's pants as he jumped over us and ran up a narrow ramp toward the parking structure.

The gunshot brought out the shopkeepers. They hung there in the doorways, fascinated and afraid until they sorted out that the man running away was the threat; we were just interesting. They watched the two of us on the ground like they would a high-speed chase on live TV, drawn in yet completely detached. *Goddamn it. I don't want to die like this, with blank staring faces watching me like I was the evening news.*

The Asian girl was lying next to me rolled into a protective ball, stunned. She turned and looked first at my face and then at my stomach and my hands pressed tight against it; I was afraid that if I pulled them away I would start to bleed and never stop.

"Are you all right?" she asked quickly.

"I am the evening news," I breathed, staring up at the tiny

patch of sky I could see through the concrete structures. "I can't believe it," I added. The sky, I noticed, was the same color as the stone.

"What?" She sounded confused.

I turned my head and looked at her. "I don't know. I don't think so," I answered her question belatedly. "Can you get my cell phone out of my purse and call for help?"

She turned to one of the boutique girls who had ventured closer for a better view of the action and screamed at her in Japanese. Not one of my languages, Japanese, but I caught "911" at the end of it. The onlooker seemed shocked to be drawn into our movie. I mean, here she was, enjoying the entertainment, and suddenly a character from the drama had called her by name and barked an order at her. She reconciled herself to this new reality in a few seconds and took off back into her shop, to the phone I hoped.

Then the girl turned back to me; with her assailant gone she became a confident, capable woman. She took off her raincoat and rolled it up, putting it under my feet. Then she put her hands over mine and looked into my eyes.

"Let me see," she said.

I nodded. There was nothing else to do. I pulled my hands away.

"I don't see anything," she told me.

"Here," I gestured, pointing to where the pain was, low on my right side. Efficiently but gently, she pulled down the edge of my slacks, I was conscious of the rain, light now, falling on my bare skin.

"It's just a scratch," she said, "but it looks like a nasty bruise is coming up. Maybe some internal bleeding, we need to get you to a hospital."

"What?" I sputtered. "Where's the round?"

"I don't know," she said, shrugging, "maybe it bounced off you." She pulled the edges of my white mackintosh, now sadly limp and dingy, over me. Then she retrieved my dented umbrella and held it over my face.

Quite a crowd had gathered now, and I was disgusted to see several of them had video cameras running. What a world.

"By the way," said my capable nurse, "my name is Aya, Aya Aikosha."

"Nice to meet you, Aya. I'm Callaway Wilde."

"Thank you, Ms. Wilde." Her beautiful dark eyes searched mine. "That was very brave. Thank you."

"Oh, that." I dismissed it, for the second time that day thinking of the man who had tried to kill me a year ago and ended up dead on the sidewalk. "That was nothing." I waved a hand. "Call me Cally."

Chapter 2

I was sitting up in the ambulance, feeling much better in the knowledge that my skin didn't have any new holes in it, when an unmarked car pulled up with the lights flashing. Doors slammed, and across the damp street strode a man so striking and masculine my heart skipped a beat just to look at him. He walked straight to the door of the ambulance, flashed his detective's badge at the uniformed officer, and stepped up into the back of the ambulance.

"What the hell happened here?" His quiet anger shocked me. The detective put his strong hand under my chin, pulled my face up, and kissed me hard. It took my breath away.

His eyes flashed with heat. "Hi, honey, get some shopping done?"

"Oh, you know," I answered Evan, "just a few books, knick-knacks, slippers, and oh yeah, I almost bought a bullet." I felt some hot tears start to well up, but it was too late for that.

"I'm really glad you decided not to." He smiled softly, knowing me so well. "You okay?"

"I'm fine. I thought I got shot, but I guess I just took the corner of some heavy literature in the stomach."

"Some books get you right in the gut." He kissed me again. "Feel like walking, Cally?" he asked.

I looked to the paramedic, who shrugged. "Up to you," he said.

"Let's go take a look," Evan said.

He helped me down from the ambulance and kept his arm around me, holding tighter than usual. We walked in step back to the crime scene, and he whipped out the badge again, clipping it to his jacket pocket as he stepped up to his crumpled-looking downtown counterpart, a woman with a hard face and clumpy mascara.

He extended a hand. "Evan Paley, North Hollywood, do you mind if I look around?"

The makeup seemed to weigh down her lids suddenly as she eyed him narrowly. "Nadine Sewell, Rampart. What brings you downtown, Detective?" She had noted his protective arm on me, and I'm sure the question was pure form.

"Do you mind, Detective Sewell?" He leaned in and pretended to be secretive. "I'm trying to impress my girlfriend."

"Go right ahead, hell, impress me while you're at it. I can't make much sense of it." She sighed deeply. "This is a tough gig, the locals aren't very good at sharing."

"Locals?" Evan asked.

She smiled with one side of her mouth. "It's a cultural thing, I guess." One shoulder followed her mouth in a half shrug. "The Japanese-Americans around here don't trust us much."

"Go figure," commiserated Evan. I think I was the only one who caught the sarcasm. He turned to me. "They don't trust us."

"They're probably still sensitive about that internment camp thing," I said to Evan.

"Gun-shy, you think?" Shaking his head in false confusion, he repeated, "Go figure."

"I mean; we didn't trust *them,*" I said, expounding on a theme.

"What the hell are you talking about?" Detective Sewell asked.

"I don't know," said Evan as he raised a finger and pointed to the crime scene. "I'm going to 'go figure.'"

"You do that." It finally dawned on her that she was a bit slow on the pickup. She scowled and turned, taking two steps away from us.

"He shot at you," Evan said to me.

"Oh yes." My hand went to my stomach protectively.

"Did you shoot at him?" Evan's mouth twitched, and Detective Sewell's head whipped around.

"No . . . I don't *think* so," I said slowly, giving him the evil eye.

"Well, that's novel," quipped Evan.

I shifted my weight onto my left foot and came down hard on his small toe in his expensive loafer.

"Ow! Excuse me, running joke." He grimaced and then asked the eavesdropping detective, "Did you find the bullet?"

"Not just yet," Detective Sewell said sourly and wandered away to light a cigarette. Evan turned to me.

"Tell it."

So I did. Knowing he would want every detail, no matter how seemingly insignificant, I told him everything I could think to tell. He walked over to the books, which were sitting upright in the rain, and tilted the pile. He crooked a finger at me, and I stooped down.

There it was: a clean dark hole right through the back cover of *Japanese Country Inns.* The beautiful snow-swathed inn featured in the photo of the oversize book didn't look quite so inviting soaking wet with a bullet in it.

Evan smiled at me, and I fought a wave of nausea. "Mightier than the sword," he muttered. "Oh, Detective Sewell!" he beckoned in a singsong voice.

She was impressed, but she didn't look too pleased about it.

"Where's the woman who was assaulted?" Evan asked her pleasantly.

"The *other* woman who was assaulted?" I chimed in.

"Yes, the other one," Evan agreed. "Could we speak to her?"

Detective Sewell considered this for a moment and then countered with a question directed at me. "Could you tell me what you were doing down in Little Tokyo today? It's a drive from the west side, isn't it?"

"Just being a good citizen," I answered.

"Very good, not many people would willingly involve themselves in a shooting." Her insinuation seemed to be that I had brought it on myself.

Evan couldn't resist. "Much less *several* shoo—"

"I didn't know he had a gun," I said, overriding him. "I would hope most people would do *something* if they saw a woman being assaulted. But that wasn't what I meant. I'm on jury duty."

"Oh," she said, as though I were one of *those* suckers who wasn't smart enough to come up with a excuse to get out of it.

"And I like sushi," I said, to let her know I wasn't. "Oh, I was supposed to be back at one-thirty, I've got to get over there or, at least, call in." I lifted my left hand to check the time and looked down at my wrist. "Oh shit," I said.

"What time is it?" asked Evan.

"Time to get a new Timex," I answered, taking off the smashed watch before he could see that it was the one he gave me. I covertly dropped it into my raincoat pocket. But I should have known better; Evan doesn't miss a trick.

"Time for me to get you a new Timex," he said magnanimously. I pulled my cell phone out of my bag and fished out my jury badge. Evan motioned that he was going to speak to some of the witnesses and moved off while I dialed the number on the back of the card and gave my excuse.

"Uh, hi, this is Callaway Wilde, I have, um, well, I've been involved in a crime and I won't be able to come in this afternoon." It sounded so lame.

"Uh-huh," the bored voice responded, and she might as well have added, Yeah, right. But she was amenable. "When do you think you might be able to come in?"

"How about tomorrow?"

"Eight-forty-five. But call in tonight to see if we need you. Could I have your juror number please?" She couldn't care less. I gave it and hung up. I stood around, feeling lost for a while until Evan came back and took my arm gently again. "Let's go talk to your damsel in distress, shall we?"

She was in one of the boutiques, the one with the audience-member-slash-shopgirl who had called the police. They were having a tense conversation in the sliding discordant tones of their native language. But Aya switched to flawless English and a quick smile when she saw me coming toward her.

The sharp light in her eye flattened a little when Evan showed his badge, but the smile's inflection never wavered.

"Nice to meet you, Detective Paley." She took his hand and shook it earnestly. "What can I do for you?"

I looked at him; he hadn't missed the change in her eyes, it was something he looked for, and he'd taught me to do the same. "Well, Ms. Aikosha, I'm sure you've answered plenty of questions already."

"A few." She sighed.

"Can you just sum up for me what you've told the detectives?" Evan asked directly.

A long breath escaped her, and she looked to me. I nodded encouragingly. "It's okay—my boyfriend," I said. She appraised him quickly and gave me her glance of sterling approval.

"Well. I am a medical student, my guardian owns a hotel here in the area, and I often come down for lunch or a visit."

"Do you live with your guardian?"

"No. I have a condominium in Santa Monica." She gave the address, and I recognized it as a luxury complex near the beach. Nice digs for a struggling student.

"So you live alone?" he asked, and I didn't like that question. It seemed a little personal.

"Yes."

"Where do you go to school?" Evan asked.

"USC. That . . . man, he grabbed me as I was coming down the stairs there and pushed me into the corner, and he was threatening me, saying really nasty things. And then"—she looked at me—"you came, and I guess you told him what happened then."

"What kind of 'nasty things'?"

"Sexual things, mostly, about what he'd like to do to me." Her eyes glazed a little, but she stayed perfectly reserved.

Evan's eyebrow had gone up, just a little. "You don't seem to feel overly upset."

Her eyes flashed at that. "Do you mean by his gun or his twisted mental health?" she asked angrily. Revealing that she wasn't quite as unruffled as she pretended, nor as much a victim.

Damn, I liked her.

"Either." Evan shrugged.

She took a deep breath and collected herself. She seemed to be embarrassed to have shown any emotion at all. "I'm okay, it was so quick. I know there are sick people in the world, *that* doesn't shock me; it was very scary being the object of that sickness." She was angry, and as much as she tried to contain it, it was seeping out toward Evan.

"I'm sure it was," Evan said, so sincerely that it neutralized her. "Had you ever seen him before?"

"No." But her eyes flicked away.

"Are you sure?" Evan asked evenly.

"Yes, I think so. I've given as accurate a description as I can to the other detectives; I hope you can find him."

"We will certainly try. Thank you for your time." They exchanged a smile that I thought lingered a second too long. Evan whipped out his card. "If you think of anything else or if you see him again, call me."

Aya's smile moved down to the card and then at me. "Did you know that in the Buddhist culture when you save a life it means you have changed fate and you become responsible for that life?"

"Well, I . . . ," I sputtered, "I don't know if I saved your life exactly."

She laughed, a lovely sound, and put her hand on my arm. "But how about, as an alternative, if I take you both to dinner at my guardian's hotel? It's the Sakura-no Hana, right around the corner. It has the finest Japanese restaurant in L.A."

Looking to Evan, I could see that he was intrigued by more than the food. Something about this assault was interesting him. I wondered jealously if it was the nymphlike quality of its victim. He nodded at me.

"As a thank-you," she added.

What could I say that wouldn't make me look as insecure as I felt? "Great. We'd love it." I'd keep an eye on this one. In fact, I decided she'd better call me instead of Evan. I took the card back from her and wrote my private line number.

"Wonderful, I will call you." She looked down at the card. "Tomorrow?"

"That'll do," I said.

"Good, and we will pick a date." She said good-bye with a slight, regal bow.

Starting to turn, I glanced at Evan and caught him watching the attractive Aya. I fought down the angry twinge as we exited together. Back outside, Evan stood for a moment looking at the crime scene, turning this way and that, his intelligent eyes scanning the details.

"What?" I asked finally.

"She's not very good at sharing," he said.

Chapter 3

As I pulled into my vast driveway the subtle outdoor lighting came on. The magnificent live oak in my front yard was illuminated from below, and the house looked magnificent. It was huge. God, I loved this place. It had been my father's before he died three years ago, and it was so like him—solid, quality, warm, and so handsome, so welcoming to me. The house always seemed glad to see me, to let me know I completed it, just as my father had always made me feel. I felt a stab of pain as the rent left by his loss opened in me once again. I wished fervently, as I had countless times, to still have him instead of all the money and companies that I had inherited.

But life was funny. He died, I got close to $200 million in assets and quickly found myself defending my right to keep it from all my relations, including my own mother. Another pang—of a totally different timbre—pierced my chest, and I had to push it back. I still had to deal with that loss, but not now, not yet. Her absence was both too old and deep, and too recent.

I hurried into the house, into the comfort of my father's lingering presence, to try to fill the arctic hollow in my chest.

My butler, Deirdre, met me at the door, and it was as she was taking in the state of my coat that I remembered the note. I felt suddenly self-conscious and stopped her before she could routinely check the pockets, since I was notorious for leaving things in them.

"Deedee, wait." I took the muddy white Burberry back and felt in the right-hand pocket. The small neatly folded paper was still there, and I awkwardly palmed it, then I took out the smashed watch and relinquished the mackintosh.

"Shall I send this to the cleaners or dispose of it?" Deirdre asked without so much as raising an eyebrow. That's Deirdre; she's British and would consider it bad form to inquire about anything as personal as why I was mud wrestling while on jury duty.

I turned, and her eyes went to the rest of my sodden look. "Let's try the cleaners Deedee, at least for the shirt and the coat, toss the pants, they got torn." She allowed herself a slight question in her eyes, just a flicker, but I thought it deserved an answer. "I got in a fight at school today, Deirdre." I smiled. "It's okay though, my boyfriend is going to beat them up for me."

She inclined her head slightly in a nod, as though I had given the most satisfactory explanation in the world, but though I knew she was dying to know what had happened, all she said was, "Will Detective Paley be joining you for dinner?"

"I think the good detective will be stopping by."

"Dinner will be served at seven-thirty in the breakfast room, if that meets with your approval." She seemed to feel slighted at the lack of forthcoming information.

"Approval granted. At ease, Deirdre, it's been a tough day." I didn't want her getting insulted because I wouldn't satisfy her curiosity, so even though I didn't want to get into it, I gave her a brief summary. "I tried to help out a girl who was being assaulted by a man. He got away, but so did she, if you know what I mean. Okay?"

I could see she was appeased, but she didn't drop her formality. She seldom, if ever, does. "I will draw you a hot bath. Would you care for a glass of wine?" It was the olive branch.

"No, thank you, I'll have a single malt scotch. In a very heavy glass."

She didn't approve of my drinking liquor, since I'd had a tendency to overuse specific stimulants in my past, and her nostrils flared almost imperceptibly to show this.

"For medicinal purposes," I concluded and started up the long sweeping staircase.

"I'll have Joseph bring it up directly." Joseph was the underbutler. Sending him was Deirdre's way of succumbing without surrendering. At the top of the stairs I looked back down over the railing. Deirdre had evaporated, as usual. As I was moving down the hall to the master bedroom I unfolded the note.

There was a Japanese character on the top, stark and beautiful; I had no idea what it meant. Underneath were the simple words:

winter rain glistens
on a jewel, entranced,
I cannot look away

Beneath that was a phone number, gracefully written.

It took my breath away.

I was floating in a sea of milk bath, thinking about my relationship with Evan. It was wonderful—he was strong, funny, and independently wealthy, and he seemed to know me so well. You wouldn't think it would be important for him to have money when I had so much, but that's exactly why it was. Men of normal means found my money either overly attractive or emasculating, and I wasn't interested in sharing the attention or nurturing the insecure.

Why did I love having the secret of that note? I had always kept an open-door policy in my relationships, open behind me, like an escape hatch. Yet Evan was everything I wanted, wasn't he? We'd been seeing each other for eight months, and we both still had our own homes. I wondered what the next step might be. The word *marriage* flitted into, and was promptly hurtled out of, my mind.

The door flew open, and my eighteen-year-old half-sister, Sabrina, bounded in.

"What happened to your raincoat?" she asked loudly in her native southern drawl. "I saw it in the kitchen, but Deirdre won't tell me anything, she never will." She perched her Rita Hayworth body on the edge of the tub and trailed her hand in the water.

I watched her fondly, wondering how she'd become such a fixture when ten months ago we hadn't been aware of each other's existence; it had been my half-brother, Binford, who found her. I sighed. What a difference a year makes.

"Hello, Sabrina, nice to see you too."

"I'm sorry. Hi. Okay, now what *happened?*"

Not wanting to remind her of an ugly nightmare from our recent past when both of us had faced attackers, or frankly, repeat the story, I told her that I was splashed by an inconsiderate motorist, and she was sufficiently incensed.

"Ooh, I just hate people like that! Did they even stop and say they were sorry?"

"Sadly, no," I said. "Downtown at First and Broadway at least, chivalry is dead."

Her eyes twinkled, but she kept her voice level and quipped, "Well, it's too close to the legal district."

"Wow, college is good for you," I enthused. "Your cynicism is coming right along. Next thing you'll be going to flag burnings, having your first beer . . ."

She slapped the water with her hand and splashed me, but she looked proud. "So, what were you thinking about when I came in?"

Squirming at the thought of revealing my uncomfortable thoughts about Evan, I said evasively, "Just having a private moment."

"About what?"

"Something *private,* hence the term," I told her pointedly.

"Come on, you can tell me," she urged.

It was different, having a sister; my defenses were constantly being assaulted by her well-meaning infiltrations. Before Sabrina, I had pretty much been an island to myself, and I had gotten damn good at it, but she, and Evan, had been building bridges. "Okay, okay," I grumbled. "I was thinking about Evan."

She watched me expectantly, and when I didn't elaborate, she splashed me again.

"Okay! Jesus," I said as I wiped my eyes with a dry washcloth. "I've been wondering how long we can go on the status quo. I mean, it's been a long time, and I've given him closet space, hell, a key to my house, but I hardly ever go to his house. When I do, I have to be invited and take anything I need. The least he could do is give me a token drawer."

"Why don't you ask him to move in here?" she asked, with her usual simple common sense.

"Ask him to give up his house?" I said, an unreasonable panic stabbing at me. Granted, it did grate on me when we were together and he said "I've got to go home." A huge part of me wanted home to be with me, certainly not a place from which I was excluded, still . . .

"Why not?" she persisted.

"Because . . . then I'm committed," I confessed tentatively, as much to myself as to her.

"You should be if you let *him* go." She splashed me once more for good measure, and this time I got her back. She retreated from the room squealing with laughter, leaving me to dwell on the subject of cohabitation, which gave me a sense of vertigo. I had always only had to answer to myself.

But what *was* next? I raised my hand out of the water and pushed my hair back off my forehead, trying to wipe away my inadequacies. I hated to admit it, because I detested weakness, but I was scared of what might happen, what I might feel, what I could lose. And I knew that I was missing something, I was holding back.

The door to the bathroom opened again, and the topic of contemplation came in; he had a sandwich in one hand.

"Oh no, you're not staying for dinner," I lamented. He worked so many hours that I took it personally. It left me alone more than I bargained for, and I like to be alone, sometimes. But I want to choose the sometimes.

"A man's gotta work," he said, his eyes searching the surface of the water appreciatively.

"But all night?" I took a deep breath, and my inflated lungs brought my breasts up through the shiny white surface of the water. In spite of the warm water my nipples were erect; Evan has that lasting effect on me. "Can I ask you something?" I said.

"Sure." He looked like he'd rather do something else.

"Why don't we ever go to your house?"

He looked surprised. "I just thought it was easier for you to be here."

"Oh," I said, and it was a loaded *oh.*

"Why?" He sounded slightly squeamish.

I joked it off. "Oh, no reason, I was just wondering if maybe you needed an escape pod, or maybe a love nest for your other girlfriends."

He laughed, "Yes, that's its, that's where I take all my other lovers in my extensive spare time."

"I see. How many are there?"

"Oh I've cut way back. I'm down to the last couple dozen."

His eyes were watching what he could see of my body in the

milky water as he put down his snack and took off the long dark trench coat I called the "Sam Spade." Part of me wanted to not let him detour, to ask him more directly how he felt about me, but I didn't have the nerve. The other part of me was aroused, and that part was winning.

Next the jacket came off. The gun in the shoulder holster stayed where it was though, dangerous and quiet. He unfastened the cuffs of his crisp blue Armani shirt, but instead of starting on the buttons of the front he rolled up his sleeves. He knelt down on the double plush rug in front of the oversize bath and put one finger on my mouth. I kissed it and then let it slip in and sucked it very gently. Watching him. His eyes were on my mouth, and his lips followed his look. I kissed him wetly but kept the rest of my body submerged.

He pulled his face back and let his hands slide in, under the water, over my body, cupping one breast and then the other. His right hand moved around my waist, and his left slid across my stomach and down. He placed the palm of his strong hand against the curve of my lower back and lifted me slightly so that my whole body was revealed, halfway in, halfway out, dripping glistening droplets along curves, forming gemlike pools in the crevices of my navel and my collarbone. His left hand swept these away as he smoothed a long caress down my body, following his hand with his eyes. A long humming sigh escaped him. He kissed the fingertips of his left hand and touched them to the darkening bruise on my abdomen. Then slowly he let me sink down again, but his hands stayed with me, moving, insistent, and firm. I closed my eyes and felt him watch me.

And then his beeper went off. As he stood up, he checked it and frowned, dried his hands, picked up his sandwich, winked at me, and left me in the lurch with not even a general idea of when he'd be back.

As I felt the loneliness he left with me saturate my body, a nagging thought came with it, This feels familiar.

Two months before I had stood by my mother's grave and whispered, "You couldn't give me what I needed. You didn't have it in you to be what I desperately wanted you to be, and I had to let you go, I'm sorry." And then I had turned and walked away.

Time and time again in my life, I had hoped for something real from Rudy, opened myself up to her, only to be kebabbed again when she disappointed me. My fault. You think I would have learned.

And what had she left me with? If there was one thing I resented more than anything else, it was this: wanting something that I couldn't have.

Chapter 4

The next day found me released from jury duty. Calling the evening before, I had heard a recorded message that I was no longer needed. I wasn't likely to have been selected for anything interesting anyway, having been the intended victim of more than one violent crime myself. I thought I could be unbiased, but I doubt very much that a public defender would agree.

It was a good thing not to have to get up early, as I hadn't slept well. The assault the day before had reared its ugly visuals every time I let myself try to sleep, and it had also brought back a year-old nightmare I had hoped I had exorcised. I had woken three times last night in a sweat, each time the phantom smell of gunpowder and blood sharp in my nose and mouth, the unforgettable blasts from both our guns drumming against my ears. The dark blue-red of fresh blood on the sidewalk stuck in my mind like a stain on my brain that, even months later, I could not wash clean. The images had haunted me until, even awake, I could see the man's face behind the barrel of the gun he aimed point-blank at me.

I pulled myself out of bed but couldn't entirely shake off the exhaustion or the vicious gnawing angst that yesterday's events had churned up. So much ugliness had made itself a part of me—the knowledge of the unexpected depth of people's avarice, the violence they were capable of, and the deaths I had witnessed. The last led me to think about my mother's final days as I contemplated my reflection in the vanity mirror. We had talked then, finally, as honestly as a lifetime of mistrust would allow, until she had been unable to speak or even to breathe. I saw in my face the shadow of how the hard things had stayed with me.

But I had survived them. So I took my scarred heart and nervous system and threw them into a new day. What else was there to do?

After ten o'clock I checked my messages, and Aya had called. I dialed the number she left, and she answered right away. I hadn't noticed how sexy her voice was the day before, distracted by how sexy the rest of her was I guess. Thinking that that was one more thing Evan could find attractive about her, I resented her for a minute and then said hello.

"I'm so glad you called. I was afraid that you might want to put aside the whole incident and forget about it, and me," she said.

"Oh, I don't think forgetting about it is an option. Not for a little while, anyway," I answered, seeing all over again yesterday's attacker, the spittle in the corner of his mouth, and hearing the echo of his gun firing. I shook it off.

"Well, let's try to put it behind us now." She laughed. "It ended well anyway."

"Did it?" It didn't seem over, since that guy was running around shooting his gun at people, but to each his own, I guess.

"Will you and Detective Paley join me for dinner, perhaps on Saturday?" She spoke so correctly that it made me conscious of my own lazy enunciation and slang.

"Love to. He's off on Saturdays. But you'll have to call him Evan if we're going to break bread, or rice, together."

She laughed again, which made me feel that I was funny, very kind of her. "If we break rice, we won't be having a very big meal. Can you come in the afternoon and let me treat you to a shiatsu massage in the spa and then we'll dine in the restaurant?" she asked.

"We'd love to join you, but I'll be glad to pay for it."

The laugh, so musical, so sexy. "No, I insist. Besides I won't pay either, it's my uncle's hotel."

"I thought you said it was your guardian's hotel," I said.

" 'Uncle' is a term of respect and affection; he is no actual blood relation, but he is my legal guardian," she explained.

"Right. The guardian. It's so charming and Old World." It sounded insulting after I said it. I hadn't meant it that way.

"It is Old World! Didn't you know we came over on the *Mayflower?"* She laughed, amused. "I shall see you at the Sakura-no Hana Hotel on San Pedro at five o'clock on Saturday."

"What do I need to bring?"

"Your man, your lovely self, and your tension," she answered quickly, "and I'll let you take two of them home with you."

"Which two?"

"You decide." She laughed again, but it was deeper and more mischievous. "And don't forget your corset. Old World fashion is new again."

"I'm picking one out to go with my pinafore now," I said, laughing with her. "Saturday then, I'll look forward to it."

"As will I, with great anticipation." Her voice dropped into a purr.

My eyebrows went up a little. Was she flirting, or just being flattering?

"Let's hope you look back on it with great fondness," I plagiarized.

She laughed again, and I realized I *was* looking forward to it. With great curiosity.

• • •

The spa, on the third floor of the Sakura-no Hana Hotel was simple, very clean, and esthetically pleasing—white tiles, neatly stacked white towels, soaking tubs filled with steaming hot mineral water—and the whole space was filled with a soothing cool mist.

I put my clothes in the locker assigned to me and put the key into the pocket of a cushy white terry cloth bathrobe that I took with me but didn't put on, as the temperature of the room was perfect on my naked skin.

Lowering myself into one of the tubs, I sucked in a rich moist breath of steam as the heat hit my most sensitive parts and then sighed it out as I sank up to my breasts and then my neck. I lay back and let my eyes blur on a skylight shrouded by the steam.

I stayed that way for a long time until I heard a voice.

"Callaway?"

I sat up a bit, instinctively covering myself, and turned around in my tub to see the most gorgeous naked woman I had ever laid eyes on.

It was Aya. Oh boy was it. Her long dark hair was up in a loose knot, and pieces of it fell to her shoulders. Although she was fairly petite, she was exquisitely proportioned, with long legs and a tiny waist. I found it hard not to look at her breasts. They were absolutely perfect. She came up to the edge of the tub and smiled down at me.

"Comfortable?" she asked.

"Yes, quite, thank you." Althought that wasn't exactly true. I've always appreciated female beauty and even sexuality. I'm not attracted to women, as a rule. But when she kneeled at the edge of the tub and reached out to brush a piece of hair off my forehead as though it were the most natural thing in the world to do, I felt uncomfortably aware of our nakedness.

On the other hand, I don't think I've ever seen a woman more comfortable with nudity than Aya, her own as well as mine. "I'm going in the steam, then. Join me?" she asked.

"In a minute. Thank you for inviting me today. It's a real treat," I said, far more casually than I felt.

"It gets better." She smiled disarmingly. "Is Detective Paley here?"

"Yes, Evan's over in the men's spa."

"How delightful. I'm sorry he couldn't join us in the women's spa," she said. Again the simple delivery, no obvious sexual pretext, but it was impossible to look at her and not think of sex. I watched her long elegant body walk back down the stairs, wondering at the lines of her body and the silkiness of her hair and skin. Then she opened the glass door, and the milky fog enveloped her.

"Wow," I muttered. Should I go in the steam? A glance around told me there was no one else in the place. Was she coming on to me? I had to admit I was a little afraid that she might be. And that decided it. I wouldn't *avoid* going in because of a feverish imagination.

But first, I took a cold shower.

While the cold water was shocking and exhilarating me simultaneously, I asked myself what was going on. For eight months I hadn't even thought about being with anyone besides Evan, and now, in the past two days I had flirted, albeit wordlessly, with a handsome man and now was questioning if a *woman* was coming on to me. Was it the way he had looked at Aya that made me hope she was attracted to me instead of to Evan? I always was competitive.

The icy water and the cold sober thoughts had me shivering, and by then I was ready to go into the steam room. I couldn't see anything except white air when I first went in. But as I moved forward I could see Aya lying on her stomach on the higher of the two tiers, the steam forming droplets of water that followed the map of her body. She turned her head to me and smiled.

"Warm," I said lamely and laid my towel on the lower level.

"Mmmm. Yes," she answered lethargically.

It was too hot to converse. So I contented myself with leaning my back carefully against the wall and stretching my legs out in front of me so that I could watch Aya through half-closed eyes. I breathed slowly and deeply and found that I could enjoy looking at her, without comparing myself to her, without feeling that just because she was very sexy I needed to be uncomfortable sitting naked next to her.

I closed my eyes and leaned my head back. And then I felt her hand on my thigh. I opened my eyes quickly, and she was running the palm of her hand along my leg from my thigh down toward my knee.

"You have beautiful legs," she said. "Very strong. Do you run?" She folded her arm back up to prop her face on her hand and wait for an answer.

"No, I have a gym at home, I work out and I love to swim." I was so confused. Her touch had been so sure and exploring, and yet was it sexual?

"Ah, that explains the strength and the long lines." She put her head back down and fell quiet. After several sweaty minutes the oppressive atmosphere was too much for me.

"See you out there," I said. As I left I appreciated watching her form being caressed by the tendrils of steam.

A Japanese woman in a white T-shirt and pants came in as I was putting on some lotion.

"Ms. Wield?" She struggled with my name.

"Yes, Wilde, that's me."

"This way," she invited, and helped me into my robe before kneeling down to hold my slippers while I put my feet into them. Now that's service.

She was a wonderful masseuse; an hour later I had forgotten everything but the insistent pressure all over my body that painfully demanded I relax, let go. When she said we were done, I sighed and sat up. It didn't seem possible that sixty minutes had passed.

She retrieved my robe from a hook on the wall, and I padded back to the lockers, pulling my key from the pocket. Placing it in the odd circular keyhole I opened the small door and then stepped back and looked to see if it was the right number on the locker.

Yes, number nine, and there were my clothes and bag, but right in the front was a small elegant black shopping bag with the name BULGARI printed in gold on the front.

Very curious, I thought as I took it out and peeked inside. There was a box, black, also with the same designer name on the top. I pulled the cubical jewelry box out and snapped it open.

Inside was the watch I had admired in the jewelry shop on the day of the shooting in Little Tokyo. As I was standing there with my mouth open, Aya spoke from behind me.

"Did you do some shopping on your way in today?"

"Aya," I turned to her, "this is too much. I can't take this," I said flatly.

She looked confused. "I'm sorry?"

"I don't know how you knew I wanted this, but I can't take it," I reiterated.

"I *didn't* know you wanted it. I didn't give it to you," she said, looking slightly affronted, as though I had accused her of something. "I would certainly not have gone in your locker, not for any reason."

Now I was confused. "This isn't from you?" I asked.

"No," she said, and she leaned over to look at the watch. "I wonder who it is from. Clearly someone very generous."

I sat down on one of the chaise longues with the watch in my hand and thought about it. Who had known I tried on this watch? Who had seen me?

"Wait a minute," I said, flashing on the face of the handsome stranger through the jewelry store window. But my common sense quickly dismissed the extravagant notion. How would he, whoever he was, know I was here and get it into my locker? And, nice as the haiku had been, such an expensive gift to someone you haven't even met would have been an overly grand gesture. It was a romantic thought, but then I had a better one.

"What?" Aya asked, intrigued.

"It must be Evan." My face flushed with pleasure. "He knows I smashed my watch, and he went to talk to the shopkeepers right after the attack. I'll bet that minx of a sales girl told him right away which watch I wanted." I laughed at the irony of her making the sale after all. Good for her.

"But how did he get it in here?" Aya asked.

"Oh, that doesn't surprise me, he has his ways." I looked at her pointedly.

"I'm not sure I want to know what you mean by that. But it will look lovely on you, and it is very grand of him, a detective." She was too polite to say it, but I knew she meant the cost of the watch.

"A detective of private means," I said by way of explanation.

"So his work . . . ?"

"Is what he always wanted to do," I finished.

With a glance to the watch and then to me she said, "It is a fortunate man who has what he always wanted." She looked me slyly up and down to make it clear she wasn't referring to his profession or his money.

I smiled gratefully at the compliment and dressed for dinner, eager to make sure, even with the sensuous Aya beside me, that I remained exactly what he wanted.

Chapter 5

"That was terrific," Evan said, in way of thanks to Aya when we met in the hall outside the spa.

"I'm so pleased you enjoyed it," she answered. "Now, the restaurant is on the top floor of the hotel. Shall we go eat?"

"Yes please," Evan said, but when he offered me his arm, I planted a kiss on his warm mouth.

"Thank you, Evan," I said.

"You're welcome." He kissed me back but squinted at me. "What for?"

I flashed the watch in his face and smiled.

"Nice watch, new?" he asked, observing me.

"Nice try. I love it, it's beautiful." I kissed him again.

"I'm delighted to accept your gratitude, especially in any physical form, but I didn't give you that watch."

"It was in my locker, after the massage." I was confused now.

"Is there a note?"

"No, well, actually I first thought it was from Aya." I turned to her, and she nodded to confirm my story. "But when she said it wasn't I just assumed it was from you," I said.

Evan released me and walked briskly back to the desk with Aya and me on his heels.

"Excuse me. But did anyone else go into the woman's spa while Ms. Wilde was having her massage?" he asked, politely but with professional firmness.

The man at the desk looked surprised at the inquiry. "Yes, there is one woman here now, she is having massage. She is very respectable customer from Japan." He seemed to remember himself. "Is there a problem?"

Evan made an effort to explain. "Someone left a gift in Ms. Wilde's locker. We would like to know who had access to the locker area."

"No one. Only the staff and myself and one cleaning person working now." He was apologetic. "I'm so sorry, I don't understand."

"Were you here the entire time, at the desk?" Evan asked him.

"I went into the back room, to get waters. But I was only gone for a very short minutes."

"It's okay," I said. "No harm done." I looked to Evan, "I mean, nothing's missing, I checked: all my jewelry, money, cards, you name it. Untouched."

"I wonder," Evan said, and pulling out his cell phone, he punched a single digit as he thanked the spa manager and gestured Aya and me down the hall. "Cally, let me have your wallet." I could hear the electronic noise of a ringing line, and then someone answered. "Joey, hey, it's Evan. Listen I need you to run a quick check on some cards, see if there's any action." He wrapped up the call quickly and then snapped the phone closed as we stepped onto the elevator. Aya pushed the button for the top floor of the hotel.

"You think someone is going to steal my credit card number and leave me a six-thousand-dollar watch?" I asked him, smiling.

"Just need to be safe. It is, of course, *you* we're talking about," he swiped back.

"I am not a jinx." I pouted. "When Evan first met me," I told Aya, "some things happened . . ."

"People got shot," Evan said flippantly.

"*Some* people got shot, okay, yes, but they were trying to shoot *me* at the time," I said, shooting him with a nasty look.

"Granted," allowed Evan.

"And it was very scary for a little while."

Aya nodded. "So that's how you met, I was wondering," she said charmingly, smiling from Evan to me. "And there are those of us, present company included, who are not strangers to being shot at."

"So there," I snorted at Evan and tossed my head defiantly.

Mercifully the elevator doors opened, and we came out onto the top floor of the hotel, into a restaurant so serene in design and feeling that no argument could last. Two beautiful Japanese women in kimonos came forward immediately. After placing their hands into a stone bowl on a low side table, they approached Evan and me with their hands outstretched. I pulled back a little as one of them reached for my face, but her movements were so nurturing and her expression so welcoming that I succumbed, and she patted my face with lightly scented lemon water. The effect was instantly reviving and refreshing. The woman bowed, smiling and welcoming me in soft, lilting Japanese, then she backed away, gesturing to a door, a sliding paper screen.

"Wow." Evan sighed. "That wouldn't be a bad way to wake up in the morning."

He was still watching the pretty girls in the kimonos, but so obviously that it was only to tease me. All I said was, "In your dreams."

Aya bowed back and received the same treatment, but with more grace than I had. It was not a custom I had been aware of. I made a mental note to self—be ready next time.

I did know enough to take off my shoes before we went into the private dining room. We sat, Evan and I cross-legged, Aya on her knees.

"If you don't mind, I took the liberty of ordering a special dinner for us, but if there is anything you would like, please ask for it," she said. The waitress was pouring cold sake from an iced glass carafe into small beautifully blown glasses. We sipped; it was delicious.

"This is a special premium sake, one best known for its light floral notes. Do you like it?"

"Yum," I hummed.

"It's from the Fushimi region, yes?" asked Evan.

"Very good." She shared a smile with Evan. I felt left out.

"Oh, you think you're so smart," I said. "Fushimi is known more for its sakes with fruity citrus flavors, Niigata is where the best floral sakes come from."

"Better," said Aya, laughing.

"I stand corrected," Evan said begrudgingly and then added in a low voice, "know-it-all."

"Show-off," I returned. We punched each other affectionately under the table.

The meal was served in a small black box, one for each of us. The box had several drawers with tiny handles. I watched Aya as she moved her hands to the first one on the bottom. She slid it open, revealing a tiny plate holding a single piece of sushi and a small white flower. She picked up her chopsticks and placed them on either side of the morsel, lifting it gently, as though she might injure the delicate flavor by squeezing too hard. She placed it, whole, in her mouth, the food never touching her lips.

Evan and I followed her lead gratefully, but it was impossible not to feel awkward and somewhat clumsy next to her delicate movements. The food was exquisite, each bite a different sensation and experience.

Watching Aya's flawless manners I grew curious about where

she had learned them, how she'd been raised. "Aya, where is your family?" I asked, indirectly.

"Minnesota." She smiled. "It's very cold there right now."

"So you are here studying medicine? They must be very proud," I told her.

"They are." She sounded vaguely unsure. "Though, they are very traditional and do not completely understand why I choose to take a 'man's' place." I could hear the loneliness of being misunderstood in her voice.

I didn't want to get too personal, I knew that wouldn't be good form, but I was so curious about this smart classy young woman. "Your parents can't disapprove too much if they are paying for medical school, that's not inexpensive."

Aya's smile stayed on her lips but died in her eyes. "They do not pay for my education. They could not afford it, even if they believed in it."

"Are you on scholarship?" I asked, impressed.

"Partial scholarship, the rest of my tuition is sponsored by my uncle."

Evan piped in, "Let's hear it for wealthy relations." He raised his glass.

"His name is Korosu, and he and I are not related. I refer to Korosu as my uncle in respect and affection only. He is traditionally what is called a guardian."

"So, your 'uncle,' who isn't a real relation, is paying for med school?" I asked. Then added quickly, "You don't have to answer that, it's none of my business."

But she was already nodding and dismissing my awkwardness. "Yes, it is partly a tradition. Korosu has no children of his own, and it is partly the repayment of a debt." She took a sip of her sake.

Evan was watching her closely; he said casually, "Whose debt?"

"Sorry?" Aya turned to him.

"Whose debt, his or yours?" He raised his glass again, and then he changed the subject to signify that he did not expect an answer.

After dinner we walked in contented quiet to the parking garage. Our cars were on different levels, and Aya protested that she would be fine on her own, but Evan insisted that we walk with her.

We were headed back to the stairway, after saying good night, when we heard her car alarm go off. Pausing, we waited for her to disarm it, but it didn't stop. Evan backed up a couple of steps and looked over to see if she was all right.

Then he started running. I followed, a little more slowly, confused. As Evan got closer to Aya's car, I saw him draw his gun. A man materialized from the space between Aya's car and an SUV and knocked Evan flat to the ground. The alarm was still screaming, and over that, Evan was shouting at me to get down as he rolled away from the man and jumped to his feet; now I could hear Aya too, calling for help. I ducked down behind the SUV, and peeking through the back window I saw Aya and the same ugly, angry-faced man who had assaulted both of us the day before. He had her arm and was trying to force her into the car.

Evan's gun, which had gone flying, was lying on the ground. The attacker had his own gun drawn and kept watching Evan to be sure that he didn't go for his weapon. He succeeded in shoving Aya into the passenger seat of her own car by the sheer force of his size and weight. She was fighting like a cat. He hit her so hard that I winced and moved forward, but Evan shouted, and I stopped myself, watching anxiously. Aya cowered in the front seat, holding her hands over her head protectively. The car alarm was still blaring mercilessly, and it was so loud it felt like constant, rhythmic blows to the head.

The man started to get in after her, and when he was halfway in, Evan made his move. While I watched with my heart beating in my throat, he sprang up, seized the car door, and jammed it hard against the man's leg.

The man howled in pain and anger. Forgetting Aya for a moment, he threw his weight back against the door and pushed Evan against the next car, pinning him. Both men were pushing with both hands and with all their strength, rendering the gun momentarily unusable; the attacker couldn't shoot while he was using his gun hand to hold the door. He and Evan were pinned in a lethal struggle; if the man could free up his gun, Evan was a point-blank target. Rage overtook my fear, and running out into the open space, I snatched up Evan's gun, screaming over the excruciating noise of the alarm as I went, "Aya! Get out of the car! Run!"

As I reached the pistol and took its weight into my hand, I turned and saw the fear on Evan's face, and at the same time, I saw why. The man was fumbling to get his gun pointed at me. Evan yelled and punched him hard in the face and then pushed himself clear, moving away from the man and the car, moving toward me. The man reeled, recovered, came two steps out of the car, and pointed his gun at Evan's back. In my vision, everything except the attacker went black. As though looking down a tunnel, I saw his face contort with fury as he started to squeeze the trigger, and then his head snapped back, a bullet hole in the middle of his forehead, right where I had aimed it.

Even as he started to crumble, his gun fired. I saw Evan's face contract in pain as he dropped, hitting the cement hard and clutching at his lower leg. I kept Evan's gun trained on the body between the two cars as Aya got out the other side and ran toward us, one hand on her brow where a nasty lump was already starting to swell.

She dropped down next to Evan, and after one more check to see that our recurring nightmare was still dead, I joined her.

Aya ran her hand over Evan's leg as she leaned down, using

her teeth to start a rip in Evan's pants, which she then tore away. It was impressive.

There was a bullet hole in his calf, off to one side. It was bleeding but not too profusely. Aya reached behind her head and yanked her white knit shirt off in one clean motion. She folded it quickly into a long strip and bound the wound tightly. She knelt there in a lace bra and a skirt and smiled at Evan as comfortably as though lingerie and bullet wounds were the fashion basics of the season.

I pulled Evan back against my knees after he had seen the damage and Aya's lovely breasts. "You're going to be okay, she's good with this stuff," I said. "She took care of me when I got shot, remember?" I had to speak loudly because the horn of the car was still bleating at painful decibels. Aya rose, and giving wide berth to the dead man, she went to the open passenger-side door and crawled inside. The alarm stopped abruptly. Then I heard her on her phone, urgently but efficiently giving our location and situation.

In the ringing silence Evan said, "You didn't get shot, remember?" The pain was evident in his voice. He looked to the man laid out on the cement then up at me. "I was going to kill the son of a bitch." He sounded disappointed.

"I know you were," I said supportively. "But you were busy and I was just standing there. Now be quiet and lay still." I tried to sound confident, but I was terrified that he would go into shock, bleed to death, leave me.

I found his hand and held tight. He squeezed back so hard I had to bite my lip to keep from crying out. "Where's the ambulance?" I said instead, feeling tears of panic well up.

Evan closed his eyes and grimaced, his whole body tensing. I wiped the sweat from his brow with my free hand, and he opened his eyes to look at the body again.

"Same guy?" he asked.

"Yes. It's the man who attacked Aya before."

Evan looked as though he expected this and squinted up at Aya, who was coming back with her cell phone in her hand. Crooking his thumb at me, he said, “I told you she was a jinx.”

Aya looked from Evan to me. Then she took a deep breath, and the exhalation was more of a shudder, “No,” she said. “That would be me.”

Chapter 6

"Oh my God, Evan, I just can't believe it, is he awlright?" Sabrina howled as she came into the emergency waiting room.

Every time I look at her I have to shake my head. She was Marilyn Monroe. I mean, really. She had the same full body, the breathy voice with an added southern flair, and that innocence that drove men wild. I was slim and jaded. Except for both of us being blonde and attractive, we couldn't have been more different. While she was being raised by a perfectly lovely middle-class family in Shreveport, Louisiana, I'd been spending my teen years in wealthy Los Angeles, ignorant of her existence. In the eight months we'd lived together we'd made some progress closing the cultural gap between us. She was working on my cynicism, and I was working on her naïveté. That had to go.

"He'll be fine, the doctor told me there's no permanent damage." I met her and submitted to one of her nurturing hugs. She was soft, but nice and firm. The kind of body men adored and women said was fat, because they were jealous.

"What happened?" she drawled, her huge baby blue eyes fixed on mine.

"He was helping a girl in trouble, occupational hazard. Where have you been?" I asked, a little annoyed that it had taken her so long to come to my side. Now that I had a sister I expected her to be there for me. Otherwise why have a pesky younger sibling?

"I was studying anatomy with a friend," she said.

With effort, I skipped the obvious joke. "How can you do that?" I asked. "I never understood that. How can you study *with* somebody? You've only got one brain. I mean, what? Do you each read half a chapter and then hold hands and try to suck it up by osmosis?"

"No, silly, we ask each other questions and talk about it, see how much we absorbed." She smiled shyly. "Now tell me what the doctor said."

Evan, I told her, needed to stay off the leg for at least three weeks. The round had missed the bone and major arteries, but it had made a nice mess of the muscle, and that needed time to heal. I could take him home in a couple of days.

Ooh boy, I thought to myself, I was going to have him home. Flat on his back, one of my favorite positions. I turned to Sabrina. "Let's go get some coffee in the cafeteria and then we'll go wait for him in his room, they're going to transfer him." As we walked down the corridor together, I watched her out of the corner of my eye; her time in L.A. had changed her, just slightly, but over her simple pine-frame personality there was a new coat of designer color.

"So whom were you studying with?" I asked.

"A friend," she answered and blushed profusely.

"You liar," I said and smacked her on the shoulder. "It's a boy, isn't it?"

She blushed again. "I just met him, so it's not like we're together or anything. And he's really nice."

"And cute?" I asked. Sabrina's romantic history read like a bad soap opera—extortion, murder plots, total deception from the man she thought loved her. It was all part of the machinations that had brought us together, and she'd been unattached for the time she'd been with me. This was the first I'd seen her spread her plumage to attract a mate, even if it was a tentative fluffing.

She turned to me as we stopped at the cafeteria, and her eyes opened wider than the doors. "He's a doll." She said it as one long breathy exhalation, her mouth a pink, pouty O, her cheeks flushed rosy, and her black lashes framing her baby blue eyes. She looked so much like a porcelain plaything herself that I just laughed.

"Perfect," I said. "His and hers. Anatomically correct." She didn't get it. That's what was so wonderful about her. If I couldn't claim her for my own, I would have hated her with an insecure vengeance. "Come on, what do you want?" We walked up to the self-serve counter.

"Cappuccino," she said, like it was a beverage she had had every day of her life instead of just finding out that it existed.

I couldn't look at her; I was afraid I would laugh. "I don't think you can get a real one here. It's just going to be the instant, too-sweet, vending-machine kind." I took a shot at educating and dissuading her.

"Oh," she said, and for a minute I thought she had picked up on my hint. But no. "That's the good kind," she said enthusiastically, grabbing a cup, two extra packets of saccharine, and a package of Twinkies. "You want me to make you one?"

"No thanks." I smiled at her. "I had a five-pound sack of sugar for lunch."

Chapter 7

The next day Sabrina had left for classes, and I was sitting on the sofa of the spacious eighth-floor room at Cedar's Sinai that I'd had Evan upgraded to. Extra space, special menu, special price, but it was worth it. He was sleeping in his bed, and I was sitting, looking out the window.

I had spent another restless night on the sofa, yanked awake again and again by the memories of gun explosions, of two different men with a bullet hole in each of them, the emotional overload of knowing I had fired the fatal rounds. Both faces, the man yesterday and the other man, a year before, had melded into one ugly angry mass. My nightmare was morphing, reinforced, into a composite monster. I was trying to find something to focus on, other than that, when I heard a soft voice at the door.

"May I come in?" It was Aya, holding a beautiful orchid arrangement with origami cranes placed artfully around the base. It was simple and elegant. So was she, in a flawless linen skirt and top. I recognized it as Chanel. Costly, her wardrobe. The bump on her forehead was well disguised with makeup and a soft sweep of hair.

I rose and came to meet her, whispering, "Of course, but Evan is sleeping, so why don't we go out where we can talk."

We closed the door quietly and settled ourselves in some comfortable chairs. The area was done in a toneless medium blue with nothing to snag the eye or recommend it decoratively—meant to be calming I suspect.

"How are you doing today?" I asked as a neutral opener; the last few days must have been traumatic for her, to say the least.

"I am alive and well, because of you." She smiled at me with genuine respect and affection, and I thought I saw a hint of trepidation. "It was amazing, what you did." She looked down at her hands, still holding the gift. "I know that I can never repay you, but I do know that I would like to try."

"Look, Aya, I did what I did yesterday to save Evan's life. Not that I wouldn't have helped you," I stumbled through an explanation. "I don't mean that, but I don't want you to feel indebted to me in any way. You aren't."

"I didn't mean that," she answered and looked up at me hopefully. "I meant that I would be honored to be your friend."

I wasn't sure what to say. Friendship is something earned, over time. "Well, friendships are based on shared experiences, and we've definitely shared some interesting experiences. But I do have to warn you, I'm not known for having lots of close girlfriends. I've always been a bit of a loner. Nothing personal, my friends, the few that I have are . . . well . . ."

Across the room the elevator doors opened, and my best friend, Ginny, appeared. Ginny is a stunningly beautiful black girl with long tiny braids and bare arms that showed off her sinewy strength and a small scar where she had taken a bullet saving my life. She saw me in an instant and shrieked, "Girl! I hate this place; why are we here *again?!*"

"Well," I said to Aya, "they're persistent." Ginny crossed to me and slapped me hard on the shoulder as I stood to greet her. I caught my balance before making introductions. "Ginny, this is Aya. Aya, exhibit number one: Ginny."

"It is a pleasure to meet you." Aya bowed slightly, in her formal way. In that second that she looked away, Ginny shot me a 'what the hell is up with this chick?' look but had a pleasant smile ready when Aya straightened up and offered her hand.

"Charmed, I'm sure," Ginny mugged.

"Aya is the lady who was being attacked when Evan was shot. I told you about her when I called you," I added helpfully.

"Oh, yeah." Ginny nodded, and then she spun on me. "Are you okay?"

"I'm fine, now." I gazed into her face. "I can't believe I had to do that again."

Ginny put her arms around me and pulled me against her. We stayed that way for a moment, and then she released me with her arms and her simple words. "You did what you had to do, and Evan and you and this woman are alive because of it."

I wiped the tears away and nodded. She had short-circuited a long painful journey for me, and I was grateful beyond words.

Knowing it would have embarrassed me to try to find those words, she deflected the attention away from me and onto Evan. "And what is wrong with that man? Did he just throw that gun away on purpose? What was he thinking? Didn't he pay attention to his basic training? We both took those LAPD pistol classes, we could have told him to keep the gun. Hell, any idiot could figure that out. Rule number one in a firefight: you need a gun! And I'll tell you something else . . ." She railed on for a little longer while Aya watched her, mesmerized by her strength and energy. Ginny is a bit overwhelming at first. Well, actually, she's always overwhelming.

During a brief pause while Ginny was inhaling I turned to Aya and said, "See what I mean. I didn't exactly have a choice."

"What?" Ginny's eyes narrowed and slid from me to Aya. "You've been talking about me?"

"Yes, but more as a force than as an individual," I explained.

"Oh, fine then," she dismissed. "Look, can we go in and see the patient, or do we have to stand out here in this fabulous decorator showroom all day?" Ginny wrinkled her nose at the ugly room, crossed her arms, and cocked her head at me.

"He's sleeping," Aya offered.

"Well, wake him up! The girls are here." Ginny waved a presentational hand in the air.

"Let's go in and see if he's up for a visit," I suggested.

They followed me to the door of the room, and I looked around the corner. I saw Evan's eyes flutter, and his right hand went up to run through his hair. The three of us filed in and lined up next to his bed, watching him as he awoke. He opened his eyes and scanned all three faces smiling down at him. He closed his eyes and then opened them again.

"What the hell is this?" he asked in a raspy, waking-up voice.

"You have visitors," I said softly.

Evan squinted up at me, adjusting to the light streaming in from the big windows. "Can we offer them some tap water, and get a cup of coffee and some morphine for me?"

"Sure," I said. "Oral or intravenous?"

"Intravenous would be great, thanks."

While I went to the phone Ginny launched into Evan, in a slightly softer tone of voice, I noticed. She works as a stuntwoman in films, big films. She's known for her high falls, fight scenes, and insane driving. Evan, of course, was a real-life detective; he didn't have a stunt double, a fight choreographer, or the benefit of a second take. But he listened to her critique of his performance last evening.

After coffee and opiates, Evan seemed to achieve the perfect balance of alert numbness that eludes many of us, try as we might to attain it. He was sitting up in his bed with his wrapped leg elevated, and he kept looking to Aya, who had perched herself on the edge of a chair. But though I looked for it, I didn't see attraction in Evan's eyes; I saw suspicion.

Ginny was sitting next to Evan by the bed, and she reached into her large bag, pulled out a green and white box, and laid it carefully in Evan's lap.

Evan's smile was genuine. "Krispy Kremes. How sweet, you remembered."

"You have no idea how much self-control I showed bringing those over here. When I picked them up they were *warm,* and you know what a warm Krispy Kreme will do to me. I made the girl tape the box closed before she gave it to me, so that you would get all twelve." Ginny looked pleased with herself.

"Would you like one?" Evan asked innocently.

"You know it!" she responded. "Pass that back over here, I'll just slit that tape for you." She readied a rapierlike acrylic nail.

We all had one of the donuts, except Evan, who was not in need of a sugar rush, being filled to the brim with narcotics. Little melt-in-the-mouth orbs of bliss, I could have eaten the whole dozen.

"Did you speak to the delightful Detective Sewell?" Evan asked, his eyes locked on Aya.

It's hard to eat a donut without it touching your lips, but she was doing it, tearing off bite-size pieces and placing them onto her tongue. She finished the morsel she had, wiped her mouth gently with a tissue, and turned all of her attention to Evan.

"Yes, she questioned me for quite a while this morning." She sighed softly. "I hope that I was helpful."

"I hope so too," Evan replied simply. "Did she ID our guy?"

"His name was Leon Sarno," I filled in, having spent some time with Detective Sewell myself since last night. "She tells me he was a semilegitimate businessman."

"Did you know him?" Evan asked Aya without acknowledging my response.

I overrode my initial response to being ignored, extreme pissiness, and watched Aya for signs of surprise or lying.

"I have never heard the name before," she said, and she didn't change the direction of her eyes.

"And you had never seen him before he assaulted you in the shopping arcade?" Evan asked.

"No." But this time her eyes shot off to the left. She was either lying or had had to search for the answer. Evan had taught me to watch for that too.

"Are you sure?" he pressed.

She was silent for a minute, and then Aya sighed quietly and tears came to her eyes, but she did not look away as she answered evenly. "No, I'm not sure. I think that I had seen him, at the hotel." No one spoke; it was strangely apparent that she was being brave. "I had seen him with Korosu. I did not tell you before because I did not want to involve my uncle or his business with this type of person and because I was not certain. Korosu is very reputable and respected. That is very important to us. Do you understand?"

"You don't want me to talk to him," Evan guessed, and she nodded. I was impressed at how easily he had picked that up.

"It would bring him dishonor," she concluded.

"It brought me a bullet," Evan said without wavering, pausing long enough for her to feel the weight of his silence. "But moving on from that; why was he with this man, Leon, if he was so"—Evan paused, and I could see that he was beginning to struggle for words—"distasteful?"

"I don't know, exactly, but I think that the man had some kind of business with my uncle."

"What?" Evan pressed, but I heard the word slur slightly, and I could see his eyes were beginning to glaze. The morphine drip was hitting its stride.

"I'm not sure," Aya said, and her eyes went discreetly to Ginny.

"Listen, honey," I intervened, "why don't you talk to Aya when you're not on narcotics. Okay?" I saw that, as sloppy as his thought process was getting, he understood that Aya did not want to talk in front of a stranger.

"You think?" He smiled, and his head lolled back before he could catch it, as though for a second his neck had fallen asleep on the job. "Maybe I'll just shut my eyes for a minute." I smiled at him and kissed his brow. The drug was beginning to take full effect, and the caffeine was no longer in the race.

His eyes closed, then fluttered opened again, and he said in a peanut butter–thick voice, "Thanks for coming, ladies." He smiled crookedly and focused with difficulty on Ginny. "Keep the gun, keep the gun," he repeated, and then he was out.

Chapter 8

It was two days later when I brought Evan home and wheeled him out to sit at the pool while I took a swim.

I dove in, swam half a length of the large pool underwater, and surfaced in time to see Deirdre coming down the cypress-lined path.

"Deedee, come on in, water's fine," I called, though I knew she wouldn't, even if it was 110 in the shade and she was heat-stroking.

"Thank you, ma'am. I must decline. I do not have my bathing costume at hand. A Ms. Aikosha is in the sitting room. Are you at home?" she asked.

Evan's head came up a little, and I saw him straighten up. "What do you think, honey?" I asked him. "Are we here?"

He was watching my body with a covetous eye. "Well, I was planning on being very busy, very soon," he said more to me than to my butler.

I smiled slyly. "I like that," I said. We let the promise of sex crackle between us while Deirdre stood waiting. "But, we have a guest." Making him wait was a good thing. His work was always making me wait. I turned to Deirdre. "Send her on out, and follow her closely with a pitcher of something with ice in it, and three tall glasses."

"Would strawberry lemonade be satisfactory?" She pronounced *strawberry* in that two-syllable way that the British have. Straw-bree.

"Just the thing," agreed Evan and then fell into a pensive state as Deirdre started back to the house.

"You seem suspicious of Aya," I said to him. "Why?"

The way he turned back to me made it clear I had interrupted a line of thought. He looked distracted but answered, "Just a hunch after the first attack, but when a man she said she didn't know came after her a second time, his being a stranger starts to look unlikely. Then she told us that 'maybe' she had seen him with her guardian, this Korosu guy. And that doesn't sound kosher either. This guy's paying for her to go to medical school out of the goodness of his heart?" He looked at me knowingly. "Something's up," he said.

"Maybe she's trying to protect this Korosu?" I offered.

"Could be," he agreed, but without conviction. Before we could go into it more I spotted Deirdre returning, leading Aya down the walk.

Climbing out of the pool, I stood there dripping wet and waited for them to get closer.

"Do you have a bathing costume at hand?" I called to Aya and glanced at my butler. No reaction. I didn't expect one, of course. Deirdre merely handed me a thick white towel in an imperial fashion and then faded away.

"No, I don't." She smiled gratefully. "I forgot my corset as well."

"And I notice you've exposed your ankles." I tried to look disapproving and severe, difficult to pull off while wearing nothing but a Brazilian bikini. "Brazen hussy."

She laughed and said, "What's the Old World coming to?" Then switching smoothly into sincerity, she added, "I'm sorry to interrupt your day."

Evan didn't smile. "I'm curious to know why." To soften his directness, I offered her a seat.

She took it and arranged herself in an attentive pose, as though even the way she relaxed was practiced to perfection.

"Would you like something to drink? Deirdre's bringing lemonade, but I think I have just about everything else," I offered as I took the edge of the other lounge, making a concerted effort to sit up straight for a change.

"She has *absolutely* everything else." Evan leaned forward as best he could and dropped his voice conspiratorially. "I know because I checked." As wealthy as he is, he still enjoyed ribbing me about my plenty. Like there's so much difference between his twenty million and my few odd hundred million. I mean, c'mon, twenty million will buy you all the soda flavors they make.

"Lemonade sounds delicious, thank you," Aya answered. "How is your leg healing?" she inquired politely.

"It'll be a relief to be able to be back on top again." He looked at me heatedly, and I smiled back, my eyes wide and my lashes batting innocently. "But I'm guessing that checking on the state of my health is only one reason you came here today."

Her smile was one of relief. A breeze wafted across the pool, chilling my damp skin and brushing Aya's midnight black hair against her cheek; it behaved like moiré satin, moving in a silky sheet that rippled and shone like a solid surface. I found myself trying to smooth my own petulant mane into submission with both hands, but, like the rest of me, it was not very good at being obedient. Maybe hair is an indicator for the personality, like frogs are for the environment.

"That is not true. Your health is my every reason for being here. First, to inquire about it returning, and second to discuss the reason for its decline."

It took me a minute to catch up with that, but I did get it. I guess Evan was tracking because he said nothing, just waited for her to continue.

"Something has happened to my uncle, and he would never ask for help, especially not from the police. But I am afraid after what's happened, and I don't know where else to go. I'm hoping that you can advise me," she said guardedly.

"I don't know if I can or not." Evan was using his firm you're-gonna-have-to-do-better-than-that voice. I'd heard that tone a few times myself.

"I must explain more about the situation, I know that." She paused as Deirdre materialized behind her. She hadn't been aware of the soft-footed servant's approach. I could see that it startled her, but she covered her reaction well.

"Thank you, Deirdre, just the thing," I said and made small talk about the delicious dinner Aya had treated us to until the lemonade was served. I would trust Deirdre with the location of an Iraqi weapons depot, but I understood that Aya wouldn't be comfortable revealing anything in mixed company, so I waited until she left. "You were saying," I continued when we were alone again.

"My guardian has a second ward," she began. "Her name is Shika. She's very lovely but also very young and didn't have much knowledge of a world like Los Angeles when she came here from Japan." Aya smoothed her perfect skirt and took a slow sip of her lemonade. "She was going to school, a very good girls' high school, and living with a family in the Hills."

"If Korosu is her guardian, why doesn't she live with him?" Evan interjected.

Aya looked surprised to be interrupted but recovered quickly. "Because Korosu is a single man who prefers to live alone; and without a chaperone it wouldn't be proper for her to stay in his home." Evan nodded, and she continued her story. "This living arrangement started when she was sixteen, she's nineteen now."

She fixed her eyes on her crystal glass and the beads of moisture gathering on it. "At the school she had a classmate who was South American. This girl's father, although very wealthy, was of questionable ethics."

I glanced at Evan, and he nodded noncommitally.

"The father introduced Shika to a friend, a very rich and powerful man. Pretending to visit her schoolmate, Shika started to spend time with this man. The family that she lived with noticed that she was staying out later and her grades began to drop. Finally, they contacted my guardian, who spoke to Shika."

At this juncture Aya's mouth tightened, and she came close to showing disapproval. "She was very disrespectful of my uncle. She told him that she did not need him or his assistance, and she left him very distressed. That night she didn't go home."

As though drawn together by the force of her gaze, tiny beads of condensation had grown into one long slow drop trailing down the glass. Aya picked it up and studied the light coming through it with rapt intensity.

"We looked for her, of course, but she had left the country with this man. It was several months before we found her." Aya took her focus off the drop and looked up at us.

"And when you did?" Evan prompted.

"She was not herself." Aya avoided a direct answer, and took another careful sip, eyes focused ahead of her on the table.

"Who was she?" I asked, trying not to be impatient or caustic.

"She was a cocaine addict, very ill, and very confused." Aya sighed. "My guardian took her away from the South American man and put her in a hospital. The man was very angry; he regarded Shika as his property, not as a person who needed help. We had to hide her from him. The man that you killed worked for him. He was looking for her."

"Why didn't you tell us that the first time?" Evan wanted to know.

"Please understand, I did not know that man was involved

with Shika when he first harassed me. I thought I might have seen him, but I wasn't sure."

"I think you were sure," Evan told her flatly.

She started to protest but then said, "That's true. Last night, he asked for Shika by name, but I didn't tell you because I was protecting my uncle."

"Protecting Korosu from what?" Evan asked, and when she seemed reluctant to respond, he looked as if he were on the edge of losing his temper. I watched him check himself and add, "I can't help you if you don't tell me everything. Whom are you protecting Koroso from?" he repeated.

She hesitated again, then nodded and said, "From any association with the Colombian man."

"Colombian. Who is he?" Asked Evan intensely, in a voice that would not be denied an answer.

"His name is Antonio Gades," she said in the same even tone, but she might as well have shouted it at Evan, who jerked upright, as though the chair he was sitting on had been jolted with electricity.

"Antonio Gades sent his hit man to get this girl back because he thinks he owns her, and Korosu left you exposed to this guy?" He was incredulous.

"My uncle was trying to protect Shika. He risked himself, personally and professionally, to do that. It was never his intention to put me in danger. He was not aware that they knew who I was."

"He must have known *after* the first assault."

"He's out of the country, but now he does know, and that is the reason that I am here."

"How did you get involved?" Evan wanted to know. "Why would they come after you?"

She shrugged, a frustrated gesture. "I have thought about that. I have been like a big sister to Shika, and we used to do things together, health club, spas, that kind of thing. I get mail for her from those businesses at my address, maybe they tracked that?"

"Could be," Evan said distractedly.

"Who's Antonio Gades?" I asked, lost again.

Evan turned to me and said shortly, "He's a bad guy, honey," and I understood that he would explain later.

But I wanted to know now. I tried another source. "Aya?"

"I don't know much about him except what I have been told," she sidestepped.

"Which is?" I insisted.

"People say he is Colombian Mafia. That is all I know," she concluded.

"Is he?" I turned to Evan.

He sighed and caved in. "Maybe, probably. The drug syndicates have replaced much of the Italian Mafia; they are ruthless, organized, and big business, and this guy is one of the major players and . . ." Whatever the "and" was, he let that thought drop. "The FBI can't get anything solid on him, because he travels all over the world and is never anywhere near the action when they find it." He tapped his fingers on the arm of his teak lounge chair. "You said Shika left the country with him for several months. Where did they go?"

Aya, watching the sunlight on the cypress trees as the breeze ruffled them gently, answered thoughtfully, "I'm not sure, different places in Europe; I heard Spain mentioned and, of course, Colombia."

"Why does he want her back?" Evan demanded.

"I'm not sure."

"Guess," he suggested.

"I think he might be angry that Korosu took away something he considered his property." There was a spitting quality to the last word, as though it tasted bitter.

"So Gades is pissed off?"

"It's only a guess, but it seems that way, doesn't it?" Aya

seemed to defer to Evan's superior skill of deduction. But he said nothing.

"Where is Shika now?" I asked; it seemed to be the logical progression.

"Hiding," Aya answered.

"How's she doing?" I inquired, remembering the painful road back from my own addiction.

"She is much better. It has been several months, and her physical health is mostly restored, but she has a long way to go before she has faced the shame of it all." Aya said it simply, and I knew exactly how Shika felt. It's a long way back from hating yourself that much, and I hadn't had the cultural onus of "dishonor" to confront that she did, just my personal demons.

"Is she safe?" Evan asked.

"I think so," Aya responded. "I hope so."

"And where is this Korosu?"

"He is in Malaysia on business. He'll return in two days, but he's afraid I'm in danger and wants me to stay somewhere safe, to get some help, discreetly, until he returns. That is why I have come to you."

Evan leaned forward, toward her. "So you have his *permission* to be here?"

"I have his blessing." She didn't take the bait. "And I'm asking for your help."

Evan's eyes cut to mine with a meaningful glance.

"Aya, would you please do me a favor and ask Deirdre to come out? You'll find her in the kitchen." I gave her directions, and she went without comment.

Evan watched her go and then said, "You sure know how to find trouble." His annoyance spiked the statement.

The annoyance was contagious, and I caught it fast. "Oh please, you would have done the same thing if you saw someone being attacked."

"I've got a badge." His eyes flashed at me.

"Oh, so I should have let her get beat up, or shot? What did you want me to do?" I was indignant; he was blaming me!

"You carry a cell phone, you could have called for help," he said with finality.

I opened my mouth to spit fire at him, I was so angry, but before I could work up a flame he held up a hand.

"I'm sorry." He brought his hand up and massaged his brow. "I know you did what you thought was best." I didn't believe him. "But right now we have to decide what the hell is going on, and what to do about it."

He looked so worried and serious that I let my retort drop, temporarily mastering my outrage with a deep cooling breath.

After several of those breaths I was able to change focus. "Is she in danger?"

"Absolutely," Evan said emphatically. "So is this Shika, and Uncle Korosu, whether he knows it or not."

I was trying to figure it out for myself. "What did this Leon guy want from Aya?"

"Good question. My guess is the first time he meant to scare her into telling him where Shika was, which you interrupted."

I bit back a defensive onslaught.

"The second time he was trying to take her—"

"Kidnap her?" I overlapped, alarmed.

"Yes, maybe thinking to trade one for the other, that's how these guys work, they go personal. If Gades thought Korosu cared more about Aya, he would use that."

"For God's sake they're women, not dry goods!" I exclaimed, affronted at the idea of women being bartered.

"To men like Gades, it's the same thing. And it sounds like he's taken a personal interest in her, which means he'd be incensed if *she* left *him.*" His eyes caught mine piercingly, and I knew he shared my sense of impotent rage at the injustice, and I softened slightly when he said, "God I'd love to nail one of these bastards."

But I was still annoyed at him for blaming me, and knowing

it would cut him as much as it would be a voice of reason, I said, "He's a little out of your league, isn't he?"

Evan deflated, and I was instantly sorry. "Yes, damn it," he said. His whole body sagged, and his handsome face looked lined and tired.

I tried to make light of it. "Why do you want this guy so badly?" I asked. "I mean it's not your neck of the woods."

"But it filters down to me!" he said. "I see all the crime and the despair caused by this guy and others just like him."

"It's just that you make it sound personal."

Evan gave me an appreciative smile. "In a way it is. A friend of mine, a guy who went through police academy with me, just hit the missing persons list. His name is Charles Chopin, nice guy. I became a detective, and he moved on to the FBI. Last I heard he was working undercover with Gades's syndicate. I can't get any details, of course, it's all hushed up, but I do know he was supposed to report in and he didn't." His face was strained with worry, and then he seemed to try to shake it off. "Cally, try to understand this too. I became a detective because there is something about people hurting other people that infuriates me, call it an overactive sense of justice. I love the puzzle of it all too, finding the pieces and figuring out the answer. It's a challenge, a chess match that I like to win.

"But, more often than not, we don't win. I have stacks of files of unsolved cases on my desk. And you know what the majority of those are? Drug-related murders. Half of them are kids, kids who get the dangerous jobs of delivering and selling the drugs. Kids who get started on drugs when they are seven and eight years old and are dead of overdoses or gang fights by fourteen. The guys who supply that poison, who profit from all that chaos, just get some new teenagers to fill in the spots when the bodies have been dragged away. I want one of those pieces of dirt. Hell, I want all of them, but I'll start with one of those bastards who makes life suck for so many people and never has to answer for it."

I waited for a minute to be sure that he was finished and then I said. "So it *is* personal."

He smiled at me again a little sheepishly. "Yeah. I guess it is." He looked past me, past the patio and the pool, and I watched him go. "I've seen some things that I wish I had never seen."

"So Gades is out of your jurisdiction?" I rephrased my earlier question to bring him back.

"Yes." He sounded bitterly resigned.

"But Aya isn't." I watched him get it. He returned to me, the pool, the morning, and a small smile crept over his mouth and into his eyes.

"What?"

I shrugged innocently. "A woman was attacked in Los Angeles, her attacker committed that crime in Los Angeles, its *your* job to solve *that* crime, Detective."

"And how do you propose I do that? It's still technically Detective Sewell's case," he reminded me.

"Aya needs protection. What if she stays here?"

Evan looked at me like I was crazy. "No way. I don't trust her," he told me. "She didn't tell us everything she knew up front, and I'm not sure she still has."

"Maybe she doesn't trust us yet," I suggested.

"I am not putting you in danger," he told me firmly.

Down the walk I spotted Aya returning, with Deidre close behind her. Evan followed my look and sat back, shaking his head. "Just for a couple of days," I whispered to him, " 'til guardian uncle gets back."

When the two ladies got to us they stood, waiting for a moment while Evan watched me closely. Finally, he spoke.

"Aya, Callaway has made a very generous offer to let you stay with her until your uncle returns."

Aya moved her head slightly but in a quick-enough motion for me to detect alarm.

"I didn't mean to impose, I couldn't, that would be too

much," she said in a rush. "I was only hoping you could advise me, or recommend someone to help."

"Find you a bodyguard, you mean?" I asked.

"What about Ginny?" Evan offered. "She's fun."

"What about you?" I asked Evan and then said to Aya, "he's on leave."

"Good idea," Evan said and pretended to think it through. "I'll have to lay flat the entire time, of course, and I'll be on painkillers, but as long as I don't have to focus, think coherently, or stand upright, I'll be good."

"The horizontal hit man," I agreed enthusiastically.

Aya was looking from one of us to the other, trying to decide if we were crazy or insulting her. I wanted her to be sure we were not the latter, so I cut it out.

"I'm sorry, Aya, but we're going a little stir-crazy here." I amended that thought. "Well, he is anyway; I'm fine. Perfectly normal."

"Whatever that might be." Evan nodded amicably.

"We want to help you," I said. "We kind of have a vested interest in this whole thing now."

"Too bad it wasn't bulletproof vested." Evan sighed. "But, seriously, as long as I've got a leg to stand on, this *one* leg anyway," he joked wryly, "I'm in. In fact"—his tone changed to a more serious one—"you're not safe right now. So at least until Korosu returns, I think it's a good idea."

"You need to go pick up some things," I said to Aya, overriding her mouth opening to protest. Evan cut his eyes warningly to me—he didn't like that idea at all. "Or we could send someone else and have Deirdre go ahead and check you in," I amended. "What do you think, honey . . . ," I asked Evan. "Shall we put her next to Sabrina?"

"I'd put her next to Sabrina, she'll love having company."

"I can't impose," Aya insisted, her natural as well as her practiced calm slightly ruffled by now.

"Impose?" I asked, turning deliberately to look at my ten-bedroom house.

She followed my glance, opened her mouth, and then shut it again. She was looking for a good reason, and there wasn't one that I could see, and then she spoke. "I can't stay with you."

"Why not?" I asked.

"Because I am the only one who knows where Shika is."

"Oh boy," Evan said. "So to find Shika, they have to have you. This gets better and better." He was tapping his fingers on the armrest. "I'm gonna have to call for backup," he finally said.

"I don't want to involve the police, please," Aya pleaded.

"I *am* the police," Evan pointed out, "and I am involved." He gestured to his left leg, wrapped thickly in gauze from his ankle all the way up to his shin. "I'm up to my knees in involved."

"Well, up to your knee anyway," I agreed. "Will they be watching Aya's place do you think?"

Evan nodded soberly and asked Aya, "Where is she?"

"She is with a different family in San Francisco until my uncle returns," she revealed. "I took her there to be safe after the first attack."

Evan's attention narrowed as she said that and I got it too. *Aya had said that Leon didn't mention Shika during the first attack, that she didn't make the connection. Why would she feel the need to take Shika away after that attack?* But all Evan said was, "I don't think Gades knows that she's there yet or he wouldn't have sent Leon back to you. I think he sent this one hired flunky to do a job he thought would be easy, and he won't make that mistake again. In the interest of the safety of everyone in this household we will leave Shika in San Francisco for a while. Meanwhile, is there someone, beside you, who can look after your place while you stay here? I don't want you going back there."

"I have a housekeeper, she can put together my clothes, but I don't know about other things I need," Aya said, beginning to object.

"Don't worry, the guest room bathrooms are fully stocked, and anything else you need we can buy," I interjected.

"Believe me, it's best if you don't leave yourself exposed right now," Evan added. "All joking aside"—his voice was stern and serious—"this guy is a badass, you probably know that much, and it's not a good idea to underestimate him."

"You think he might find out that Aya's here?" I asked him.

Evan looked at me with his sharp blue eyes, and they were as humorless as daytime drama. "If he's taking this personally, baby, he already knows."

Chapter 9

"Wow, you're pretty," Sabrina said as she was shaking Aya's hand later that same evening.

"Thank you," Aya said politely, though she looked a little disconcerted by Sabrina's unconventional greeting. "I consider that a vast compliment from a woman as beautiful as yourself."

"It's a lovefest, I just knew it," I commented. I had introduced Aya as an old friend of mine who was staying with us for a few days, and that had piqued Sabrina's interest because I didn't have many old friends. Or new ones for that matter.

I asked Sabrina to help Aya get settled in and went to check on Evan.

I found him in the library. He and his partner, Curtis, sat facing each other in front of the fireplace in leather armchairs. Curtis was attractive in a Marlboro man way; not what you'd call a pretty boy. He was a little rough-looking, with salt-and-pepper gray hair and a dry sense of humor that could crush you like a sledgehammer. He was as sharp as they come. He was a man's man, Evan spoke of him with deep respect, and had told me of two separate times when Curtis had saved his life—once with smarts and once with sheer all-out ballsy guts. I liked him; to tell the truth, he impressed the hell out of me and turned me on a little. I supposed I was partial to detectives, understandable given the supreme pleasure I derived from my relationship with Evan. The two of them had been closeted in there for a couple of hours talking strategy. I got the idea pretty quickly that Curtis wanted something on this guy as badly as Evan did. The two men stopped talking when I entered the room.

"Go on," I encouraged. "Don't let me interrupt. I've come to light the fire." I got down on my knees and struck one of the long wooden matches I kept in an eighteenth-century coal scuttle on the floor. Holding it under the stacked kindling, I watched the flame take hold and begin to climb up the logs. Behind me, Evan and Curtis picked up their conversation, filling the grand space with the deeper timbre of male voices. The sound filled an empty space in me as well—a hole carved by the painful loss of my father.

"But he can't just want her back for his ego," Curtis was saying.

"Can't he? You've seen the stuff these guys have done because somebody looked at them the wrong way."

"I know how these animals behave. How many times have I said I'm a glorified zookeeper? I hunt them down, I put them in the cages, and I shovel the shit they leave behind. Hell, I'm an animal behavior *expert.* But from what you're telling me about the condition she was in, he should have been pretty much done with this girl; he'd used her up and it was time to toss her out with the trash. Why would he want to get her back?"

"Personal thing against this girl's guardian?" asked Evan.

"Could be, but from the way Gades met this Shika, it doesn't sound like it. How reliable is this source of info?"

Evan paused before he answered. "I don't know. I've had the routine checks run on her, she looks as clean as Plexiglas."

That surprised me. I knew he thought Aya wasn't telling him everything but not that he thought she was lying. I turned away from the growing warmth. "Are you saying you don't believe what Aya *has* told us?" I asked.

"Do I ever?" He raised his brows at me in a question, and I shook my head. "One of many occupational hazards. I think she's telling part of what she knows, anyway." His eyes glinted. "I'm guessing this other girl, Shika, knows a lot more."

"Yep," Curtis agreed, and with a body-sliding glance at me on my knees, he stood up. "Well, I'll get started then. We'll find out where Gades personally has been in the last month or so."

"Thanks for coming over, Curtis." Evan stretched out his hand. "You'll forgive me if I don't get up," he added dryly.

Curtis switched his eyes to Evan and I saw it in a flash—a look of genuine affection as he shook the hand offered to him, and then he looked back to me and winked. Only a real man could flirt disarmingly with a woman in front of her lover and be so likable. Still on my knees, I smiled in a sexy way and leaned over to offer him my hand, exposing a bit of lace with the move. "Good night, Curtis, thank you so much." I squeezed his hand meaningfully and then released it.

He smiled back. "Good night, don't do anything I wouldn't do." He was starting out the door when it opened and Ginny took the room.

"Hi!" she said in her full-throttle voice. "I came as soon as I got the call . . ." She spotted Curtis. "Oh, hi." She focused on him as though she were looking through binoculars and hit the stabilizer. "And you are?"

"Curtis, Curtis Rossmore. I'm Evan's partner in crime solving."

Ginny offered a hand. I saw Curtis wince appreciatively at the strength of her grip. "I'm Ginny, Callaway's partner in crime."

"It's nice to see you," he said.

"I don't believe we've met."

"We haven't, but I'm still very pleased to see you. It was worth the wait." He gave her an appreciative look, then he nodded his head to us all and exited. Ginny stood looking after him for a minute and then pivoted back to face us.

"Hello, Ginny," Evan said formally. "We'll be with you in just a minute."

Ginny frowned and spun again. "Dismissed! I come flying over here and get sent away. Fine." She flounced to the door and then turned back and said in a fast, unconcerned voice, "I need a glass of wine and a long steam anyway, you guys want me to bring you something?"

"Not just yet, thanks," I told her. She made an indifferent noise and left.

Evan was watching me with an experienced eye. "You little tease," he reproached me. "What the hell was that?" It looked, for just a moment, like he was going to take my flirting seriously, but a moment was all it took for me to move to him on my knees, to kiss the inside of his thighs, and look up, from that willingly submissive place, into his gorgeous sculpted face.

"Tease?" I asked, and then my voice dropped an octave. "That wasn't tease, that was being nice. *This* is tease." I put my hands on the outside of his thighs and let my breasts rest against his crotch. Then, slowly, I used my teeth to open his jeans, one button at a time, pushing aside the rough blue cotton as I went, not using my hands until I had to pull the denim over his hips. One pant leg was slit up the side to leave room for his bandaged leg, and I carefully eased them around his wounded leg. Then I put my hands behind my back and touched him only with my mouth and my breasts, letting him unbutton my blouse and lift my breasts easily out of the bra so that softest skin was on skin. I moved and kissed and sucked until I felt my reward was almost there, but then his hands moved around my waist and he lifted me, pulling my skirt up around my waist, my panties down and off, and then pulling me down on top of him, oh so nice. My knees fitting easily on both sides of him in the oversize chair. His eyes half closed, but his gaze remained intense while I surrounded him. So ready, so easy. I controlled the movements and the timing until his hands took hold of my waist and held me tighter against him, and our orgasms came together, wild and huge.

Afterward I snuggled against him and we watched the fire while our breathing settled down. I felt it was time to bring up a subject we both were avoiding, but I wouldn't, I couldn't, bring it up directly.

"So, how long do you think Aya should stay here? Just until her guardian gets back?"

"He hasn't done a very good job so far of protecting her, and I think this might be an actual shot at getting something to stick on Antonio Gades."

"What do you mean?" I was curious.

"Look, Gades wants Shika back, so it makes sense that she *knows* something about him, something about his business. It might just be his ego, because this Korosu guy took her away from him, but I get a gut feeling it's more than that. So if we can find out what 'it' is and nail this guy, Aya could be the goose, and Shika just might be the golden egg." He turned and kissed the top of my head; I didn't look up at him but braced myself instead.

"So, you should probably stay here for that whole time, not keep going back to your place, right?" I kept my voice even with a practiced effort.

"Should I?" His voice had changed. It was softer, more searching.

"I mean you have to, don't you?"

"No. The smartest thing would be to put Aya and Shika in a safe house somewhere else and keep a watch on them there. First we have to talk to Shika, find out if she really knows anything." He left that hanging. "Cally?"

"Yes?" I answered.

"Are you asking me to stay here for a while?" He was smiling softly, like he wanted to make me say it first.

I wouldn't take the bait. "It'd be okay, I guess. I'm getting used to you."

"I'm getting used to you." He smiled, and I smiled back. It didn't seem like much, but it would have to do for now. I was tempted, for the hundredth time, to say the three little vulnerable words, but I'd be damned if I was going to say them first.

I was thinking to myself that there was a good reason I haven't gotten close to anyone, when Evan said it.

"There's a reason I've never gotten close to anyone." Hearing him confess my thoughts was novel, and I was all ears. "Being with someone makes me vulnerable. Do you understand?" I didn't really know how he meant that, and my face must have showed it, because he said, "If I'm on my own, there's no one who can be hurt to influence me."

I nodded, disappointed to discover he considered me a liability. It smacked of being told that our relationship was a disability to him.

"And there's something else." His voice dropped to a very quiet personal place, and I knew that he was going to tell me something he had never told anyone. "I want you to know that I've done some things that no 'nice guy' would ever do." He fell quiet, and I sensed that he was afraid to continue.

"So have I," I said at last, but standing on the ledge together wasn't enough. We needed to step off the edge into the void. "Tell me one of those things," I said and braced myself.

He looked at me for a moment, and I saw how hard it was for him to let me in. I sensed that if I recoiled there would be no going back. "I shot a man who was seducing young, very young girls. He was getting them addicted to smack and then turning them into prostitutes. He had some kind of protection, and nobody could get a conviction on him. He knew how to play the system, and every time we got him on something he'd slip out of it. He even bragged how he'd do it again, how nobody could stop him." I could hear the anger and the hatred in his voice, and something else, fear that he would frighten me away.

A little chill went through me, but I kept my voice steady. "Did you kill him?"

"No," Evan said without hesitation. "I had threatened him to try to stop him. He thought I was bluffing, that my hands were tied because I was a cop. But I did what I had said I would, and that made it very clear that I meant my next threat." He stopped there, and I could almost hear his teeth grit.

"What was that?" I asked softly.

"That I would kill him if he ever told anyone it was me."

"But did that stop him?" I asked.

"Yes." There was a pause while Evan took a deep breath and threw his weight into thin air. "*Where* I shot him, didn't leave much to brag about."

I thought for a minute about what it would take to do that. It was too horrific to hold in my head. And then I thought about the hell on earth my life had been when I was an addict, about the kind of person I had been then, self-loathing and desperate, and the men who had taken advantage of that. I found his eyes with mine and smiled gently.

My hand went to his chest, and as I laid my palm against it, he exhaled, and I felt the space between us close as the dark side in each of us recognized the other.

"Good for you," I said quietly.

Chapter 10

The light off the blue water of the pool was blinding when you first came around the cypress trees and your irises ran smack up against all that glistening, undulating brilliance. I saw Evan pause and lean against one of his crutches as he fumbled for the reflective sunglasses in his pocket. Deirdre waited patiently behind him. Once he had the mirrors in place and his balance intact again, he just stood and took it all in.

Ginny, Aya, Sabrina, and myself were all in bikinis, lying on pool floats. I was keenly aware of my immediate competition and just as confident of my belle-of-the-ball status. They looked great, but Evan's gaze landed on me, and stayed there.

"Don't I have nice pool accessories?" I asked, waving a hand in the general direction of the other contestants.

"I *must* get the name of your pool man," Evan said wryly. "My guy offered me a waterfall and a pond option, even said he'd throw in some pollywogs. I certainly didn't see this kind of fauna in his brochure."

"Did you just refer to us as some kind of algae?" asked Ginny.

"No, algae would be flora, I'd say we fall into the exotic fauna division," I explained. "Although, technically, Evan did compare us to an amphibian."

"He called us frogs?" boomed Ginny.

In contrast, Aya's voice was a pretty soprano. "If I stay in the water much longer I might turn into one."

Evan pretended to ward off Ginny's assault. "Whoa there, I might put you in the water nymph category, or possibly some kind of goddesses of the deep, but that's as low as I'd care to go."

"I'll take that," I mused. "Ginny?"

"Which one am I?" She slid her sunglasses down her nose and peered at him across the water.

"You are one deep goddess, Miss Ginny." Evan flashed that flawless smile at her, and she kept it.

"We were just talking about why a man, like Gades, would mistreat a girl so badly," I filled in. "I'm saying he used the drugs to hook her in, then he didn't care enough about her to not let her destroy herself."

Aya turned her face quickly to one side, as though she'd been struck a painful blow; I felt terrible for being so insensitive.

Evan didn't notice her reaction; he was trying to get comfortable on the chaise as Deirdre propped a cushion under his leg. She then proceeded to line up other chairs and put the terry covers on them.

But Ginny had seen Aya's reaction, and I was grateful when she turned the focus from Shika to me.

"Gee, I wonder what could make you think that," Ginny said and pointed a finger at me. "Could it possibly be because of what you went through?"

She and I argued for a while about whether or not my opinion was based entirely on my own jaded experiences until I conceded that it probably was. But I made her admit that there were lots of men out there who were incapable of seeing a woman as anything but a sexual object, men who would never value a woman for anything else.

At this point Sabrina popped up with a bit of wisdom. "But don't you think some girls see themselves that way?" We shut up and looked at her. She blushed. "I mean, I'm just saying," she drawled, "I know some girls, at school and back home in Louisiana, who see *themselves* only as something pretty and sexy, and they use that all the time. I knew one girl who had herself a rich older boyfriend, and she was always bragging about what he bought her, and how when she wanted something special she got new lingerie and did these new tricks. I mean, she's not making any bones about it, she wants something, and the only thing she offers for it is *s-e-x.* She doesn't respect him at all." Sabrina finished her dissertation and then put her pouty lips around the straw in her orange soda and sucked.

There was a quiet while we all contemplated the wisdom of children.

"Tricks?" asked Evan. "What kind of tricks, exactly?"

I splashed him from my floaty. "That's enough out of you. I know what you mean, Sabrina. It doesn't seem honest, but at least everyone is getting something out of it." I thought for a minute and then said, "I mean, I'm sure the boyfriend knows what's going on, right?"

"Uh-uh." She shook her head. "He thought she loved him. Isn't that just so sad?" Sabrina looked as though she actually might cry.

"Come on, guys aren't that stupid, are they, Evan?" I looked up at him.

"When it comes to a pretty girl, *most men,*" he said, accentuating those last two words to give himself an out, "are dumb as rocks. They will believe anything a woman tells him."

"I agree!" yelled Ginny. "I'm not saying anything against men, individually, you understand, but as a group, they're remote controlled by just the suggested promise of large breasts and a tight ass. Look at our whole society." She gestured to the shrubbery, as though it represented a microcosm of our social structure and beer advertisements; but I knew what she meant. The man with the prettiest girl won the grand prize.

"And then, there's Richard E," I said, and looked at Evan and Ginny.

"Richard Evans?" asked Sabrina. "He's so handsome, and famous." She sighed.

I did have a few famous friends. It was hard to live in my neighborhood in L.A. and not know a few celebrities. Sabrina was totally taken with this particular rock star friend; he was very gracious to her, even though she behaved like a lovesick twelve-year-old when he stopped by. It was embarrassing really, but I brushed it off.

"You've met Richard, I think, Sabrina," I said, and Evan snorted a laugh. "He sometimes hires a girl to go out with him, and/or have sex with him." I dropped the bomb on her in a casual voice.

"With a *prostitute?"* sputtered Sabrina, and her whole world rocked. Well, her blow-up raft did anyway. "Why on earth would he do that? He could go out with any girl he wanted, girls are lining up to go on a date with him."

"Exactly," I said. "But they never leave. If he goes out with a girl once, he can't ever get rid of her, they cling, and they stake a claim. The other way, he can call, meet a beautiful girl, go out, have sex, or not. And she leaves. And they both get what they wanted. He got some company, and she got a couple thousand dollars. Mutual respect all the way around."

"Korosu has the same problem," Aya said. When I looked at her in surprise she added, "He is not a famous rock star, but he is very wealthy, and he says it is difficult to know when a woman is interested in him or his financial holdings."

"I can relate to that," I told her.

Evan was watching Aya, but he said, "She's not referring to me, of course."

Aya smiled. "I know she is not talking about you, that's very clear."

"Of course it's very clear," Evan insisted, "I'm not after her money, I'm after her butler." Deirdre looked up from where she was cranking open a huge canvas umbrella and gave him an admonishing smile.

Sabrina was back on Richard. "But why would someone like Richard want a prostitute? They're so"—Sabrina searched for the word—*"dirty."*

Ginny looked at Sabrina. "Girl, he's not picking up hookers on Hollywood Boulevard. We're talking about high-class operators. Girls like us, who need help with the rent sometimes."

"Girls like *us?* I could never do something like that." Sabrina shuddered. "Have sex with someone you don't even know?"

"What if you knew it was Richard Evans?" Ginny taunted.

Sabrina didn't answer. She just looked at Ginny with surprise on her face and then burst out laughing. "Well, if it was him, he wouldn't have to pay me."

"Thank you, Miss Louisiana," Ginny said, laughing.

"But a nice girl who was smart, she wouldn't do that, I mean, would she?" Sabrina pressed. It was a whole new world to her, and she was fascinated.

"I did," Ginny said, and even though she had said it mostly for the shock value, I knew that it was true. It went over big.

"You did not! You liar!" Sabrina breathed.

Ginny didn't look at Evan, but she held up her hand in his direction in a "stop" position. "You"—she addressed him from her watery throne—"are not here. *You,* detective man, did not hear this. *You* will be called a bald-faced liar if I ever have this thrown back at me."

"I hereby stamp 'out of service' across my forehead," he said and started to whistle softly.

"Listen to me, petticoat girl, it's a tough world out there, and we don't all have billionairesses for sisters. Getting started out here is tough, and I don't wait tables. So, when a friend of mine, whose face you have seen on many, many advertisements and billboards but who also has some slow months, came to me and asked me if I wanted to 'work,' I said I'd check it out." Ginny trapped some water in the cup of her hand and let it dribble over her chest, making her audience wait before she continued.

"So, she takes me to this house in Beverly Hills, gates, dogs, security cameras, you name it, to meet her madam. And guess what was in that house?" She stuck her face toward Sabrina and waited.

"What?" My naive sibling was hooked.

"Cats. Persian cats, a couple dozen of them, it was a cathouse. And there was a very obese woman whose name was Dona, and she was the *real* Beverly Hills madam. Now, in order for me to even be allowed into the house, my friend had to tell her that I was a working girl from another city. So, this Dona looks me up and down once, and asks me if I want to work right then, I mean, right that minute, upstairs in that house. I make up some excuse because I'm too scared, and so she explains the terms for future reference. Five hundred to get them off, once and only once; they pay per orgasm. If they want a night, it's two thousand, flat fee. She gets three hundred out of every thousand dollars the girls collect. I must bring it to her the day following the date, she'll call me. I get up to go and turn around, and who do I see standing there? Well, out of respect for the detective *who is not actually here,* I won't name names, but suffice to say, that the client I turned down that afternoon was a movie star that I would have given my left tit to sleep with."

"Who?" Sabrina was beside herself.

"I'm not saying, but his last film was about race cars," Ginny said smugly.

"No way!"

"Way. So I left, and when Dona did call a couple days later with a date, it was somebody good."

"Him?" Sabrina asked, wide-eyed.

"No, not someone in the public eye but someone good. Real good. He took me out to the finest restaurant, treated me like gold, asked me to go down on him, and gave me twenty-five hundred dollars."

Sabrina's poor little face was torn in half, it didn't know whether to be horrified or delighted, it was doing calisthenics trying to meet halfway, it looked a little painful.

"And, he wanted to see me again. I saw him once a week for one whole summer, and I only had one other 'client,' whose whole deal was making sure I got off, thank you very much, and I got myself set up so that I never had to do it again." Ginny settled back on her float and smiled. "And you know the best part?"

"What?" Sabrina asked her, spellbound.

"They were so fucking grateful." She sighed wistfully. "I've never felt that appreciated by any guy I sucked off for free."

Sabrina looked shocked, affronted, and delighted all at once. Then she said simply, "I don't believe I would have told that last part."

I burst out laughing so hard I almost fell into the water. Turning to Evan, I saw he was looking pointedly at Aya. I followed that look quickly. She didn't seem to share my amusement; in fact she looked highly uncomfortable. Her eyes were fixed on the water beside her.

Evan asked his question before I could formulate mine. "Aya, what are you thinking about?"

The smile came quickly back to her face, and she looked from him to Ginny and then to Sabrina and me. "I was thinking how wonderful it is that you can be so honest with each other," she said, and the smile still graced us, but a melancholy note played in her eyes. Still, there was harmony in it, a sweet sad song.

"Can't you be honest with your friends?" I beat Evan to it this time.

"In the culture in which I was raised, privacy is within a person. It is not considered good form to bare yourself. I don't mean to criticize, not at all, I think it's wonderful," she said enthusiastically. "It's so nice that you all trust each other."

It was Sabrina who broke it all down for us again. "But, Aya, don't you trust us?" The size of her eyes reflected the vulnerability of her heart.

Aya's eyes filled with tears, and for just a moment I thought that all her most hidden pain would flow out, that stories would be told, confessions released, but her mouth spoke only three words. "With my life."

Chapter 11

Monday morning I was coming down the front stairs when I saw Evan, Sabrina, Aya, and a young man I didn't know standing by the front door. Aya was speaking to Evan, a little aside, I couldn't make out her words, but her tone was honey, and she touched his arm often as she spoke. He was smiling bemusedly down at her; finally he put his hand on the small of her back and walked her out the open door.

A cold metal spike passed through my chest. Sabrina was talking to the young man, whom I took to be a fellow student. He was dressed in jeans and had a backpack slung casually over one shoulder so that it wouldn't catch on his long ponytail.

I moved into the open entrance hall, trying to get a straight view of Evan and Aya's little tête-à-tête, but Sabrina intercepted me as they stepped outside. "Callaway, this is Detective Storm. Isn't it amazing how much he looks like a college student?"

"Amazing," I muttered, distracted. "Nice to meet you. Where did Evan go?" I leaned around them and saw him closing the door of a blue sedan I kept as an extra car. He had recommended

Aya drive it instead of her own, as an added precaution. As she drove away he came back in.

"Get going you two," he said to Sabrina and the young man, and to Detective Storm he added, "Stay on her."

Before the door had even closed behind them the gate phone sounded. As I picked it up, Evan said, "I'm expecting a delivery" just as Deirdre appeared in the hallway and told him that Detective Curtis was on the phone. He hurried down the hall after her.

The messenger handed over a thin brown envelope and took away my signature. Still wondering what the hell I had just witnessed between Evan and Aya, and feeling shaky about how to bring it up to Evan, I walked the envelope into the breakfast room, where he was on the speakerphone with Curtis. I handed him the envelope and then stood looking out through the Tiffany windows at the gardeners working. One of the men was pruning the row of olive trees growing in giant terra-cotta pots that lined the moss path.

Though I had often enjoyed this view of the gardens and the fountain that lay beyond them, today I was really listening to Evan's conversation with Curtis. They were talking about Gades. It seemed he was out of the country right now, connected to several big businessmen and politicians who might be protecting him. He always had someone else do the actual deal and was seldom without the company of one or more beautiful women. He kept several homes, including a penthouse condo in Westwood, was a golf enthusiast collecting memberships at exclusive clubs around the world, and was a very good soccer player at one time. He loved to bet on sports events, especially soccer, and he didn't like to lose, at anything.

Except for the criminal aspect, he sounded a lot like my dad.

Evan opened the envelope I had given him while he was talking and gestured to me to take a look. I opened the itinerary and saw three reservations, first-class, to San Francisco for Evan Paley, Aya Aikosha, and Callaway Wilde. There was also a hotel booking at the Fairmont, two rooms, one was the honeymoon suite.

Evan said good-bye and hung up, watching me all the while. I tried not to look as tense as I felt.

"How sweet," I commented. "You're taking me on a business trip."

"Not officially business. I'm still on leave, remember?" He smiled. "Besides, the department doesn't generally pay for suites."

"So it's a romantic getaway . . . for three?" I egged.

"Well, we might want to find Shika while we're there. And since Aya is the only one who knows where she is . . ." He let it drop off.

Trying for casual humor to cover my hopefully irrational panic about his attention to Aya I said, "But then we're going to have to get a sitter, and we can't stay out late; I say we leave the kid at home."

"Think of it as quality family time, honey," Evan said and then, apparently sensing that I was at least halfway serious, his voice changed. "Cally, I need to talk to this girl, and I don't know if she'll talk to me without Aya there. I have to find out what she knows, if anything, about Gades. If it's nothing, then we send Aya home, forget about South American badassess, and cruise across the Golden Gate on a rented Harley."

"Yeah? Who's driving?"

"Well, you of course, I won't be able to change gears." He opened his arms, and I went to sit stiffly next to him on the settee by the stained glass windows. "Say you'll come with me," he said with that mellifluous voice that melted me and made me slippery. Still I resisted; I wanted an explanation.

"Why don't you just take Aya?" I asked. "I'm sure she'll show you a good time."

Evan pulled back a bit. He seemed to be more amused by my petulance than put off by it. But he also looked surprised.

"What are you talking about?" he asked.

"You two sure looked cozy enough at the front door. It didn't look to me like she'd mind going off somewhere with you."

Evan took his arms from around me, crossed them, and sighed. "I don't think I could afford her," he said.

"I'm sure her tastes aren't too expensive for you."

He looked angry for a flash and then said, "She wanted something from me this morning."

"No kidding." I sounded immature and I knew it.

"She wanted me not to send a detective with her, she thought it would look suspicious."

"Oh please," I said. "That guy looked more like a med student than she did."

Evan was looking at me like I was missing something obvious; I felt like it was the other way around. "Why would she think she could manipulate me if she acted coy? Think, Cally, what debt is between Aya and her guardian?"

"I don't know, maybe her family lent him money." At least he acknowledged her behavior by the door, that was something. Now what about his?

"If they had that kind of money why is it through 'Korosu's generosity' that she is going to medical school. Why aren't they paying for it?" He was gazing steadily at me. I was getting angry that he was diverting the conversation, but somewhere in me a warning light went on; he didn't look guilty of anything, and I was about to look stupid.

So instead of snapping I tried to answer his question. "Maybe she did something for him?" That could be it; I didn't care much right now.

"You're getting warmer."

"Saved his life?" I asked impatiently.

"Colder."

"She's his lover," I said, as though it was obvious.

"No," Evan surprised me by saying. "But you're getting warmer."

"What does this have to do with the way she was playing up to you at the door?" I wanted an answer.

"Think, now." Evan was leaning toward me. He placed his hand on the inside of my thigh and started to run his fingertips lightly up and down.

"Stop that," I said, but I didn't move away.

"Now concentrate." His hand moved higher, the movements got smaller but more insistent, and my eyes narrowed. I definitely found it distracting. *"He* owes *her* a debt, what could that be for? She's Japanese, attractive, trained to be ladylike and entertaining." His lips went to my neck, kissing me the way he knew would please me.

My resistance was weakening. I wanted to answer, to stay focused on his questions and be smart, but he was distracting me, doing everything he knew I liked . . .

"She's his geisha," I said. My eyes flickering open for a moment to see Evan intently focused on the pleasure I was feeling.

"Bingo," he said and went for my neck again.

"Wait, wait, wait!" I sat up and shifted away from him so that I could think about something beside his hands. "You're telling me she's a geisha med student?" I looked at him dubiously. "C'mon."

He looked very disappointed and tried to move next to me again, but I straight-armed his chest and stopped him. "It's not that bizarre," he said. "I'm guessing she came here to the States with him, fairly young, and has since decided she wants something more out of her life."

"Okay, that I totally get, and I salute her for it. But she will not get away with geisha-ing her sexy self all over you." I stood up and straightened my skirt. "And I saw the way you put your hand on her back, you're not getting off that easily."

His eyes crinkled into a naughty smile. "Looks like nobody's getting off right now."

"Evan, I'm serious." I was upset.

"I'm sorry, I know you are. I was just getting her moving outside, and by the by, she did not get her way. The detective went with her," he added pointedly.

Still uncomfortable with the way he had touched her, I looked away, out the windows again. There were my gardeners working steadily, all three of them. "Evan?" I said, suddenly alarmed. "Do you have a detective that looks like a gardener?"

In two seconds he was on his feet and scanning the yard. "Which one?" he asked quickly. "Don't point at him," he added sharply as I started to raise my arm.

"The one closest to us." I cut my eyes to him, trying not to look alarmed. But the man had seen us focusing on him; he started to walk toward the fountain, away from us, and Evan moved as fast as his injured leg would allow to the doorway. The man glanced back over his shoulder, and seeing Evan yank open the door, he bolted, disappearing rapidly over the edge of the lawn where it sloped down to the wall of my property, hidden from our view.

Evan grabbed one of his crutches, drew his gun, and hastened out into the yard. He stopped and looked around where the man had been pretending to work. Stooping down suddenly, he picked something up.

"What is it?" I asked. "What did he drop?"

Evan scowled and threw away a small twig. "Nothing."

I couldn't agree with that. He *had* left something behind, and I couldn't see it, but I sure could feel it.

Fear.

Chapter 12

After Evan had my security company check the property and they found no one lurking, we relaxed a little bit. And when Sabrina and Aya got back to the house safe and sound I felt much better. I'd had vagrants on the grounds before, but I doubted that the intruder was unrelated to our houseguest; it looked like it was time to bring in more security.

Leaving Evan to give instructions to the two extra security men we hired, I crossed back through the marble entry hall and went up the stairway. Stopping at one of the doors along the hall, I knocked. Aya answered right away, asking me to come in. When I saw her, she was standing politely in the open French door of her balcony. A thick textbook and a notebook were lying open on the small table outside.

"I didn't mean to interrupt your studying," I said, "but I wanted to talk to you."

"Please." She moved her hand in a graceful arc toward the chair. "I'm the guest, but I will be so bold as to invite you to sit."

I sat, realizing that I had never been on this balcony before.

"Isn't it lovely?" Aya said softly, looking out. "Beauty and peaceful surroundings are important to you. You know, in a way, your thinking is very Japanese," she told me softly.

I took in the view; far away the ocean lent its shimmer to the horizon, and closer by, a waterfall in the garden cascaded down a rock wall producing different lilting voices in languid conversation.

"It's so important to have a sanctuary," reflected Aya, and I noticed that she let her voice mix into the sound of the falling water, rather than compete with it, or try to override it. She was more like a new instrument blending into an orchestrated piece.

"Yes, it is." I looked around for a moment. "I'm not sure I've ever been in this room," I joked.

She nodded agreeably but said nothing, no push, no filler, just sitting. I could have stayed like that for a long time. Aya made me comfortable in my own home. Unfortunately, I was far too Western a woman to stay silent for long.

"I wanted to ask you something," I said, interrupting the stillness again.

"Please," she encouraged.

Now that I got down to it, I didn't know what I wanted to ask her exactly. As usual I had formed a vague idea but no definite plan of action. I wanted to ask if she was a geisha, but now that seemed rude. I felt the blood rise in my face and struggled for wording for a moment before deciding that it would save tons of embarrassment if I weren't distressed about it.

"I want to know about what you do," I said finally, "and I don't mean medical school, I mean what you do for your guardian. What you owe him and what he owes you." I fumbled on. "I'm not judging or anything you understand. Part of me wants to know to get to the bottom of this craziness and part of me is, well, frankly curious."

She was watching me with wary eyes. "What do you want to know?" she asked.

I sighed. I guess I would have to be blunt after all. "I want to know if you're a geisha, and I want to know what that means."

"Ah," she said, and she turned her eyes away from the harshness of the question. "Yes, I am what you would call a 'geisha,' a very modern version of geisha. I was trained in Japan from my tenth birthday. My guardian chose me from among many girls in my school and offered to pay for my training and also to help my family, who, as I said, are not wealthy, come to the United States. It's not easy to learn the arts, dancing, how to play musical instruments, and how to move and behave when entertaining. Being geisha is very respected in Japan. Here people would consider it something else. American men would not understand." As she spoke I was envisioning a man in his late sixties walking along a row of schoolgirls picking out the ones he wanted. I had to admit that I, an American woman, was having trouble understanding that.

"Why?"

"Because if a woman takes money from a man they expect it to be sexual."

I raised an eyebrow. "Isn't it?"

She still didn't look at me; her eyes took on that soft-focus quality that I had seen before. "Yes, but most likely not in the way you think."

"Forgive me," I apologized, "but I don't understand. Do you not have sex with the man?"

"If I choose to give that gift and receive that pleasure, then I might. And there are games that are played, sexual games, with light touching and dancing, but most of those are performed fully clothed." She raised her eyes just a bit and focused even farther away, where the mist met the shore.

"Is it exclusive?"

"Sorry?" she asked.

"Do you only, uh, geisha for Korosu?"

Her look stayed focused far away. "No."

"So that's how you can afford to live the way you do?"

"Yes, my house is paid very well for my services, and I receive a generous allowance from them," she said this as though it were common practice.

But I didn't get it. "Your house?"

"Yes, traditionally in Japan it would have been where I lived, and the other people there would have been considered my family; Shika is my 'little sister,' it is part of the custom for a geisha to pick an apprentice and help her. Mainly try to guide her, give her advice, and most importantly, to introduce her around so that she becomes well known. That's why I spent a good deal of time with Shika. But here, the 'house' is usually a working group, run by an older woman, usually ex-geisha, who functions as a sort of business manager. She makes all the arrangements and takes care of the payments."

"How many of you are there? Here, I mean, working for your 'uncle'?"

At this her eyes came back to me. "I do not work for Korosu. He was my sponsor, and my legal guardian when I came here at fifteen to go to school. He does not take any money from me, or anyone else. In fact, he feels indebted to me for the training I undertook, and he made a promise to me to help me with whatever else I chose to do when I came of age. That's why he pays for my school. He is a man of his word."

I asked, "But if it's not exclusively for him, why would he go through all that trouble?"

She smiled at me now, like I was a child who needed things explained to me. "Because he is a connoisseur of beauty, and of . . . many things." She glanced away. "And because it brings pleasure to so many."

"Really?" Other aging men who bought sex, I assumed. I know I sounded skeptical, but I found it hard to believe that it didn't help him in some way.

"I know what you think," Aya said self-consciously, "and part of it is true. It helps his business, yes. He is very highly regarded for *many* reasons, and that is one. There are men from Japan who choose to bring their business to him because of his respect for tradition."

"Wow, I guess it's a little hotel that's big on service," I commented.

"The hotel is a small investment for my guardian," Aya continued smoothly. "It's simply a place to provide an elegant retreat for his guests and business associates. He has said so, many times."

This was getting interesting. "Really?" I said again, more authentically this time. "And does he expect you to 'geisha' for him?"

I knew my question was awkward, but though she rose easily to the coarseness of the inquiry, I could see the effort it took to reveal herself to me. "He reserved the right to be the first. But I had the right to refuse if I chose." Her voice shook slightly, and she shifted in her chair.

I wanted to ask her if she did refuse, but I could already see what this conversation was costing her. She was very uncomfortable.

She had told us at the pool that in her culture being open wasn't "good form." So all I said was, "Listen, Aya, thank you, for confiding in me what you have." I started to rise.

She stopped me with her comment. "I want to trust you," she began, paused, and then continued. "I would like to be able to talk about it with someone." Smiling shyly she added in a softly defensive tone. "I am not ashamed, you understand."

"You shouldn't be," I commented automatically, "and if I've offended you or gone too far, please tell me."

"No, it's all right." She looked at me mischievously. "You want to know if I refused him, don't you?" Her eyes sparkled when she said it.

"Well, yeah, but you don't have to tell me."

"I didn't." She looked pleasantly scandalized that she had told me, and she whispered the next part, "I didn't want to. I was very lucky to have such an exceptional partner for my first experience; as I said, he is a connoisseur of many things." She nodded proudly and then added in a girlish voice of shared confidence, "It was great."

That surprised me. Maybe it was my Western value of youth and beauty that made the whole thing seem distasteful. I really didn't judge the money exchange part, but it was hard to imagine this young woman enjoying herself sexually with some soft old guy. But she had taken a chance trusting me with that secret, and I didn't want to push it, so I asked, "And what is his business?"

"Investing, importing, international money market, many things. He's also deeply committed to several charities helping people both here and in Japan." She smiled and turned her palms up. "It's my wish to return to Japan and work in the children's hospital that he established there. At least for part of each year."

"An international financier, philanthropist, and sex expert." I smiled. "My kinda guy. I'd have to get over the multiple-decade age-difference thing though." I turned to look out over the garden and asked the question I had really come to ask. "What is it like?"

She was quiet for a moment, and then she said the one thing I would never have expected her to say. "Powerful."

That I didn't get. I could relate to the sense of power that being sexually desired gives you, of course, but my limited understanding was that she was paid to be subservient, to make the man feel more important than she was. I gurgled a little in the absence of an appropriate comment. She laughed and looked at me slyly.

"It's part of being a woman to make a man feel like a man. It's natural. Understand that I am only with men who truly respect geisha. They pay my house a great deal of money for me to be charming and gentle, to be ladylike. I'm honored to be regarded that way, mostly because they feel honored to be with me." She inclined her head in that noble way she had.

"Wow, things are different in Japan," I said.

At this her face saddened. "I wish that were true in the sense that you mean it. But we also have prostitutes and men who do not respect women and women who do not respect themselves. But true geishas don't fall into the group of women who rely completely on men who desire them sexually. Also, in many other ways, women have much farther to go to be considered equal to men there than here. That's another reason I choose to be a doctor." I saw a moment of fierceness in her eyes and realized that being respected, as an equal by men in her culture, was a greater personal challenge than she yet understood.

"You'll make a good one," I said. I gave her a moment and listened to the waterfall. "There is another reason I wanted to speak with you. Evan has decided to go to San Francisco and talk to Shika."

I saw the tension pass through her body, it was almost imperceptible, a split-second cessation of movement, a frozen pause in her fluidity. "When?" She asked.

"It's nothing to be afraid of, we'll be very careful. We leave tomorrow afternoon, you'll be back on Sunday, in time for classes on Monday." I didn't want her to worry about that.

She smiled, her eyes flickered down for a moment as she thought of something. "I'll be ready, but I have one request, perhaps you could speak to Evan about it for me?"

"Sure, what is it?"

She leaned in so that she had to look up into my face and

touched my knee in a gesture of supplication. I recognized the move as the one I had used myself on Evan when he thought I was flirting with Curtis. "I would like to see Shika first, to explain to her who you are and that you are trying to protect her. She is afraid, understandably, and also ashamed of her weaknesses. I want to be sure that she will speak with you and tell you what you need to know." Her eyes had dropped away from mine, as though she knew she were asking too much, more than she deserved. She was appealing to me to help her in this, yet I wasn't sure Evan would go for it. He liked to get people's first reaction.

"I understand; I'll mention it to him."

"I'd be glad to make this request myself, but I think that, because you know Evan so well, you will know so much better how to ask. And as a woman, I know you will understand how Shika feels." Her eyes came up to mine now, soft and needy. I felt an overwhelming desire to grant her this, to be on her side, to champion her cause.

"Don't worry, I'll talk to him." I smiled reassuringly and then stood up, and saying I'd see her at dinner, I made my exit.

I had reached the top of the stairs, resolved to go straight to Evan and make sure Aya got her first visit, when a funny suspicion came over me. It wasn't that I didn't agree with Aya, I did; I understood what she was asking, and I thought it was a good idea. I empathized with Shika having to dredge up her worst memories to strangers with no introduction, so I was okay with the request itself. It was Aya's approach, the appeal, the body language, the helpless eyes that I found uncomfortably familiar. I had used them myself to such great effect time and time again.

"Did she just work me?" I wondered out loud and was surprised to get an answer.

"I shall need to know the question to answer that." I jumped and turned to see Deirdre as she emerged from my bedroom with a vase of flowers that needed to be replaced. She fell into step behind me as we descended the main staircase into the entrance hall, our voices, muffled at first by the plush Berber carpet on the stairs, amplified as we touched down on the cream marble floor and crossed together toward the kitchen.

"Oh, I was just wondering: can a zebra change into *and out of* its stripes? Or, once they have been tattooed on, will no amount of laser surgery remove them?" I said.

"Your wandering observation is cryptic, but not undecipherable, considering the background of your guest."

"Did you go online?" I teased Deirdre. Of course she had known Aya's occupation; the staff always knows first.

"No, but I went into your library. I find books so much more esthetically pleasing than the hum of a hard drive," she answered. "Also, when I heard her playing the samisen in her room, very skillfully, I might add, I came to my own conclusion. The question you are debating, however, is not a cultural but a universal one. If an individual has trained themselves to, shall we say, 'behave' a certain way to succeed in one field, can they break away from that behavior?"

"Well, if that's what I'm asking, then, I think yes, in this case," I began. "For the simple reason that I met Aya outside of her, uh, work and she's already chosen a new line of work."

"Yet, the influences of her profession remain, I think, intact," Deirdre pointed out.

"You've noticed that too?" I asked. "She has a way of making me feel more clever and funny than I am."

"And she does it so effortlessly that if you ever noticed she was in control at all, it wasn't until later." Deirdre stepped ahead of me and held the swinging door to the kitchen open while I passed through. "I believe Miss Aya to be a genuinely thoughtful and kind person, I take that into consideration," Deirdre expounded, "but she is also a professional at creating an illusion."

I remembered my own sad version of that, trying to always be what a man wanted me to be, a sexual creature, because that was how he valued me. "After a while the line between who you really are and who you are pretending to be moves toward the wrong goalpost, if you know what I mean." I stopped at the huge center island of the kitchen and picked out a piece of fruit from the wooden bowl that sat in the center. "In my case, the line actually moved all the way across the field until I was running touchdowns for the wrong team. But, and this is a big 'but,' *she* is aware of what she's doing. She knows where the line of scrimmage is, I think."

I took a bite of the pear, and its firm soft flesh surrendered in a satisfying burst of ripeness. "Yum," I said with my mouth full and took another bite. It was really sweet, almost too sweet.

Deirdre went to one of the Sub-Zero refrigerators and took out a white paper wrapped package while she spoke.

"True, she seems to be fully conscious of her actions and their effect. And I believe that she respects you because you are the kind of person she would like to be—respected," said Deirdre as she unwrapped a huge wedge of cheese and chose a large knife from the wooden block.

"What does that mean?" I asked.

"It means, that my impression of Miss Aya is that she wants to be respected in the same way that you are, she wants to make something of herself." Deirdre placed a sliver of the hard cheese on a small china plate, placed it in front of me, and followed it with a linen napkin while I let that compute. "I think you'll find this complements the sweetness of the pear," she said.

I picked it up, took a bite of the strong-smelling sheep's milk cheddar, and marveled at the way two distinctly different flavors could improve each other. "Yum," I said again.

"However, she has also trained herself to behave in a way that will not achieve her ultimate goal of respecting herself and being respected," continued Deirdre. "She might find it hard, whatever profession she now chooses, not to 'run the same plays,' to use your analogy of American football, because those 'plays' have provided results for her. Many people find it difficult to change sides in the middle of the game." She rewrapped the cheese and wiped the counter clean.

I held up my slice of cheese in one hand and the remains of the pear in the other. "So, you're saying her game plan and goals don't go together?"

"I'm saying, old habits die hard." That was all Deirdre would commit to.

Chapter 13

Still miffed by Evan's attention to Aya, I had donned the Bulgari watch for the trip to San Fransciso. I sat next to Evan in first class, with Aya in the seat behind us, and brooded. Although the watch was unlikely to be an anonymous gift from the handsome stranger, I liked to think that it was; it gave me a sense of autonomy. So what if things don't work out with Evan, I told myself, he's not the only fabulous man on the market.

So why was I miserable when there was any kind of rift between us? I was surprised when Aya asked Evan if he would mind switching seats with her so she could talk to me. I watched the way her hand stroked his arm as she spoke, and I made a point of looking at my watch to see what time it was. Evan noted the cold look on my face and the watch, and changed seats without comment.

When she was settled next to me she smiled shyly and gave my arm the same treatment. "I hope you don't mind," she said apologetically.

"Not at all, things have been a bit tense with the two of us anyway," I confided in a voice low enough that Evan wouldn't be able to catch it.

"I noticed that. I hope everything is all right?"

"Fine. No big deal," I told her. "These things happen."

"I was curious," she said, also in a conspiring tone, "did you speak to Detective Paley, I mean, Evan, about what we discussed?"

She wanted something. I experienced a sense of relief that she had gone through me instead of him to try to get it. "Yes, he wasn't very happy about it, but he said five minutes."

Her face brightened. "Oh, what a relief, I've been so worried about Shika. You can't imagine how she feels about men now, especially men with power over her, she's just terrified."

"Well, hopefully you'll be able to tell her what nice people we are." I laughed, but Aya looked at me seriously.

"It's true, you know. You are." She sighed. "It's been very enlightening to watch you two together, it's wonderful to see the equal footing you have, you're so lucky." There was no resentment in her voice, only a sense of longing. "It's as though you don't have to try to guess about each other, you don't have to work at making each other happy."

I laughed again, this time at myself. "Oh God. I'm better than I thought if it looks *that* good. Aya, I can't tell you the work this relationship has been for me. Not Evan, I don't mean he's a lot of work, it's more me trying to get over a history of not trusting anyone and always thinking it was me against the world." I felt overwhelmed at the task. "And I refuse to play at something," I said finally.

Aya opened her eyes wider, and then her mouth curved into a sly smile as her eyes narrowed. She leaned in to me and lowered her voice even more. "Oh, now, sometimes, a man has to be handled. You and I both know that, I've seen you, you're very good at it." She giggled and squeezed my hand quickly. "Sometimes it's just so much easier than a confrontation."

I was taken aback, but only for a moment. I thought of how I had appeased Evan's jealously over Curtis in the library a few days before and the many times I had softened his mood, brittle from a harsh day at work, by speaking soothingly and sitting near him quietly until he responded. The way I had made him think that giving Aya a few minutes with Shika alone would be a generous thing for him to do.

"You know," I said, "you're right. Somewhere along the way I have learned how to handle a man when he needs it." I'd never thought of it that way, it didn't seem like a bad thing when you were just trying to calm someone or get close to them.

"And I'll bet," said Aya, her eyes twinkling, "that there are times when he handles you."

I hated to admit to myself that I could be so unsuspecting; but she was dead-on.

The FASTEN SEAT BELT sign came on, and Aya rose so that Evan could sit next to me for the approach to San Francisco International Airport. When he was comfortable I took his hand in mine, and although I didn't really look at him, I didn't let go until we were safely on the ground.

Chapter 14

A few hours later, Evan and I stood on a landing outside an apartment door while Aya took her designated five minutes. Evan was raising his hand to knock when Aya opened the door to us, revealing a million-dollar view of the bay through an uninterrupted window of huge glass panels that ran from the floor to the ceiling. In front of this architectural masterpiece sat Shika.

Like Aya, Shika appeared to have an innate sexiness, but Shika also possessed an awkwardness that betrayed both her youth and her nervousness.

Aya watched each of us intently, as though she felt responsible for all of our actions. Shika tried to meet our eyes but with only limited success. When she spoke her voice shook a little, but she smiled softly and answered Evan's questions as helpfully as she could. He was asking about Gades in a professional, impersonal way; I knew this was to help her answer the same way. The damaged quality about her made it clear that she was still emotionally distraught over her experience.

"He was not what you think," she was saying in a voice both gentle and fearful. For some reason I thought of delicate flower petals on scorched earth. "He was very strong, and he had a bad temper, yes." She nodded and appealed to Evan with a look I had seen before, when Aya asked for a favor. I wondered if I looked like that when I wanted something. "But he was sometimes very different, he could make people understand themselves in a way they didn't before," she said, her voice trailing up at the end, signifying that she knew the thought was incomplete.

"Really," Evan said, leaving it open ended.

"Yes, for instance, if there was going to be a fight, he could stop it, he could speak to the men who were angry, and they would hear him. Or if someone came to us with a bad intention, he could diffuse it."

"How?" Evan asked.

"Because he didn't speak *down* to anyone. He knew how to make them hear, to make them feel that he had been like them, and had risen above it. I don't know how to describe it exactly." There was a fondness in her voice.

"So, you think highly of Antonio Gades?" Evan asked flatly.

Her eyes fluttered away at this. "No, not anymore, but there was something about him, something special." She appealed again. "Do you understand?"

"I think so," Evan said. "He has a great deal of charm, street smarts, and possibility, but he doesn't use it for good. He didn't choose that. He has chosen to use that charisma for profit and power."

Shika smiled at him. "Yes, I believe that you do understand."

Evan smiled back, but only politely. "Shika, I need to know why he is trying so hard to get you back. Why he would try to hurt Aya."

Shika's gaze flew to her friend in the corner, and it was instantly clear that she had not known about the attack. "He wants me back?" she asked, and it was at once fearful and laced with hope.

Aya spoke to Shika in Japanese, smooth and firm; it sounded like she was comforting, calming, and warning all in one lilting sentence.

Aya turned to Evan. "She must not go back, she does not understand."

"I do understand," Shika said in a very small voice. "I am grateful to Aya and my guardian for helping me. I know how shamefully I have behaved." A large tear rolled down her cheek, though she never blinked.

It was my turn to try to comfort Shika as others had comforted me. "It's not your fault, not the drugs anyway. They rule you completely, not the other way around; this is something I understand," I said to her.

She gave me a thankful look, but there was no forgiveness of herself in the glance.

"I need to know if there is a reason for Gades to be worried about you," Evan said. "Something you could know that would make him vulnerable."

"No, nothing. I don't know." She sputtered a little. "I, uh, I can't think of anything." Her eyes went to Aya for help, but Aya did not look at her, just focused on the water behind Shika. Shika looked lost, both in the expression on her face and in her chair by the glass. She seemed afloat in a vast blue sea.

"They almost always spoke in Spanish around me," she said finally because she knew we were waiting for more. "And I only understood a very little bit. I'm sorry." Her doe eyes went to Aya again. "I just can't help you. I'm sorry."

Evan sighed and looked at her curiously. "You only understand a little bit of Spanish?" he asked. "School?"

She nodded again.

"Did you pretend to understand more than you did?" he asked gently.

Another tear came from her eye. I half expected it to splash right into the ocean around her. "Yes," she whispered. "I did."

"But, what *did* you understand?" Evan asked, more softly still.

"The word *coca,* and they spoke often about places." Shika studied her folded hands with intense interest.

Evan said nothing, just stayed absolutely motionless, eyes on Shika. The silence among us lasted longer than it took me to draw three deep calming breaths. Finally she spoke, her lips moving but no other part of her stirred.

"San Pedro," she breathed. "The port of San Pedro."

Evan leaned in again. "What else? Were there dates or details?"

Shika remained silent, her face closed. It was impossible to tell if she was trying to remember, completely ignorant, or just refusing to say anything further. In the void, Aya's voice came sharply to our ears. She spoke in Japanese, not loudly but with great conviction. She seemed unhappy with Shika and to be letting her know it in no uncertain terms.

Evan cut her off. "What are you saying to her?"

Aya was quick to apologize. "Please forgive my impatience, but I was reminding her how much you are trying to help. I will speak in English, I am sorry, that was very rude." She turned to Shika and spoke to her, stressing the sentence. *"You understand what I said to you."*

"Yes, I understand you," Shika said to Aya, though she did not look at her. "But I can only remember one other thing. I do not know if it is important or not."

"Everything you can remember is important, every detail," said Evan encouragingly.

"They used a word often, seemed to think it was funny. Maybe it was a joke or something. But the word was *tina.* I don't know what it means." She looked up to Evan and myself and shrugged her pretty shoulders.

At this point Aya stood and walked quietly around behind Shika; she placed her hand on Shika's arm, stroking it absently while looking with an unfocused expression at the floor between herself and us. The gesture was delicate and precious to see. It was a lovely picture. The two gentle beauties, and all of San Francisco Bay's blue mist beyond them.

And then the blue mist beyond them shattered. One second it was as clear as though the glass wasn't even there, and the next it was nothing but a kaleidoscope of distorted colors. In an explosion of light and noise the giant wall of glass disintegrated and fell in one wavelike tenth of a second. It happened so fast I didn't have time to close my fascinated eyes; I saw both the women hunch instinctively forward away from the pebbles of glass that rained down on them. Then I was hit from the side, and I found myself underneath Evan on the painful glass gravel that covered the floor. By some miracle it hadn't cut me or the other women to shreds. We stayed, shocked and still, for a full hour-long second, and then Evan reacted first.

"Don't move, don't raise your head, no matter what," he hissed in my ear. And then I felt him rise off of me. "Get down!" he shouted at Aya and Shika. "Get flat and cover your heads!" He moved toward them on his hands and knees, pulling his gun as he went past them, getting between the two women and the ledge of the building. "Now, start crawling, all of you, toward the hall, hug the floor, and I mean crawl. Stay on your bellies and move, now!"

Evan has a way about him in emergencies that you don't question. In prehistoric days, he definitely would have been the grunting male with the biggest club. Even by today's standards, as gentle as he could be, you knew he was dangerous when aroused, and he was in full arousal now, not the kind I preferred, but it was working for me on a real basic level right at the moment. I crawled, I hugged, I moved. I had reached the back wall directly across from the shattered window before I turned to make sure the other two were crawling to meet me, and to see what Evan was doing.

Where the window had been there was now just a pile of clear shiny rubble and a line where the glass had been secured into the floor. Evan was lying across that line at the very lip of the concrete ledge. Through my panic, I saw him freeze on something, and I followed his gaze. On the roof of the building down the street on the right, there was a figure in black holding a rifle. My heart somersaulted into my mouth.

"Oh shit," I said in an exploratory manner, not too sure I should be speaking at all.

"I see him," Evan said curtly, his eyes still locked on the man, who seemed to be holding the rifle upright, not pointed at us. Evan was watching him down the sight of his gun.

"Evan, get away from there!" I was terrified for him, he was completely exposed and was facing a rifle with a handgun for God's sake.

"Call nine-one-one," he enunciated really clearly and then added, "and get the fuck out of the room." The man on the roof moved his gun into shooting position. Evan spoke and rolled at the same time. "No, get the fuck out of the room and *then* call nine-one-one." He got to us, and we all started to move when the arm of the chair next to Aya's head exploded, throwing feathers into the air. Shika dove into the safety of the hallway, but Aya froze a few feet short of the passage and put her arms over her head. I moved in behind her and grabbed her around the waist, pulling up hard, using my legs and falling backward into the hallway with her on top of me. Evan hit the floor beside us just as a good portion of the wall behind us turned to dust. It was so strange, not hearing any shots but seeing the effect of the impacts. I looked back at the feathers from the chair arm settling on top of the tiny glass shards.

I tried not to picture bits of one of our brains settling on the ground instead of the feathers. Shika looked both confused and terrified. Two emotions I heartily seconded. Aya rolled off of me and scrambled farther down the hall. I reached for my cell phone and realized it was in my bag, in the breezeway that had once been the apartment's living room.

Evan was already on his cell, and he rattled off all the pertinent information I would have never thought of. I waited until he flipped it closed, and then we all looked at one another.

"So?" I said, so shaken and nervous that I couldn't stop my mouth. "We've got a foursome, how about a round of bridge?" The two women looked at me with an appropriate reflection of my insanity. "Mah-jongg?" I tried.

"I've got an idea," Evan said. He was busy investigating the hallway. It ran at a right angle to the living room, sharing the back wall so the room to the right had the same view as the glass wall of the living room.

"Oh good, nobody liked mine." I was so grateful that he was speaking, that he was there, that he was alive in the world.

"You stay here and I'm going into that bedroom to see if I can get a clear shot at him." He started awkwardly forward on hands and knees again, his injured leg obviously paining him, staying low as he went through a door on the right side of the hallway. I moved down so that, without exposing myself to the window, I could see him go to the far corner and rest his back against the wall next to the window. He turned his head and looked out over the sill. Between him and the window was an opalescent sheer drapery. He could see through it, but it was unlikely anyone could see in from a distance. I hoped. I thought with an icy jolt that the rifle, obviously very high powered, must have an effective scope. He reached up and unfastened the latch, sliding the window open a few inches.

"Evan be—" The window next to him shattered with a terrific noise. Shika screamed, and I pushed her farther back behind me.

"Cally?" Evan called.

"Yes?" I answered quickly, eager to be useful but other than trying not to breathe I couldn't think of anything remotely helpful.

"Do you have a mirror?" he asked.

"There's one in my purse in the living room. Want me to get it?" I asked.

"Don't be a smart-ass," he snapped at me. I didn't mean to, it just came naturally.

"In the bathroom, there." Shika pointed at a doorway on the left side of the hallway a few feet closer to us than the bedroom doorway.

"I'll get one," I volunteered and crawled through the door. The second drawer I opened was filled with makeup, and I grabbed a large compact and crawled back into the hall, trying to smile at Aya and Shika, who were both hugging their knees in a self-protective attempt to shrink into the wall behind them. "Got it," I said to Evan.

"Okay, no, don't throw it to me," Evan said as I prepared to toss it. "Now listen to me, I need both hands to fire from this range, and I may only have a second or two to aim, so I need you to spot for me. But *only do this* if you can stay down and not let your head clear the sill." In his eyes was extreme fear for me.

"Can't you just wait for backup?" I didn't want him taking that chance with his life, much less mine.

"There are other people in this building, most likely going to their windows right now."

He was right; we weren't the only ones in danger. I took a deep breath and repeated my father's mantra silently to myself: *you can do it, nothing to it.* To Evan I said, "I can do it."

He nodded at me. "I know you can. Now, go to the other side of this window and use the mirror to try and see him. And Cally," he said urgently as I started to move.

"Yeah?" I answered, looking up at him hopefully.

"Be careful."

I smiled and winked conspiratorially to make him think I was neither disappointed nor mortified, and did my snake impression until I got to the wall to the right of the window. Once there, I opened the compact and very slowly held it out at an angle to see what I could see.

It was disorienting at first, trying to see such a large view in such a tiny square, but I adjusted and steadied my shaking hand enough to tilt it minuscule fractions until I saw the gunman, passed him up, went back.

"Got him!" I breathed, trying not to move.

I had to speak softly for fear of losing the image on my tiny screen.

"What's he doing?" Evan demanded.

"He's leaning down on his elbows, maybe, yes, I think he's got binoculars and he's looking this way," I replied. It was a guess but a fairly educated one. As I started to shake again, so did the image in the glass, and I squeezed tighter to steady it. "Now he's put the binoculars down, and he's leaning over."

As soon as I said that, Evan turned and came up on his knees. Staying behind the curtain he took his forty-five in both hands, and keeping his head as low as possible, he aimed. I could see him past my hand but I tried to focus on the shooter in my tiny screen. My hand started to shake again, and I dropped my arm once to stop it, then I had to find the view again. I got the rooftop, the exit from the building onto the roof came into view as I adjusted a quark left, and there he was, no, it wasn't him. It was someone else, standing with an arm outstretched, a tiny bit farther, and then the gunman came into view. And then I heard the shot, not from Evan's gun, but a tiny pop from far away, and I heard Evan curse at the same time. Within seconds, the man in black had crumpled to the roof and the newcomer had crossed over to the fallen figure, leaned down, and then run back into the exit, disappearing as suddenly as he had appeared. Evan rose up a few inches higher now, trying to get a view of what was happening.

I took my cue from him and raised myself to look out the window.

"Get down!" Evan barked at me, and I did.

"Who was that?" I asked him, bewildered and shaking from the adrenaline overdose in my body.

Evan fell, exhausted, back against the wall, reaching a hand to his leg, still bandaged under his pants. I crawled across to him, avoiding the glass shards on the carpet and tried to help him take the weight off his injured limb. "Looks like somebody sent us a guardian angel," he said through gritted teeth.

"An *angel,"* I asked pointedly, "who just shot a man point-blank in the back of the head?" Evan's look conceded that it was a question of perspective.

I could hear Aya crying softly and sirens walling with increasing volume as they neared us. Over the windowsill I saw the unmistakably dead figure in black sprawled on the tar and gravel rooftop.

From *my* perspective the whole scene seemed not so much sent from heaven as summoned from hell.

Chapter 15

When the San Francisco SWAT team and assorted members of the police force arrived, we spent the better part of an hour answering questions, and then Evan sent Aya and Shika back to the hotel with two SFPD uniforms. He tried to send me, saying it was safer, but I begged to differ; I was pretty sure that the safest place in the city was next to *him* surrounded by the SWAT team. He couldn't argue with that, so, after a short wait while they finished "sweeping" the building for the second gunman and found nothing suspicious, I went with him to see what had happened on the other roof. Some heavily armed, very serious-looking men, with terrific physiques, escorted us up in the elevator.

The roof was swarming with dark uniforms. Some of them were in position, looking out over the street, and some of them were looking at us in a not-so-friendly way. I felt a bit conspicuous in my pale blue linen slacks and my silk shirt, and probably the Gucci slip-ons were a little impractical for day-to-day police work. "Hi!" I said self-consciously. Nobody answered so I added, "Thanks for coming."

Evan cleared his throat to cover the silence that accompanied their incredulous looks and gave me one of those "maybe you should let me do the talking" glances. I couldn't have agreed more.

In the corner of the tar-and-gravel-covered roof lay a body, next to it was a rifle with what looked to me like a long-range sight and a silencer. I'm not exactly a weapons expert, but it didn't take one to see that this was some serious firepower. The body was facedown, slight of build, and wearing black gloves. The only other thing I could make out was short-cropped black hair, except where the hair was missing. I looked away quickly.

The photographer was just finishing up as we approached. The SFPD detective who had questioned us in the other building nodded to Evan and ignored me. We had told him everything we knew about Antonio Gades and the situation with Shika. Evan had explained that he thought this was a professional hit man hired by Gades to silence Shika. He expected the hit man was Colombian as well. Evan's San Francisco counterpart had rubbed his brow and shaken his head. The detective looked at me now. He seemed hesitant to continue with me there.

"It's all right, she's seen it before," Evan said, vouching for me, and I was sorry that it was true. Nonetheless I focused hard on a spot of gravel just beyond the body in case I couldn't take it when they turned him over.

"Go ahead," said the detective. "Roll him."

A member of the forensics team put one rubber-gloved hand under a shoulder of the body and another under the hip and lifted. The body seemed light, and it flipped easily.

My eyes flickered to the face and away and then went back and fixated.

The local spoke. "You did say 'Colombian' drug lord?" He said it very dryly.

"Yes, I did," Evan answered smoothly, but I could tell he was shaken. I know I was.

The body's nationality wasn't South American. It was Asian. And there was something else. Even with the impression from the gravel on the face, you could tell she had been very pretty.

Chapter 16

When it was all over but the questioning we got back to the hotel suite and I sank deeply into the huge tub with Evan. He propped his bandaged leg up out of the water and got on the phone. When, in ten minutes, he was still on the phone with Curtis and I was still shaking, I climbed out of the bath and went to the minibar. Rum always had a calming effect on me, and I mixed two little bottles with some orange juice in a large glass. As I stepped back into the tub Evan put his hand on my calf, and I felt him rub appreciatively. He was looking at the wall as he focused his attention on what Curtis was saying on the other end of the phone line, but he let his hand slide up my leg, across my ass, and around my back as I joined him horizontally again. His hands were large and strong; God I loved his touch.

I was halfway through my relaxant when he finished the call. He hung up and turned his considerable focus and attention to me.

"Find out anything?" I asked. In response he put his arms around me, pulling my head against his damp chest.

"Yes. A little." His chest vibrated slightly when he spoke, the rich texture of his voice resonating through him and into me. "She was a professional, imported from a city to our south."

"Los Angeles?" I asked sitting up again.

"Good guess. All false documentation on her of course. We ID'd her from her prints, but there was also a receipt in her back pocket from a certain hotel in Little Tokyo." He dropped his chin and looked at me for a second before he took the glass from my hand, took a drink, and grimaced at the intense alcoholic content.

"I wanted a little help calming down." I said, justifying myself with the guilt of an addict.

"It's okay, Cally, I don't blame you. In fact . . ." He took another big swig and grimaced as he handed it back to me.

"So she's obviously connected with Uncle K in some way?" I prompted.

"It's the 'obvious' part that bothers me," Evan continued.

"So you don't think he had anything to do with it?" I asked.

"I don't know. My understanding is that, until Aya brought Shika to San Franscico, he knew where she was, he could have had her killed at any time, so that doesn't make sense. Unless he's smarter than we think and he wants to make us believe it wasn't him. I think it's more likely that this hit person went to the hotel to find a trail for Shika or Aya. But . . ."

"It bothers you."

"Yes. These professionals are really careful about covering their tracks. Why the hell would she have a receipt with the name of the hotel on it in her back pocket? Its just not right."

"What if it was planted?"

Evan looked at me fondly. "Exactly. What if Gades hired the shooter and wanted to make it look like Korosu. That would work with the theory of him wanting to get back at Korosu for taking Shika, *and* it would silence Shika as well."

"We'll have to go meet this venerable elder, won't we?" I asked.

"I will, yes," he said grimly.

I let that slide. "Anything else?"

"The rounds were very high caliber stuff. Hollow-point slugs, designed to explode on contact. That's the only thing that would shatter that thick glass the way it did."

"Yeah, I noticed the way the chair arm disintegrated." My teeth started to chatter again as I tried not to think of what would have happened if the chair had been my head, and I took the glass away from Evan and took a sip to unclench my molars.

"Obviously she was a professional. That much is apparent. 'Who hired her?' is the question. What would help us answer that is knowing this: was she already in San Francisco, or did we bring her?"

"I know I didn't invite her," I said, trying for a levity I did not feel.

"No, I meant more like a virus we picked up," Evan said grimly.

"Is it contagious?" I asked.

"Very good question." He kissed my head. I liked it. It reminded me how much I enjoyed being alive.

"And if it is contagious," I said, continuing along my private thought process, "is it fatal?"

"*Very* good question," Evan repeated. "And here's another one. Who the fuck killed her? And why?" He turned to me and wiped a bead of water off my chin. "Listen to me. I want you out of this. This guy Gades, and maybe somebody else too, seems to be after Shika, in the most terminal way. We don't know why, but I've got to find out. If it is Gades, which looks likely, he used Aya to find her, and I helped him. He's smart."

"So are you," I said, encouraging him and kissing him quickly on the mouth. He returned the kiss, but his eyes were far away.

"Actually, I've been very stupid." He was angry, and when

Evan got angry he got quiet and scary. I had to remember that he wasn't angry with me. "I put you in a lot of danger, and I won't make that mistake again. I want you to go away for a while."

I sat up and got in front of him on my knees. "Why? He's not after me!"

"C'mon, you are much smarter than that." He reached up and brushed a piece of hair off my face. "I don't like you being caught up in this."

"I'm not too crazy about you being involved in this either if it comes to that," I said, "but I'll be damned if I'm going to leave you with this chick I picked up in Little Tokyo." I crossed my arms under my breasts, and it served to plump them up rather nicely. "No. We are in this together, like it or not."

He smiled at me and stroked one breast as he looked at me lovingly.

"Listen to me. These are dark people, they don't play by rules, and I may have to break a few myself to stay in this game." I could see that he was crossing out of the conversational comfort zone; there were aspects of Evan and his "work" that we didn't discuss.

"So, if you follow procedure on this case, your hands will be tied, right?" I asked.

"Yes."

"Then why don't I invite Aya *and* Shika to stay with me, that way you can control the situation?"

"Callaway, no—" Evan insisted vehemently.

"You're already in this," I cut in, "and you're going to have to put them somewhere safe." He started to protest, but I put a finger to his lips. "Listen, for a minute, just listen. The 'hell' you talked about that men like Gades create, I've been there. I'm one of the lucky few who's been to that hell and come back again." There were things about my past we didn't discuss either.

"I know you want to help Shika and Aya, but Callaway, it's too dangerous."

"Then walk away," I told him bluntly.

He looked pained. "I can't."

"Then be smart," I insisted, "and make him come to you. You said yourself he's got people inside—informants, politicians. If you let someone else into this, those woman are dead; we both know that." Taking his hands and never wavering in my gaze I said, "I am not afraid."

He was watching me with a tortured expression. Then he spoke to me in a voice I had never heard before. For a second I thought he was going to say "it." "If anything were to happen to you, it would end me."

I leaned forward instinctively to protect him, wrapping my arms around his head and drawing him onto my chest. "Oh, Evan," I told him with total confidence, "you would never let that happen." And as wonderful as it was to see how he felt about me, I was still disappointed that he couldn't say he loved me.

Chapter 17

"Okay, listen up. These are the rules." Evan came manfully into the library, his limp barely noticeable. It was two days since the shooting in San Francisco, and we were back at my house in L.A. with Aya and Shika. Ginny, who had a phobia of being left out of anything, had insisted on being there as well, and of course Sabrina. We all stopped our chattering and looked up at Evan when he spoke.

"Ooh, the rules," Ginny said ominously, turning to Sabrina. "Now you listen up, you have a little trouble with this part."

"I do not!" Sabrina objected.

Evan rolled on before an argument could break out. "The house is now fully guarded, nobody, and I mean nobody"—he looked pointedly at me—"leaves without an escort and permission."

"What if I have a note from my parents?" asked Ginny.

"I'll give you a hall pass. You are here only because our very stubborn hostess insisted on having you," Evan said. "But"—I got another look—"and this is a big 'but,' even you two don't leave without a police driver. Do you understand?"

"No leaving," Ginny nodded. "Got it, but did you say somebody's got a big butt?"

"Okay, okay," Evan chided gently before we careened too far out of control. "Ladies, this is a very serious business, I'm afraid."

"We know it is," Ginny said, sobering appropriately to the situation.

"Okay then." Evan waited to be sure everyone was settled before he continued. "Now to make this work, I've established safe zones in the house and on the grounds. On the west side of the house you may each approach the windows, but on the east side, facing the street, no one is to stand in a window or doorway. Understood?"

We all murmured or nodded as suited us.

"The pool and pool house area are safe unless I let you know otherwise. The west garden is fine. But please don't wander around the sides of the house or on the front grounds." He went on to explain the reasons. The house was on a sloping hillside. On the back, or west side where we had a full view of the ocean a few miles away, it would be extremely difficult for anyone to get a shot in range from that direction, since past my property, the ground fell away steeply. Impossible really. There were two police officers and two private guards on the property twenty-fours hours a day.

Aya spoke up now. "This is too much. I am sure my uncle could find Shika a safe place in Japan," she insisted.

Evan glanced quickly at me. I knew he was thinking of the Sakura-no Hana Hotel receipt in the shooter's back pocket, and said, "We need to talk about that. It's time to meet this 'uncle.'"

Aya nodded reluctantly. "But he is still out of the country, he'll return on Wednesday."

Evan sighed unhappily. It looked like it was going to be a long two days until Wednesday.

• • •

I was in my library alone a few hours later making some business calls when the door opened without a knock. I looked up, vaguely annoyed.

"What 'cha doing?" Ginny asked as she swung around the corner.

Indicating that I was on the phone by pointing to the receiver against my ear and waving the contract in my hand seemed to get the message across.

"Oh, I can wait for a minute," she said, and with two long strides for momentum she cleared the arm of the sofa and landed with her legs outstretched and her hands behind her head, in a perfectly reclined position; she's very athletic.

"Are you bored, already?" I asked when I wrapped up the call.

"Yes. Entertain me." She sat up eagerly.

"Shall I sing for you?" I asked.

"God, no." She recoiled. "So what's up with the Asian contingency?"

"I'm not completely sure."

"You seem consistently uncertain these days," she said and added pointedly, "how unlike you."

"Oh, I know *why* they're here," I said. "Evan really wants to get this particular bad guy."

"Mm, hmm." She nodded. "And *that's* interesting."

"What?"

"Evan wanting to help these two poor ugly women out." She was clearly on to me.

"Don't think I haven't thought of that," I said quickly. "But I fell in with Aya first, and got him involved, and now this guy, Gades, turns out to be someone that's really dangerous and worth taking down." I fumbled a little, unsure of my own motivation. "Maybe I'm having superwoman crime-fighting fantasies, you think?"

She sat upright and her eyes lit up. "Since you ask me what I think, I'll tell you."

"Oh boy."

"I think, that you see a lot of yourself in Aya; she's beautiful, regarded as valuable for her sexuality, and you want to help her. That's number one. Number two, Shika, she's a drug addict who needs saving, ring any bells? Then there's the big payoff. Boyfriend moves in for an undesignated amount of time without you having to offer or commit yourself." She threw up her hands. "Am I brilliant, or what?"

"Or what! Maybe some people need help and I can provide that."

Ginny cleared her throat and stared me down.

"Okay, I admit it," I said after her accusing silence. "I'm not exactly a mother duck. But I'm not *that* bad."

She stopped glaring and sighed. "No, you're not that bad. But girl, if you can't tell Evan how you feel, you can't expect him to know."

My turn to sigh. "I know, but I've been wondering about myself. I mean just before Aya's attack, I was down in Little Tokyo and I saw this incredibly handsome man. You know when you catch someone's eye and inside you go 'boom.' Well I went boom, and I really liked it. Hell, I realized I *miss* my insides going boom. I'm just not sure I'm ready to be with one man."

"Fool! 'Boom' my ass. Being with somebody doesn't mean you will never be attracted to someone else, it just means you don't act on it, *because it's not worth it.*"

I agreed to shut her up, but I wasn't so sure that it worked that way with me. I thought about the haiku and the way it made me feel when I read it: breathless. I was glad I'd kept it, I would call that number if things didn't work out with Evan. It couldn't hurt to have an option. And a secret. "Anyway, if Evan wanted to live with me, he'd stop changing the subject when it comes up."

"That man is hooked, you know it, I know it, he knows it,

maybe it's time for somebody to admit they know it, to not be afraid to say it. What do you think?"

"Well, it's not going to be me," I insisted. "Why should I put myself on the line?" But even as I said the words I could hear Aya's soft voice in my head, saying, "sometimes men just have to be handled, it's so much easier than a confrontation."

"It doesn't have to be you," Ginny said, and I felt better. "It has to be both of you." And I felt worse than before.

I heard a soft knock and was relieved at the out. "Yes?"

Deirdre opened the door and announced the arrival of a private shopper she'd sent to buy wardrobes for my guests, as they had arrived with very few personal belongings. I asked her to send the things up and sent Ginny to see what the shopper had brought for her.

Pleased with myself, I went back to my calls, the last of which was to one of my company accountants. I was unhappy with her choice of banks and the interest rates involved. When you are talking about the kind of numbers I play with, banks have a tendency to negotiate.

Evan came in while I was wrapping it up and listened in for a minute before nodding his approval. Evan doesn't deal with his family's money as firsthand as I do; his brother and sister handle most of his inheritance, they enjoy it more, but he knows what's going on. High finance involves being really good at math, reading people, and keeping multiple strategies in play. Some people like playing the game more than others. Evan's chosen games were played for higher stakes, life and death. I respected him for it. Secretly, I even envied him.

"Hi, you look as antsy as Ginny," I said to him as he leaned over to kiss me nice and soft and slow.

"I'm sure I'll have plenty to do soon enough." He kissed me more deeply and put his right hand on my breast, caressing me. I don't think he realized that he always greeted me that way. A kiss and a fondle. I didn't want to make him aware of it because then he might stop. "What are you smiling at?" he asked.

"Something Ginny said about us," I answered. It was honest enough.

He straightened up quickly. "If it's okay, Curtis is joining us for dinner," he said. "We have a few things to go over." He waved a stack of files as thick as my leg and grimaced.

"A little light reading?" I asked, disappointed that he hadn't asked me what Ginny said.

"Oh, riveting stuff, really." With a stiff gait he crossed to one of the big armchairs in front of my desk and sank into it. "We're trying to find some connection between Gades and the shooter on the roof. The San Francisco detectives have come up with nothing."

"So, are you officially back at work?" I asked him.

"Part-time, I'm still on medical leave, so most of my cases have been reassigned."

"Is Curtis working, or just curious?" I smiled.

"Both, I imagine." I watched him remember the last time Curtis had been in this room. "He looked at Ginny like she was the light at the end of the tunnel."

I laughed. "The light in *that* tunnel is a locomotive coming the other way." I shifted at my desk, braced myself to bring up the living-together subject and plunged in. "And speaking of big scary things—"

"Hold on," he interrupted. He smiled and let his eyes travel down as far as the very large secretary desk would allow, about my waist. "Come out from behind that desk," he ordered. So manful, I loved that. I thought again of what Aya had said, this time about feeling power from being vulnerable, and I understood.

"Take off the dress," he said a moment later. "Leave the heels on." His voice was rich with lust, and it felt electric to hear it. With my back still to him, I slid both straps off my shoulders and with a slight shimmy I let the slippery garment float down around my ankles. I stepped deliberately out of the pretty folds.

"Turn around" was his next direction. "Real slow."

It might have been his command, but it was exactly what I wanted: his attention, his lust, his adoration. I loved it, I needed it, I missed it.

There was a discreet knock at the door, and I sighed, regretfully pulling the dress easily back on before calling, "Yes?"

Deirdre came in again. "Detective Curtis," she announced and turned, but there was no one there.

"Where'd he go?" I asked.

She looked back out into the hallway, and then, with only the slightest visible sign of approval, she said, "He seems to have been diverted."

Evan and I looked at each other knowingly. As he stood to go to the door, I got in, "Evan, I do want to talk to you about something."

"Sure," he answered, but he kept moving across the room, and I followed. Ginny was sitting on the stairs, and Curtis was talking to her through the balustrade.

"Excuse me," Curtis said to Ginny with a regretful smile. Turning to Evan, he echoed my sentiment: "We need to talk."

Unlike me, Curtis got the okay.

"Let's do it," Evan said, motioning to the library. Curtis, looking grim, nodded a polite hello to me as they passed. I crossed over and slumped down on the stair next to Ginny.

"How'd it go?" she asked.

"It didn't," I said before our attention was drawn to the top of the stairwell.

Sabrina and Shika were there, both in new outfits, and Sabrina drawled, "It's the fall fashion line." She struck a pose I assumed she thought was very vogue, and Shika giggled, looking both delighted and self-conscious.

Getting to my feet I applauded. "Very nice, you both look

very pretty. I'll see you all at dinner." Passing them on the stairs, I went to my bedroom.

I went straight to my dressing table and opened the top drawer; still neatly folded was the note I had found in my umbrella on the rainy day in Little Tokyo.

Reading it brought a rush of blood through my body. Somehow it made me feel better, having the romantic missive, so I carried it into the bathroom and set it on the vanity.

What did I want? Could I be with only one person for the rest of my life? I thought about the handsome stranger in Little Tokyo, and that lead me to think about the assault. What in the hell had I gotten us all into? I truly did feel a sense of protectiveness toward Shika and Aya, but I had a greater responsibility not to endanger Sabrina, Ginny, and my staff, which, it seemed certain, I was doing.

I shook my head and groaned, trying to push out some of the tension with the aggravated sound as I drew a hot bath, throwing in some milky oil and lighting a few candles. Sinking gratefully into the cocooning heat, I let it embrace and support me.

But though I soaked thoughtfully for half an hour, only one incomplete answer grew clear and calm in my mind. I didn't know what I wanted or expected to happen with Evan; but I couldn't imagine being without him.

There was a knock on my bedroom door, so soft I could barely hear it.

"Come in, Deirdre," I called out as loudly as I could muster in my relaxed state and waited. I didn't hear footsteps approaching, didn't expect to. She wore soft-soled shoes to be less obtrusive, but when the figure appeared next to my bath I was very surprised to see not Deirdre but Aya standing there.

"Hi," I said, surprised. "What's up?" I was curious. It seemed out of character for her to visit my room uninvited.

"I don't mean to intrude, but I wanted to talk to someone. I felt"—she paused and looked at one of the candles—"afraid."

I let that hang for a minute, and then I sat up a little and rolled my neck in a circle, trying to loosen it up. "Well, I can't say I blame you. I'm feeling a little pressure myself. Are you afraid because we will talk to your guardian the day after tomorrow?" I asked.

"Partly, yes. I suppose he is, in a very unusual way, a father figure to me, and I don't want to fail him," she confided.

"How would you be failing him?" I asked. "Have a seat." I gestured to the stool next to the vanity.

"I suppose it's not really rational is it? But my own parents have never understood me," she explained as she sat down and pulled her legs up onto the chair, exposing her smooth bare legs all the way to the top of her thigh where a sheer lace panty edge disappeared the way G-strings do. "They are very, how can I put this, traditional, he's the man and she serves him. Of course they mean well, but they don't understand about the kind of success I would like to have."

"It must be hard for you," I commiserated, thinking about her situation. "You've given yourself very high standards, and you're rocking the boat, people don't always like that." As I said it, I was amazed at how much we had in common.

"It can be difficult sometimes," she admitted reluctantly, "but I'm grateful to my uncle and I don't want to cause problems."

"You can be very grateful and thankful for your blessings but still have every right to feel that it's been a difficult path. Let's face it; it sucks not to have somebody there to help you, to understand what you're going through, to . . . well, not to have someone to bitch to. We all need that, Aya, it's called support."

"I guess I haven't really had anyone to 'bitch' to," she said and looked at me sadly.

"Feel free to begin." I smiled at her. "Bitch away. Believe me, not having anyone who can empathize is something I know a little bit about." I was serious about that. I knew what it was like to be told you don't have the right to be unhappy.

"I don't want to have to answer to anyone," she said tentatively, like she was not quite sure how to bitch.

"Got that," I said. "You're on the right path, I think. It's tough because you have to rely on people to get you there. Kind of a catch-twenty-two. But there's a definite stop date on that reliance"—I smiled at her—"so you've got that going for you."

"Thank God." She smiled back. "But it makes me angry when men act like they're just naturally smarter than any woman." She looked angry when she said it, almost irrationally so. I knew how that felt too. "They especially act that way if you're pretty."

"That's a toughy." I sighed. "If you're sexy, it's hard for men not to see you in a sexual way. It's like you said when you talked about being a geisha; it's natural. I guess what we look for is a man who sees *that* and all our other good qualities." I sighed again, dramatically. "Qualities far too numerous for us to list here. Although, being smart, successful, funny, *and* gorgeous *and* sexy doesn't suck." I laughed.

"Yes, I suppose it's a curse," she said, joking back, and then she looked serious again. "But sometimes there are people who *value* you, but they will never acknowledge you as an equal. That's what I hate the most." She was thinking of someone in particular, I could see that.

"I have one thing to offer there. I deal with people's misconceptions of me all the time, and after many years of careful analysis, deliberation, analysis, and painstaking strategizing, this is my enlightened advice: fuck 'em. It's their problem. I know it's infuriating, but remember that people like that don't deserve to be around someone as special as you. If you're like me"—I leaned forward a little and watched her flashing black eyes—"and I suspect you probably are, then you want to teach them a lesson, make them see the error of their ways."

"Exactly!" she said with the most vehemence I had ever heard her use. "I want them to admit I'm every bit as good as they are!" Her face was set in a fixated rage.

"But they probably won't. Ever. Even if they did, they wouldn't mean it. Maddening, I know, but you have to learn to say 'Fuck them, it's their loss,' *and here's the key:* learn to enjoy doing it."

She was looking at me with an odd combination of repressed fury and bewilderment. Like she both couldn't fathom that I would know what she was talking about and was shocked that I had a plan to actually deal with it. But while I was formulating how to broach a discussion of her new emotional palette, all the anger and confusion seemed to melt off her face, and she started to laugh, that melodic sound that I had heard when we first met.

"Fuck them," she said and laughed so hard tears came to her eyes. The laugh had a hysterical edginess to it. If I hadn't understood from my own experiences how much she had been repressing and holding back all this time, I would have suspected she was unstable.

I watched her, very pleased to see her opening up, but fascinated by the unsettling display of raw feeling. She quieted down and leaned her head on the vanity.

"Thank you," she said when the fit had subsided.

"Sure. Anytime," I said flippantly and dunked my head under the surface of the bath. When I slid back up and pushed the water from my eyes, I saw Aya holding the haiku note in her hand.

She looked up at me. "I'm sorry, I shouldn't have read this, but where did you get it?"

I told her about the handsome man and finding the note, but I wasn't willing to share its impact on me. "I just found it in my pocket before my bath and threw it on the table," I lied.

She looked amazed. "I know this signature," she said, pointing to the bold Japanese character above the lines of poetry.

"You do?" I asked, shocked.

I heard Evan's footfall and his voice.

"Cally?"

I felt panicked, irrationally guilty. Aya looked from my face to the note in her hand and then folded it again and slid it under a hand towel.

"We're in here," I said and looked at Aya, who smiled innocently at me.

"We?" Evan asked, and he appeared at the doorway. "Am I interrupting?" he asked smoothly as he took in the scene with a scan from my naked body to Aya's shapely legs all the way up to the edge of the lace string of her panties and what they didn't cover.

"No, not at all, we're just having some girl talk," I partially lied and smiled at him.

"Well, don't let me stop you. I'll go downstairs and, uh, take a cold shower or something."

"No, please," said Aya, "I should leave you two." She rose, and her thin dress fell to the top of her thigh but clung to her skin, slightly moist from the heat of the room, revealing more of her perfect curves. I watched Evan watch her. His eyes slid quickly down her body, and then he looked straight to me and didn't look back at her. Though my logical mind told me it would have been impossible to expect him not to appreciate her, I flashed on his hand on the small of her back and resented his attention to her, however brief.

I pretended to be busy with a sponge for a minute until I couldn't avoid looking at Evan anymore. "So what did Curtis say?"

"We got a track on the shooter in San Francisco. I need to go talk to some people."

"Who?" I asked.

He didn't answer. Instead he peeled off his shirt, and I had a chance to watch the V shape of his torso and the slight ripples of his toned stomach. I enjoyed a moment of pure physical coveting, anticipating the deliciousness of pressing up against him, but when he was naked he turned on the shower. "I'll try not to be too late. Curtis is going to stay until I get back," he said as he stepped in and closed the door behind him.

I climbed out of the bath, wrapped myself in a cashmere robe, and with a glance at the steamed-up glass shower walls, retrieved the note from under the towel and looked at the phone number.

Maybe tomorrow I'd call. It wouldn't hurt to say hello.

Chapter 18

I sat up in bed abruptly as the light went on. Evan was standing by the switch.

"What?" I asked him, covering my eyes from the sudden brightness, the urgency of his movements ringing alarms in my sleepy nervous system.

"Sabrina and Shika apparently snuck out." He looked seriously put out.

Anger flared up in me; where the hell had *he* been? "Oh, Evan. I know they shouldn't have, but they're so young, and they must feel cooped up and bored here. They probably just went to the mall or the Foster's Freeze. And maybe they just wanted to keep it a secret too," I said, referring to his mysterious destination.

Evan crossed to me and put his hands on my shoulders. "And they're not back."

"What?" I tried to focus on the bedside clock: 4:47 A.M. "Where are they?" My brain started flashing: red alert, red alert!

"We don't know. Sabrina's cell phone is turned off, if she's even got it, and all we know is that Curtis and Ginny heard the door chimes to the kitchen go off at around ten; they assumed it was Joseph the under-butler leaving for the evening. They were apparently too absorbed to bother to check," Evan said, growling. He was not a happy man.

"Did they take Sabrina's car?"

"No, damn it. If they had, the black-and-white outside would have seen them. They must have snuck over the fence."

I crossed to my dressing area and whipped out some jeans and a T-shirt. "We've got to go look for them." I couldn't think straight. Mostly my brain was spinning. *God damn it! What were you thinking, Sabrina?*

"First, we need to figure out where to start," he said, and as usual, his sense and his calm brought my brain's revolutions per minute down from a high-pitched whine.

I dressed in a flash and followed him down the hallway. Aya came sleepily to the door of her room when I knocked. "What's wrong?" she asked nervously after searching our faces.

"Shika's gone. It looks as though she snuck out with Sabrina," Evan told her briskly. Aya's hand flew up to her mouth, and she gasped as he continued. "Please come down to the kitchen right away. We need to try and guess where they would have gone." She nodded, and gathering her robe around her, she joined us down the stairwell.

My heart was thumping in my throat; I kept thinking of the shooter on the building and the ruthlessness of the criminals Evan was up against. I was trying not to picture Sabrina surrounded by people with no regard for human life. I kept hearing Evan's words when I told him they weren't after me—"come on, you're smarter than that." By the time we got to the kitchen I was praying that I wasn't smart at all because the girls' disappearance was adding up to only one thing to me—a hideous nightmare.

Ginny was already in the kitchen. I could see from the look

on her face that she'd been having similar thoughts; she was scared, and she was furious.

"I should have strapped that girl down in her bed. She's got no sense at all," she fumed.

"I realized they were gone when I got back twenty minutes ago. Curtis met me at the door, and he told me that the only person who went in or out was Joseph," Evan told us.

Curtis, who was seated next to Ginny, scowled angrily. "But I didn't fucking check."

"So I did," Evan went on, "and Joseph had been in his apartment over the garage since about eight o'clock, so the chimes at ten weren't him coming in or out. Then Curtis and I went to check for everyone else. Ginny woke up when I opened her door, but Shika and Sabrina's beds were empty, not even slept in."

Aya sat with her hands folded, an unidentifiable look on her face. Was it panic? Guilt? "How do you know someone didn't take them?" she asked, in a tight voice.

"Because there's no sign of struggle, *at all,"* Evan said conclusively, "and there were too many people here to make that a feasible possibility."

"And because the two of them were giggling about something all evening," Curtis said disgustedly.

"And they both got dressed and put makeup on." Ginny looked like she wanted to slap someone, mostly herself. "I thought they were just fooling around."

"I should have guessed that they were up to something." Curtis smacked his hand down hard on the table. "It was obvious, damn it!"

Evan's face was a mask, but I sensed that was only a front for my benefit, as well as an effort to gain control of the situation. "Okay, they snuck out, and they're not back. Everything—bars clubs, even coffeehouses—closed around two A.M. at the latest. Let's focus on where to start looking." I could see his brain working furiously. "Most likely they would have walked into the village, right? I'll have anything that's open twenty-four hours checked."

"What were they thinking?" I said in angst. "Shika especially. Isn't it enough that when she stands next to walls they spontaneously explode? She knows these people, better than any of us!"

"Okay, let's not jump to the worst conclusion," Evan said levelly.

The phone rang, and we all jumped to the worst conclusion. Evan picked it up on the next ring.

"Sabrina, where the hell are you?" he growled into the phone.

"Put her on speaker!" I insisted.

Evan complied, and suddenly Sabrina's drawl was echoing around the room. "I'm sorry to wake you up, but I thought you might be worried."

"We're all awake, and we're all very worried," I said loudly enough for my voice to carry to the phone.

"We're on our way back . . ." She sounded indignant.

"Are you okay?" Ginny screamed across the room.

"We're fine now," Sabrina replied, all breathy and excited.

"Are you sure?" Ginny repeated the question.

"Oh yeah."

"Good," Ginny said a little more softly, "because when you get home"—she drew a breath and then shouted so loudly that I covered my ears—"I'm going to smack you so hard I'll knock you all the way back to that fucking trailer park!"

Evan took advantage of the shocked silence to ask the obvious question. "What do you mean you're all right *now?*"

"Well . . ." There was a pause, and then her words, usually slowed by her southern drawl, gushed out enthusiastically. "I know we shouldn't have done it, I realize that now. Of course, it's easy to see later that something wasn't that smart, but it just seemed like fun at the time. I mean, we didn't know what was gonna happen, how could we? *Now* we do, sure. But you know how it is, Shika and I were bored, and we thought we'd just go out for a little while. It was my idea, she didn't want to at first, but I said, 'just a coffee or something', and she said, 'no, we shouldn't because Mr. Paley said no.' But I said, 'oh, come on, it'll be fun, we'll be back before they even know we're gone and Evan is really nice and he won't be mad at us, and who's even going to know we were gone?' So she said 'well okay' and I said 'great, it'll be fun' and—"

"Sabrina?" I interrupted.

"Hi, Cally!"

"Sabrina, what time is it?" It was all I could do to keep my voice calm.

"Almost five o'clock in the morning."

"And I'm up, but my patience sleeps until nine, so get on with it!"

"Okay, but I'm trying to make the point that it was my idea, it wasn't hers; she didn't want to go. I thought of it and I said to her 'let's go' and she said, 'no,' and I don't want you to be mad at her 'cause it was my idea." Clearly she was going to tell this story her way.

I rubbed my aching temples and said, slowly and clearly, "What happened?"

"So, we go out to the street, and start walking down toward Westwood village, and these two guys stop and ask us if we want a ride. They're real well dressed and very polite, and I think it's a good idea, because it's a long walk, but Shika gets all scared and grabs my arm and says, 'run.' I don't know what's going on, but next thing, Shika's pulling me through some other people's azalea bushes, I think that's what they were, they were some kind of low plants with flowers on 'em, anyway then I hear this crashing noise behind us. And then . . ." She took a deep breath and paused for what I think was her idea of dramatic effect.

"Then *what?*" I insisted. Evan put his hand out, indicating that if we were quiet we might actually get to hear what happened.

"And then somebody grabbed me around the waist and just, like, picked me up! It was one of those men from the car, and the other one had Shika by the arm, and she was fighting like a wildcat. She's little, but she was kicking and screaming, and yellin' and flailing around—"

"Sabrina," Evan interjected. "Are you safe now, where are you? I'm going to send a car to pick you up."

"Oh, no, we're almost home now. We're fine. I mean, we're okay. So, I mean, if you guys will let me, I'd *like* to finish telling you what happened." She actually sounded put out.

I wanted to reach through the phone and rip her hair out. Evan was a more patient soul. Breeding or training, I don't know which.

"Please," he encouraged.

She hurled herself back into it. "Okay. So, next thing I know they are dragging us toward the car, and this man is trying to put something over my face that smells funny. And the other guy has the same thing, and he does get this cloth over Shika's nose and she goes all limp, like she's dead or something, so now I start really screaming."

"Of course, you must have been scared," I put in when she was inhaling for the next run-on sentence.

"No! Not scared, now I'm *mad.* Can I please tell my story?"

Where my once naive baby sister had acquired this cocky new attitude, I had no idea. I bit my lip to stop myself from biting her head off. "You go right ahead."

"Thank you. So, I kick this guy really hard, and he starts saying something, I don't know what it is, but I think it's probably not very nice, in Spanish. But I manage to break away from him, and I start after the guy who's carrying Shika now. I get him by the hair and start pulling like I'm plucking a chicken, and he is so surprised he almost drops her and that's when the other guy grabs me again, but I will not let go of that handful of hair and so we're all spinning around and it's just crazy confusion. Then, like something out of a movie, these two *other* guys jump over that same shrubbery and one of them hits the guy grabbing me real hard. So now the guy carrying Shika does drop her and he pulls a gun, but the other new guy, the younger one"—she dropped her voice to a secretive level, as though he were there and she didn't want him to hear—"who is really cute"—she went back to her full voice—"he kicks the gun out of that man's hand, I mean, whammo! Smack! Those two Spanish-speaking men ran off and jumped back in their car and took off. Can you believe that?"

She paused, wanting a reaction I suppose, but nobody seemed to even have taken in what she said. The air in the kitchen crackled with the static from the speakerphone and our disbelief for a few seconds, and then I addressed the room in general.

"What did she say?" I asked. The other faces at the table looked as befuddled as I felt. All except Evan, who jumped in on the opening like he was snatching an insect out of thin air.

"Did you get a license number?" he asked. "Even a portion of it?"

"No," Sabrina continued, "because *now* I'm looking at Shika, lying on the ground, and these two new guys, I don't know who they are." She dropped her voice secretively again. "But they are definitely not Spanish. The older guy picks up Shika, neat as you please, and asks me, very politely, if I would come with him please, and seeing how he just saved us from being kidnapped and all, I thought I probably should, so I did."

"Where did you go?" Evan asked, as though he was hearing about a trip to Yosemite, but his lips were tight and his brow was contracted. Though I'm sure I still looked stunned on the outside, inside I was waking up to a new anger—*who the fuck was messing with my sister?*

"We went to this really nice house, not too far from Cally's, and waited for Shika to wake up. A doctor came and looked at us both, and I kept wanting to call ya'll, but this nice man, his name is Korosu, he didn't want me to."

There was a quick breath to my right, and I looked at Aya in time to see her recover her composure.

"He said that I shouldn't call until he was sure things were okay, and that he would take us home as soon as she was feeling better. And guess what? We're pulling up outside the gate right now. I'll see you in a minute. Now, don't be too mad, okay?" She clicked off before any of us had time to even absorb it all, much less decipher how we felt.

Evan hit the gate code and picked up a walkie-talkie from the table. "There's a car coming up the drive, follow it in." Then he moved with purpose to the front hall. We followed.

He threw the door open, and we all peered out into the misty marine night. We heard the cars coming before we could see them. Next to me I felt Evan's arm move as he reached for his gun; he kept it in his hand but put his arm down by his side and shifted in front of me. As we watched, an expensive sedan pulled up the driveway followed by the black-and-white. The back door of the sedan flew open, and Sabrina jumped out; she seemed pleased to have been part of such a grand adventure. She ran up and hugged me; I was so relieved to see her safe and intact that it didn't occur to me to reprimand her right then. Shika followed her, considerably more chagrined. The front passenger-door opened, and a very handsome young Japanese man chaperoned her to the door; presumably the "really cute" one. Last, the driver-side door opened and a tall dark-haired figure emerged and walked slowly around the car. Something about his gait seemed familiar to me, it was dark and foggy still, but as he came to us he entered the ring of light and the mist cleared.

Holy shit.

Chapter 19

It was the same handsome stranger I had locked eyes with outside the bookstore in Little Tokyo on the day that had started all of this. His eyes, as they caught mine, had the same effect on me now as they had then.

Boom.

Next to me Aya bowed deeply to him and then spoke.

"Allow me the great honor of presenting to you Korosu, my guardian."

He stepped up onto the front step and, bowing, offered his hand to me. I took it in absolute surprise. I didn't know what to say.

Aya was continuing. "Uncle Korosu-san, allow me to introduce you to my generous hostess, Callaway Wilde. And to Detective Evan Paley."

Korosu bowed slightly to Evan and extended his hand to him. Evan made no secret of putting his gun away before he took the offered hand and shook it. As usual, he missed nothing. "It seems you two have met," he said, looking from Korosu to me.

"Uh, no actually," I stammered.

"I admired Ms. Wilde from a distance and was very grateful to her for her bravery in helping Aya. But no, we have never met." His voice was very pleasing, smooth, and gentle.

I remembered my manners, the watch, and the haiku note all at once. No wonder Aya had recognized the character on the note.

"Please, come in," I said, turning to hide the hot blush that was burning my face.

Evan dispatched the gang, including the handsome young stranger, to the kitchen where, the staff having been roused, they were to eat breakfast and wait to talk to us. Evan, Curtis, Korosu, and I settled in the library, where Deirdre had set up coffee and, thoughtfully, tea. The first wisps of light were illuminating the mist outside. Being up at this time of day always gave me the unpleasant sense memory of being coked out at dawn. I shook it off and served the caffeine.

"Thank you for bringing the ladies back safely," I said to Korosu. As I handed him a mug of tea, our fingers brushed, and I felt my cheeks grow hot again.

"Yes, we're all grateful, but I am curious about how you happened to be there." Evan, I was relieved to see, was watching Korosu's face, instead of mine.

"I was not there. I have had two men who work as bodyguards for me keeping an eye on your house. Please forgive me, but I am unfortunately familiar with the 'business dealings' of Antonio Gades and I wanted to ensure the safety of my nieces."

"How familiar are you with those dealings?" Evan inquired. Curtis shifted in the chair next to Evan and, if possible, focused on Korosu even more intently than Evan did. He remained quiet, letting Evan ask the questions, yet his presence was as innocuous as an armed nuclear weapon. With both of them there, the situation took on the heightened feeling of an interrogation.

Korosu sighed, and rather than it sounding like a surrender or exhaustion he seemed to gather strength from the gesture. "I have been fighting his attempts to draw me into those dealings." He looked directly at Evan as he spoke. It was seldom that I saw a man who could equal Evan's gaze and masculinity; it was damned exciting to watch. "I do not think it was an accident that Shika became involved with him. I believe that he targeted her to get to me."

"Why, exactly?" Evan wanted details.

"He wanted my cooperation," Korosu answered evenly. "We all know what he is involved in. The fact that the government is watching him makes it more difficult for him to import and sell drugs. I have a very reputable import business that also import-exports from the legitimate South American trade industry. He came to me with a proposition. He was very adamant that I not refuse it."

"I can guess what the proposition was, but I'd like you to tell me."

"He wanted to use my company to move a large crated shipment in the next month."

"Did he specify a large shipment of what?" Curtis asked hopefully.

"We never got that far. He was flatly refused from the very beginning."

"What do you import?"

"Mostly high-end electronics. But I have separate companies that cover many other things, flavor concentrates used for juice drinks, home furnishings, even bathroom fixtures."

"Why you?" Evan persisted. "There must be thousands of businesses that would be more than happy to extend their net worth. Half of the Asian businesses in Chinatown exist to launder money on a small scale. We know all about that. So why not go to one of them?"

"Because most of them would not be capable of conducting these transactions on the scale that Gades works in. For all I know he does work with others, I am not interested in that. It is my belief that it is because I am so reputable that I became his choice."

"Are you that honest?" Evan smiled dubiously.

"Yes," Korosu answered without hesitation. "My reputation is everything to me."

"What about the girls?" Evan asked.

"There is nothing illegal or immoral in what Aya and Shika choose to do. They are free to do whatever they want at any time." He spoke with a calm confidence, giving the impression that it would take a great deal to ruffle his charming feathers. "It is only your conditioning in Western puritanical beliefs that gives you cause to judge them, and me. But, if you knew the truth"—he offered us all the option of rising above our limitations—"if you were to truly investigate what they do, and be willing to compare it honestly with the way your society operates in regards to beautiful women, I think you might not judge us so harshly." His smile was neither condescending nor apologetic.

What surprised me most was how natural and unrehearsed he sounded. I would have expected him to get defensive or challenging, but he did neither, just addressed the subject eloquently. I looked to see Evan's reaction; I knew Korosu's explanation had sounded good to me.

"Well, that's a discussion for another time, perhaps." Evan managed to sound neither convinced nor disbelieving. I wouldn't have thought that was possible. "Why does he want Shika now?"

"I don't know." Korosu's striking face tightened with concern.

"Why didn't he go after you or your family personally? That's his usual style, I'm sorry to say."

"What does that mean?" I interrupted. *"Didn't* Gades go to him personally?"

They both looked at me and then at each other. Curtis was the one who answered; I had almost forgotten he was there. "Gades *approached* Korosu personally but was refused. Usually, if they don't get what they want, they go after someone's family. They make it clear what will happen to them if you continue to refuse to do what they want."

"I do not have a family, but I care very much about my 'girls' as you refer to them," Korosu answered. His black eyes shone, endearing him to me. "Very much."

"Why Shika in particular? I trust there are others." Evan left it open.

So did Korosu. "He had a connection to Shika, and perhaps because she is the youngest and in many ways, the most vulnerable and impressionable." He looked directly at me as he continued. "She is not yet geisha. I do not think now that she will ever be."

"Is that a disappointment to you?" I asked softly, since he seemed to be addressing me.

"Not at all. Very few women are truly suited to the craft. Many do not succeed or simply choose another lifestyle. I want for her to be happy, I am here to protect and support her, either way." He let his intonation fall on the last two words.

"And on that note," Evan said, leaning in and waiting for Korosu to look directly at him, "been in San Francisco lately?"

"I did not try to kill her, or you," he said without flinching. "I do not kill people." For the first time, a flicker of anger touched his demeanor.

"The shooter had your hotel address in her pocket," Evan stabbed.

"I find that very incriminating," Korosu jabbed back.

"So do I."

"But not for me."

"What," I broke in, "are you talking about?"

Korosu stood and walked to the window, where the dim gray light seemed to give him a visible aura. "I think that information was placed on that woman. I also think the choice of the shooter was meant to paint a target on me." He paused, and I watched him fill himself with the beauty of the dawn. It made him somehow bigger, calmer, stronger. "Gades is very clever. I am sorry that he has come into all of our lives, but perhaps there is, as there always is, a reason for this." As I watched him, I felt a strange connection to him; I was being drawn by his presence into a feeling of believing and belonging. It was a strong pull on a cellular level.

He turned and faced us, an imposing figure, partially silhouetted by the light behind him. "It is very easy, when we are not personally affected by a problem, to turn our face away. Perhaps there is something we can do, something we are meant to do." He looked at me, and the air between us evaporated, I could *feel* him; I had to avert my eyes.

"Like what?" As Evan asked, I turned and looked at him, and I thought about the fact that Evan could easily turn his face away from the vicious crimes we all heard about every day, but he had made a choice to confront them instead. I was proud.

"Stop him," said Korosu. And it sounded so simple.

"Sounds good." Evan stood up and offered me his hand to help me up. "Callaway, could I ask you to go and bring Shika in to speak with us?" He was leading me to the doorway. He turned back to Korosu, who still stood framed in the library windows, his shiny hair wreathed in morning light, black and gold against the gray mist. "If you'll excuse us for a moment," he said to Korosu and Curtis and pulled me out the door.

"Wow," I said when he had closed the door behind us. "That's not what I expected at all."

"No?" Evan smiled. "Didn't you think he would be smart?"

It was obvious, of course. "Well, I suppose he would have to be, to be so successful, but he seems so, I don't know, respectable, and so . . . young."

"And charming?" Evan asked.

I pretended not to hear that and hurried on. "He certainly is convincing."

"We have a little saying down at the precinct that I think might be applicable for you here." Evan's eyes glinted. "Don't believe a fucking word they say."

"Oh, that's pithy," I commented, feeling a little stupid but knowing he was right.

"Of course that doesn't mean he's not telling the truth," he added, confusing me all to hell. "Go get Shika, and listen, Cally." He looked into my eyes, and I realized he was counting on me for something important. "Watch her reaction, understand?"

"To what?" I asked.

"To the fact that we want to talk to her before anyone else."

"Okay, Kemo Sabe." I started to turn away, but my motion was arrested. Evan pulled me back and kissed me firmly, pressing his body against me. "Don't think I didn't notice the way you and Korosu looked at each other." He put his hand in the back of my hair and pulled me toward him, there was a sense of ownership about it that appealed to me. "When you told me you were shopping, I assumed you meant for shoes."

I feigned complete ignorance to cover my confusion and embarrassment, which he seemed to find transparent and amusing. On the one hand I was surprised at myself for feeling attracted to Korosu, on the other hand I was pissed off at Evan's assumption of exclusivity.

"Where did *you* go tonight?" I asked him.

His face closed and his mouth tightened. "I had to see someone."

I wasn't letting him off with that. "Who?" I demanded.

"Callaway." His hands tightened on my arms so that it almost hurt. "I have to find out who hired the shooter in San Francisco. *Somebody* knows, and I have to go through some, let's just say, unofficial channels to find out who. That means people I know who are . . . well, nobody in your social circle," he finished grimly.

"Oh." I didn't know what more to say to that, but I didn't like being in the dark. I hated him having a secret. It made me want to have one.

"I did find out something else though." Something he could tell me I supposed. "An undercover narcotic agent told me that there's a big shipment coming in of cocaine. There's been lots of activity, distributors being lined up, deals made to move a massive amount of product. Word is, it'll be the first of the month."

"That's a few days from now."

"I know." He was still holding me, but his eyes had moved far off.

"May I go now?" I asked.

"Almost." He smiled knowingly; that pissed me off more. "But first, you need to kiss me." He wasn't going to let me go angry, let me place another brick on those fortifications from my past. I knew he was doing it, and I resented that he had to, hated myself for being such a baby. "Please?" he asked nicely.

"I just kissed you." I pulled away a little, but he had broken through the masonry.

"No, I kissed *you,* "he insisted.

"Oh, all right." I set aside the trowel and mortar, for now. Somehow he always found a way through to me. I kissed him, but with a certain amount of coolness.

"Now, you may go." He released me.

So I went, muttering to myself about why he should get to tell me what to do.

Before I got to the swinging kitchen doors I could hear the eager voices. Ginny seemed to have gotten over her anger and was complimenting Sabrina on her use of force, vocally and otherwise, with the two would-be abductors. They all looked up at me from the table as I swung open the heavy painted door.

"Shika, Evan wants to see you *first.* "I stressed the word and tried to watch her face closely, but it was hard not to be drawn to Aya's response. Her head swung away from me and her mouth tightened; it was a quick knee-jerk movement that ended as quickly as it began with a strong glassy stare at the tabletop. I wondered what that was about. Was it because her junior was being summoned before her? Was there some kind of pecking order that she felt needed to be respected? Shika's gaze changed only slightly, from already feeling bad for what she'd done to afraid she was now going to be reprimanded for it. She nodded and stood, joining me at the door without speaking.

Halfway across the entrance hall she stopped. I turned back to her. "Are you okay?" I asked, concerned at the light sweat that had polished her face.

"I'm afraid of them."

"Who?"

"Those men." Her voice was so thin that my heart opened at a small seam. She'd been so misused.

"You can trust Evan," I told her, but she looked terrified at the thought.

"He's going to be very angry." Her eyes were like saucers.

"No, he won't, not if you help him. Detective Paley and Detective Rossmore are here to protect you, you shouldn't have snuck out but—"

"No, I mean Korosu; he'll want to kill me." She was shaking. I put an arm over her shoulders and squeezed reassuringly.

"Nobody," I said with conviction, "is going to touch you or be cruel to you with me here. Do you trust me?"

She looked up and searched my face before nodding and steadying herself.

"Okay." I smiled at her. "Ready? I won't leave you."

"Okay." She smiled back, though her lips trembled, and then with a visible effort she adjusted her features and started forward.

We walked back to the library and I knocked once, quickly, to alert the men of our presence, and then opened the door. Evan watched Shika carefully as she crossed the large room and bowed to Korosu, who inclined his head slightly to acknowledge her bow and presence but his expression displayed nothing. At no time did Shika make eye contact with him.

"Shika, I need you to tell me what you know about what happened tonight, and a little more besides," Evan began, motioning that she should sit.

"I am so sorry," Shika started, and I saw a large tear escape her left eye and travel down her shapely cheek. "I did not mean to put Sabrina in any danger. I am so sorry."

Korosu stood now and crossed to her. He stood in front of her for a moment without speaking. He seemed huge and powerful in front of her slight fragile figure. At first it seemed that he was very angry, and I watched Evan shift his weight, ready to stop him if he tried to strike her. Her face was down and tears were dropping freely onto her lap now. But when Korosu did lift his hand it was to set it softly on the top of her head.

"You are forgiven. You have done something foolish, and yes you should have known better. You know these people think nothing of cruelty. But you didn't mean for anything bad to happen." He took his hand away now and called her by name. "Shika?"

She looked slowly up at him and said in a voice still filled with shame, "I'm sorry."

"We all know that and we're not here to blame you. Detective Paley is asking you to help him now. I have not asked you what happened while you were with Gades before today because I know you weren't ready to talk about it, and that—whatever happened—it was beyond your control. I'm sure you have learned a great deal, and I can see that you have suffered too much. As far as I'm concerned, your debt is paid, but you need to tell the detectives what you know. Will you?" He smiled kindly at her.

She raised her hands, palms up, in a tender gesture of supplication. "I'll try."

"Good," Korosu said. "Thank you." He turned back to his chair and sat down, nodding to Evan and Curtis to proceed as they needed.

"Have a seat," Evan said to Shika, and then he turned to me. "Why don't you go back to the kitchen, Cally?"

Panic flickered over Shika's face. I looked at the three imposing, grim men facing this one frightened girl, and I bristled.

"No thank you, I think I'll stay." I dared him to ask me to leave again by refusing to even look at him as I planted myself on the same side of the room as Shika and folded my arms defiantly across my chest.

"Shika." Evan spoke softly but firmly. "Is it true that you have not talked to Korosu about what happened in the time you were with Gades or what happened earlier tonight?"

She glanced up, surprised at the question, and then said, "Yes, it's true."

"Who tried to take you tonight?" Evan asked. "Did you recognize them?"

Shika's breath shook raggedly as she tried visibly to gain control of herself. "It was two men, both of them work for Antonio. One is called Luis and one is called Jorge. I do not know their last names, but I was always frightened of them when they were with us."

"Were they with you often?" Evan asked.

"Yes. But they would leave sometimes for a few days and then come back. Sometimes Antonio would be very angry with them." Her eyes kept darting to Curtis, as though she was most afraid of him. Maybe because she didn't know him.

Evan sat back for a minute and squinted at her. "Were you ever afraid of Gades?"

There was a pause while Shika seemed to be sorting out what words to use to answer that question. I pretended to clear my throat and adjust a pillow to pull the nerve-wracking focus off of her for a few seconds. Evan shot me a look; I ignored him, looking instead at Korosu, who seemed to acknowledge my effort on Shika's behalf with a slight knowing smile in his eyes.

"Ye-s." Shika spoke haltingly. "Most of the time he was kind and charming, especially when we would travel together; but sometimes he would get angry and I wouldn't know why. It was as though he couldn't control it."

"That sounds very frightening," Evan commiserated.

"It was, but then everything would be okay again, except . . ."

"Except what?" Evan didn't let her pause.

"Except once." Tears were back in her eyes, and she looked to me in what seemed to be an appeal. I smiled, hoping it was a sympathetic, reassuring smile.

Her voice went very small, like air escaping from a tiny leak. "I saw him hurt someone once."

An icy jolt shot through my body. This could be it, I thought, this could be why he wants her dead.

"Can you tell us about it?" Evan's voice was strained and eager. I glanced at him, and he was rigid in his chair.

Shika sighed in a terrified way and then took another breath. "A man came to the house. He had been there before. Antonio was always very friendly to him, but Antonio had heard something about him, and he was angry."

"What had he heard?" Evan wanted to know.

"I'm not sure." Shika's eyes went from Evan to Curtis like a nervous hummingbird. "But I think that he was some kind of informant."

Evan seemed to hesitate and Curtis spoke up at last. "What was this man's name?"

"I don't remember; no wait, he had a name like that old-time movie star, Charlie Chaplin, that wasn't it, but something like that." I remembered Evan telling me about his friend Charles Chopin; an icy finger touched my spine.

Curtis and Evan exchanged a black look before returning

their attention to Shika, who continued. "This day we were outside by the pool. We were . . ." She paused, gripping the arms of her chair so tightly that her fingers whitened, and then continued in a steady stream, as though any further interruptions would sap any small strength she had mustered to tell this story. "We were doing cocaine, and Antonio asked me to go and get some more. I went inside and was on my way back out when I heard them shouting at each other. I stood there, looking through the glass doors, not knowing what to do. Antonio was so angry he kept hitting his own chest with his fist. And then he turned away, and the other man stood up and put his hand on Antonio's shoulder."

Her eyes had glazed, and she was speaking in a lilting monotone. I could tell she had detached herself as much as possible, but the veins on her neck were strained. "Then I saw Antonio pick up a candleholder from the table next to him, made of iron, very heavy; he swung it hard and hit the man on the head, and he kept doing it, even after the man fell down on the ground." She took a few short shallow breaths, and I saw Evan close his eyes while Curtis's hand went to his chin. But neither of them spoke, so Shika went on. "I don't know why I kept watching, I couldn't help it. There was blood everywhere, and then Antonio straightened up, he looked, I don't know . . . I don't know . . . I guess, calm again. Like nothing had happened. He picked up a towel, and as he started to wipe the blood off himself he walked toward me."

She stared straight ahead, a look of horrified distance locked in her eyes. "I remember just before he got to the door, he looked up at his reflection in the glass, and there was blood on his face, splatters . . ." Her throat was closing up, but she forced herself to continue. "He stopped to wipe it away and he . . . he . . . he checked his hair." She seemed to not believe it herself as she said it. "And then he opened the door and I was standing there, holding the mirror with a big pile of cocaine on it."

"And what happened then?" Evan demanded. The sound of his voice jolted her, as it did me.

"I smiled," she said, and the shame of that moment was etched onto her face. "I smiled at him"—she shook her head disbelievingly—"and tried to pretend that I hadn't seen anything. I didn't know what else to do." Her eyes were shining with tears that wouldn't fall because she did not blink.

"Did he know you saw him kill the other man?" Evan asked, coldly, insistently.

"He must have, but he didn't say anything. He just told me to stay in the kitchen while he took a shower. When we went outside, maybe an hour later, the man's body was gone." She unclenched one hand from the armrest and waved it vaguely in the air, as if she were wiping away the bloody images. "No man, no blood, no candleholders, just clean white towels and lounge chairs. I guess I convinced myself that I hadn't really seen anything. But that was when I knew I had to leave. The next day, when Antonio left, I called Aya and she came . . ." Her throat seemed to seal itself; she neither spoke nor moved for a moment.

And then she fell apart; we watched her shatter as thoroughly as a crystal goblet hurled to a concrete floor. Her tears came, and her body shook silently. Crossing quickly to her I sat on the arm of her chair, pulled her head down against me, and encircled her with my arms as best I could. I turned to Evan. "Don't you think maybe that's enough for now?" I asked him.

"Korosu, may I speak to you outside for a moment?" Evan stood stiffly, Curtis followed, and as the door closed behind the three men, Shika let the sobs come, her body convulsing as the pain took her again and again.

I was so focused on Shika's emotional state that it was a full minute before it occurred to me to think of Evan's. As a detective, he had just listened to a detailed description of a man's head being pummeled with a heavy metal object until he was dead. But outweighing the value of having an eyewitness, aside from the importance of possessing evidence that could put Gades away, one thought hovered ominously, casting an unredeemable pall over any possible benefit.

Evan's friend had been brutally murdered.

Chapter 20

I sent Shika upstairs to bathe her face and went to find Evan. I opened the door of the breakfast room and walked into a charged exchange going on inside.

"Did you know about this murder? Is that why he wants Shika, to silence her?" Evan was asking angrily as he stood over Aya and Korosu with his back to the stained glass windows.

Korosu's answer was measured and stern with a dangerous lilt. "This is the first I have heard about it. I was as ignorant as you were, Detective."

Evan's eyes flashed at the implied insult, but he turned to Aya. "And you?"

She also returned his gaze unflinchingly, but she let a second or two pass before she responded. "I knew she was traumatized by things she had seen, but I did not intrude on her privacy to ask her specifics. That would have been very rude."

Evan's volume increased. "I think that Shika withholding information about a murder supersedes her right to common courtesy, wouldn't you say?" There was bitterness in his voice.

I could see the pain he was in. "Evan," I interjected from the doorway, "it's not their fault."

He spun on me and said forcibly, "They've been harboring a murder witness!"

I felt as though I'd been slapped. "They didn't know about the murder! And they were trying to save her life!"

"You need to stay out of this," Evan said dangerously.

Curtis stood up and took a step forward. "Okay, everybody settle down."

Evan drew himself back in with an obvious effort. "We'll establish if there are grounds for supression of evidence later," Evan said to Korosu and Aya, the warning clear in his tone. "The question now is how to proceed *legally* with this new information." I didn't like the dubious way he said the word *legally*.

"If," said Aya after a stressful pause, "she is telling the truth."

Evan's eyes locked on Aya. "Why do you think that she isn't?"

"I know that she was very disoriented when she came to me, she had no idea what day or even month it was. I don't believe she had slept in many days, so one possibility is that she didn't see things clearly," Aya speculated.

"What's another possibility?" Evan demanded tersely.

"That she's not telling us everything." Aya didn't miss a beat.

Korosu stood up and turned away. The notion clearly upset him.

"Why would she keep something from us?" Evan stayed on track.

"I don't know. Like you, I'm wondering why she didn't tell us this before." Aya's mouth tightened, and she seemed to find the next statement distasteful as it crossed her lips. "She actually seems quite taken with him."

I had to agree with that. Shika had said things like "most of the time he was kind and charming," and in San Fransisco she had said there was "something special" about him. And she hadn't told us about his violence before, although she had had every opportunity to do so.

Evan sighed. "It wouldn't be the first time we've seen this happen. In some twisted way, the girlfriend thinks the bad guy is really good at heart. Part of it is usually that someone very powerful is paying a lot of attention to her. And this Gades"—he spit the name—"by all reports, can be persuasive and even charming."

I was wondering, What next? I mean, how long do we stay holed up here? Until the guy was wiped off the planet? I was not anxious to force Aya and Shika out into the cold, but the situation was getting far too serious for my house to hold.

"What can we do *now?*" I asked pointedly.

"We need to get the ladies out of here," Curtis said matter-of-factly.

Evan looked at Korosu. "You wouldn't know of any small hotels with an available room would you?"

"How many rooms will you need?" he responded.

"Two should be fine: one for the police and one for Shika. I think Aya can get back to her life now, if you have someone to keep an eye on her. Now that they know where Shika is, there doesn't seem to be any further danger to Aya. Do you agree?"

Korosu thought for a few seconds and then nodded. "Is Shika's testimony enough to put him away?"

Evan's right hand tensed into a fist as he spoke. "I doubt it. There's no body, there's no other material evidence at all, and a good defense lawyer, several of whom he probably keeps on retainer, will rip Shika to shreds in a courtroom. She'll look like nothing but a hallucinating junkie when they get through with her." He rubbed his eyes, and I thought about the pile of unsolved murder files on his desk at the precinct. It was damn near impossible to get a conviction at all these days, much less when somebody had millions to twist the evidence. But this seemed so conclusive.

"But she's an eyewitness!" I insisted.

"She won't be a good witness," Aya said, and shared a look with Evan that stung me.

"And if you think she's a target now," Evan laughed without a trace of humor, "just wait until she's the key witness in a trial. I wouldn't offer even odds that your hotel would be left standing."

Curtis stirred, and all of us looked to him expectantly. He looked at Evan and said, "What if he thought he had killed her?"

"How?" asked Korosu.

"The last time they saw her, she was unconscious, right?"

"Wait, wait, wait." Evan was holding out his hand, thinking as he crossed back to the table and sat down. "She was in the car when you came back though."

Korosu nodded but said, "I made them both lay down when we got near the house, just in case; he's already employed one sniper for the job. It's very doubtful that they saw either of the women return."

Evan looked at me and then at Korosu with an even, piercing glare. "This is assuming I believe Gades hired the sniper and that I trust you," he said to him.

"I've always been a bit presumptuous," Korosu responded, and though he didn't exactly turn to me, his body language clearly included me in the remark.

"This would be a bad time to assume anything," Evan said, making himself clear. "Although Shika's story seems to suggest that you aren't the one who wants her dead."

"Well, that's something." Korosu smiled wryly at Evan. His charisma and his personal power made it hard not to like him.

"It's an idea," Evan admitted reluctantly.

"It's a good one," I said, without taking my eyes off of Korosu. He met my look and I couldn't pull it away.

Aya asked, "How would you make that happen?"

"Fake death certificate, some kind of service, attended by you," Evan said to her and Korosu. "We could get her a new identity after that, but I can't move her for a while. She'd have to disappear for at least a month, maybe two." He noticed the way Korosu and I were watching each other and I broke away.

"That's a long time to stay in a hotel room," I said, hating the idea myself.

Aya smiled and said soothingly, "It's a very nice hotel, and she's made a lot of trouble for many people." She appealed to Evan for confirmation. "If I am not mistaken, she could go to prison, yes?"

He looked at her and narrowed his eyes. "Yes, she's confessed to illegal drug use, and withholding information on first-degree murder."

"Then she shall 'do her time' as you say, in luxury." Aya smiled to us again. "I think she'll see the wisdom of this."

Evan considered the suggestion for a long beat and then looked to me. I avoided his eyes and spoke to Korosu. "Food's good," I offered.

"Okay," Evan agreed. "For now, nobody leaves, nobody says or does anything. You two"—he pointed at Aya and Korosu—"are in mourning, do you understand?"

"Yes," they chorused. It was a lovely harmony, resonant and smooth.

"As far as anyone knows, Korosu, you came here to tell us about her death. Aya, what would you do?"

"I would go to the temple to pray for her."

"Then get ready, I'll send you with one of the officers to do that."

She rose, bowed to us all, most deeply to Korosu, who nodded back, and left the room.

"I will make funeral arrangements," Korosu offered. "Fortunately, Buddhist funeral services are performed after cremation, so we will not need to produce a body. And I will inform her family in Japan of the situation and the need for secrecy."

"Good. I'll get the death certificate," Evan said. "I'll have to let my lieutenant in on this, but nobody else; if Gades found out about Chopin, he must have an informant somewhere in police business." He and Curtis looked at each other grimly again, and I knew they were thinking of their friend and wondering who had betrayed him.

"I'll tell Sabrina to keep her mouth shut," I volunteered.

Evan said to me, "Very important. Don't forget the staff."

"Oh, don't worry about them, every one of them is the soul of discretion." Unwittingly, I looked again at Korosu and a flash of sparks flushed my cheeks.

Evan noted my glance and then said to me in a flat voice, "I'll remember that."

I could have reassured him with a smile but I let that hang. Let him sweat a little, it's good for him.

Chapter 21

Korosu and I were the first to the entrance hall at the appointed departure time. To cover my unease at being alone with him for the first time, I switched into rehearsed hostess mode.

"Let me get your coat." I crossed quickly to the hidden door of the coat closet and found his overcoat; it was the finest cashmere, and it smelled faintly of subtle masculine cologne. I turned to give it to him only to find him behind me, close enough to breathe the same inviting scent on him. I did so, trying not to seem too obvious. Afraid he would see his effect on me, I didn't look up at his face; instead I focused on a dark silk pocket handkerchief in his breast pocket. I was so close to him that I could make out a discreet monogram stitched onto the fabric in the same color thread, a small Japanese character that I recognized from the haiku.

"I'll take that, thank you," he said in a low sultry voice, but he didn't move away. The open closet door blocked us from anyone's view and the sense of intimacy excited me.

Raising my eyes to meet his I said simply. "You're welcome."

Taking the coat, he draped it over one arm and then reached out and ran his hand down my arm, experimentally letting the fingertips trail. It sent a thrill, and a wave of guilt, through me. Very softly he said, "What an amazing woman you are."

From the other side of the door, in the entrance hall, I heard footsteps coming down the stairs. Korosu smiled, winked at me, and backed away. I busied myself closing the closet and, hopefully, leaving my disarranged feelings inside of it, before joining Aya and Deirdre at the door.

Aya and Korosu left through the front door, doing an excellent acting job, I thought.

Shika and Sabrina hugged with tears in their eyes and promised to see each other again when this was all over, like sorority girls on graduation night. And then Shika was escorted into the garage, where she lay on the floor in the back of a black-and-white, and then she was gone as well.

I was worried for the women but relieved to close the door behind them. The police, who had been watching the house, were released by Evan. Things were back to semi-normal. I walked into the entrance hall and whooped, "Alone at last!"

"Yeah, right, you, me, and the cast of a manor-house murder." Ginny spoke from the top of the stairs.

Deirdre entered from the kitchen. "You did it!" I said, pointing at her.

"Did I?" She raised a brow. "And might I inquire what 'it' would be?"

I shrugged. "I don't know, but you're the butler, you guys are always guilty."

"I'm sorry to hear that." She faded back into the kitchen.

Ginny was on her way down the stairs. "Let's get out of the house. Isn't your standing tee time in about an hour?" she asked.

"Brilliant idea, I'll get the clubs."

"I'll get the car," she said and almost ran into Evan and Curtis, who were coming down the hall from the garage.

"Where are you off to?" Evan asked her.

"Golfing. I feel the need to get out in the open air and hit something really hard. Want to come?" She smiled evilly at him.

He shuddered slightly. "I've got to go down to the precinct. Thanks, though. After tonight, I am officially back at work."

"Oh well," I said, trying to sound casual about it.

Ginny's voice turned smooth as honey, and I had to suppress a smile as she asked Curtis, "How about you?"

"Can't," he said, eyeing her as though she were a delectable treat. "Much as I'd like to hit on something." Ginny smiled, and I would say from the unbreakable eye contact between them that it was a rain check.

A feeling of familiar disappointment came over me. "I guess that means you'll be going back to your house tonight?" I asked Evan, and my voice sounded colder than I meant it to.

Ginny made a noise that sounded like "uh-oh," and Curtis said to her, far too loudly, "So, you golf," and they moved a little ways down the hall, away from the possible shrapnel.

Evan approached and put one arm around me. "Would you like me to come back here?"

"Whatever you need to do." I tried to sound disinterested, but I couldn't keep from producing a fake smile.

"What would you like?" he pressed.

"You do what you need to do," I insisted.

"So you don't care?" He pulled me harder up against him.

I wasn't falling for it. In fact, I let some real coldness creep over me as I thought about him snapping at me earlier, telling me to keep out of it when I had defended Aya and Korosu. "Look, you don't answer to me, I'm fine with that. Just let me know if you're coming, if it's not too much trouble, okay?" I smiled insincerely again and called out to Ginny, "Ready?"

Evan let go of me. "Fine, I'll call you later." He crossed into the library without looking back, leaving me feeling like an incapable fuckup. Curtis muttered a good-bye and followed him.

Ginny watched them go and then looked at me. "That was real inviting."

"I know, shut up," I said. She just stood there looking at me, so I snapped at her. "Okay, so I suck at this relationship thing, okay? Are you happy now?" I wanted to be angry at her, to make it her fault, but we both knew it wasn't, so she let the strike roll off of her, bless her. "But it's not just *my* fault," I continued. "I'm not going to beg him to stay, he can go where he wants to. I don't care."

I started down the hall, and she fell in behind me. "Okay, you don't care," she said as we reached the garage and I hurled the two bags of clubs into the trunk. "I buy that," she added as I slammed the trunk closed with all my might. "But I do have a question."

"Yes you can drive," I said to her, and she climbed into the driver's seat.

"Another question."

"What?" I asked, annoyed at myself for sounding so sharp.

"What *do* you want?" she asked me when I had settled next to her and cursed the seat belt a sufficient number of times, as it kept catching when I repeatedly tried to yank it out too fast. Then while I muttered that the world was plotting against me, she continued, cutting off my tortured sigh. "I'm just saying that it can be helpful to ask yourself what you're feeling and how you want to resolve something, that's all." Her look as she started the engine and pressed the garage door opener was inquisitive as well as accusing.

Sulking, I turned forward as we headed out onto the drive. "You don't have to talk to me like I'm in kindergarten, you know," I said, wondering if my coat closet encounter with Korosu had contributed to my response.

"I know." She smiled at me. "You're a grown-up. Relationship-wise, however, your growth is somewhat stunted, you must admit." She was speaking in the most infuriating voice. What pissed me off the most was that she was right, I knew it, and I hated hearing it.

"So," she persisted, "what *do* you want to happen with Evan?"

"I don't fucking know!" I said. My heart was swirling as my brain tried hard to get control over my childish reaction, and I couldn't take anymore reprimanding at the moment.

"Well, give it some thought," she said imperially, and when I growled at her she added quickly, "I mean, I think. Don't you?"

As we came around the curve to the front of the house, the object of my confusion was standing in the drive. He moved to my side of the car as Ginny came to a stop.

I took my time rolling down the window so that he would see I was perfectly uninterested in his presence.

He leaned down and looked into my eyes. "I'll be back later tonight and I would very much like to see you."

It took a deep breath and a wobbly baby step, but I managed to move past my metal coating and say honestly, "I want to see you too. Thank you." I smiled openly at him, and received his kiss with a flood of relief.

Sometimes the baby steps get us the farthest. I felt an immediate rush of connection to Evan. The pressure of his hand and the glint in his eyes told me he felt the same.

"I'm sorry I can be so silly," I whispered in his ear, not wanting to share the confession with Ginny.

"You're the least silly person I've ever known," Evan whispered back. He kissed my hand with his eyes tightly closed and then looked up at Ginny. "You be careful, okay?"

"She'll be home for dinner," Ginny told him, and we pulled away.

Leaning back in my seat I felt immensely proud of myself. "He's an awful damn good one," I said to my friend.

She looked over at me with a pause that said I wasn't pulling the polyester over her eyes. "You stay out of trouble."

"What does that mean?"

"Oh, please, I've known you for a long time. If I've seen you work a man once, I've seen it a hundred times. You stay away from Handsome Asian Stranger Man."

"What are you talking about?" I feigned annoyance, but she knew me so well.

"If you fuck up your relationship with Evan, somebody who loves you very much is going to leave your life forever," she warned.

"You think Evan would do that?" I said, suddenly struck by the very real possibility.

"I'm not talking about Evan." Ginny looked at me meaningfully. "I'm talking about me."

Chapter 22

We chatted on the way to the first hole. It was a perfect day, sunny, a smooth breeze strong enough to cool the skin but not enough to reroute your ball.

I took a practice swing and then lined up my shot. Ginny put in her inevitable two cents and I adjusted my stance accordingly, and then let it rip. It was a lovely sight; a tiny white spot arching up and then slowly down far away across the green expanse. I turned proudly to Ginny, and she fed my ego with a wry smile, then she proceeded to knock the skin off her ball, sending it half again the distance of mine.

"Am I just a natural or what?" Ginny whooped.

"Or what," I muttered and climbed sourly into the golf cart. I tried not to look at Ginny flexing her arm muscles at me as we started off. I'd taught her to play when we first met, and with her natural athleticism she'd caught up to me with a vengeance.

At the fifth hole there was a male foursome ahead of us, and the first golfer was balancing his ball on the tee. So we pulled up and sat back to watch. A gold watch flashed on the wrist of the man as he swung his driver with a practiced precision, and an unusual amount of strength. As he untwisted and turned to face us, I smiled at him.

"Beautiful," I said. Meaning the shot, but I could have said the same about his golden eyes and his white teeth. He had wavy brown hair with natural highlights, a little longish but neatly cut and styled. His physique was strong and solid, yet lean, and he moved off the tee with the grace of a predator. One word summed up his entire presence, *leonine.* I heard Ginny next to me make a long sexy throaty sound to voice her opinion of him.

"Thank you," he said graciously. I detected an accent so slight I couldn't place it. He kept coming toward me until he was at his own cart, level with ours. As he put his club in the bag, his eyes were watching me, toying with my obvious approval. "Hello, ladies."

"Two hundred and twenty yards, I'd say, straight down. I'd be happy with that," I said.

"Two hundred yards would make any woman happy, if she could ever do it," he answered. The assumption of superior male athleticism stung me in an old competitive place; Ginny's growl implied she'd been rubbed the wrong way as well.

She looked at me and didn't bother to lower her voice. "Cocky son of a bitch, isn't he?"

"Well . . ." I looked straight at her, ignoring the stiffness that had come into the man's body language, and began to explain as if to a small child. "You see, some men have this thing where they think that because they have a . . . you know." I gestured to my crotch.

"Oh," Ginny's eyes widened, "a hoo-ha."

"Yes, a hoo-ha. Well, they think that because they have a hoo-ha that they can hit a little white ball better than someone who hasn't a hoo-ha." I nodded seriously.

"Do they hit the ball with the hoo-ha?" Ginny asked.

"Ah, I don't think so."

"Then why would having a hoo-ha make you better than a non-hoo-ha-haver?"

"I don't know." Maintaining my neutral expression with difficulty, I turned to the man, who was now standing with his arms crossed next to his bag watching us with unabashed interest. "Do you?" I asked him and smiled sweetly.

I looked at the other three men, none of whom had spoken. It was instantly clear they were with the man I was addressing, and not the other way around.

"What a charming way of calling me a chauvinist," he said disarmingly, but I thought I detected a tic in his mood that kept him teetering precariously between amusement and insult. I'm pretty sure if we hadn't been two unusually attractive women he would have plunged over into angry disgust right away.

"Oh, I wouldn't do that," I said to him. "Would you?" I asked Ginny.

"Not yet, no." She smiled. "You gentlemen gonna be a while?"

"Would you ladies like to play through?" he asked.

Ginny smiled at me and then said to him, "How kind, thank you." She climbed out of the golf cart and sauntered around to the back, affecting a lazy sexiness. She put a forefinger on her full mouth and stuck her butt out as she gazed into her bag to pick a club. It was such an obvious pose that I had to pretend to fix my glove to keep from bursting out laughing.

"Now which of you little ol' clubs wants to come out and play?" She looked up at me, and I turned in my seat to face her. "Is this one of those big bad holes, one of those, you know, those . . ."

"Par five," I confirmed.

"Ooh, that's so scary." She put both her feet together and arched her back in a Vargas pose. Not one of the men had taken his eyes off her. Ginny whipped out a club, sashayed all the way to the woman's tee, put the pointed end of the tee in her mouth and wet it before leaning over, knees locked, ass up, to push it sensuously into the earth.

"Get in there, all the way, deeper," she said as she eased it in. Then she placed her ball, straightened up, and smacked the fire out of it. She wasn't much for finesse, but range she could do. The men watched the little white speck disappear and then watched her sashay back to the cart. I put my head down on the wheel for a minute to control a spasm of laughter and then pulled myself together.

I took my club and could feel the challenging watchfulness of the men, men unused to a woman who could compete with them. I felt the satisfaction of knowing I could rival them in most aspects of what they would consider masculine territory. It was unlikely that they had my money, my business success, or my sexual prowess. They certainly didn't have my ass. My drive followed Ginny's down the fairway. It smacked, bounced, and rolled on, at least two hundred yards. I didn't look at them as I stooped to recover my tee, but the silence was most eloquent. I walked back to the cart and smiled at the man who stood waiting.

His eyes were smiling now, but he held himself in a way that let me know he was on to me.

"I think I might get my score whipped by a lady today." He smiled.

"Oh, I wouldn't bet on it," I tossed out coyly.

"Maybe we should." His voice was very quiet, yet it had strength and rumble in it. I liked it, in spite of the obvious arrogance. I knew his type, European old school, confident of male superiority. I felt a surge of desire to knock his pretty teeth out.

"Did he just dare you?" asked Ginny. "Doesn't he know you're the queen of this playground?"

"A wager?" I asked the man.

"A wager, I think, is in order," he answered, placing a hand on the roof of my cart as he leaned down a little, smiling. "I'll give you two strokes."

"That's interesting." Now for the kill. "How about five?"

"Five strokes? That would be generous after what I just saw." He sounded surprised.

"No, I don't want any strokes; I meant shall we play for five?"

"Not much of a gambler are you?" he asked.

"Not enough you think? How about fifteen?" I smiled back sweetly.

He looked, for just a flash, pitying, which made me flare with anger and determination. "Fifteen to the winner. We'll compare score cards at the clubhouse?"

"Of course. I'll wait for you. Take your time."

I started to pull away and then braked and turned back innocently. "Oh, you do know I mean fifteen *hundred,* don't you?" I batted my lashes.

He put his head back and laughed; it was a rough rolling masculine sound from deep in his chest. "My mistake then." He looked into my eyes. "I thought we were speaking in *thousands.*"

I pulled myself together in the space of a head snap. "Done. Fifteen thousand," I said. "I wouldn't want you to be mistaken. Men hate that, I understand." I winked, pushed the accelerator, and we passed on.

"That's a hell of a bet," Ginny said. "I think he may have baited you a little."

"You think he's that good?" I asked, not liking the idea of a stupid bet; it's against my business ethics.

"Damn, I don't know." Ginny sat for a minute with her eyes narrowed and her mouth pursed out. Then she punched me hard in the arm and let out a resounding war cry. "Let's shrink his hoo-ha!"

Back at the clubhouse I waited with my scorecard. A seventy-two. A score I had only shot once before. While I was waiting I sounded out the club pro about my adversary.

Robert, the pro, was a handsome man in his sixties who had

taught me to play at thirteen and beaten me soundly for over twenty years since, though the gap in our scores has closed steadily until it was only a stroke or two.

"Who was the guy who teed off right before me?" I asked him. "I've never seen him here."

"About ten years ago the club opened a very few memberships for an exorbitant amount of money; he bought one. He's seldom here though; I hear he travels a lot for his business. I think he lives in Switzerland."

"Banking?" I asked.

"Telecommunications, best I can make out. Anyway, I heard him talking about some new technology, sounded something like that. I can't keep up with all the members."

I caught his smirk. He knew just about everything about just about every golfer at the club, maybe not all their business, but who was dating whom and whose marriage was on the rocks.

Robert looked serious. "Some of his guests seem a little shady, if you know what I mean. Aren't you dating that detective? I thought that was pretty steady." He was going for the inside scoop.

"This is a golf course, not a singles' bar. We have a little bet going, that's all. Girls against the boys. That kind of thing." I winked, and Robert didn't believe a word I said. Considering the looks of the male lion and my history of one-month relationships, I couldn't blame him.

"Can he beat me?" I couldn't help asking.

"Not likely, he's strong but doesn't keep his cool real well. Unlike some ice princesses we may know." He wiggled his eyebrows at me.

"Are you calling me cold, Robert?" I asked in mock indignation.

"In person, no. In cleats? You're a buffet table centerpiece at an Alaskan wedding. I'm not saying that's a bad thing, you understand." He rubbed my arm affectionately and walked away to greet a new foursome.

My challenger and his group rolled in shortly afterward, and I held out my card with one hand and reached for his with the other. I looked down and saw his score, a twin to my own seventy-two.

"Well, well, everybody wins. How nice," I said casually, deeply disappointed.

"But I gave you two strokes, so you have me," he offered.

"Nice try, I didn't take them." Was he testing me? "Did you really think I would take you up on that because I'm a woman?"

"I don't play with women, as a rule." He picked it up. "Especially not women who are scratch. But you are obviously an exception."

"Well, that's the first time I ever got stroked for not getting strokes, if you know what I mean." I was fully expecting the hit now.

He walked around me, very close, to take a bottle of water being offered to him by one of his friends. There's something about a man who smells good when he's hot that stirs up my primeval soup. He turned as the friend backed away and leaned down to speak softly in my ear. I could feel the warmth of his body, and he had that dangerous magnetism that crossed lines and threw switches.

"I would like to play you again, Ms. Wilde," he said, and I was not surprised he'd learned my name, I was well known here, but I was surprised to feel his hand take mine. He raised it quickly to his lips, and after a soft kiss his eyes met mine across it. "Perhaps we shall have another game soon, a different game, but I'm afraid I must leave the country on business at present."

"I'm sorry I didn't catch *your* name," I said, catching my breath in spite of myself at the same time. This guy might be an arrogant asshole, but he was a very *charming* arrogant asshole.

"You may call me Anthony." He bowed slightly without releasing my hand or my eyes, and then he turned and left with that striking, rolling gait. His friends, looking curiously like subservient bodyguards now, trailed behind him. He stopped at the door and turned. "I should mention, however, that most people call me Antonio." He flashed a smile and left.

I stood frozen. I was still holding his scorecard in my hand and I forced myself to look down at it. There, written in pencil across the top was his last name: Gades.

"Jesus Christ" was all I could muster through my locked jaw. "Antonio Gades."

Chapter 23

"How did he know?" I almost screamed at Evan.

"What they don't know they find out," he repeated.

"So he set the whole thing up?" I was still incredulous.

"Sure. He wants us to know exactly how easy it is to get to us," Evan spat out angrily and aimed a vicious kick at the ottoman.

"Evan, the doctor said to be careful."

"Yeah, I know." I could see from the grimace on his face the pain it had cost him to vent his frustration, but he looked as though he'd like to throw the thing through the window. "God damn it! I swear I'll get that bastard!" Evan was incensed, angrier than I'd ever seen him.

It had scared him that Gades got to me, scared him that Gades had picked me, pissed him off that he hadn't been there to protect me. I was watching him take the situation and shake it into submission.

For my own part, I was trying to stuff an octagonal impression into a linear space. Gades had been so refined and so charming. My left hand covered the spot on my right that he had kissed. Could that man really be responsible for the brutal murder Shika had told us about? Instinctively, I knew that he could. I brushed the top of my hand against my thigh to try to wipe it clean.

"What should we do?" I asked.

"I was hoping that Shika's and Aya's leaving this house would be enough to keep him away from you." His face and his voice were brittle. "There's no reason for him to think you're involved, past letting them stay with you."

"Do you think he wanted to scare me because he's worried that she told us what she knows?" I asked him.

"Men like Gades don't worry about people knowing things, they worry about people being able to prove it. I think he was letting us know he could get to us. He's making it personal. Men like this don't have rules; you can't deal with them like normal people. They don't go away once they smell blood, or fear." He stared at the floor so intently I felt sure he could see right through it. "They're monsters. They don't die like mortals."

"So, what do we do?" I asked cautiously, afraid of intruding.

He looked slowly up at me, and my heart was hit by a blast of icy wind.

"We run a stake through his heart," he said through gritted teeth.

And I knew, as surely as I had ever known anything, that one of them was going to die.

Chapter 24

It was incongruous to be wearing black on such a beautiful day. I looked at Aya across the small gathering of people and watched a tear slide down her cheek as the monks in saffron chanted a haunting prayer. Damn, she's good, I thought to myself and wondered briefly about believing everything she and Shika had told us before I pushed the suspicion out of my head.

After the simple service, Korosu bowed deeply to the monks, presented them with an envelope, and walked over to where Evan and I stood. Aya remained in the garden as the mourners faded back to a respectful distance, and then she knelt near the little shrine and bowed her head with the grace of a compassionate angel.

I watched her from the edge of the path.

"That was very beautiful," I said, touched by the ceremony in spite of its lack of validity.

"Let's hope it was also very convincing," Evan added under his breath. He extended his hand to Korosu, who took it with equal strength; they did not smile or break eye contact. "He didn't come."

"No."

"I didn't really expect him to expose himself." Evan sounded disappointed. "But I'm positive he's been informed about it. He's probably keeping an eye on you," he said to Korosu, "which means he's got someone watching us right now."

"I would like to speak to you," Korosu said, and his tone implied he meant "not here."

Evan's eyes cut left and right before he responded. "Come out to the car." Then he turned to me; I was still watching Aya, feeling an odd melancholy.

"I'd like to stay here for a few minutes, if it's okay," I told him. He glanced around again, and I found myself looking at Korosu.

When our eyes met the click was almost audible. I had to look down when I felt Evan's watchful gaze return to me and heard him say, "That's fine." Nodding, I turned away.

I made for a bench near a small pond a few feet away. Across the water I could see Aya; she was still kneeling, the breeze playing her hair like a black silk banner. I wondered what she could be feeling at a fake funeral for a friend and hoped it was a sense of relief that she was out of danger. My gaze drifted to a twisted pine surrounded by pebbles raked into a wave pattern and my mind drifted comfortably. When I turned back toward Aya my sense of well-being evaporated like a drop of water on a hot coal.

She was not alone.

And she clearly hadn't heard the man in a dark suit approach her from behind; I watched her startled reaction as he lay a hand on her shoulder and spoke to her.

Her eyes flew open, but she did not turn around or look up at him. Instead she stared straight ahead. I didn't need to be close enough to make out the face to know who it was. The leonine gait and the strength in his stance gave him away: Gades.

Coming to my feet, I looked quickly behind me, but the temple grounds were deserted. As I watched, Aya struggled under Gades's hand, as though he were hurting her, and I saw her lips move in a single-word response. My brain was racing, searching desperately for options. *What can I do?*

Before I could think of anything, Gades took his hand off of Aya's shoulder and reached across his chest, into his jacket. Maybe if I called out, or just made myself known, he would leave. *Or maybe he'll kill us both.* Shoving the fear aside enough to move, I started forward.

"Aya!" I called, and they both looked up at me. As I kept walking toward them, Gades's pulled his hand back out of his jacket and there was no gun in it, only a handkerchief, blindingly white in the sun. Aya was still on the ground; she hadn't turned to him. She looked up at me with fear in her eyes.

After a cursory glance, Gades ignored me; he was staring at the shrine, his whole body stiff with grief. Disbelieving, I watched him wipe tears from his face. No one spoke, or moved for a full two minutes. Finally his eyes rose to mine, and the pain on his face was undeniable. Without breaking eye contact, he nodded his head slightly.

"Ms. Wilde," he said, acknowledging me. His eyes glinted dangerously, and he spoke in a dead, even voice. "Tell your boyfriend to mind his own business or he'll be dealing with me." He raised his hand and struck Aya sharply on the side of the head. As she fell to one side, I lunged forward to protect her from another blow, but he shifted in front of her and faced me squarely, raising his hand and pointing a finger at me as if to say "you're next." He turned and walked back the way he had come, with long, strong strides, and his shoulders braced tightly against the grief that shook them.

Aya swayed slightly and put her hands on the ground in front of her. Then she rose and took my arm. "Let's go," she whispered. "Please."

Neither of us breathed until we were in the car with Evan.

After we'd both piled in, Aya covered her face with her hands, her shoulders shaking as she cried silently.

"Are you okay?" Evan asked, disturbed.

"No," I answered quickly. "Gades showed up, he went right to Aya and said something to her. I was too far away to hear, and then he struck her."

"Are you hurt?" Evan asked.

She shook her head no, but her hand went up to press against her hair.

Evan asked sternly, "What did he say?"

Aya took a moment to compose herself. "He wanted to know if it was true—if she was really dead. I told him yes." She slowly pulled in a lungful of air, as though it was filled with painful glass shards.

"What else?"

"He wanted to know if it was an overdose," she added.

"What did you say?" I asked, amazed at how quickly she had cut the flow of fear, at how skillfully she had controlled her emotions. It seemed unhealthy, in an all-too-familiar way.

She looked up at me and then at Evan, "I said yes. It seemed to make sense."

Evan was nodding. "Yes, good, that was smart of you." He included me in his next query. "How did he react?"

I waited for her to answer first, since I had not been privy to the exchange. She answered clearly and with some anger in her voice. "He was angry, and upset."

I told Evan about Gades's threat and then added, "Evan, he was *really* upset. Does that make sense?" I still felt confused; who was this guy? "If I didn't know anything about him, I would say he really cared for her, he looked like he'd lost someone in his family."

Evan's eyes had gone narrow, and he looked to Aya again. "What did he say, *exactly?*"

Aya's brow furrowed, as though straining to remember each word. "He said, 'So, I've lost her.' It was such a selfish way to put it, as though he was only concerned that she wasn't there for him." Her voice was steady, too steady, but her nostrils flared as she spoke. "And then after I answered the questions I told you about, he said, 'I should have known.' And that's when Callaway called out."

Evan's cell phone appeared in his hand, and he punched a number. "Curtis," he said quickly, "we had a visitor. Did anyone see him?" There was a quick pause and then, "Damn, he must have come over the wall. I guess he wanted to see for himself. Okay, thanks." He put the phone back in his pocket and started the car. "Are you okay?" he asked Aya.

"I will be. I was just startled. For a moment I thought it was the other man, Leon, and then I realized that of course it couldn't be, but sometimes I have nightmares." She stared out the window and didn't say any more.

"I know," I told her touching her leg, "I have nightmares about the man who attacked me too. Even though he's dead, he still haunts me. But Leon can't hurt you anymore, it's okay, you're safe now." I smiled at her but avoided making eye contact with Evan. I knew a look between us would betray what we were both thinking.

None of us were safe.

Chapter 25

The next few days were anxious but mercifully uneventful. We heard from Aya, who checked in to say that she was fine, which was good. And I didn't see much of Evan, which wasn't. My neck and shoulders were so tightened by tension that I took to rolling my head constantly from side to side to try to relieve it. Ginny and Sabrina both commented on the motion, the latter out of curiosity, the former to inquire if I had taken up modern dance.

I was sick and tired of jumping at shadows and decided we all needed to get out. I wanted a massage and knew just where to get one. Remembering how good, but unexpectedly painful, the shiatsu massage at Korosu's hotel had been the first time, I found myself snickering derisively at the thought of Ginny wincing and cursing beneath a female muscle-bound shiatsu master. She thought she was so tough; she was tough, of course, but it wouldn't be bad for her to get brought down a tiny notch. I also couldn't help but notice an increase in my pulse at the thought that I might cross paths with Korosu again, but I dismissed the excitement as inconsequential, because I wanted to.

I called the Sakura-no Hana Hotel and Spa and booked three simultaneous hour-long massages in the early evening. Specifying no preference in masseuses other than a particularly strong one for Ms. Virginia. That would show *her* smart ass. Figuring we could sneak in and out without Aya knowing, I deliberately didn't call her; I wanted to pay this time and not impose on her hospitality.

We were greeted with bows at the hotel, and I was welcomed back with full recognition; so much for sneaking in and out. My masseuse, Hiro, turned out to be a slight woman; Ginny's was a man who, I was glad to see, could easily have played left tackle. When we were called in for our massages after a long hot soak, we put on our T-shirts and cotton shorts and I winked at Ginny. "You're gonna love this," I told her. Sabrina looked scared, so I added to her, "Don't worry, we'll all be in the same room."

Hiro smiled and spoke in gruff broken English. "They be in same room, but we very busy, you have private room," she said to me. She nodded and repeated, "Yes, private."

"Oh," I said, "I guess we picked a popular night." We all followed Hiro into the main room, and then she led me through a curtained doorway into a small darker room, lit with two white candles that infused the room with the scent of greenery.

She left me to get settled, facedown, and when she returned I felt the focused pressure of hands on my back. I was impressed by the strength and the size of her hands as she worked at releasing the tension in my neck and shoulders.

Slowly, expertly, she moved her hands down my back, gliding and kneading until I felt malleable again. This massage was far more skillful than my first at this spa, and the first time here had been great. This was different, though, more sensuous and knowing. For a time there was a circular rhythmic pressure on the small of my back that was building up a different kind of pressure. I thought of Evan on top of me, moving with that same rhythm, and the heat increased, the lack of sexual release in the last couple of weeks was driving me to distraction; to stop myself from getting carried away I opened my eyes, and took in the limited view of the floor through the small opening in the massage table.

What I saw was not Hiro's white-socked feet in slip-on shoes but a man's shoes, expensive ones. I didn't dare move, but my body went rigid. Noticeably so, apparently, because he spoke a few soothing words, and I recognized the smooth masculine voice right away. Raising my head suddenly I looked up at him.

"Korosu?"

"Relax, lay down," he said again in a soothing, commanding voice. So I did, conscious suddenly of the loose cotton boxers and shapeless shirt that I was wearing.

"How did you know I was here?" I didn't know what else to ask, like maybe, "Why are you rubbing my body?" or, "Damn, how do you make that feel so good?"

"You called to make a reservation, it's a very small hotel." He was wearing his suit slacks but had stripped down to a fine white cotton T-shirt himself. His arms were delicious, and the rest of him looked really good too. "As you didn't specify a masseuse and I have taken some pains to master the art, I had hoped you wouldn't mind."

"Uhm, okay." I put my face back down before it reddened and gave me away. *It's just a massage, no big deal.* But every touch was charged, his hands were expert, and though none of his movements were overtly sexual, it was all arousing, and when his skillful fingers pressed against the back of my thighs and worked their way up across my ass, it took all my self-control to keep my body still. I understood completely what Aya had meant when she said that he was a connoisseur of many things, that she had been lucky to have him as her first lover. I lay there and played a new visual of Korosu and Aya skillfully pleasing each other, and tried not to press back against him.

"Turn over, please," Korosu whispered, so close that I could feel his warm breath on my ear. Then he held the sheet up slightly for me to do so. My nipples were so hard they were singing a high note in an aria through the thin cotton T-shirt. Trying to pretend I didn't notice, I snuck a glance up at him as I settled and saw that he was smiling down at my body with the pleasure of a collector coveting a find. Nice.

Somehow, I got through the rest of the massage without writhing or having an orgasm, showing a great deal of self-control, I thought. Finally he asked me to sit up and rubbed my shoulders once more with his face very close to mine, and I was trying desperately to win the struggle to refuse him when he kissed me.

He got up behind me on the table and worked the last of the knots where my neck met my shoulder, smoothing out and down until his hands came to rest on my upper arms. And then I felt his lips brush the back of my neck. I took in a sharp breath and felt the thrill all the way up and down my spine, and then the curtain behind him parted and Ginny stuck her head in. Her inquisitive smile twisted instantly into a suspicious pursed mouth. Korosu slapped his hands down on my shoulders with a hollow sound, then stepped off the table, bowed without lowering his eyes, and left.

I fell back on the table, completely, overwhelmingly relieved to be snatched from the jaws of temptation *and* deeply disappointed for exactly the same reason.

When I went to pay the bill, it was, of course, already taken care of, so I tipped Ginny's and Sabrina's masseuses and toyed with the idea of leaving something for Korosu as a private joke, maybe my phone number, but I knew that was dancing on dynamite.

He had left me something, a note inviting us to dine in the restaurant, regretting that he would not be able to join us, as business called. It was signed with the same strong symbol as the haiku. I smiled to myself and asked my partners if they were hungry.

"Will you be joining us," Ginny asked me, "or will you be eating in a private room?" Her insinuation made me feel guilty, and I wasn't.

Was I?

Sabrina lifted a piece of raw fish she had speared with a fork—all my efforts to coax her fingers to manipulate the chopsticks had failed—and looked at it dubiously. Then she put it down and regarded a tempura shrimp as though it were from another planet before taking a tentative bite. Her face lit up. "Oh, it's a fried shrimp!" She looked victorious. "I like these, they're especially good with hush puppies."

Ginny, as a counterpoint, was slurping raw oysters with obvious relish. When I offered her a mushroom delicacy, she wrinkled her nose. "You know I don't do fungus," she said and expertly snabbed a sea urchin sushi between her chopsticks.

"Is this place great, or what?" I asked them both.

Ginny nodded enthusiastically and finished the morsel before she spoke. "I can't believe I never knew this hotel was here. It's like a little hidden oasis. Kyoto, California."

We were dining at one of the private tables, enclosed by sliding paper screen doors, sitting on silk cushions in our stocking feet.

"Korosu certainly does a good job keeping it secret. The clientele seems to be exclusively Japanese, and rich," I added, thinking of the menu with no prices on it. If you had to ask, you couldn't afford it. That got me thinking about the price of a relationship; I missed Evan, and I was pissed at him for being so busy that he made me miss him.

My cell phone sounded its annoying musical scale and a recorded woman's voice said, "you have an incoming call, you have an incoming call." The caller ID read BOYFRIEND.

"Hi there," I responded eagerly.

"Hi." I could tell he missed me too, just from that one syllable. "Where are you?"

Guilty. I hadn't thought about it up till now, but it occurred to me before I answered that Evan might not like us coming down here. "Uhm, we're in Little Tokyo."

"Who is?"

"Me, Ginny, and Sabrina."

"Where?" he asked, and I could tell he already knew.

"Sakura-no Hana." I was feeling defensive. "We came for massages and now we're having dinner. Why? Is that not okay?"

"Is it just you three?" He was asking if Korosu was with me, I thought, it gave me a little twinge of pleasure to know that he was jealous.

"Just us."

"Then I think it's fine," he said, deflating my puffiness, "as long as you feel it's respectful of our recent loss." His sincerity was perfectly played.

"I do," I answered, making a mental note to remind Sabrina not to mention anything while we were here, and there was a pause on the line. Finally I said, "Will I be seeing you this evening?" and braced myself to be disappointed.

"I'd like that very much." His voice was saturated with innuendo.

"So would I." Now I was saturated myself, his voice still had that simple power over me, and I needed contact with Evan to keep me from doing something rash if I saw Korosu again tonight.

"How was your massage?" he asked, and for just a second I wondered if he knew who my masseuse had been.

"Actually, it was great, but distracting, if you know what I mean." Sometimes vagueness pays.

"I do know. I often feel that way when I think about you," he said, and I smiled. He knew where I lived all right. "I'll be at your house in about an hour, good?"

"Very good." We signed off, and I turned to Ginny and Sabrina, who were both staring unabashedly at me. "What?" I asked coyly.

Ginny kept watching me, but she leaned her shoulder into Sabrina's and addressed her. "She's got that gooey look, don't you think?"

"Like sugar on pie," Sabrina answered knowingly.

I hated being so easy to read. "What? So? He's coming over and we haven't had much private time lately, what with house-guests and international drug cartels popping up left and right."

"Mm-hmm." Ginny looked at me. "You're in, hook, line, and sinker, and here's the best part." She turned to Sabrina now and started talking to her like I wasn't even there. "It's been eight months, hell, damn close to nine, and she hasn't driven him off, pissed him off, thrown him out, gotten bored with him, or screwed anyone else." She shot me an evil squint. "And she better not," she threatened. I thought of Korosu's hands on the small of my back as she continued. "It's like a miracle," she concluded.

"Amen," Sabrina answered solemnly, and they both turned back to look at me. Ginny reached onto the plate in front of her and put a piece of sushi in her mouth, like popcorn at a movie, without ever taking her eyes off me.

"Fuck off," I said, laughing, but inside I was glowing, and secretly, I was overjoyed that even with the temptation of Korosu, I still wanted Evan.

I left a hundred-dollar tip, on the way out, and we were halfway through the lobby when I saw Korosu outside the sliding glass doors. He was speaking to a shabbily dressed man, who looked like one of the many vagrants who called the downtown streets their home, and as I watched, Korosu took money from his pocket and handed it over to the man who shuffled drunkenly away. Then he turned, and looking as sleek and masculine as the tasteful decor of his hotel, Korosu crossed to us and bowed politely. Sabrina returned the gesture unself-consciously; I was impressed by her composure.

"How was dinner?" he asked.

"Delightful."

"Amazing."

"Yummy."

The three responses were simultaneous, and we all laughed at ourselves. Korosu's eyes rested on me. "I hope you will come back and be my guest again soon." I felt a hot blush rise on my face, and it doubled when I saw Ginny frown at it. Just then, an attractive, sharply dressed woman approached Korosu with a phone in her hand. He turned to her. "Yes?"

"Sorry to interrupt, but it's the ship-to-shore call you've been expecting," she said to him and held out the phone.

Korosu took it quickly, and excusing himself, he strode away to take the call.

I managed to steer the other two to the exit. Once through the doors, Ginny's black eyes tried to lure mine into a snare, which I successfully avoided, but only for a short time.

As we came into the parking lot I saw the vagrant; he was counting the crisp bills Korosu had given him. It was a very generous handout.

When we were all in the car Ginny lassoed me directly. "Okay, what's up with Korosu-san?" she asked.

"What do you mean?" I tried another evasive tactic. It failed.

"I mean, why was he rubbing on you?"

"You got a massage from Shika's uncle?" Sabrina asked, "I thought he *owned* the hotel."

We ignored her. "He wanted to give me the massage, he's grateful to me, and he's an expert at it," I fumbled.

"I'll just bet he is," she said as though it were my fault.

I felt genuinely indignant. "I didn't even know it was him until it was halfway through," I said, defending myself.

Ginny sat back against her seat and sighed. "Damn. You've got to be so careful what you wish for."

"What does that mean?" I asked her.

"For a long time I've been wanting you to find somebody with enough personality and power to handle you." She was shaking her head as though she had failed. "But I should have been more specific, *one* man, not two."

I smiled at her, more reassuringly than I felt. "Just do me a favor?"

"I will *not* cover for you." She was emphatic.

I laughed. "No. Not that."

"What?" she asked, suspiciously.

"Get me home to Evan," I told her, "and hurry."

Chapter 26

But when I got home, I couldn't find him; he wasn't in the living room, the kitchen, library, or the den. Meeting Deirdre in the entrance hall I asked her where Evan was, and she told me he had gone upstairs to take a shower.

I started casually up the stairs until I could be sure Deirdre had retreated into the kitchen, and then I shot off, taking the wide staircase two steps at a time. I slowed down outside my bedroom and pretended to be breathing normally, as I imagined him spread out naked on my bed, waiting for me like the juicy snack he was. I slipped off my top and stepped out of the silk pants I was wearing, leaving on the heels and the G-string; he needed something to take off. I slithered in, ready to admire and be admired, but the bed was empty. The room was dimly lit, and I glanced about. He wasn't in the sitting area, not by the fireplace, maybe he was just out of the shower . . . even better. I'd surprise him.

But he wasn't in the bathroom either. The glass was steamy and warm, a sensation I seconded, but there was no man to match my mood. The door across from the bathroom was open, and light flickered through it, candlelight.

Ah, my mirrored dressing room—an octagonal affair, eight hidden closets, all behind floor-to-ceiling mirrored doors. In the middle of the circular room was a silk ottoman, six feet in diameter. And as I entered through the doorway from my bathroom I got nine terrific views of the naked man I desired most in the world, stretched out on that ottoman, lit sensuously by candles, one on the floor in front of each wall, and the crystal chandelier on its lowest, most glowing, setting. I took my time admiring each of the eight angles of Evan in reproduction and then feasted my eyes on the real thing. He was stretched out on his side, and he had obviously been thinking about me.

"Miss me?" I asked softly, my senses overwhelmed by him.

He offered a glass of champagne. The bottle sat in a crystal ice bucket, and another glass sat beside it. I took two slow steps in, accepted the proffered glass with an outstretched arm, and sipped thoughtfully, letting my tongue touch the cold bubbly liquid before warming it in my mouth. Keeping my eyes on him, I circled slowly around him, keeping a few feet of distance between us, watching as his eyes followed my reflection in each mirror.

"Yes, I did miss you."

"Was it hard?" I asked.

"It is now," he answered, and I moved to him. "Finish that," he said. I threw back the rest of the amber elixir. Evan took my empty glass and set it on the floor. Almost immediately the potion went to my head, and the delicious dizziness was accentuated by the movement of Evan sweeping me easily off my feet and underneath him.

I could get a good view in about three of the mirrors, and that was plenty. Our lovemaking was intense, and being able to see him, inspired, as it were, by watching us together, was a double turn-on. The toned strength of his arms and his shoulders as he held his body above mine, the small of his back as he thrust into me, had me screaming and grasping at him in moments.

We settled down slowly onto our sides, and I nestled my back up against his chest. He kissed my neck and wrapped his arms around me, curling us both into a yin-yang symbol of intimacy. I would have given him anything at that moment.

"I want to ask you something." He spoke softly, into my ear.

My heart thumped loudly. "Yes?"

"What kind of man do you think I am?" He sounded serious; it certainly wasn't what I'd been expecting. I'm not really sure what I *was* expecting, but I guess I assumed it would be more about me.

"Um, well, that's kind of hard to sum up in a sentence," I stalled.

"I'll give you a paragraph." He raised himself up on one elbow as I turned to him. This was serious, I could tell, and I knew I could play my old game and say something flattering and romantic, or I could be as honest as possible.

"Okay." I thought for a moment, tracing the line of his forehead down his nose to his lips where I pressed lightly, a kiss of the fingertips. "I think that I have never known a man who made me feel as safe as you do. I don't mean physically, I mean emotionally, but who also makes me feel like I'm in the gravest danger I have ever known." I took a deep breath and tried to explain this to myself as well as to him. "You scare the shit out of me. Every time you peel off one of my defenses I'm left looking at all my fucked-up faults and . . . well, let's just say, not being perfect is as difficult for me as it is an extreme understatement." He smiled at that confession, as though that were his favorite thing about me. "You're an amazing thing," I found myself saying. "Always better than I thought you were."

He leaned in and kissed me. "Thank you."

"And what I want most in the world is to make you happy." As I said it, I realized for the first time that it was true.

His face looked confused, a thin happy veneer stretched over deep pain. "Callaway, I know you want a commitment from me, I'm not stupid. But you have to understand *who I am.* You worry about not being perfect, I'm a man who has *hurt* people and felt it was the right thing to do." His eyes went distant and he looked away. "And when I have to, I'll do it again."

I put my hand under his chin, rough with the shadow of his beard pushing through at the end of the day, and lifted his face to look at me. "I love you," I said, and felt the sensation pulse through me and into him. "I love everything you are. Do you understand?"

"Yes," he said, and I waited with my heart laid out on a salver for him to say it back. "But can you live with what you know about me?"

That part was easy, of course I could, the question was, how long would I have to wait before he could say he loved me?

And then the answer came to me. "I can do anything," I said.

Chapter 27

The knock came seconds after I had switched off the bedside lamp and nestled into Evan's warm humid embrace. Evan was instantly alert. He turned on the light and pulled on his shorts as he crossed the room, opening the door to reveal Deirdre, in a dark blue flannel dressing gown. "Yes, Deirdre, what is it?"

We both knew she would never wake us unless there was an emergency. She didn't disappoint. "I'm sorry to disturb you, but Ms. Aya is here, and I think you should see her." When we hesitated she added, "Right away. She's is in the kitchen, and she's been assaulted."

"What?" I flew out of bed and beat Evan in throwing on pants and a sweatshirt, but only by a few seconds, and I barely had to pause by the door for him to fall in beside me as we started down the hall. The inclination was to run, but Evan placed a firm hand on my arm, and I matched his quick unpanicked pace, which was far more sensible and productive.

She was freshly bruised; her left eye looked like an unopened bud, pink and swollen. Tomorrow it would blossom into a violet plume fringed in greenery. Her bottom lip was split. Deirdre had given her an ice pack from the freezer, wrapped in a dishtowel so white it could have been sanitized for her protection.

Rushing around to the chair next to her, I laid my arm gently around her shoulders, careful not to apply too much weight. "What the hell happened?" I blurted out.

She looked up at me with her one good eye, and then it filled with tears and she couldn't maintain the gaze. Evan, once again, struck the experienced note and his voice was calm and unruffled.

"It's okay, you're safe now, take as much time as you need and then tell us what happened." Smooth, reassuring, confidence-gaining, he was just so damn capable.

Her voice, when it came a moment later, crawled out, escaped like a tiny bird from the clutches of a house cat. "It was Korosu."

"What?" I spurted. Evan shushed me with a look.

"What happened?" Again, complete calm and patience from Evan.

"I have never seen him this way before. I went to talk to him, at his home, and those men were there." She gulped a small, frightened breath.

"What men?" Evan asked, keeping his voice calm.

"Gades, and two others."

Trying my best to mimic Evan's composure, I asked in a forced steady voice, "What was Gades doing with Korosu?"

"I don't know." She cried for a moment as though her heart was breaking. "From what I heard, I think they were making a deal of some kind. They were talking about a shipment, that's the word they used, coming into San Pedro, something about changing at sea, I didn't understand." She raised her eyes to us, one of them barely visible, and the pleading in them was intense. "Have I been wrong? How could I be so blind? I have involved you, because I refused to see that Korosu could be corrupt." And then she lowered her face gingerly into the towel and cried harder, with hurt, guilty sobs.

I looked up at Evan, but he was watching her intently. "Aya?" he addressed her softly after giving her a few seconds. "What happened next?"

With an effort, she came back to us. "Korosu saw me, there in the doorway, and he knew I had heard something." She gulped again, seemingly to swallow back down a cold surge of emotions from deep inside. "Gades got up and said something about too many ears, and Korosu said not to worry, that he could take care of it." Her eyes glazed over, as though she were seeing the scene before her, and then continued. "I was so afraid. Gades and the two men with him left, but as he went past me, I felt a chill. I knew he wanted to kill me and I knew he could, but he went out and then . . ." She seemed to lose her nerve.

"And then?" Evan encouraged.

"I made a mistake." She took a deep breath, sucking it over the broken skin of her lower lip. "I told Korosu that I was afraid for him and what he had become involved in, and he beat me, told me never to tell anyone what I had seen or he would kill me." She looked up at us with the pleading eyes of a puppy at a shelter. "He cannot know I came to you. Please! But I'm so afraid, and I had to warn you, it's my fault you've been drawn into this."

"He won't know," Evan soothed firmly. "Don't worry, and Aya, thank you." He nodded his head. "I know how difficult this is for you, but you have done the right thing by coming to us." He patted her shoulder and then asked, "What exactly did you hear Korosu and Gades discussing?"

"Nothing specific other than that a shipment was coming into San Pedro, soon, it sounded like maybe next week. They stopped talking when they saw me in the doorway." She looked as though she wished she had more to offer. "I'm sorry."

Evan seemed to take all the information in stride. For my part, I was horrified.

"You sit here for a few minutes, and then I think we need to get you to a doctor."

Aya shook her head. "I just want to take some ibuprofen and lie down somewhere safe." Her tears were still coming but in a slower, steadier stream. "I didn't lose consciousness, and there's no broken bones, so that's all a doctor will tell me to do."

Evan smiled at her. "I forgot we have a med student for a patient." He considered her diagnosis. "Okay, but do you mind if I take a Polaroid of you in case we need it for evidence later?"

"All right. Just let me touch up my makeup." Ruefully, she attempted a sarcastic smile and then winced at the movement.

"We'll get the camera," he said, gesturing with a slight jerk of his head that I should go with him. Reluctant to leave Aya hurting inside and out, I got up. Deirdre had hovered in the background the whole time, and now she moved in to fill the chair beside Aya.

Out in the hallway, I gave vent to some of my scrambled thoughts. "Korosu? He just doesn't seem capable of something like this. God I guess you never know."

"He's a very successful businessman," Evan said, "and drugs are a very successful business, that part isn't too unbelievable. The story he told about Gades coming to him to use his import company and him refusing was a good one, it covered anyone who happened to have seen them meeting, but now, with Aya hearing them talk about a specific shipment . . ." His voice dropped off and then he picked up again. "He has already demonstrated, with the women, that he's willing to live outside the law. Although . . ." He let the thought hang as he opened the library door and ushered me inside. "It does seem out of character for him to use force on Aya, personally, anyway." He moved pensively to the desk. "Why now? If she's known him for so long and never had any clue of a violent side or nature, why wouldn't he have one of his men, like the ones who kicked ass saving Sabrina and Shika, do it?"

I wondered about that, it was a good point. Trying to come up with a theory that would fit, I offered the only thing that came to mind. "He's cornered, desperate?"

Evan looked pleased, I was proud. "Good. Yes, that would work."

"But he seemed so sincere when he talked about being honorable."

"What did I tell you, about that little saying we have at the station?" he asked.

"'Don't believe a fucking word they say,'" I repeated.

"But your theory would work again there. If Gades has something on Korosu, or is forcing his hand somehow, then Korosu would naturally be stressed and desperate, not a comfortable position for a man who is used to being completely in charge."

"No," I agreed, thinking of his mastery over the massage I'd had earlier that day, flinching at the thought that he could have hurt me, just as easily as he had excited me. Of course the same was true of Evan, but that never occurred to me either.

"What about Shika?" I felt a new and sudden fear; she was almost completely in Korosu's control.

"I've been considering that. We have an officer with her, and I don't think there's any reason for Korosu to involve her again."

"But you can't leave her there!" I insisted.

"I have to for right now, or Korosu will know that Aya came to us." He took my hand in his and said, "Cally, trust me, I know it's hard and I'm aware that it's a calculated risk, but I really do believe she's all right and I'll pull her out the minute I can."

Reluctantly I agreed.

And then I remembered something else. "Evan."

"What?"

"When the three of us went to Sakura-no Hana for massages yesterday"—I paused and wondered if it was after midnight before going on—"or this evening, whenever. Anyway, as we were leaving the hotel, Korosu met us in the lobby and an assistant of his interrupted us with a ship-to-shore call." I was thinking about what Aya had said—"something about changing at sea."

Evan said nothing but picked up the phone and punched a group of numbers with nothing but a glance at the keypad. "Curtis? Sorry to wake you, but we've got a development, can you get over here? Thanks."

He hung up and looked absently at me. It took him a few seconds to register that I was smiling.

"What?" he asked.

"You didn't tell him you were at my house, you just knew he'd assume?" I tested.

He smiled back. "I haven't seen much of my house lately." He paused and then said, "I'm pretty sure I still have one, but I can't really remember where it is."

There was a knock on the library door. "Yes, Deirdre?" I called out, loudly enough to carry across the large room.

But the face that appeared was Ginny's. "What the hell is going on?" she asked, sleepily, her hundreds of tiny braids pulled up on her head with a royal blue silk scarf that I recognized as one of my own.

"Aya was beaten up by Korosu," I replied simply, feeling that I might as well get right to the point. "She's in the kitchen."

Ginny blinked twice and then seemed completely awake, "Oh shit. Anything I can do?"

"Probably," I said, confident in her supportive strength.

"I'm on it," she nodded and closed the door again. I could hear her footsteps across the hall and then the creak of the kitchen door.

It was another rough night, and I had just crossed into my third hour of sleep when my bedroom door flew open. While I was squinting at the sudden light and trying to focus on the source of the invasion, Sabrina leaped onto the bed and started firing questions. "Oh my God! Why didn't you wake me up? What about Shika?"

"Uhm, yeah." I tried to shovel the sleepy sand out of my brain. "Why don't you go ask Deirdre to bring me my coffee and get yourself some breakfast, and then we'll talk about it, okay?" All I wanted was five more minutes of sleep, and like a junkie, I would have done anything to get it.

"I can't eat breakfast!" she exclaimed, flopping back onto the bed and jolting me more awake. "I'm worried about my friend!"

"Okay, okay." I pulled myself up and punched the intercom buzzer on the phone for Deirdre, who responded to my desperate request for a double cappuccino with her usual efficiency.

"We've got to go get her, she's in danger!"

"First of all, I'm not going anywhere until I have my coffee." Sabrina opened her mouth for another onslaught, but I rushed on. "Curtis and Evan went over all this last night, and they don't think she's in that much danger. Remember, Gades thinks she's dead. Korosu is smart, really smart, and that means that if he keeps Shika under his hat, he's got leverage against Gades. Korosu doesn't seem to have any reason to hurt Shika. If he did, he could have done it well before now," I told her, repeating what I'd heard. Curtis had agreed with Evan's assessment and they had decided to leave things status quo. "Listen, I know you're worried about her, so am I, but we have to trust Evan, he really does know what he's doing." She looked doubtful. "Okay?" I prodded.

She seemed to settle, intellectually anyway, on the outcome, but her eyes, though calmer, were still concerned.

"But I'm worried about her, I can't just do nothing," she stated simply and truthfully, as always.

"Yes, you can. You have to, Sabrina." I reached over and took her hand. She squeezed mine tightly and her eyes filled with frustrated tears. "We cannot let Korosu know that Aya came to us, it would endanger everyone. You don't want Aya to get hurt again, do you?"

"Of course not!" She looked horrified at the idea.

"Then you have to be patient." I pulled a tissue out of the box by the bed and offered it to her. She released my hand to take it and blew her nose comically, with no sense of embarrassment. "Now, Aya is going to stay here, and we don't want to publicize that fact, so it would really help a great deal if you would go to school, as usual, and when you're home, you could spend some time cheering her up."

She liked that. Having a useful purpose and a plan of action suited her more than worrying ineffectually. "Okay." She sighed.

"But she's finally sleeping, and we need to let her rest now."

Sabrina nodded, "But we have to help her *and* Shika." Her face was set, she was calm now, and there was a mature determination in her voice as she said, "We have to."

I nodded back and looked out at the uncertain day, thinking of Evan's resolve and the plans that he and Curtis had laid the night before. "Don't worry," I told her grimly, "we will."

Chapter 28

"Good morning, Curtis," I said when I entered the kitchen an hour later. He was seated at the table with Evan, and though exhausted, he smiled at me.

"Good morning, Callaway. I seem to be straining your hospitality," Curtis said as he turned back to his coffee.

"Strain away, I'm glad you're here." I poured myself a mug and couldn't resist adding, "And I don't think I'm the only one."

"I know," he said and then stage-whispered, "Deirdre's had a crush on me since first we met. But it's the bachelor's life for me."

"A blow to womankind everywhere," Deirdre quipped from the counter where she stood. I flipped through the mail as I went to join them at the table.

"We'll see about that," I whispered to Evan. Then in my normal voice I asked, "Did Sabrina get off to class?" I was wondering if I should recount her reaction to last night's events.

"She left about half an hour ago," he answered and added, "reluctantly. She seemed to think we should all form a posse and ride into town to rescue Shika."

"Don't make fun of her, I'm worried about Shika too," I confided. "I know it all seems logical, the things you discussed last night, and I agree with all the salient points, but what if . . ." I hated to say it, but it was a fear that was irritating me, and it needed voicing. "What if Korosu hands over Shika as part of the deal Aya said she overheard him making with Gades?"

Evan sighed, and Curtis didn't look at either of us, but I saw him draw a deep breath as well. "Then it's probably too late." From the deadness in Evan's tone I realized that he had already thought this through and landed at the same tortured answer. "And remember we've got an officer with her, and so far, everything is all right. I'm still gambling that Korosu's keeping Shika under his hat as a bargaining chip. I plan on dropping in on Korosu, with the guise of questioning Shika later on today." I pulled away from him in alarm, but he kept his arm firmly around me. "I won't let him know Aya's here, but it would look suspicious if I didn't follow up on Shika."

Woodenly, I nodded. It was true, and if they were going to get Gades and Korosu, they would need to keep a close watch and gather more information. Evan and Curtis resumed their discussion. I picked up that the FBI had been notified and were available if things escalated or more definitive information became available. Apparently, so far, everything that had happened fell under the heading of local crime, and that meant Curtis and Evan's jurisdiction.

Which made me decidedly uncomfortable. I knew that Evan's job was sometimes dangerous, but in the time that I had known him, at least, he had not faced anything as potentially lethal as this case. Deirdre came into the kitchen, and I joined her over at the counter, taking my mail with me.

"Is Aya sleeping?"

"Soundly, I checked on her a few minutes ago."

"Good, let her sleep. Is Ginny up?" I asked.

"Yes, ma'am. She is in the gym, lifting something that could easily be the front axle of a small lorry."

I laughed as I slit open an envelope, an invitation to a showing at the Getty Museum. As a major contributor I was often invited to special events, and this one looked interesting, but I knew I wouldn't have the time.

"Deirdre? Would you like these tickets to a cocktail party and art opening at the Getty? They're for a Friday night, your night off, and it's a special exhibition of illustrated manuscripts. I don't know if you'd be interested or not." I was teasing her; she had a fascination for books of all kinds, especially illuminated.

"That would be most generous of you." There was definitely a covetous glint in her eye.

"I'll leave them on my dressing table upstairs after I *répondez, s'il vous plaît.*"

Changing into some sweats and a stretch top, I headed outside. The gym was connected to the garages and opened onto the west garden. Loud music was blaring through the open French doors. Salt-n-Pepa, I think it was.

My first move was to ease the strain on my ears with the master volume dial, then I said my good mornings to Ginny, who was on the StairMaster, and went to do some stretching on the mats in front of the mirrored wall.

Neither of us had mentioned her extended stay with me; I found it very comforting to have her around, and she seemed to be settling into protective big-sister mode. I suppose, being blessed with a large extended family, it came naturally to her, although she may have chosen a word other than *blessed* if it were left to her to describe her multiple siblings.

She stepped off the machine and swabbed her face with a small towel before joining me on the mats. "So, Aya's back."

"How'd it go last night?" I asked her.

"She'll be okay. We had the 'it's not your fault' talk." She sighed. "I gave her a sleeping pill, she'll be out until at least noon."

"She must feel so betrayed," I said.

Ginny looked at me sideways. "Girl, she's damaged, and I'm not just talking about her face." She looked grim when she added, "But she's smart and very determined. I told her not to let Korosu mess up any more of her life with a bunch of emotional baggage."

"Did she hear that?"

Ginny smile. "She swore to it with a vengeance."

"Anger's good," I noted, nodding. "Way better than being a victim."

"Meanwhile, can we *safely* assume that the attraction to this Asian-Ralph-Lauren-model-wealthy-industrialist-combo-guy is no longer a threat to your relationship with Evan?"

I sighed and stopped myself from giving a flippant denial. I used the time it took to climb onto the StairMaster and start the program to check up on what that question meant to me. Pointless to deny it—I could have gone after Korosu, lied to Evan, kept one on the side. It was my pattern, but I was no longer blissfully ignorant of that pattern.

"You know, Ginny, I want something different than I used to." After throwing that out I fell silent while I sorted my feelings again, simultaneously conserving my breath for an uphill section of the program. When the difficulty level flattened out, I said, "Used to be, I didn't want to let anybody get too close to me, I didn't like feeling . . ." I exhaled hard, fighting a stitch in my left side, searching for the right word.

"Say it!" Ginny teased from the mats, where she was pressing her chest against the floor between her spread-eagle legs. "You know what it is, you were afraid to be . . . imperfect!"

"Shut up. I was not." I laughed at her.

She did a quick impression of me being cool; flipping her hair and striking a pose. "I don't need him, I don't need anybody. From a distance, I look perfect. And perfect is cool." It wasn't a bad simulation, and it was painful to watch.

"Okay, I get it. To let someone get close, you have to let them see that you might have some faults, and that's not real comfortable for me."

She snorted loudly.

"All right. I hate it, I hate that," I admitted with massive reluctance. "I'm *supposed* to be perfect," I revealed. "And we don't need to go into why my mother only noticed my existence when I was exceptional and thereby made her look good." I dismissed her knowing look with a wave of my hand. "Ergo I think if I'm not perfect I don't exist, thanks to Rudy. Let's not get into my inverted Oedipal psychosis, not right now, thank you." I reflected and then continued, "It's not that I think I *am* perfect, you understand, exactly the opposite." I leaned onto the bars to take some of the burn off my thighs and sighed a curse. "Fuck, maybe that *is* why I'm so afraid."

"Probably," she said simply.

"Is that supposed to be comforting?" I asked, resisting the urge to throw my water bottle at her.

She surprised me by saying, "Yes, actually. Frankly, I think you'll find it's a great relief to be able to say, 'Hey, I fucked up.' Or maybe, 'I suck at this.' Or even just, 'I don't know and that's okay.'"

"Well, I've got lots of things that I suck at. The good news is Evan doesn't seem to mind. He even seems to think more of me when I flop around trying to find a way to communicate or to get over myself."

"And, let me guess," she continued as she stretched her foot up over her head, "he allows you to see his faults and you don't think any less of him for that."

I stared at her. "How do you know these things?" I asked, astounded.

"Hey, I watch Dr. Phil," she joked, but I knew she was far wiser than me in many ways. "Now hush, I'm focusing."

Leaving her to zone out or send messages to the universe or whatever the hell she did when she closed her eyes and dismissed me, I trudged onward and for a change gave myself up to thinking about Ginny's relationship situation.

She was a handful herself, and although men adored her beauty and her confidence, very few could handle her octane level. Men with less going on were soon left in the dust, and a man with an equal amount of charisma just created too damn much kinetic energy in the same room. What she needed, I always thought, was the brilliant, pithy type. The kind who would let her shine without being wallpaper, stay included with a sharp wit and the occasional outstanding accomplishment. Rare, yes, but it would take an exceptional man to balance my friend. In a word: Curtis.

Three deep exhalations alerted me to her returned attention.

"How come, if you know so much, you aren't with someone?" I asked, leadingly.

Her eyes opened and twinkled at me. "How do you know I'm not?"

"Because you would *tell* me," I insisted.

"You haven't asked. Not lately, anyway."

"Are you?" I asked, incredulous, insulted. How dare she have a boyfriend and not tell me.

"No." She closed her eyes, and resumed her yoga breathing, taking short quick breaths. "Now leave me alone, I'm achieving a Zen state."

Laughing, I climbed down off the machine and poked at her once. "But you like Curtis," I said in my playground voice. The only response I got was a long drawn-out "ohm" and a little smile that played in the corners of her mouth.

I was glad she was interested, I thought as I crossed back to the house. Deirdre intercepted me at the doorway, remote phone in hand.

"Who is it?" I asked, assuming it would be my assistant, Kelly, about a board meeting I had asked her to postpone.

"A young man, a friend of Miss Sabrina's, he is inquiring into her whereabouts."

"She's at school, in class," I said dismissively, surprised that Deirdre hadn't just handled this without bothering me.

"So I told the gentleman, and he, in turn, informed me in a whisper that she was not."

"Why in a whisper? And how does he know she's not in class?" I asked skeptically.

"Because class is where he is telephoning from," she answered both my questions, extending the phone to within easy reach. I snatched it away.

"Hello? Who is this?"

"Hi, it's Aaron, I'm a friend of Sabrina's," came the whispered young voice. "Is this her sister?"

"This is Callaway, yes." Somehow it was still strange to me to accept the sibling label from outsiders. "Are you telling me she isn't there?"

"No, she wasn't in biology either. We're supposed to have lunch and study and she doesn't have her cell phone on. Is she there?"

It seemed as though Deirdre had already answered this, but I sucked back a biting remark and started walking toward the kitchen and Evan as I answered, "No, she left this morning, supposedly for school; tell you what, I'll tell her to call you, Aaron, and would you do me a favor?"

"Uh, sure." He didn't sound too sure.

"Let me know if she calls or shows up, just because, you know, I worry," I said, as though it was no big deal. But I was more than worried, I was afraid.

I was halfway through the entrance hall when I ended the call and picked up speed, almost knocking over my under-butler, Joseph, as he came out of the kitchen, carrying a stack of freshly laundered towels.

"Sorry, Joseph," I muttered and ducked around him. "Evan!" I called out, and he and Curtis both responded to the urgency in my voice, stopping midsentence and directing their considerable combined attention on me from the kitchen table. "Sabrina never showed up at school."

"Damn it!" Evan said, rising on the curse. Curtis was in concert with him, already on his feet, gathering his papers. "That means one of two things," Evan began.

"Neither of them good," Curtis finished for him; they had been partners for a long time.

"What two things?" asked Ginny, who had come in through the garage door in time to pick up on the tension and the last split sentence.

"Sabrina's not at school," I told her, worried.

"She's disappeared again?" Ginny exclaimed. "I knew it! She's gone down there to see her little buddy, hasn't she?" She directed the question to the gentlemen. "She's going to blow it for everyone."

"Or she's been kidnapped," Curtis said. Ginny's impending diatribe halted, suspended in her mouth, which hung open until she snapped it shut and crossed to me, putting her arm around my shoulders.

"Let's go," Evan said to Curtis, pausing only to give me a quick firm embrace that held little reassurance.

"Okay, let's not leap to the worst conclusion," Ginny repeated Evan's words from the last time Sabrina had gone missing.

"I won't, I promise, maybe she just went shopping or something. Cut classes for the fun of it," I suggested.

Ginny looked hopeful. "Does she do that often?"

"Never." I crushed the thought. I exhaled and forced some calm into myself. "But we can always hope she was in a car accident or something," I added, feebly illustrating the desperation I felt.

Ginny and I sat around as long as I could stand it, and then we both agreed we needed to do something besides spasm nervously every time the phone rang.

I went into my office to try to focus on some business that needed immediate attention and Ginny left to meet with a director about stunt doubling the lead actress in his next film, promising to bolt back the second she was through negotiating and sucking up.

The call from Evan came while I was on the line with the CEO of a bank. I was so nervous to hear what he had to say that as I was switching over, I disconnected the head of a major financial institution. Oh well.

"Which one is it?" I asked without saying hello.

He hesitated, trying to catch up with me, then he answered grimly, "It looks like both." I gasped, and he went on quickly. "But we're not sure about the second yet. We know she came down to the Sakura-no Hana and asked at the front desk which room Shika was in. They told her they had no such person and she *explained to them* the situation. Everyone heard her. If Gades had any kind of feelers out at all, which I'm sure he did, he knows." He sighed. I stayed silent, wanting him to tell me what he knew as rapidly as possible.

"Now," he continued, "what we *don't* know is what happened next. She got huffy and upset and left the hotel, and a few people in the shopping mall saw her, but we don't know where she is now. Her car is here in the parking garage, the cell phone is in it. All we can do is wait."

"Maybe she's just wandering around, upset," I suggested optimistically.

"Maybe." His tone squelched my positive attitude.

"Oh, Evan," I said, trying not to panic, "what can we do?"

There was a crackling silence while he must have debated what to say and then: "Curtis and I are still looking around. I've got someone posted on her car, we should know something soon, one way or the other. You can wait there, in case there's a call."

"Oh good," I said sarcastically, "I feel so much better being such a big help." I was snapping at him in my frustration.

"Callaway." His voice was soothing, full of compassion for me. "We could find out something any minute, or it could be the longest day of your life, but *I am here,* do you understand?"

"Yes." I spoke through a wet rag of emotion. Evan understood that I was so used to being alone, to pretending that I could take on every problem and handle the density of them all by myself, that having someone stand beside me and take a corner of the weight was both difficult for me and an infinite relief. "Thank you," I said, the words thick and soggy in my mouth.

"I'll call you the second I hear anything," he finished. "Hang in there, I know it's hard."

I nodded. Of course, he couldn't see me, but I couldn't speak—and then I hung up.

My hands came up and my face went down, meeting each other halfway as a sob escaped like too much pressure on a valve. After indulging for a few moments, I realized that I should call Ginny. I reached for the tissue box, wiping away the tears and taking a deep settling breath. As I turned toward the phone, my blood crystallized.

At the edge of my desk, stood the devil himself.

Chapter 29

When Gades had come in or how long he had stood there I did not know. Petrified, I watched him, unable to move or speak.

He regarded me oddly, as though he was sorry for what I was going through, and then he moved, walking slowly around behind me. He turned my chair to face him and leaned down until he was very close to my face; terrified as I was, he didn't seem to be threatening me. He looked . . . compassionate, as though he knew everything about me, yet in his eyes there was something mesmerizing and poisonous.

"She's all right," he said thoughtfully. "It's such a shame to put you through this. I apologize, I didn't mean for you to get involved in all this." His hand brushed my cheek. "I would have liked very much to meet you under different circumstances," and for a moment I thought he was going to kiss me, but he stood up and kept moving, with intent, around the desk. I glanced at the phone, but somehow I knew it would be futile to reach for it. For all his deliberate slowness, it was impossible not to know that my attempt to act would be no match for his swift and final reaction.

"But I find that you have involved yourself," he continued, still moving, pacing stealthily around the huge desk. "And you have something that I want."

I found my voice, dragged it out of its hiding place, and shoved it forward. "What is that?" I asked, pointlessly.

A flash of rage spiked across his face before his features resettled. "I don't have time for games. I am a businessman, and though I enjoy betting, I rarely bet against the odds." He turned the corner and headed back toward me, still stalking. "I will exchange your sister for Shika. I'll leave you the instructions—do not make the mistake of betting on the wrong side."

"Why do you want Shika?" I found myself asking him, but inside, I was asking myself a different question. How can I possibly trade one life for another?

"That does not concern you, or anyone, except she and I." He was near me again, and he stopped, reaching down to pull me up, close against him, taking my face in one hand while he looked down into my eyes. The power in him was hypnotic. "I will not hurt her."

I blinked but found it impossible to dismiss him as a liar. "Why should I believe you?" I asked him.

He smiled slightly and ran his thumb over my lips; it was a sensuous and yearning movement, causing a stirring in the lower part of my body. His danger and strength were confusingly exciting. "Because I could have done it already," he whispered. "Easily."

"But you tried to kill her, or us, in San Francisco," I murmured. He moved his hand around behind the back of my neck and drew me in toward him, laying his face against my hair. He was so close I could feel his lips move as he spoke; yet his voice was barely even a whisper, so soft that even though he spoke a fraction of an inch from my ear I barely heard him.

I think he said, "I took care of the sniper." His lips brushed my temple. "I've been protecting Shika all along."

The words jolted and surprised me, but not as much as a second sensation—the feeling that a man of such strength and power could touch so gently, speak in such a sacred hush, and offer comfort and even pleasure, in this moment.

"I believe you," I said, and it was true. I didn't know why, but I did.

"Then believe this, Callaway," he breathed into my ear. "Next week you and your boyfriend need to take a vacation. If I catch any of you interfering with my business, you'll be dead." And then he pulled away, held my face inches from his between both hands as he searched my eyes, then disappeared through the open French door before I could settle the reeling in my brain.

I sat down hard, gasping for air, as though I'd held my breath during the whole strange interlude without knowing it. My mind was a swirling misty vortex blanketed in confusion. What had just happened? *What did he say?* I fought to remember exactly, trying to hold on to the solidity of information in spite of the whirlpool of sensations, the pull of which I was swimming against.

I'll leave you the instructions. I remembered that. Where? I stood up and searched around. The envelope lay on the floor on the other side of the desk; he must have dropped it there as he circled. I lunged forward and stopped myself just before I grabbed the crisp white legal-size package. *Evan, call Evan!*

I lunged again, this time without cessation, and the phone was shaking in my hand as my brain struggled to recall the familiar digits. After three tries, I was successful.

"Yes?" Evan knew it was me and his voice was as impatient as he ever allowed it to be. "Did Gades call?"

"No," I choked out, "he was here, Evan, he was here, and he wants to trade Sabrina for Shika. He left a note, I didn't touch it—can you come? Will you come, please?" I was babbling, but I couldn't seem to pull back on the reins.

"I'm on my way," Evan cut in. "Callaway, where is he now, are you safe?"

"He's gone. Yes, I'm safe," I replied definitively. Somehow I knew that he was gone and that he wouldn't hurt me, not now anyway.

"When did he go?"

"Just a few seconds, uh minutes ago, I think," I said. Time was undulating, impossible for me to track.

I could hear Evan shouting to Curtis, something about getting a car to my house, but I knew it was futile. Gades was gone, seeping into the underground from whence he had emerged. "Are you alone?"

"Yes. I mean, the staff is here, but not in the room."

"Get to them, right now. Do you hear me? Callaway, get everyone in the house together in one room and stay there. Do you have your gun?"

I glanced down at the desk drawer that concealed a lockbox with a loaded nine-millimeter inside. It was with a vague sense of discovery that I remembered it was there; its presence hadn't even occurred to me when Gades was with me. Even now it seemed a pathetic tool against his methods: sheer power and presence.

"Yes, I have it," I said absently, without making a move to retrieve it. *What's the point?*

"Good, take it, and go, *now,*" he ordered, and something awoke in me. If Gades had gotten in, had his men also? Had anyone been harmed?

"All right, I'm going, and Evan?" I said before he hung up.

"What?"

"Hurry," I pleaded.

"Like the wind," he said and was gone.

I dropped the phone, got my gun, and ran out of the library, terrified of what I might find.

Chapter 30

I blasted through the kitchen door, calling out loudly for Deirdre. She was on her feet, heading calmly in my direction in response to the shouted summons, but she halted instantly when she saw the gun.

Counting the people seated at the table eating lunch or working around the room, I ascertained that the entire staff was present and accounted for. I relaxed, quickly dropping the pistol to my side after removing the round from the chamber and clicking the safety down.

"I apologize, but I've had an unannounced visitor," I said to their shocked faces, before realizing finally that one face was missing. "Where's Aya?" I asked Deirdre.

"I am here," came her lyrical voice from behind me. She had obviously just woken up. She was in a silk robe and slippers. "I heard you calling out and came to see . . ."

The explanation ceased when she caught sight of the gun. Terrified, her eyes flickered quickly around the room and landed on me. "What is it?" she asked. "Korosu? Does he know I'm here?" Her eyes had opened wide, the pupils dilating suddenly, like tiny saucers of ink. Evan had taught me to watch for that as a sign of true fear; in this case, it was hard to miss.

"No, no, it's okay, it's not Korosu," I said, going to her protectively; it was painful to watch her hunted look. But I did have to explain the rest of the situation, and it wouldn't be easy.

"All right, everyone please sit down at the table, I need to tell you something." After they had arranged themselves as quickly as possible, I filled them in on Sabrina's indiscretion and subsequent disappearance, ending with Gades's visit and his offer.

When I finished I looked at each person at the table individually, trying to sum up their reactions. I looked at Aya last. She was staring straight ahead, mouth set in a line of anger, but tears were coming steadily from eyes that didn't blink.

She must have sensed my focus, because without looking at me she said, "It's my fault. I have brought this on everyone. I should never have involved you, I should never have trusted Korosu. My whole life is a lie." She took a strained breath and then went on. "Because of my ignorance Sabrina is in danger." Now she looked at me and then dropped her head. "I beg your forgiveness, although I do not deserve it."

"That's enough of that," I snapped loudly, and the level of my anger surprised me. Aya looked up, shocked and curious. "Don't you dare blame yourself for this," I told her. "You've been misled. Evan and I were just as taken in. And as far as Sabrina goes—she's gotten *herself* into this, remember that. And last, but certainly not least, Evan really wants to get this guy Gades, and if he does, you will have helped him much more than we have helped you. So that's the last we'll hear of this." I nodded, turned back to the rest of the table, and stood, signifying that we were done.

"I need to call Ginny and fill her in. If the phone rings, *I will answer it,* all right?"

Nods and yeses met me quickly. Aya was still looking at me as though she had never seen me before. I would have bet big money that she didn't know it was possible for a woman to assert herself with that much strength and conviction and get away with it.

The sound of a siren and then the crunch of wheels on the driveway outside told us Evan had returned. I opened the front door just as he reached it with his gun drawn.

I hurried to him, saying, "It's okay, everyone's fine. Nobody saw anything, except me."

He placed his gun back in his holster and wrapped his arms around me, shivering slightly in spite of his strength. I remembered what he had once told me about what would happen if he lost me, about crossing the line and not looking back. I squeezed him tightly around the middle.

"I'm okay, really."

He pulled back enough to look directly at me, then, seeming to be satisfied, he took my hand and said, "Let's see what he left us."

Curtis was explaining the situation to Ginny, who had just arrived as Evan was slitting open the envelope.

It contained a single sheet of paper. On it was a time, an address, a date. There was also a Polaroid picture of Sabrina, walking out of the hotel, wearing the outfit she had donned this morning.

"Well." Curtis spoke first. "I suppose he wanted us to know definitively that he had her. It's not like we doubted him."

"What's the address?" Ginny wanted to know.

He told us and then said, "It's in the wholesale food district, south of Chinatown. It's this afternoon," Curtis went on, speaking to Evan. "Trying to keep us off guard, you think?"

"No time to involve the FBI. He doesn't want us to have time to deliberate." Evan's businesslike face told me that the second thing was one wish Gades wasn't going to get. His brow was creased and his eyes were fixed points of concentration.

"It's eleven-fifteen," Curtis said. "He's set the meeting for five-thirty. Right in the middle of rush hour, lots of people around; he's smart."

"Why is that smart?" I asked, conscious of my naïveté.

Evan turned and started pacing, too deep in thought to be aware of my query, but Curtis answered me. "Because it enables him to fade in and out of crowded streets as well as confine us in the use of force or any kind of dragnet. It's damn near impossible to pull a single man out of a crowd without a large informed force, impossible to shoot at someone without endangering bystanders, and we don't even know who's going to show up, except that it's God damned unlikely to be our man himself."

Ginny pitched in now. "You can't just be thinking of handing Shika over to them. I mean, part of me thinks we should, that it's her fault to start with, and I want Sabrina back, but it's still not right!"

There was a sound at the door, a movement, and we all spun around, but although it was opened a few inches, there didn't seem to be anyone beyond it. Curtis silenced us all with a hand gesture then covered the large room in a few quick strides and pulled the door open with an abrupt jerk.

"Who are you?" he asked, and I started over hurriedly when I heard the voice of my housekeeper, who sounded afraid.

"I am Carmen. I work for Ms. Wilde," she was saying when I reached the two of them.

"It's okay," I said soothingly to Curtis. "My housekeeper, she's supposed to be here now."

"Sorry, Carmen, we're all a little jumpy." Curtis started to withdraw and then addressed her again. "Did you see anyone else in this hall in the last few minutes?"

"I see first Ms. Deirdre and then Miss Aya going up the stairs." Carmen pointed to the large curving staircase at the far end of the vast entry hall; it was hard to imagine someone hearing *anything* from that distance, much less the details of a quiet conversation.

"All right, thank you," Curtis said, and he carefully closed the door behind us before we rejoined Evan and Ginny, who was looking at Curtis with a wide-eyed breathlessness. I knew that look—a take-charge man is quite a revelation to the liberated woman.

Evan was looking at me. He took my hand as I came back over to him and sat me down next to him on the sofa. "Callaway, tell me exactly what happened, what he said, what he did, everything you can remember."

So I did, trying to include everything, except for the strange connection I felt with him, that disturbing sense of respect and attraction he inspired. Somehow, it was difficult to remember exact things that had been said; the fear I had been feeling seemed to have created a kind of distortion filter. Evan, of course, understood and was patient with my repeated backtracking and insertions. Finally, I got through it as best I could. Gades's warning about staying out of his business next week sent Curtis and Evan into a flurry of discussion. But there was one thought I was trying to assimilate, something that hadn't made sense to me, that I had barely heard.

"Evan," I said, interrupting his conference with Curtis. "There *is* something else he said, something I didn't understand, still don't."

"What is it?" He came quickly back to me.

"He said, at least *I think* he said 'I took care of the sniper.' He meant in San Francisco of course, and he said 'I've been protecting her all along.'"

"Protecting Shika? Is that what he meant?"

"I think so. It was right after he told me he wouldn't hurt her and I said something about his having already tried to do so. He, uh, whispered it, really softly, in my ear, and I was so"—I looked for a word that would reveal how afraid I had been without exposing my inexplicable arousal caused by the same intimate proximity—"um, distracted by him being so close to me, it was scary."

"I'm sure it was." Evan pulled me in up against him protectively. "You did great, as usual, keeping your cool."

"Thanks." But the word and the sentiment were muffled in his chest and I felt a quick snap of anger that he would expect any less of me. I pulled away and straightened up. Evan didn't notice; he had jumped to his feet again.

Curtis watched him with a patient intensity that, in spite of the seriousness of the situation, almost betrayed a touch of amusement. I gathered that this was their pattern, Evan serving the ideas and Curtis returning volleys by either shooting them down or keeping them in play.

"Okay." Evan stopped pacing and turned to Curtis, who uncrossed his arms and waited to return the first serve.

"If we wire Shika, we can surround the building and pick them up after the exchange with proof of kidnapping," Evan began.

"He'll expect all of that." Curtis let Evan know his ball had tipped the net. A let.

"If we show up without Shika, Sabrina will never materialize," Evan tried.

"True." The ball was in play. Curtis was mesmerizing in his intensity and calm, and Ginny was fascinated. She'd become blasé about even the biggest, baddest movie stars, but she was now watching a real man handle a very real dangerous situation. There was no script, no acting, and no contest.

"Something is strange, though; he can't really expect us to hand over one innocent girl for another," Evan said.

"He's counting on the emotional connection between Callaway and Sabrina to outweigh the legalities, and moral implications. That's his style, to go personal; we know that," Curtis said, as though reciting something from a rule book.

"So, let him think that. Shika has to go voluntarily, of course, and we have to move in *before* the exchange. The minute they produce Sabrina," Evan offered.

I interjected at this point. "Shika will be terrified. Will she go?"

It was Ginny who responded from the umpire's seat, an empirical judgment. "She'll go, her honor and her affection for Sabrina will demand it." Curtis caught her eye and nodded, he looked impressed. The air between them was wavy with heat.

But I was worried about something else. "What about Korosu? Will he allow it?"

Evan looked at me as though he was running out of patience. "Shika and Aya are both over eighteen, and he has physically assaulted one of them, something I'll have to contend with after we've dealt with the bigger picture."

"But you promised Aya that you wouldn't."

"I promised her I wouldn't involve the police," he said coldly, and not necessarily to me. Ginny looked at me, and I could see I'd have to explain that later.

Curtis added, "And if we can nail Korosu for collusion with Antonio Gades, it's incidental. He'll be going away and not coming back." Evan nodded his agreement. "We've got to pinpoint the date the drugs arrive. Next week narrows it down, but I need an exact date."

"It's more than we had," Evan said.

"What did Korosu say when you saw him today?" I wanted them to focus on getting Sabrina back. I assumed that he had spoken with him as planned.

"We didn't see him. He left town for the day, on business. He's supposed to call us before two o'clock," Curtis said, as though it would be a cold day in hell when that happened. "Of course, as soon as he speaks to his people he'll know what's going on with Sabrina, if he doesn't already."

"We can't very well expect him to have known about Sabrina's sudden attack of indiscretion." Evan sighed. "Clever as he may be, I don't think he anticipated or planned that."

"Do you think he's involved?" Curtis asked.

"With Sabrina's kidnapping?" Evan asked, and the words cut my heart. He let the question hang while he considered the complication before answering definitively. "No. It's just not his style, too public." He and Curtis exchanged a black look, and I knew there was more. "What if," Evan went on, "and remember, we're making educated guesses here, Korosu isn't working with Gades. What if he found out some information from Shika and he's somehow using it to counter Gades, or even *to pirate a shipment.*"

"That makes sense, and it explains the ship-to-shore call," Curtis interjected.

"Exactly," Evan concurred. He turned and started his slow deliberate tracking again, a tiger at the edge of his cage. "But it sounds like, from what Aya overheard, that Korosu is working with Gades now, or is at least pretending to. So why did Gades take Sabrina?"

"Because Gades didn't know Korosu had Shika, and now he's pissed," Curtis said morbidly. "That explains why Korosu left town suddenly, and if he *is* stealing a shipment, he might think Gades is about to find out."

"So Shika's in danger again," said Ginny grimly. The two men looked at each other but didn't speak.

"You know something," I said, "you know something you're not telling me." I dared Evan not to respond.

With a sigh Evan looked down at the floor and then to Curtis. I spun on Curtis. "What is it? Tell me!"

Curtis was watching Evan, who nodded once briefly, before he answered. "We have information that points to Korosu as the person who hired the hit woman in San Francisco. The person who made the connection was an associate of his."

"What? When?" I sputtered.

Evan stepped in. "Just a short time ago. Remember when I

went out the night Sabrina and Shika snuck off?" I inclined my head in mute remembrance. "I . . . put out some feelers, and word came back this morning. It's not definitive, but it's very incriminating."

"And you left Shika with him?" I was reeling.

"She's under police protection, and we were discussing how to get her out of there when this came up."

It was too much. "Please," I pleaded, my head spinning. "I just want Sabrina back safely."

Evan looked as though he felt the same way. "I've got to send Shika in. I'll put a chopper up and place as many undercover officers as possible in the area, then we can decide how best to move in," Evan concluded.

Curtis shifted uncomfortably and said the two things we were all thinking. "So, your plan, as I understand it, is to bring them Shika, hope they produce Sabrina, and assume they won't hurt either one of them before we can get around to arresting everybody in a hundred-yard radius? Is that about right?"

"Do you have a better idea?" Evan asked coolly.

"Nothing leaps to mind," Curtis said. "It's completely illegal for us to involve a civilian by offering her up as bait, of course, but considering she's already in the hands of someone who wants to kill her and the lack of an alternative, I'm going to go with—simple yet brilliant."

Evan turned slowly, pivoting with a thought that was turning, changing, 180 degrees. When he had come all the way around he looked up at us as though seeing us for the first time. "Everybody wants Shika." He gazed from us up to the ceiling, as though there were writing there that would clear this whole thing up. "Shika is the connection."

"We've established that," Curtis agreed, "she's connected to every player."

"Shika *knows* something," Evan began, "something *other than the murder*. She has information, shit, she may not even know she has it, but whatever that information is, it's worth a big-ass pile of cash, probably in the form of several semis filled with raw, pure cocaine. Cocaine that apparently arrives within the next seven days." He spun again, this time to face me.

"Do you remember what she said, in San Francisco when we first met her, right before the window shattered? She had overheard something." He already knew what it was; I could see that.

"San Pedro," Curtis filled in. "But shit, that's the biggest import spot in the United States, it's not exactly a pinpoint lead."

"Something else," Evan said, railroading over him. "She said something else, she'd overheard them say *tina.* It seemed inconsequential at the time."

"My Spanish is extremely rudimentary, but the reason it seemed inconsequential when she said it, is because it *is. Tina* means 'bathtub,'" I concluded dismissively.

But far from dismissing it, Evan leapt on it. "Bathtub. Yes, that's right. Good." He resumed his stealthy pacing.

"Good?" Ginny looked at me, then she looked at Curtis. "Bathtub is good? Why?"

"Shhh," Curtis hushed her with a sound and a hand on her arm, which he left there; it was obvious Evan was on to something.

"Now, when we talked to Korosu, what did he tell us?" Evan didn't seem to want an answer, which was okay, because I know I didn't have one. But he did. "He told us what he imported."

I started to list what I could remember. "Mostly electronics, gourmet foods, home furnishings—"

Evan cut me off. "He said *bathroom fixtures.*"

Curtis came to his feet. "The process."

"Yes, that's it." Evan had locked eyes with his partner. "You've got it."

"I don't get it," Ginny said, and you could have photocopied the sentence from me.

But Curtis was lit up now, and he explained to Ginny and me

quickly and without humor: "There's a new process that the drug importers have been using. We've only heard about it—by the time we usually deal with the stuff it's been cut and separated into anything from a kilo to a half gram—but they've developed a new way to mix the cocaine with another substance and mold tons of it into something resembling Fiberglas in a huge variety of shapes, countertops, sinks . . ."

"Bathtubs," I said, getting it.

"Right," Evan broke in. "And once the items get past customs they use a reverse process to break it down and remove the extra compound, cut the cocaine, and deliver it to our musicians and schoolchildren."

"And Shika doesn't understand what it is she knows, does she?" I asked Evan.

"No. If Korosu's been in on this from the beginning, part of his role has been to keep her out of the way."

"So that's why he sent her into exile in San Fran," Curtis mused. "He didn't want anyone else making the connection, one way or the other."

"Maybe. If he figured it out for himself and is jumping the shipment, he needs to make sure Gades doesn't know that." Evan was juggling so many balls it was making me dizzy to watch him. The possibilities were mind-boggling.

"Most likely," Evan went on, "he didn't expect the complication of Aya getting involved. Letting her come to us was probably a ruse to keep her out of the way, and try to make himself look innocent; what better alibi then asking a detective for help? Although, remember how adamant she was that he didn't want us to involve the police?" he said pointedly. Evan narrowed his eyes and shook his head, as though it just didn't add up yet. He started to put on his jacket, and Curtis followed suit. "We'll deal with the hows and whys after we get both Sabrina and Shika to safety. First we'll go get Shika."

"I want to come with you," I said, rising.

Ginny was next to me. "I ain't staying here by myself."

"There is no reason for you two to go." Evan sighed and put a hand on each of our arms respectively. "Please, understand that this is strictly police business now."

But it was my sister and I was terrified for her, I had to help. My mind was flashing through possibilities. I found one and grabbed on to it. "Shika doesn't trust you, she doesn't trust men, and with damn good reason. But she might trust me, and if I ask her to help Sabrina, I don't think she'll be able to refuse me."

Evan wavered. I could feel Ginny lean in, waiting as he teetered on the edge of decision.

It was Curtis who spoke up for me. "She's got a point."

"All right, but just Callaway. Ginny, I'm sorry, but you have to stay here."

"No fair!" she said, but I could see that she knew, as frightened and concerned as she was for Sabrina, there was no reason for her to come. "Okay, okay, I'll just sit here and vibrate." She flopped down on the sofa again.

Suddenly we heard a soft knock at the door. "Yes?" I called out.

The handle turned, and Deirdre moved into the room a cautious half-step. "I'm sorry to intrude," she said.

"It's all right." I rose and went to meet her so Evan and Curtis could continue their feverish planning. I gestured for Ginny to join me. "What is it?" I asked when we were out in the hallway.

"Ms. Aya just left."

"She what?" Ginny exclaimed.

"She was upset. She told me she was going to the temple to pray."

"She blames herself for this whole mess," I told Ginny, sighing.

"And that really worries me," said Ginny. "The girl is in a bad way," she added, almost to herself.

I got a bad feeling from the tone of her voice. "Are you suggesting she'd consider hurting herself?" I addressed the question to both women.

Deirdre's brow twisted, and she sighed as well. "She clearly sees herself at fault, and you know how seriously she feels about debt and responsibility." She shook her head and looked at both Ginny and me with worried eyes. "She was very distraught when she left."

I looked back at Evan, he was holding his head with both hands, and Curtis was speaking rapidly to him. The last thing I wanted was to distract him with something else that might not even be important.

My head was swimming; I was already so wound up with concern for Sabrina there almost wasn't any room left inside me to be worried about someone else. "Oh God," I moaned, "I do not want to add this to Evan's plate right now."

Ginny must have sensed my overload. "I can go to the temple and keep an eye on her," she offered.

I thought about it. "Aya needs some time to deal with all the shit that's been heaped up on her, and praying isn't a bad idea, but it wouldn't hurt if you were close by."

"Done." Ginny turned and went up the stairs.

Watching Ginny go, I felt relieved that she would be watching over Aya, and then I thought of Sabrina and how terrified she must be, and my throat swelled and pulsed as my heart tried to climb up through it.

Chapter 31

The high-speed ride downtown didn't do much to improve my palpitations. When we finally reached the Sakura-no Hana, it took all my self-control to walk, not run, through the lobby. We did run down the hallway toward Shika's room. Evan knocked four times.

We stood there.

He knocked again.

No response.

Evan and Curtis both drew their guns, Evan using his other hand to move me behind him and up against the wall. Once he had placed me out of any potential harm's way, he pulled an electronic key from his breast pocket. Even in my extra-crispy state I thought, He has a key to a geisha's hotel room? Nice, I thought, irrationally of course. I'll have your ass later. Evan didn't notice; he was busy sliding the key in the lock, and after a vague hum and click he and Curtis watched each other from their positions on either side of the doorway, backs against the hall wall. A quick nod from Curtis sent them both into action, Evan turning the handle and throwing the door open and Curtis spinning and sinking to one knee in the doorway with both hands extended, his gun pointed into the room.

There was a body on the floor, a woman's body, with black hair pulled up into a knot on the back of her head. She was lying next to the bed with her face up against the bedspread.

"Shika!" I called out and tried to get past Evan, but even as he blocked me and advanced first, I could see it wasn't Shika. The body type was too solid.

Evan finished checking the bathroom, closets, any and all spaces that could hide a human before reholstering his gun and leaning over the body.

Moving to the floor next to him, I waited while he checked for a pulse. "She's alive," he said, the relief evident in his voice. His hands reached gently under her shoulder and hip, and I instinctively supported her head and neck as he flipped her over.

"Damn it," Evan cursed. Curtis was already on his cell phone.

"We have an officer down, requesting medical transport." He was giving the address while I was processing that info.

"She's an officer?" I asked as I grabbed two pillows from the bed to support her head.

"Officer Giles."

"Where's Shika?" I asked desperately.

"Gone."

"What about Sabrina?" I asked Evan, choking back a sob when we were in the car. "Gades isn't going to believe we don't have Shika. What can we do?"

"Let me think for a minute," he said, and it was such a reasonable request that I didn't take offense. The paramedics thought that Officer Giles had been unconscious for only a short time, but it looked like she wasn't going to come around soon. Bad news for her and us; she couldn't give Evan any information about what had happened.

I spent the quiet time doing some thinking of my own. I wasn't going to lose Sabrina. Eight months ago when I'd found out I had a sister, I hadn't been keen on the idea at first, but now that I'd gotten attached to her, I sure as shit was going to keep her. I clenched my fists and tried to calm myself as I thought of the menace that permeated Gades and radiated from him. He personified the kind of danger that women are attracted to and are so often injured by, and I shivered at the thought of placing myself in that sphere again, but I knew I was better equipped to handle it than my small-town sibling.

"I know," I said quietly, fired by absolute conviction. "I'll do it."

Evan pulled himself out of the flow of his thoughts and focused on me. "Do what?"

"Pretend to be Shika. I'll just put on a wig and some sunglasses. I'm a little bigger than she is, but proportionately we're about the same. As long as they don't get too close, it should work."

Evan was looking at me thoughtfully. "That's a good idea."

"It is?" The words came out an octave higher than I had intended; I hadn't expected my plan to be received without resistance.

"Yes." Evan smiled at me. "But not you."

"Oh." I felt a wave of relief in spite of my resolve. "Who?"

"Someone convincing enough to buy us the time we need to move in close enough to get Sabrina."

"Aya?" I asked.

He drew his breath in sharply and then shook his head. "I can't put her in danger, as long as she's at the house, she's safe."

"Well, she's not exactly at the house." I told him and then rushed on guiltily, "Deirdre told us Aya'd gone to the temple while you and Curtis were planning; Ginny was going to follow her over there."

"Shit!" he exclaimed. "I've got to get to the switch zone and position officers. We've only got an hour and a half. I don't have time to run after her; and I need to know where she is, right now."

"I'll call Ginny." I speed-dialed her cell phone number, and she answered with a curse.

"I'm stuck in fucking traffic!"

"How long until you get downtown?" I asked her.

"As soon as I hit an exit off of Satan's freeway south, I'll be there in fifteen minutes."

"Okay, hurry, but don't hurt yourself," I told her, thinking of her stunt-driving tactics. I hung up. "She said fifteen minutes."

"Shit," Evan cursed softly. "She could be gone by then."

"I'll go," I said. That I could do. "The temple's a block from here. I'll just walk over."

Evan considered it, his eyes filled with personal concern. "All right, that will work. But get her and go straight home with Ginny when she gets there, do you understand?"

"Yes."

"Okay, call me right away when you find her. I'll find an undercover officer to take Shika's place."

"Do you have any really pretty Asian ones?" I asked, struggling to divert myself, if only for a few seconds.

He sighed and picked up easily on my feeble joking. "Unfortunately no," he teased me, halfheartedly. "I've always thought we should recruit a whole lot more." I punched him in the solar plexus, and he pretended to wheeze. "I *used* to think that, I mean. Not anymore of course."

I smiled at him bravely and my eyes filled with tears. "I'm afraid for Sabrina," I whispered.

Evan leaned in even closer. "We will get her back, do you understand?"

"Yes."

"Do you believe me?"

I couldn't lie, not even to make him feel better or encourage myself. “I know you’ll do everything in your power to make it true,” I told him.

“He is going down,” Evan said to me, and the dark part of his soul crept up into his voice.

And I knew that in spite of all Gades’s power, he had met his match.

Chapter 32

I was deep in thought and worry as I came up the steps to the temple. The vision of Sabrina's face, terrified and confused, kept centering in my brain but not so completely that I didn't notice two men leaving the temple. I had never seen them before, but both could easily have been South American, and they had that slick thug look. As they came nearer, I tensed, but they smiled and nodded politely to me. I relaxed somewhat and returned to my fears.

Sabrina was so innocent. What could she tell them? I closed my eyes for a few steps to try and clear the ugly thoughts of what they might do to her and ran right into a man exiting the vast wooden doors of the temple.

"Sorry, I'm so sorry," I murmured as I looked up, contrite. I felt foolish, but somewhere deep inside me a caution light went on when I saw the man's face. It was the vagrant that I had watched Korosu give money to outside his hotel, and though he was dressed shabbily and his movements were those of a drunk, his eyes when they met mine were completely bright and sober.

He dropped his gaze quickly and shuffled around me. I flashed on him counting out crisp bills in the parking lot, on what I knew now about Korosu, and I rushed into the temple, terrified that the man was a plant and Korosu had gotten to Aya before I could reach her. My eyes swept the dimly lit space, searching for her.

She stood just a few steps from the door, and I called out softly to her. She spun around, startled.

"I'm sorry," I said. "Did I scare you?"

Her eyes scanned the doorway behind me. "No," she answered hastily, "I'm just relieved it's you. I suppose I'm feeling paranoid. I'm sorry."

I sighed. "You're not the only one," I told her, and simplifying my fears I said, "I just saw two guys coming out of here and immediately jumped to the conclusion that they must be Gades's men, and after you."

She looked even more startled and afraid. "What made you think that?"

"Oh, they looked South American, so naturally they must be guilty and evil." I laughed flatly. She did not. "You must have seen them, they were just coming out the door."

"I did see them, and they spoke to me," she answered, "but they were asking directions to Chinatown. I assumed they were tourists." Fear flashed across her countenance. "But do you think . . . ?"

"No. I'm sure you're right." I took a deep breath. "I just need to live through this day and then maybe I can stop hallucinating."

"Why are you here?" she asked me.

"I need a favor."

"Of course, anything, what can I do?" She was immediately concerned. Leaning toward me, she placed a gentle hand on my arm. "Please, how can I help?" Her eyes were filled with a faint hope of redeeming herself that tore at my heart, since all I was going to ask was for her to come home with me and stay out of harm's way.

"We should talk privately," I said, still unable to convince myself that my paranoia was only that. "Where's your car?"

"Parked in the alley, beside the temple," she answered. "Shall I go get it?"

"I'll come with you," I said, thinking of the men again and the gun from my office drawer, which now nestled in my purse. Better safe than bleeding, I thought to myself.

Just as we came to the corner of the building, my cell phone rang. Pausing, I snatched it out of my bag and flipped it open. The reception was iffy, so I backed up a few steps until it cleared, and then I stayed where the signal was strong. Aya pointed and mouthed "the car is right there" to me and continued on around the corner, respectful of my privacy, as always.

It was Evan, of course. "Did you find her?"

"Yes. Evan, she's desperate to help in some way. I'm sure if you asked her she would—"

"No," he cut me off. "Let me know when you're both safe at home."

"I will." Though I didn't like him overriding me, I knew time was precious now. "Everything okay on your end?"

"It's all in place."

We signed off quickly, and I hurried toward the alley. As I rounded the corner of the building, the sight that met me stopped me as quickly as if I had slammed into a glass wall. Aya was next to her car, and a man had hold of her. Even ten yards away with his back to me, I knew who the man was—Korosu's physique and impeccable suits were unmistakable. He had Aya in an armlock, and he was speaking to her angrily in Japanese; she would not meet his eyes. It looked as though terror had immobilized her.

I backed up a step, half concealing myself behind the building. My hand was still around my cell phone in my purse, and I let go and found the hilt of my gun. I brought it up and out, flipping the safety off with my thumb as I pointed it at the couple. Aya was directly behind Korosu, there was no clean shot. If I announced my presence he was sure to use her as a shield, it was an easy spin, and he already had her pinned against him.

Icy sweat hit my brow, my hand wanted to shake, but I squeezed tightly, squaring the center of Korosu's back down the sights of the nine-millimeter. I knew I couldn't shoot him, not if he was unarmed, but would he call my bluff? Aya was wincing in pain, and as he raised his hand to strike her, I knew I had to act.

"Freeze!" I shouted, and they both did. "Let her go!" It was desperate, but worth a try.

Korosu's head spun around, and a gun appeared in his hand in one swift pirouette. I tightened my finger on the trigger, praying for a second to get a clean shot before he could thrust Aya out in front of him. I watched his eyes identify first me, and then my gun. In that stop-motion time that happens when your brain is panicked, I saw him begin to move Aya. I focused tighter, raising my sights to his head as I started to squeeze the trigger that would fire a bullet and end him before he could pull her fully around to block my shot. Just before the trigger caught, I watched his arm extending, shoving Aya down *behind* him, down to the ground, and to safety. I jerked my hands up in the last two frames of the slow-motion second, releasing the trigger.

Korosu stood absolutely still now. He was holding his gun, but it was hanging limply from his outstretched hand, both his arms extended in a bizarre but noble parody of crucifixion. When most people would have flinched and cowered, his eyes were open, and he was watching me calmly. Aya lay stunned on the sidewalk behind him, forgotten by both of us in the connection of the moment.

"Are you going to shoot me?" he asked quietly. I had his chest in my sights, and at the slightest wrong movement I would fire; I would not miss.

"I don't know yet if I'm going to have to," I said.

"May I put down my gun?"

I nodded, watching his fingers intently to make sure they did not move into firing position. Holding the hilt between his thumb and fingers he laid the compact weapon down on the pavement.

"Thank you," I said; I don't know why.

With his eyes still locked on mine, he smiled sadly. "I am sorry you do not trust me."

"Do you blame me?" I asked him incredulously.

An anger showed on his face that I had not thought capable in a man who was always so serene, so in control. "No," was all he said as the emotional window quickly faded, and he composed himself again. But the irritation had been entwined with something else, something that was hard to compute quickly because it didn't belong in the mix. Belatedly, I identified the secondary emotion: regret. I thought of the haiku and the heat between us, and I felt a flash of disappointment myself.

Aya got up, and giving him a wide berth, she ran behind me and started to cry.

Korosu watched her intently. He seemed to regard her with disappointment and contempt, and it scared me to have been so deceived. Yet when he spoke I was amazed again at his self-assurance. It was as though he was trying to *connect* with me. "You, Callaway Wilde, must be careful whom you trust."

"Apparently," I flared at him, angry that he thought he could fool me, even now. "Aya's face told me that much last night." Korosu's eyes flickered to Aya and then back to me, making it obvious that he hadn't known she had come to us. "I'm sure your warning to me is meant as a threat, and I won't pretend that you don't frighten me. You're very smooth, Korosu, and very self-righteous in your justification of what you do to these young women, but you are no longer fooling anyone but yourself."

Aya started to cry harder. "Callaway, please, let's go. Please."

"And now," I continued, "we know that you're in much deeper than a little socially acceptable prostitution."

Korosu's expression had resumed its enigmatic state, and without looking away, without remorse of any kind, he *admitted* it. "Deeper than you know." There was the resonant tone of an unabashed confession and some secret power behind it, another threat.

"Please, Callaway!" Aya begged.

Korosu began, very slowly, to walk toward us. I kept my gun leveled at his chest, but I knew I couldn't fire, not at an unarmed man, not unless he physically attacked us, and I prayed he wouldn't risk that. When he was a few inches from the barrel of my gun he stopped. I was vibrating, every sinew and nerve in my body alert and screaming opposing instructions at me. *Attack! Run Away!*

"Of course," he said very softly, staring into my eyes with a confidence that was mysterious to me, "you will have to do more than suspect me. You will have to prove it." He glanced around me at Aya with a frost in his black eyes that chilled me, producing a whimper from the cowering girl, and I shifted protectively to block her from that menacing gaze. What he said was true. There was no proof, and if he killed Aya, there would be no witnesses to his meeting with Gades. But his eyes came back to me and softened. "And *that* is what I intend to make sure you cannot do."

Then he walked around me, and like a moon orbiting a planet, I turned with him, keeping the gun trained on his chest. Without any warning he stopped suddenly, and I jerked the gun up to his face, ready to react to his next movement.

His eyes dropped down to the pavement at my feet, and I braced myself for his assault.

But he didn't lunge, or swing, or any of the things I was expecting. He did, however, make a move.

He bowed.

And then he turned crisply and walked away.

"Get the gun," I said to the sobbing Aya. She scuttled quickly to where it lay on the ground and picked it up awkwardly. Holding it away from her body but never looking at it, she brought it back to me. I would give Korosu's gun to Evan.

I put both weapons in my purse but kept my hand on the hilt of mine.

"Come on," I urged Aya, moving back to her car, "give me your keys, we need to hurry."

"Why? What's going on?" Aya looked so confused and upset that I hesitated, but I didn't have time to soften it.

"I need to get you back to the house," I told her. "Obviously you're in danger, and I just want to get Sabrina back. Evan is going to have an undercover officer impersonate Shika for the tradeoff."

She nodded. "It's too dangerous for Shika to go, or she is too afraid." She looked disapproving.

"I wish one of those was the reason, but at this point Shika is no longer able to help us or anyone."

Aya's eyes widened, and I realized, too late, that I had implied more than I intended. I hastened to relieve at least the worst of her anxiety. "No, she's not dead, at least," I backtracked, wanting to be clear. "I don't have any reason to think so."

"But . . . then . . . what happened to her?" Aya stuttered.

Feeling the bile rise up into my throat, I started the car and tried to sum it up quickly. "Shika's gone, the officer who was with her was knocked out."

She nodded, looking confused and shaken.

I looked down to put the car into gear, and my heart exploded as, five inches from my head, I heard a sharp metal rapping on my window.

Chapter 33

"Jesus, Ginny," I gasped as I rolled the window down. "You scared the shit out of me." She pulled her hand back from tapping her large silver ring on the glass to plant it on her hip.

"Sorry, but you were about to drive away," she said without sounding very sorry at all.

"What are you doing here?" Aya asked. She had one hand on her chest where I thought surely, her heart was beating as fast as mine.

"I was looking for you," Ginny said to Aya with her characteristic frankness. "I thought maybe you could use someone to talk to, or just hang out with." Ginny eyed me narrowly. "But I see someone else had the same idea."

"You're late," I told my friend. Then before she could start ranting about the obscene number of cars on the road I added, "Get in the car. We'll fill you in."

An hour later Ginny and I were seeing off an undercover officer named Siebert, accompanied by Evan and Curtis. Aya had retreated to her room. Officer Siebert was Asian, pretty, and she had pulled her hair up in a soft sweep with a few strands hanging loose, the way Shika usually wore hers. The late afternoon light made the sunglasses she was wearing seem appropriate. At a glance, since they were expecting Shika, whom they hadn't seen for a few months, they might buy it.

I held Evan tightly without speaking for a long moment before he pulled away and opened the car door for Officer Siebert.

"Good luck," I said softly, more as a prayer than anything else as I watched the car pull away.

I didn't know who I was more afraid for, Evan or Sabrina. My mind couldn't acknowledge the possibility of losing them both.

Ginny pulled me back inside the house as they disappeared, and we settled ourselves in the living room.

I leaned back; she crossed her legs. I hugged a linen throw pillow, she propped her elbow up on the armrest. She sighed out, I breathed in. The clock on the mantel ticked, but time did not progress.

We looked at each other. "Did you get the address where they were going?" she asked me.

"I run a multinational finance company, juggle six conglomerate manufacturing businesses, and oversee a payroll close to our state debt." I looked at her significantly.

"Meaning?" she asked.

"I'm okay with numbers," I said. "Hell, sometimes I can even remember three in a row."

"Got a Thomas Bros. Guide?"

We checked the book of street maps, and the address was on the southeast side of Little Tokyo, 967 Oslo. It was a busy wholesale and warehouse district. Not as crowded as Chinatown, but there would be plenty of people around. We didn't look at each other; the map lay seemingly innocuous between us.

Ginny said nothing; I said nothing. There was a pause that was pregnant with twins, a pause that was punctuated by the beat of the clockworks, a pause long enough to taste test a good red wine—I could have gone for a nice glass of Australian Shiraz. Then simultaneously our eyes met, and we jumped up and headed for the garage.

As a plan, it was dangerous, it was stupid, and it was not optional. It was an impossibility for the two of us to sit on our asses and wait to hear something. There would be plenty of people around, and with a modest amount of luck, we could find a parking space on the street that would give us a vantage point to see what happened.

I stopped Deirdre in the hall on our way out to give her strict instructions not to let Aya leave the house.

"If she wants to go anywhere, wrestle her to the ground and sit on her!"

"I would prefer to use reason, ma'am, she's not stupid," Deirdre said.

"She's not very big either," Ginny told her. "So if reason doesn't work, put her Mensa ass in a headlock."

We decided to take the least flashy of my vehicles, a dark blue Nissan sedan that I kept for the staff to run errands. It would blend into traffic and was so nondescript not even Evan would notice. It was the one Aya had been driving while she was staying with me, and the seat was so far forward I could barely fit my legs in under the wheel. By the time I got it adjusted, Ginny was done rooting around in the backseat; she'd come up with two baseball hats and some heinous sunglasses.

Ginny put the glasses on; they were the Porsche ones so popular in the 1980s. She looked like a deranged fly.

"Nice look for you," I said to her.

"Don't laugh. When I met you, you were wearing these sunglasses." I think she was looking at me, but I couldn't tell behind the mirrored saucers resting on the bridge of her nose. "I thought you must have been high."

"I was," I said. Reaching into my purse I felt for Korosu's gun.

"I've got one more accessory to complete your ensemble." I found the sleek metal pistol and handed it over.

She accepted it, checked the chamber, and stuck it in the top of her pants.

"You sure it's not too much with this outfit?" she asked flatly.

"Jeans go with everything."

We smiled grimly at each other and fell quiet. We didn't speak until we reached Oslo Street.

We drove by twice, trying not to look conspicuous. There was a 965 address and a 969, but no 967. The address Gades had given didn't exist.

"It's the sidewalk," Ginny said, breaking the silence. "The address is the sidewalk, he wants to keep it public."

I found a parking space on the other side of the street a couple of car lengths down and checked my watch. Ten minutes till. If we sat in the car we would be far too obvious, especially to Evan, who would be watching for just such a setup.

"Let's get out and fade into the crowd," I said to Ginny. "We're too exposed here." We went into the closest market, directly across the street from the appointed address. It was an open warehouse, with fish laid out on long rows of iced tables. We could see across the street clearly from there and were pretending to be intensely interested in some long glassy-eyed denizens of the deep when a rough voice barked at us from behind.

"You ladies have a wholesale license?"

We snapped around, and there, wearing a smock covered in fish guts and blood, was Curtis, the fishmonger. He was so perfectly in character that he literally exuded the aroma of his adopted part.

"Well, I'm having a huge party and this place came highly recommended by my caterer," I said to him with a plea in my voice.

"Go ahead, take a look around." Curtis's eyes gave me the warning that neither of us was to break character. "But only your caterer can actually buy anything, got it?" His face was as dead serious as the mullet on ice in front of him. "And be careful, it can be dangerous in here, slippery."

"Oh we're just looking, thank you," Ginny said to him and turned away as Curtis's eyes cut hard out into the street.

In the brightness of the direct afternoon light, I watched Evan and Officer Siebert walk down the street, toward the switch point. And then I saw her, coming from the opposite direction.

Sabrina was headed directly toward Evan. There was no one beside her, but the streets were crowded, and there were two men who could have been Gades's a couple steps behind her. She was wide-eyed and walking hesitantly, in one hand she clutched a small shopping bag. Evan and Siebert were coming closer, and I watched with my heart throbbing in my throat. Ginny put her hand on my arm and I startled, jerking my arm away, before I realized it was her. I then covered her hand with my own, squeezing too hard.

Suddenly the two men behind Sabrina stopped and looked back behind them, and I saw Evan zone in on them, his one hand firmly on Siebert's arm and the other under his jacket. Curtis had disappeared from behind us, and I noted him out of the corner of my eye, holding a crate near the edge of the sidewalk, his eyes too, darting everywhere.

The gap between them was closing slowly, the time it was taking was interminable. I wanted to scream, to run to Sabrina, to grab her and hustle her to safety, but I was flash frozen. Evan stopped, pulling Siebert up short beside him. I saw two men dressed in drab brown uniforms put down their parcels and reach into their pockets.

Three yards away, the men behind Sabrina spotted what they were looking for behind them and waved furiously. Evan's gun came out and Siebert followed suit, dropping into a doorway. At the same time Sabrina spotted Evan.

"Evan! Hey! What are you doing down here?" The question

rang out from a mouth turned up into a beaming smile. "What a coincidence, huh? This is *so weird.*" Her voice was so honestly surprised and pleased to see him that the volume and tone of it carried perfectly to where we stood across the street.

Then everything happened at once. A van pulled up instantly from where it had been double-parked down the street, and Evan grabbed Sabrina and thrust her toward it. The men who had been behind Sabrina hurried away from the scene, only to be quickly grabbed and handcuffed by cops posing as two pedestrians and ushered unceremoniously into an unmarked car. Shoppers and pedestrians alike gathered to gape and point.

"What's going on? Hey! Wait! Evan!" Sabrina's voice was confused now, and she kept up a constant stream of exclamations as she was thrust into the van. Siebert jumped easily in right behind her, and the van took off.

I was left standing in the aftermath with the heavy odor of low tide and a fragmented perception of what had just happened.

Next to me, Ginny reached up and took off the offensive sunglasses. She started absentmindedly cleaning the lenses with the sleeve of her shirt. Then she put them back on and cleared her throat.

I didn't speak; my brain seemed to have disconnected from my mouth, from everything.

Ginny cleared her throat again and faced me.

"Will you slap me?" she asked calmly. "Really hard?" she added.

"What?" I asked weakly.

"Slap me. Because I must be dreaming." Ginny nodded. "Yeah, that must be it, because I *thought* I just heard your half-brained half-sister say, 'What a *coincidence.*'" Ginny's head went from a "yes" to a "no way" motion, "And she couldn't have said that in real life. I mean, not even Sabrina could have said *that,* right?"

"No," I agreed. There was no logic to it of any kind. "She was surprised to see him," I said. "I mean, it certainly looked that way."

The show was over, several other people who had obviously been undercover, including Curtis, had disappeared. The locals seemed to take it all in stride, as though a couple of women being abducted or rescued, or whatever had just happened to them, happened every other Thursday, just like clockwork, in this part of town.

"I think we can go now," Ginny concluded.

We started for the car. Partial ideas occurred to me but never solidified into a complete thought.

I walked around to the street side and started to open the driver's door when a passing car gave a warning tap at the horn. I drew back against my car, pulling the door out of the way of traffic, and looked up apologetically into the eyes of the driver—Gades.

He had slowed, and as his eyes met mine, his mouth curled into a small smile. He touched the fingers of one hand to his forehead and then out, in a respectful salute as he passed me. At the last second I realized he wasn't alone. I could see the profile of a pretty Asian girl sitting next to him in the passenger seat. She turned her face in my direction, and for just a fraction of a glance, I saw Shika, but the glimpse was too fleeting to read her expression as Gades accelerated and disappeared around the next corner.

"Well," I said to Ginny who had seen it all, "it looks like Gades faked us out. Don't I feel stupid?" But what I really felt was impotent, furious rage.

Chapter 34

Ginny and I rushed into the kitchen when we got home to find Sabrina telling Evan and Curtis what a lovely day she'd had. I could see from the way the two men looked at me that I was in trouble, but I knew my news was a bombshell.

I tried to interrupt to tell Evan about seeing Gades and Shika, but he was totally focused on Sabrina.

"Evan, listen," I tried, but he turned to me and raised his hand.

"I'll get to you in a minute," he said angrily and turned away. I wanted to hiss at him. *How dare he speak to me like a child?* I pulled myself up an inch or two taller and inflated, ready to spit venom, but Ginny put one finger against her lips and nailed me with a look that said "we did do something we shouldn't have." *Fine. Whatever.* I wanted to hear what Sabrina had to say anyway.

"I was so disappointed when I couldn't find Shika," Sabrina was telling him, "so I went to a coffee shop and tried to calm myself down with some tea. This really nice older man and his daughter at the next table noticed me crying, and they were so nice and sweet, and they wanted to know what was wrong. I told them I couldn't find my friend."

"What did they look like?" Curtis asked when she took a breath.

"Oh, nice, they looked nice," she said smiling.

Evan sighed. "Were they black, white, Asian, Hispanic?"

"Uh, white, I guess, but dark white. They were from Spain. Is that white?"

"Did they speak with an accent?"

"No," she said thoughtfully. "I don't think so. Anyway, the man's name was George, and he said he was a chef, and he wanted to know if I'd ever been to visit the wholesale food district? I told him no, and he said I really should go, and would I have lunch with them? His daughter, whose name was Juliet, was really interested in going to school at USC, and she wanted to ask me all kinds of questions. So I said yes."

"Where did you go?" Curtis asked; he had a pen out and was scribbling notes as she talked.

"To a little Italian place right there, kind of out of the way, you'd never notice it, but it was good. They both kept saying how I reminded them of his other daughter in Spain."

"What happened after you ate?" Evan prompted.

"George said he had to go buy some vegetables, and Juliet said it would be boring for her, so why didn't I go with them and keep her company?"

"How did you get there?" Curtis asked.

"They drove me, and they said they were going to drop me off after. Why are you all so mad at me?"

At this point Ginny could hold back no longer. "Haven't I taught you anything?" she railed. "This isn't Podunk, Louisiana. You can't trust strangers, you know that! It's bad enough you sit down and chitchat with these frauds, but to get into a car with them—"

"Okay, that's going to have to wait," Evan said, nixing the

reprimand. "What happened to the man and his supposed daughter?"

"I don't know. I mean they said they had to go into a gourmet place on the next street down from where you *grabbed me."* She looked accusingly at Evan, but he let her have a warning look that was half big brother and half badass cop, and she hurried on more humbly. "I didn't know they were bad guys, why should I? I thought I was playing hooky from school, and now everybody's all bent out of shape." She puffed up, and indignant tears threatened to flow from her baby blues. "And I'm *fine.* Nothing happened."

For just a moment I thought Evan was going to shake her, his face was so compressed with anger. "Listen to me, Sabrina, and listen good."

The totally uncustomary impatience in his voice stopped her self-pitying tears in midflow.

"Because of your selfishness," Evan started in, "and it *is* selfish to endanger someone because you are feeling lonely, we have lost Shika. You revealed her whereabouts and destroyed her cover and ours. I'm not going to make this easy on you because if you repeat this level of foolishness, you could get yourself killed and very likely take the rest of us with you. I'm not even going to mention the emotional hell you put Callaway and your friends through. You tell me everything you said, can think of, or know that Shika ever told you and you do it quickly and without side commentary on anyone else, and just maybe, I can find a way to save Shika's life. Do you get it?"

Sabrina's lips were trembling. She hadn't taken her eyes off of Evan, and for a second a deluge of tears and indulgent hurt threatened to break through the floodgates and engulf everything in its wake, but she made her hands into little fists and smacked them down hard on her thighs to push it all back.

"Okay." She gulped. "Let me think for a minute."

"While she's thinking," I interjected, knowing I would not be shut up now, I told him my news about seeing Gades and Shika together. Evan shook his head with self-contempt.

"I should have seen this coming, what a setup. So, when Sabrina showed up and blew the bugle, Gades moved in with a fake kidnapping as a ruse to distract us while he nabbed Shika." He stood up and paced. "But why?"

"Why what?" asked Ginny.

It was Curtis who answered. "Why would Gades want you to see Shika with him?"

I had wondered about that, about Gades whispering in my ear that he wouldn't hurt her. I remembered his eyes when he saluted me, slightly mocking.

"I think," I offered tentatively, "that he wanted us to know she was all right."

Evan stopped and turned to me. "Why do you think that?"

"Something he said, something about his attitude toward her. Hell, I don't know." I was fully aware of my ignorance. "Call it an instinct, and God knows, I've been dead wrong before." I was acutely aware of my intuition that Korosu had been a decent person, but this was different somehow. I knew that Gades was a criminal, he wasn't pretending to be an upstanding citizen like Korosu, but there was a certain *thief's honor* about Gades. "I know it seems strange, and I know he's a criminal, but I get this feeling that he's an *honest* criminal. Does that make sense?" I said, stumbling.

Curtis sighed deeply. "Unfortunately, yes."

"It's not an honesty you can count on though," Evan elaborated. "That kind of honor tends to shift with the bad guy's need or perception. But first, why do you think he wanted you to see him with her?"

"Because he honked the horn for fuck's sake!" Ginny said loudly.

"But he couldn't have known you'd be there," Curtis pointed out and added coldly, "we didn't."

Evan looked at me and then Ginny grimly but then growled with a grudging pride, "I should have known that you would be." He seemed angry with himself. "And there's a hundred other ways he could have let us know if you hadn't been there." He considered this, then he said, "So, for now, we need to zoom in on what *motive* he would have to let us see that Shika was with him."

"Uh, I have something to say now." Sabrina's guilt-ridden voice drawled from behind Evan.

We had all forgotten her entirely when we began think-tanking, and everyone looked surprised to remember that she was there.

"You said I should tell you everything Shika said, and I don't know how much y'all know already, but I can tell you this." She paused and took a breath. "She loves him. At least, she thinks she does. She knows he does bad things, and she knows she should stay away from him, but she said that he's different around her."

My heart went out to the girl. "She's very confused, Sabrina, I've been in a similar place with a man that wasn't treating me well, and I would try to justify all his behavior—" I cut myself off when I saw her reaction.

"I know a little something about that myself," she said softly, and I shut up. It had been less than a year ago when she had been hurt so ruthlessly, and I realized that this was one reason why such a quick and solid bond had formed between Sabrina and Shika. They both had been badly used by men, men who, in a pathetic way, seemed to have really loved them, and they had escaped the experiences, but not without scars.

"Did she ever say anything about his business, any specifics at all?" Evan persisted.

"Yes," Sabrina said, and we all leaned in, anxious to get the information and use it to save Shika, to stop a shipment of tons of illegal drugs.

"What did she say?" Curtis asked.

"She said that they used to travel together, and have really romantic times. They'd go to Europe and the Islands but that, wherever they were, he always went away alone for the first few days of every other month, for business, and she'd have to stay alone and wait for him. She didn't like that."

"Did she say how many days?" Evan asked sharply.

"She said he always came back by the fifth, with presents and flowers, so she said that the fifth was always their special day."

Evan glanced at the calendar on the kitchen wall; it was the twenty-eighth of April today, and I could guess what he was thinking. For Gades to be finished and back with Shika 'wherever' she was, on the fifth of the month, the shipment would have to come in on, or before, the third.

Curtis must have been doing the same math because he said, "That leaves about five days, only three if we count from May first." Evan nodded.

Sabrina continued. "She wanted to go with him, but he protected her from the business stuff." Sabrina nodded smartly. "She thought that was real considerate." She smiled, as though she thought so too.

Evan and I exchanged glances. I knew we were both thinking about what Shika had told us, about seeing him bash a man's head in with an iron candleholder.

"Yeah, very protective of him," was all Evan said. I was thinking that even if Gades did care for Shika now, if he knew Shika had seen him kill, and he must have, he would never let her go, not alive. Evan's cell phone rang, and he snapped it out. "Paley." He listened while we all eavesdropped discreetly, but strain as I might, I couldn't make out the other end of the conversation. "Okay, thanks for calling."

He closed the phone and looked at Curtis. "The two guys we picked up were clean, cousins of one of the grocers on the street, not even South American. Mexican."

A weighty silence fell on our shoulders. There didn't seem to be any real leads. Ignoring me completely, Evan motioned to Curtis, and they left the room.

I felt stranded; Evan obviously thought I had behaved like an idiot and was taking no time to even talk to me. I felt completely useless. Gades had Shika, we couldn't trace the drug shipment, Korosu had dissolved again, and now as far as both Gades and Korosu were concerned, we were all extraneous players, and better off dead.

Chapter 35

Over the next two days I didn't see Evan, and my annoyance was rapidly morphing into despair. He called once to let me know that he and Curtis were researching all of Korosu's import deliveries; so far, nothing in the bed-and-bath department was due in.

Ladies' lingerie wasn't getting any action either, I thought, pessimistically. What's the use of having a boyfriend if he didn't have time for you?

My friends were absent as well. Aya and Sabrina had resumed going to classes, Evan had a uniformed police officer accompany both of them, and Ginny was off working on a new action series. In this episode she had to jump from an RV onto an eighteen-wheel flatbed truck and fistfight someone while it was rolling down Highway 1, or some such nonsense. I wondered where they thought this stuff up. The consequence was, I was left by myself.

To break the cycle, I immersed myself in work, attacking the pile of contract approvals on my desk. Wary of going out more than absolutely necessary I had my assistant, Kelly, come to the house. In the library we locked down, and I worked her ruthlessly for hours until I noticed her trying to massage her neck when she thought I wasn't looking. An ace executive assistant, Kelly was a pert, petit brunette with a cute smile, and I thanked the universe daily for her.

"I'm sorry, Kell, I'm being a slave driver, I know, but this has to be done," I told her by way of apology. I picked up my desk phone and buzzed Deirdre. When she came on the speaker I gave her my instructions.

"Yes, ma'am?"

"Deirdre, I need a masseuse over here in two hours, have them set up in the pool house, and ice a nice bottle of wine out there as well."

"Very good." Every time she rang off that way I felt like I was in a Wodehouse novel.

Kelly looked up, hopefully, but tried to seem strictly professional. "So, a couple more hours to go today, and then you'll have a nice rubdown and I'll stop by the office to file these before I head home."

"No." I shook my head sadly.

"Oh." She looked disappointed and frazzled; I'm sure she thought I meant to leave her working while I took a break.

"No," I repeated. "The massage and the wine are for you." Her head came up, and she beamed her surprise and thanks at me. "I think if we can put in another good hour and get through the wording on this acquisition contract then you'll have plenty of time for a swim and a sauna before your 'rubdown.'"

"Let's go then." She went back to work with a renewed frenzy, and we were finished in forty-five minutes. Then I sent her off on her minispa excursion, and I went upstairs, feeling sorry for myself.

When I reached my bedroom, the private line was ringing. I snatched it up and tried to pretend I didn't care. "Hello?"

"Hi." It was Evan, and I could tell from the tone of his voice that he missed me. Good. Let him.

"Oh, hi." I feigned indifference. "What's up, working all night again?" I sounded bitter and babyish; I wished that I didn't. But I couldn't keep it out of my voice. How dare he dismiss me for days? I was too old for time-outs.

"Actually, I was hoping that we could have dinner," he said, and I could sense the caution in his manner. He was ready for me to be in a bad mood.

"Oh, is it my turn for an evening?" Sometimes my preadolescent behavior wrestled my grown-up self to the ground and sat on its head. I struggled to reason with her, but my inner child had a serious learning disability as well and would hear no reprimand.

"Okay." Evan took a deep breath; in it I could hear the effort it took for him to force down his own angry teenager, the part of him I knew wanted to tell me to fuck off. "Okay, I would like to see you tonight, would you like to see me?" His patience sounded like a net that was barely containing his flight response.

"Sure, I guess so," I told him. *What am I doing?* Why can't I just say "I miss you too?"

"Look, Callaway . . ." Whenever he called me Callaway, I knew I was in trouble. "I'm busy, and I'm stressed, and I know you probably feel like I'm not paying enough attention to you right now, and I'm not. But I'm trying. I'd like to spend the evening with you and reconnect. I miss you." Damn it, when he got honest it backed me up against my own stubborn wall and smushed me flat. I struggled against a smart-ass response.

"Cally?" he asked, "are you there?"

"Yeah, I'm here." I took a deep breath and managed to say, "I'd like that too." There, it was out. The pressure eased. "I'll have Sophie make us dinner. What time?"

"Actually"—a playfulness came into Evan's voice—"I was thinking I'd like to cook."

I laughed. "You?"

"Yes, me." He sounded indignant, "I *can* cook, you know."

"So you keep saying," I challenged.

"You just be at my house at seven, and don't worry about anything else."

"Don't worry? That makes me nervous." I'm a bit spoiled when it comes to good food. Sophie trained at the Sorbonne, and I snatched her away from one of L.A.'s better restaurants with the promise that I would eventually help her open her own. It was a promise I would keep, albeit reluctantly.

"Just be there, and be ready for a little snack before dinner," Evan said and hung up.

Chapter 36

The driveway to Evan's Westwood home was a tastefully grand affair. Huge gates, video setup.

Which gave me an idea. Stopping just down the street, I slipped off my slinky dress so that I was only in my carefully chosen black silk bra and panties. When I pulled into the wide drive I secretly praised Evan's landscape designer for the private alcove that blocked a view of me from the street. My five-inch black Jimmy Choo heels made a resonant clicking noise as I stepped up to the buzzer and pressed it before returning to the side of my car where, placing both hands on the hood, I assumed the shakedown pose and turned to look over my shoulder into the camera.

A small speaker next to the keypad was humming out an electronic buzzing as the phone rang in the house, and then I heard him answer. "Hello."

"Hello, officer." I spoke loudly so that my voice would carry the few feet to the gate phone.

"Cally?" he asked. "I can hardly hear you.

"Well then you'd better get a visual," I half shouted.

There were a few seconds of static from the speaker and then "Very nice," which was quickly followed by "Now get in here, I need to search you for weapons."

Enjoying myself, I slipped into the car, and out of my bra, so that he could search me more thoroughly. Naked except for the heels and a G-string, I drove my car up to the front of the house, where an eager man was outside waiting to claim me. As soon as I'd turned off the engine Evan pulled me out of the driver's seat and laid me across the hood of the car. He started with the snack he had promised me and then pulled me into a tight embrace, kissing me enthusiastically. I pressed my skin against his, reveling in his heat and his affection. I turned my back to his chest and wrapped his arms around my chest: he kissed the side of my face again and again, his arms protecting me from the slight chill in the air.

"Hello there," I said, nestling back against him. His hands moved to cover my breasts and then down to my hips. I leaned forward, pressing my front down on the warm metal of the car hood, and he held my waist, keeping me exactly where he wanted me.

It was exactly where I wanted to be too. His rhythm was slow and controlled but my response was almost immediate, a growl rose up in my throat and built into a long sustained carnal expression of the waves that were riding through my body. The pace of Evan's movements quickly matched my vocal intensity, and his fingers pressed hard into my flesh as I felt his body thrust against me, his tight grip increasing the fever of our orgasms.

When we finished gasping and our breathing had calmed, he kissed me luxuriously, both of us breaking only to smile contentedly.

"Hungry?" he asked.

"Suddenly I seem to be ravenous. I can't imagine how, but I must have worked up a bit of an appetite," I answered. "Enough to sample the Paley cuisine."

"Then let me show you to your table." He released me long

enough to adjust his clothes, then he swept me up into his arms and carried me through the door he'd left open in his haste to meet me.

"Love the valet," I told him as we crossed the threshold. "You don't get that kind of curb service at any ol' Denny's."

"And it's all strictly for the gratuities." He smiled at me.

"Well, I, for one, am very grateful, I'm sure."

"Customer satisfaction is job one." He set me down and stood looking at me. All I was wearing were the black heels. Not exactly demure.

"I don't suppose you could lend me a shirt or something," I said to him. "Seeing as I don't have anything of mine here." It was a jab I couldn't resist.

"If you must." He sighed and led me upstairs to his closet, a large walk-in affair, very masculine. "Help yourself." He gestured to the long rack of neatly hung button-downs.

I picked out a light blue Egyptian cotton, snooping a bit as I went. "Remind me to get my bag out of the car when we go back down, if I'm going to spend the night, that is."

"Well, I certainly hope you are." He sounded like he thought it was a done deal.

"It's a little awkward for me, what with having to pack a toothbrush and whatnot, I'm not exactly a fixture here." Could I be more obvious?

He looked uncomfortable and on the verge of defensiveness. "Are you trying to tell me something?"

"No." I spun toward him, holding the shirt up so that it covered at least half of me, and lifted my brows in innocent surprise. "Like what?"

"Like, you would like to keep some things here." He looked amused at my transparent diversion. His eyes slid downward, past my waist and lingered just below. "Or something else?"

"What are you looking at?" I asked, stepping sideways as I held my ground.

His eyes continued down to my heels, then back up until our gazes reached out to each other like silk tendrils that tied themselves skillfully into a knot. I could have towed a trailer with the strength of that double hitch.

"I'm looking at you. All of you." His voice flowed along the connection between us, and I felt the resonance of his tenor in my body.

"What do you see?" I asked, not sure if I needed to speak the words for him to hear them.

"Everything I want." He stood and came to me; the tie between us did not loosen or fall slack. Instead the strands knitted tighter as he approached. "Everything I have is yours." He said, kissed me gently. "Take it."

This depth of feeling between us was new and scary and an exhilarating place to be. I pushed my need of proof to one side, raised my face to his, and found the words I wanted to say. "All I want is to be with you."

His eyes flickered with loving warmth, a crackling blaze that softened into humor. The intensity between us had built until it must have some release. "I adore you," he said, beaming at me, "but . . ."

"What?" I started to laugh, knowing some wisecrack was coming.

His face took on an apprehensive expression. "What if you hate my cooking?"

I didn't hate it. In fact, I loved the meal he made. Rich curry and rice, so heated with spice that it was painful. He seemed worried when my face turned red, but it was delicious.

"I'm sorry, it's too hot," he apologized.

"No, it's really good," I enthused. "Are my eyeballs sweating?" I laughed and took a long drink of the Indian beer he had chosen to accompany our dinner.

"I thought you liked spicy food," he lamented.

"I do! I really do, everything tastes great. Yes, it hurts, but it hurts so good." I sucked air in through pursed lips to cool the burn on my scorched tongue. "So what's the news on Gades?"

Evan sighed and switched reluctantly to the subject. "Curtis has been tracking all arriving shipments in Korosu's import business. We've had Port Authority inspect two so far."

"And?"

"Nothing. They're clean." Evan's face stayed relaxed, but his voice betrayed his frustration. "So, so far, we've got nada."

"Have you been able to trace all of his holdings?" I asked, thinking it through from a business point of view.

"His import company is called East-West Imports. It's big, but so far, blemish free."

"What about his South American import company?" I asked, swigging beer again to coat my aching membranes. "Any zits on that one?"

"He's only got one import company," Evan said.

"No way," I responded quickly. "That just doesn't make sense, Evan. There's an entirely different set of laws for each country. Either he would have subsidiaries, all under the umbrella of East-West, or he would form other smaller licensing corporations to facilitate those specific legal restrictions. Also, it just makes sense to break up those kinds of holdings, in case of lawsuits or seizures."

Evan's hand had frozen halfway to his mouth, and he was looking at me as though I was pointing at an obvious flaw. "That's true," he said.

"You know how it works. If customs has a reason to hold or seize a cargo of some kind, they can put a freeze order on the whole company. If you're doing business on the scale Korosu does, that would be disastrous. So you want to break it up into smaller, more manageable—and less vulnerable—businesses." I smiled at him. "I'm sure your brother and sister have done the same with your holdings. The hotel construction company is different from the bank, they are separate corporations, so that if one of them is sued, the plaintiff cannot come after a separately held company." I paused. "Or you personally."

"But the research only shows one company, owned by Korosu, licensed for import."

"There's probably several different smaller import businesses, all with different names, which service different products, and/or various countries." I nodded conclusively. Must be. But maybe he's split the ownership or uses a company licensed to someone else. "As long as Korosu's name is connected *in some way,* you should be able to pull a list from the . . ."

He finished for me. " . . . from the business bureau, I know." He put his beer down without drinking from it, kissed me, and started for the phone. I felt like I had finally contributed something. Halfway across the kitchen he stopped and turned back. "What if Korosu's name isn't connected?"

"That's harder," I said. "I'm guessing you guys know how to trace stockholders and profit sharing, but there's probably a quicker way."

"What?"

"If he has an executive assistant, which he must, and it's probably the woman I saw when he got the ship-to-shore call that night, he or she might know. Whether or not they'd be cooperative is another matter." I said, as it occurred to me. He nodded and went to call Curtis. I pushed my plate back, disappointed that our evening had been interrupted.

When Evan came back and sat down I wiped my wounded mouth and forced a smile. "Well, that was lovely, I guess I'll get going now."

The corners of Evan's mouth twitched, and he canted his head curiously at me. "Why? You have somewhere you need to be?"

"Don't you?"

He reached over and took my hand. "Yes, I do. Right here, in my bed, with my arms around you all night."

"Good answer." I pulled cool air over my stinging lips again. "You wouldn't happen to have any ice cream, would you?"

He laughed. "As a matter of fact, I do." He pulled me up, and we found the freezer, two spoons, and coconut sherbet. We spent the rest of the evening curled up on the couch together. I could sense urgency in Evan's manner, I could feel the impatient pull on his attention, and we continually went back to discussing the case. As much as I needed his attention, the threat of Gades and Korosu wouldn't just go away because I felt romantic. It needed all of Evan's considerable intelligence and focus to neutralize it.

Maybe more.

Chapter 37

On the drive home the next morning my brain was swirling with conflicting emotions. Evan had been gone when I woke up, leaving a brief note and a sense of loss. I consoled myself with the memory of him saying that he wanted to be with me more, and that everything he had was mine. Yet he had still avoided saying "I love you" and made no mention of sharing households. Nice sentiment, but still squishy on solid proof. I fluctuated between thinking separate houses would be fine, that wouldn't bother me, and feeling like it was all a pathetic ruse and I wasn't falling for it, damn it.

I pulled up the drive, and the garage doors opened smoothly as I passed the side of the house. Leaving the brightness as I drove in, I was momentarily blinded, but I knew the dimensions of the space without seeing them, so I pulled forward and cut the engine.

I climbed out and started to the kitchen door.

But I only made it two steps. Next to the door, slumped

against the wall in a sitting position, was a man; the smear of blood down the white wall from the back of his head and his staring eyes told me more than I wanted to know about his vital statistics.

He was so dead.

Chapter 38

"Hi, honey, it's me," I said numbly.

"Hi." I could tell he was busy, rushed, pushed, annoyed by that stack of unsolved files on his desk, but his voice went immediately into an idling purr when he recognized my voice. That was nice. "I'm sorry I snuck out, but I hated to wake you, you looked like an angel."

"Oh, don't worry about it." I wasn't really sure how to tell him there was a body in my garage.

He sensed something was up. "What's going on, you okay?"

"Oh, yeah, I'm fine," I said unconvincingly, "but the guy in my carport is definitely not fine."

"What guy?" Evan was alarmed, so I rushed on.

"The dead one." There just wasn't an easy way. "There doesn't seem to be any danger of any kind." That sounded lame. "Well, not for me, anyway, I guess the guy parked next to my Mercedes might disagree, if he was talking, which he's not, of course." I knew I was rambling, but if I stopped being flip I was afraid I'd start screaming.

"Who is *he?*" Evan wasn't freaking out, not yet, but I could sense that he was afraid that "he" was one of my staff or friends.

So I hastened to eliminate that possibility. "I have no idea what his name is, but I think, no . . . I'm sure that I've seen him before. He was with Gades the first time I saw him at the golf course." The air crackled between us.

"Have you called the police?" Evan asked.

"Isn't that a redundant question?" I was, after all, on the phone with one of L.A.'s finest. "I hit the panic button on my alarm panel and I think the guard who showed up first went through the usual channels, if that's what you want to know."

"I'll be there as soon as I can." Evan's volume went up with urgency. "Make sure some of the staff stay with you."

"Nobody's here, it's Friday, remember? They all leave in the morning and have the day and the night off."

"Oh." The monosyllable was hard to read. It could have been disappointment that I was alone or relief that my staff was not in danger.

"And the women are all at school or work?"

"Yes."

"The security officer is with you?"

"Actually there's about six of them here now. This seems to be a special occasion for them, since they don't get to see many bodies on their usual rounds, and"—glancing out the window I saw a black-and-white speed up my driveway—"the police just got here."

"I'm glad," Evan said grimly. "I'm almost to my car, I'll be there in fifteen minutes. Don't let anyone touch anything."

"That part I remember," I responded. "I can't quite recall the rest of the routine at the moment, but I'm sure it'll come back to me."

"Are you okay?" He wanted a real answer.

"I'm not sure," I felt tears rising and gulped them back, "but I'll be better when you get here."

We signed off and I went to busy myself in the kitchen, funneling some of my urge for hysterical panic into making coffee for the law officers who continued to arrive, blaring sirens leaving a ringing silence as they turned up my drive.

The whole circus was showing in three rings by the time Evan arrived—forensics, photographers, uniforms, the place was overrun with people in white coats and rubber gloves. Evan found me huddled in a nook in the kitchen, drinking from a cup of coffee heavily whitened with Baileys.

He sat next to me and pulled me up against him; I felt nothing.

"Have you checked on the ladies?" he asked, concerned.

"Ginny's phone is off; she's on the set; I left a message. I talked to Sabrina between classes. She told me Aya was dressed and ready to go when she left the house at eight o'clock, and all of the staff were already gone or on their way out."

"Did you tell Sabrina about the body?"

"No, not yet. I couldn't reach Aya though; I got her voice mail when I called her cell. Should I be worried about her?"

"What time does she usually leave?"

"About eight-thirty," I told him.

"Let's find out how long our corpse has been in his present condition and then we'll know whether to worry or not," Evan said with a sense of urgency and left me for a few minutes.

When he came back he said. "Not very long, apparently less than an hour, and it's eleven-forty-three now. So"—he poured himself a cup of coffee—"I don't think Aya's in any danger if she left at eight-thirty." He took a cautious sip of the hot liquid and murmured to himself, "I need to make sure." He turned to me again. "Who *was* here an hour ago?"

"Nobody that I know of. I told you Sabrina said everyone was gone or leaving." My head felt a little breezy inside, as though I had left some windows open and wind was blowing through it.

"Somebody was here to show him into the afterlife." Evan's

supposition was grim. "But we need to find out who he was and what he wanted from you or one of your houseguests."

My swirling thoughts were turning rapidly to gusts. The aimless breezes were developing into gale-force winds, sweeping away logic and bending reality as they went. "But Gades has Shika, why would he send someone here?"

Evan didn't answer straightaway, instead he took a thoughtful sip of coffee and leaned against the counter. "He might think we know more than we do, or . . ." He stiffened, coming away from the counter like a string straightening on a bow that has fired its arrow.

"What?" I asked.

"When we took Shika to the hotel to hide her, she must have left things here."

"She didn't come with much, just one bag, like a carry-on bag," I said, remembering her gathering only a few items after the shooting in San Francisco.

"Let's go," he said keenly.

I jumped up and started up the service stairs off the kitchen. He was right behind me as I moved down the hall, sensing an urgency I didn't understand.

Her room was on the left before you reached the main stairwell, and it was ransacked.

We both stood in the doorway looking around. "Damn it," Evan cursed. "Whatever she had, it's gone now. And my guess is, either Gades or Korosu has it." He spun and headed back for the garage; I followed as soon as I could react.

Curtis was in the garage when we got there, and the body, zipped into its final plastic resting place, was on a stretcher going into the coroner's van.

"Did you find anything that might be Shika's on him?" Evan asked in way of greeting.

Curtis's head snapped up at the thought and he moved quickly to a worktable in the garage where there were several plastic bags, each one tagged with a number. Evan crossed with him, and without opening the bags they picked up each one and looked through the contents. I moved cautiously up beside Evan.

"What are you looking for?" I asked him.

"I don't know. If Shika did have something they wanted then whoever shot this guy probably took it." Evan scrutinized the bags as he talked. "It looks like this guy, or whoever killed him, went though her room, so she could have left something behind, something Gades or Korosu wanted. She might not have known what it was."

Curtis nodded. "It could have been something that would incriminate him, or information crucial to the shipment," he contributed. "That makes sense." He turned to me and said with exactly the same inflection, "Do I smell coffee?"

But I had frozen. In the bag Evan was holding was a small silk pocket handkerchief, and embroidered on the corner was a discreet Japanese character. Even through the clear plastic I recognized it instantly.

"Evan," I blurted out, "I know who killed him." Raising a shaking finger, I pointed at the scarf. "That's Korosu's, I saw it in his breast pocket."

"Are you sure?" he asked me.

"Positive. That character is his signature." I forgot that he would want to know how the hell I knew that, but before he could ask anything else, Curtis spoke.

"On the ground, just beside the left hand."

"So he was probably holding it. That means he could have dislodged it in a struggle, taken it from Shika's room, or . . ."

"It could have been planted on him," Curtis shrugged as though it was impossible to tell which. "How about that coffee?"

"In the kitchen. You want me to get you some?" I needed a purpose.

"No. I'll get it." Curtis continued his line of thought as we walked back through the house. "But supposing we're right about

Shika having something incriminating. Would Korosu know about that?"

My blood chilling, I said, "He's the one who had access to Shika at his hotel, and he could have found out what she had, whatever it is." I suddenly felt very insecure about drawing conclusions in my present company, so I added, "Right?"

"Could be," Evan concurred, and I was relieved. "It's also very possible that this is a warning left for all of us to reflect on."

"*Who* left?" Curtis asked as he poured milk in his coffee. "Korosu or Gades? Would Gades kill his own man?"

Evan rubbed his brow. "Yes, remember his threat to Callaway when he made his appearance here, that he would kill us if we interfered with his business this week? He's very capable of killing his own man if he thought his man failed him, or didn't do what he wanted him to do." The body was a chilling reminder that we had not exactly acquiesced to his wishes. Evan added, "It wouldn't be the first time," I didn't ask how he knew that bit of trivia.

There was a shuffling behind us and two uniformed officers appeared with Aya between them. She was holding her textbooks, as though they would shield her from further vulnerability, and her eyes were wide with fear.

"Callaway!" she called out when she saw me. "What's going on?"

"There's been a murder," Evan said quickly and simply.

Aya's face went ashen. "Sabrina?" It was a whisper, it was a prayer.

I rushed to her as I answered, "No. No. Sabrina's fine, I talked to her on her cell phone. It was a man, a man we don't know." I watched Aya exhale. She looked deflated, but infinitely relieved.

She tensed again when Evan spoke. "I'd like to see if you recognize him."

"Evan, no!" I countered protectively.

"I'm sorry, but it's important. Aya, you got a good look at the men who were with Gades, the night you walked in on his meeting with Korosu, didn't you?"

She looked nauseated. "Yes."

"It would help me very much if you recognize the body as one of them," Evan said softly.

I started to object, to tell Evan that I had already recognized the man, "Evan, I—"

His hand flew up quickly and he spoke over me, cutting me off, "It's important," he said to her. I realized he didn't want her to be influenced by my conclusion.

"I'll try." Aya swooned slightly where she stood, and I tightened my grip around her.

"You can take a few moments if you like," Evan said considerately.

"No." Aya straightened and her eyes lost their focus as we watched her fight to find the strength to face this horror. "I would like to do it now, to be done."

"That's smart, get it over with," Evan responded and led the way. A word from him and the stretcher was pulled out of the van. I stood with my arm around Aya's waist, ready to catch her if she fell. The dead man's face was etched on my memory already; it wouldn't matter if I had to look at it again. Evan gestured to the coroner and the bag was unzipped. Aya's whole body trembled, she took several quick shallow breaths, and then she nodded quickly and looked away.

"Do you recognize him?" Evan asked.

"I think so. I think he is one of the men who was there." She turned away from the body as though it were a repellent force. "I don't know his name, or anything about him."

"That's enough." Evan thanked the coroner, and the zipper closed over the death mask. "Thank you, Aya, I know that was difficult, but I needed to know if you remembered him."

"C'mon," I said to Aya, "let's get out of here." Evan caught my eye over her head, and I realized he had more questions for her. "How about we all go sit by the pool?" I tested. Evan nodded.

"Yes," Aya agreed, "I'd like to sit down."

"Aya, did you know if Shika had something in her possession that was valuable to Gades?" Evan was watching her closely. "It would have been something that could incriminate him, or information about the cocaine shipment we expect is coming in." He paused, and then added. "Something Korosu might also want or need."

"If I had known about that, I would have told you," Aya told him.

"Of course," he responded quickly. "But you might not have suspected that it was important or connected. Someone went through her room, probably either the man who was killed or his murderer."

"How did they know which room was hers?" I asked, confused.

"She's had direct contact with Korosu and Gades, so she could have told them." Evan kept his voice patient while explaining that obvious basic fact. Boy, did I feel stupid again. I wasn't contributing much of anything helpful to this whole situation. I felt useless.

"I don't know." Aya's eyes filled with frustrated tears. "I just don't even know what you're looking for."

"It's my fault, I'm asking the wrong questions." Evan seemed impatient. "Do you, by any chance, happen to know if Korosu had import companies under different names than East-West?" He didn't sound hopeful.

Aya's pretty brow furrowed, and then her eyes looked vague. "Well, I'm not sure, but he would sometimes give gifts of stock in his companies." She angled her head and cut her eyes toward the blue water of the pool. "I know he gave me some, as an investment; I'm sure he must have given some to Shika as well. But I don't think the import companies were in that group. I remember him talking business one time with a man . . ." She paused and reflected, the sunlight playing on her black eyes, sharp obsidian. " . . . They were speaking in Japanese, but . . . no, I can't remember."

"Try harder," Evan told her forcibly.

She fell silent with concentration. "The words were something like *fune me-gami.*"

"What does that mean?"

"It doesn't translate exactly and I'm not sure it's correct anyway."

"How do the words translate roughly?" asked Evan.

Aya seemed alarmed at Evan's forcefulness. She answered, "Roughly, in English it means 'ship goddess.'"

Evan already had his pad out. "Could you write that down please?"

"Of course, I will write it in Japanese and in English letters."

"Thank you." Evan waited while she performed the simple function and then he asked, "So, you are a stockholder in Korosu's companies?"

She smiled ruefully at that. "I suppose you could say it that way, a very tiny one, enough to pay a small dividend, and give me some capital for when I graduate from medical school. That was Korosu's intention." Her face clouded. "I thought it was very kind of him."

"And he did the same for Shika?" Evan persisted.

"I am not sure, it would not have been polite for me to inquire, as it was none of my business, but I would assume." She turned her gaze back to him. "I don't understand what that has to do with this."

"I don't either." Evan sighed. "But maybe it will help, I'm not sure."

"I can't think of anything else," Aya said, her eyes fading back into opaque black glass. "I'm sorry."

"You've been a huge help, thank you," Evan told her, standing up.

"I am glad I could help in a small way. I cannot help but feel I have brought all of this on you, and I am deeply sorry."

"It's not your fault," I told her again and waited for Evan to back me up. When he said nothing, I turned to see why. He was already gone.

Chapter 39

It was a subdued foursome who sat down to a dinner we had fixed ourselves that night, as the staff was off. The corpse in the garage seemed to have a diminishing effect on the appetites of Ginny, Sabrina, Aya, and myself.

The conversation was sparse, every attempt to spark one felt trite, and the subjects didn't hold our interest in our reflective moods. I pushed the food on my plate to one side and then back to another, sighed, and leaned back in my chair.

"It's funny," I began, looking fondly at each of their faces and noting with relief that Aya's bruises were healing well. "I've always planned my life as though there's a lot more of it to come, but you never know."

"How would you do it differently, if you knew it wouldn't last long?" Ginny asked.

"Oh, I don't know." It was a good question. "I know I would appreciate little things, moments, more than I do. And I would definitely spend less time on business and more time taking care of myself."

"You don't exactly nine-to-five it now," Ginny teased me.

"True," I consented, "and the truth is that I enjoy my work. I find it challenging and fun, I'd be bored without work." Warming to my subject, I began to expand my thoughts. "I would sit still more, maybe."

Both Ginny and Sabrina laughed now. "I don't think you can do that," my sibling said.

"I know, I'm overactive, I don't like wasting time."

"I think it takes a balance," Sabrina said, nodding. "Sometimes you gotta run errands, and sometimes you gotta take a bubble bath and paint your toenails." She shrugged. "That's life."

Ginny summed it up for us. "It's all good."

Aya chimed in now. "Even the bad is good." We all looked up at her, so she explained. "The theory is that we create each moment, it is all connected, if we didn't experience something as 'negative,' then we would have no point of reference for what is 'positive.'" We must have looked like a trio of idiots because she laughed and added, "At least that's what they taught me in *my* Sunday school."

Sabrina was watching her, and obviously what seemed like a common theory to me was a revelation to her; from the look on her face I could tell she was trying to translate what Aya was saying into a language she could understand. "And sometimes," she said tentatively, "things that seem bad can actually turn out to be good." She looked proud of herself. "Like how I met Callaway, that was terrible, but now I have family I didn't know I had."

"True for both of us." I picked up my glass and toasted her. "To the terrible-wonderful sister."

Aya smiled from a distant place at the exchange between us, and I recognized the sentiment behind that look: being on the outside looking in. "Very often, it is the hardest trials in life that we grow the most from." She said it simply, but in her voice there was something that suggested massive complexity.

Ginny raised her glass now. "To life's trials." We all raised our glasses over the table, and then with a glance at Sabrina, who added, "And to bubble baths."

"Here, here!" I called loudly, and the musical bell tones of crystal clinking rang out happily through the room.

"What are we drinking to?" Evan's voice added a tenor note to the chimes as he entered the room.

"Hi!" I smiled at him, thinking that part of my amended list of life changes would be to include more time with Evan. "Evil and hot soapy water, basically."

He didn't even look surprised. "Well, let me add something."

I handed him my glass, and Ginny encouraged him. "Go right ahead."

He raised his arm and spoke clearly. "To nailing two of those evils and a huge shipment of cocaine tomorrow."

"What? You found the shipment?" I asked amazed.

Evan took a drink and then pulled up a chair next to mine. He picked up my fork and took a few hungry but polite mouthfuls as he continued. "We think so, thanks to Aya." He nodded in her direction. "There is a shipment coming in of assorted housewares on Goddess Shipping lines, due in at San Pedro, pier number twenty-seven, at approximately three o'clock in the afternoon, tomorrow, the second of May; plenty of time for Gades to take care of business and get back by the fifth."

Aya looked pleased. "So, my information was helpful, I'm so glad."

"So am I." Evan's smile dimmed a bit. "Let's hope this is it."

On the cuff of Evan's blue shirt, where it extended from the jacket sleeve as he reached for my plate, there were spots, stains of something dark, and I noticed that his hand had a few shallow scratches. I took his forearm in my hands, alarmed, and asked, "Is this blood?"

"No," Evan said dismissively, but his eyes gave me a quick warning to drop it, and he changed the subject. "So with luck,

I'll have a productive day tomorrow." He smiled around the table.

"What will you do?" I was instantly nervous for him, it *was* blood. I wondered who Evan had "questioned" to get his info about tomorrow. If the shipment was the one Korosu and Gades were waiting for, it would be heavily guarded.

"We've already alerted the port authority, they will deal with most of the technical aspects of this, it's their jurisdiction. Curtis and I will be there strictly to arrest the major players in the connected crimes that are our jurisdiction."

My feelings, as I watched him, were an odd fusion of excitement—it definitely turned me on that he was eagerly willing to confront such a dangerous situation—and stark, hot fury that he would jeopardize himself regardless of my fear for him. My feelings turned somersaults until I was dizzy. I stood up.

"You okay?" Ginny asked.

I answered, "I'm just feeling jumpy all of a sudden. Just leave the dishes; the staff will take care of them when they come back in the morning. Excuse me."

As I had expected, Evan followed me from the room. I was headed through the living room toward the main staircase, but on a whim I took his hand and opened the huge doors that led to the ballroom; Evan closed them behind us. The marble floor clicked under my heels and echoed in the vast space.

Reaching the middle of the room I stopped and waited for Evan to reach me. I put my arms around him and pulled him up close. "What if something happens to you?" I whispered.

"Nothing will happen to me." Evan began to rock me with a reassuring steadiness.

"Then what happened to your hand?"

He tensed. "I wanted to talk to someone who wouldn't stand still."

"But what—?"

"No. No more questions," he said, cutting me off, but his

look went from hard to sheepish in half a second. "We talked about this, remember? If it's not okay, then—"

"I understand," I cut him off in turn, but I was asking myself how I would deal with him having a secret life. Not well. Not unless I had one too.

He smiled. "I'm going to be all right."

I let that statement sink in for a moment, memorizing it with my body and mind so that it would stay heavily ensconced throughout the coming day and on into the future. But reality and chance nagged at me.

"You can't control everything," I argued, looking up at him. "You're taking a giant gamble, every time you go to work, and I have to admit, I don't care if it's selfish, I don't like it."

He smiled gently at me. "Nobody can control everything. I worry about you every single time you leave this house, hell, sometimes even when you're here." He kissed me once quickly. "I mean, this is Callaway Wilde I'm holding in my arms."

"I am not a jinx," I insisted, but I smiled back at him.

"Not at all, you're my good-luck charm." With his left hand he encircled my waist and lifted my left hand into a waltz position. His mouth still curved in an amused smile injected with fondness, and as he began to hum he moved me easily into a dance around the grand room. I laid my head against his shoulder and spoke softly into his ear.

"Do you know what I like most about you?" I asked him when we slowed to an easy sway.

"No, tell me."

"I always want more," I told him, and it was true.

"Good," he told me, "because I intend to be around for a long time." His message was loud and clear: he would be back, and he would stay.

Provided, of course, that he lived through tomorrow.

Chapter 40

We had just slid under the Irish linen and were starting to embrace when there was a soft knock on the door. I called out, "Who is it?"

The door opened a foot; Aya was standing there, wearing a thin peach silk kimono; the light behind her in the dimly lit hall made a seductive shadow outline of her body on the folds of the fabric. "Can I talk to you?" she asked.

"Come on in." I sat up, propping a pillow behind me as Evan rose up on one elbow, looking appreciatively at Aya, I noticed.

She closed the door soundlessly behind her and came across the room toward us. Instead of sitting on one of the chairs across the room, as I had expected, she came right to the bed and perched herself on the foot of it, her robe separating as she drew her knees up enough to show her perfect legs, with those impeccably manicured petite feet. Even her feet are sexy, I thought without resentment. Evan shared a look with me that said it was impossible for him to sexually desire this woman, but she was undeniably pretty.

"I'm afraid." She said in a small voice. "I'm afraid that something very bad will happen tomorrow and it will be my fault."

"We've told you it's not your fault," Evan said deliberately.

"Yes, you've been very kind." Her eyes looked pleadingly at both of us and then filled with tears. "But I have been a fool. I have failed you."

I sat forward and put my arms around her, expecting her to resist the offered comfort, but instead she leaned against me.

Evan spoke now. "You're wrong, you know; it doesn't mean you have failed or that you are a fool, it means Korosu is not worthy of your trust, the failing is his." We exchanged a look—he hadn't told her about Korosu's scarf found next to the dead man.

She pulled back enough to smile at him. "Thank you," she said. "You have both helped me so much. I feel that I've changed in the time I've spent with you. As though now I can actually do the things I want; before I wasn't sure."

"Of course you can," I said to her. "You can do anything you want."

After Aya left to return to her own room I snuggled up to Evan.

"Well," I said. "Whatever else happens, we've helped Aya out of a very tough spot."

"True," Evan agreed as he encircled me with his arms. "Whatever else, we have done that." And then he kissed me.

Chapter 41

The sound of Evan coming out of the dressing room roused me. My eyes flew open and I was instantly wide awake.

My handsome shirtless man came to me and kissed me lightly, pulling the covers up around my shoulders. "Go back to sleep," he whispered.

"Not likely." As I recalled what would happen today my nerves felt like they were each individually attached to a hot wire. "When did you get up?"

"Early, before it got light."

"Hell, it's not really light yet now."

"I've got to go," he stated, but he didn't move from beside me. He stroked my cheek and my shoulder, tracing my arm with his finger until our hands found each other and clasped tightly. His hand was cold, he was nervous.

"Are you okay?" I asked him.

"I'm fine." His eyes sparkled with reassurance, all meant for me. I accepted the gesture without questioning.

"Good, I'll expect you home for dinner."

He laughed. "I don't know about dinner, if everything goes well in San Pedro, I'll have a pile of paperwork to get through that'll make K2 look more like a pre-K hike."

"Breakfast?" I asked hopefully.

"I think you can count on me for a midnight snack." He leaned in and kissed my neck.

"You can count on me to be one," I murmured while he was nibbling.

The banter was a thin deception. We were both afraid, but there was nothing for it but to get dressed and through the day.

But before we had finished a quick cup of coffee in the kitchen, Evan got a call from Curtis that gave us another jolt of confusion.

Evan was snapping the phone shut when I asked him what was the matter.

"Well, good news, actually." But Evan didn't look like he entirely thought so. "The officer who was assigned to Shika regained consciousness yesterday and was well enough to speak to Curtis this morning." He clenched his teeth together. "Apparently she was knocked out by Shika herself."

My head reeled, as though I too had been struck from behind. "Shika!" I was shocked. "But why?"

Evan sighed and put his hands on my upper arms. "I can only think of one reason." But he waited for me to say it.

"She wanted to go back to Gades." The realization was painful, and the words stung as they crawled out of my mouth. We had harbored her, tried to protect her from him. He had abused her and killed someone in front of her. Why would she do this?

"Remember how hopeful she looked when she heard that Gades was trying to get her back?"

How could she deceive us like this? A sense of betrayal and its hurt washed over me. "Damn her!" I exclaimed.

"She's very confused, and she's being used, very skillfully, by a master manipulator." Evan shook his head. "I know you're angry, and rightly so, but I think her behavior is more pathetic than egregious."

Even as he said it, I was working that out for myself and moving on. "So it was definitely Korosu who tried to kill her in San Francisco?"

"Looks that way," he mused.

"But Korosu could have had her killed anytime!"

"That's my problem with it." Evan was putting on his jacket. He drew his gun and checked the clip, replacing it with a practiced snap. He slid the pistol back in the holster and turned away from me. He leaned against the counter, staring motionless through the window over the sink. Recognizing the move as one in which he was lost in thought, I remained silent.

"What if," he said quietly, "what if they weren't trying to kill Shika?"

"Then who?"

"Remember when the shooter fired?" Evan turned back to me.

I would never forget the moment; the image was frozen brightly in my memory. The giant wall of glass, Shika in the chair that seemed to be floating on the bay, and Aya standing just behind her . . .

"Aya!" I exclaimed. "Aya walked over next to her, and then the wall of glass shattered." My brain was racing through the events now. "And it was near Aya that the next hit came, right beside her head. Shika was already in the hallway."

"Yes." Evan's eyes were lit up from the friction in his active mind. "But who wanted to kill Aya?" He started to pace. "Why was Aya a target?" He didn't seem to be addressing me, but I chimed in anyway.

"*If* she was," I amended; we were theorizing after all. "Maybe because she had involved us?"

"Possible, or because she had hidden Shika away from

Gades. He could have wanted revenge for that, but it's sloppy, that's not like him." Evan looked at his watch. "Maybe because Aya knew something she didn't understand, maybe Goddess Shipping and Gades didn't want anyone, especially me, connecting his shipment with that name." He looked pointedly at me, and there was a hint of melancholy in his tone. "Let's hope that's it."

"But"—I was spinning—"Gates told me that he killed the shooter." I looked at Evan for some semblance of logic.

"Yes, and that makes sense." He came to me and took my arms. "If Gades hired the woman shooter, and Aya was his target, then he would have killed the shooter for two reasons: because *she failed,* and because she was a living connection to him."

"Is Aya in danger now?"

As he considered the question, his eyes narrowed and his nostrils flared, then he said, "I don't believe so. Gades has Shika back, and he's got much bigger issues right now with the shipment coming in. I've got to go. Where is Aya?"

Deirdre had come through the kitchen door, and it was she who answered. "She's in the garden, I passed her on my way through from the pool house."

"Balance," I said softly, wishing that I had the calm to follow her example.

"She is not to leave the house today," Evan said. "She needs to stay right here."

I concurred.

Evan kissed me hard and looked into my eyes. "Pier twenty-seven here I come," he said grimly, and then he went out the door, leaving me terribly alone and afraid of that state becoming permanent.

Trying not to cry or let panic overwhelm me, I resorted to casual conversation. "How was your night off, Deirdre?"

"Excellent, thank you," she responded politely as she started to clear away the coffee cups we had all left scattered about. "The showing at the Getty was delightful and most educational, I am very grateful to you for the tickets."

"I'm glad you enjoyed it, I definitely wasn't in the mood." Now I came to the difficult part of this week's job description. "Uh, Deirdre?"

"Yes, ma'am?" She turned, politely attentive.

"We, um, had a little situation in the garage, well, to be frank and get to the point, we had a body in the garage, and although Evan had a cleanup crew come in, you may find a few . . . distasteful remnants."

One of her dark brown well-defined eyebrows went up, and though she did not comment, there would be no question of my not offering further explanation. She was responsible for the rest of the staff, and her personal safety was at stake.

"God willing, Evan is going to put an end to all of this ugliness today. We didn't know the victim personally, he seems to have been one of the bit players in the South American storyline of our current drama."

"Overplayed his part?" Her taste in humor ran toward the dry.

"Apparently so. Anyway, he 'got the hook,' as we say in vaudeville," I told her. She arched that brow higher still and I hastened to add, "Not by me. I was, thankfully, not home at the time. We think it was someone looking for something that Shika had left here. Her room is a horrendous mess, I'm sorry to say."

Deirdre's brows both dropped into a concerned frown and she looked like she was debating whether or not to speak.

"What is it?" I asked her.

"Only that I find the fact that her room was searched interesting." She set down the cups she had held suspended in the air and wiped her hands on her professional white apron. "I had said good-bye yesterday before I realized that the tickets you had given me were still on your dresser, so I came back in and went up the kitchen stairs. And as I passed Ms. Shika's room, I noticed Ms. Aya looking through her friend's things."

Confused, I asked the obvious question. "Did she see you?"

"No. I assumed it would cause her considerable embarrassment if she were to realize that I had observed her, so I went on my way—very quietly."

And Deirdre could be absolutely silent, that I knew firsthand. She worked hard at being unobtrusive and was successful to the point of being damn near invisible.

"What do you think she was looking for?" I asked her, annoyed now at being left ignorant of the details in my household.

"I don't know. I remember thinking that perhaps Shika had borrowed something of hers, or . . ."

"What?" I pressed. Evan had told me many times that no detail was unimportant.

"I thought maybe she just missed her friend and wanted something to hold on to that was hers." Deirdre looked empathetic.

"Was she wrecking the room?" I inquired, the answer to that was so important. If it was Aya who had turned that room upside down then everything else Evan had deduced was wrong. And a wrong guess could cost him his life.

"No, not at all. The room looked very neat, and it seemed she was being most discreet and careful to leave things undisturbed."

So someone else had gone through the room after her; that was something. But my blood had already started to boil. I wanted to know what the hell was going on.

I looked at Deirdre, and she flinched slightly at the ferocity of my gaze.

"Where exactly is Aya in the garden?"

Chapter 42

I found her by the fern garden fountain, her eyes open but with a distant expression in them, as though she was far from the sparkling water she regarded. Before I spoke she turned and smiled at me. "Good morning, Callaway."

"Good morning," I responded and seated myself on a stone bench near where she sat cross-legged on the ground. I knew if I tried to be subtle or polite I would fumble, and there was too much at stake for me to drop the ball.

"Aya, why didn't you tell us that you were looking through Shika's things yesterday?" I kept the anger out of my tone, but it brooked no argument; I wanted an answer.

I had expected her to flinch, to look away, to react in a guilty manner, but she remained calm.

"I didn't think it was important," she said, looking sheepishly up at me. "I'm sorry if you think I deceived you, and I know that I shouldn't have invaded her privacy, but I thought . . . I was hoping to find something that would help us to get her back. I found nothing, or I would have told you."

She may have been waiting for a response, but I held my tongue and watched as Aya's eyes filled with tears. "I understand how afraid she is, now. When she first came back, I was very hard on her. I didn't realize how desperately lonely she was and how that man had made use of her pain. She needed a friend, and I judged her harshly, but you have shown me how to be kind to someone who very much needed kindness, and patience, and an ally." She still held my gaze, and though pain and hurt passed just below the surface of her eyes, it barely made a ripple on her face. "I am ashamed. I could have helped her, but instead I made her path more difficult. Even to the extent that I wished she would be punished." She seemed to be fighting a desperate battle to stay in control.

My suspicions melted away into the cold stone as she explained her motivations.

"If I had found anything, I would have come to you immediately." She sighed, and the last part of the breath took on a musical hum broken with emotion. "I didn't really know what I was looking for, I was hoping for an address book, or phone numbers, something. There was a plastic file holder with papers, bank statements, some mail, and a small key to a jewelry box, but it all looked normal to me." She dropped her head, dispiritedly. "I should have told you yesterday that I'd looked and found nothing, of course I should have thought to do that, but I felt ashamed to have been snooping."

"Bank statements?" My brain was searching.

"And an empty envelope from a bank in the Canary Islands, but with no letter inside."

Stumbling around in the pitch-dark, the beam of my flashlight found a target; it started to come to me. "He's using her as a mule," I said.

"A what?" Aya looked confused.

"It's possible that Gades, knowing he is constantly watched, is sending Shika to set up numbered accounts to hide his money. You told me she'd been traveling, right?"

"Yes, but I'm not exactly sure where."

"I think we can guess one place; the Canary Islands are outside U.S. government supervision, and since there are no names on the accounts, it's almost impossible to trace them."

"So what did the man who"—her voice fell off momentarily—"the man you found yesterday, what did he want?"

"The bank account numbers, maybe, but Gades should have those if he set them up." I thought about it. He would certainly have those numbers somewhere else. Even if he was afraid of arrest and confiscation of records, it wasn't that hard to write down a list of numbers somewhere, coded perhaps.

But there was one thing. "Could it have been a safe-deposit box key that you saw?" I said out loud.

Aya looked enlightened. "I hadn't thought of that."

"Yes, if they kept those account numbers and records in a safe-deposit box in Shika's name, then it would be dangerous for him to keep the key, in case federal agents impounded his belongings. A safe-deposit box key would almost certainly be recognized and could possibly be traced, though I'm not sure how traceable they are." I hummed a low note to accompany the quickening of my brain. "*That* would fall under jurisdiction in this country, and if the feds got their hands on his account numbers that would pretty much finish him." I added the theories together. "And if the box was in her name, he would need her back, badly."

Aya's realization had turned to vexation. "I didn't think of that. I should have told you earlier . . ."

"Don't beat yourself up, you wouldn't have known what it was anyway, it's not like they left it tagged with the bank name and address."

"What can we do?" Aya asked.

I sighed again. "Nothing. I'll tell Evan later, but I don't see how it could help him right now. If he's lucky enough to arrest Gades today, Shika should be close by, and he can deal with our brilliant deductions then." I shared a smile with Aya. "Although, I have to warn you, Watson, that most of the time when I think I've come up with a genius observation, he's already thought of it."

"What will happen to her?" Aya's face clouded.

I reached out and took her hand, trying to connect again. "I don't know, but I do know from experience that there is much Evan can do to help someone when he feels there are extenuating circumstances. And I know he thinks there are in this case." I patted Aya's hand. "I think so too, and I also think that you should forgive yourself as well as her; you never meant her ill, I know that."

She gazed across a thousand miles and into my eyes. "No," she said after a long pause, "I never did." She stood fluidly, assuming the same perfectly relaxed posture standing as she had when sitting in meditation. When she spoke it was distant and dreamlike. "But what if she dies today?" she asked softly. "Or tomorrow?" The questions hung between us, apparitions of possibility too frightening to consider directly. She drew a sharp breath that brought us both back to the present. She smiled sympathetically at me. "It can't be easy for you to wait here for the man you love."

"It's not." I stood up next to her, the phrase "the man you love" wobbling in my head, bouncing gently off the sides like a rubber ball. We started back toward the house. "I'm going to stay close to the phone and try not to run screaming through the house."

Aya cocked her head to one side thoughtfully. "Maybe you should," she suggested.

I laughed. "It might help." We both laughed, but the humor quickly died back into solemn silence.

We parted without words, only a mutual look of concern. Aya headed up to her room while I floated aimlessly back to the kitchen.

"Perhaps some tea." Deirdre had moved on cat feet into the kitchen behind me; her voice was as soothing as the suggestion.

"Tea always helps," I said. "Will you join me?"

"Certainly." My butler spoke without hesitation, breeching the etiquette that always stood comfortably between us. There were times in women's lives when formalities must be dropped, when we stand next to each other not as employer and employee, or with any social boundaries between us, but as compassionate women, and we both recognized this as one of those moments.

We were just pouring the steaming cuppa' when Ginny came in. Though she would have dismissed such a notion as "sentimental woman shit," I knew she had turned down work today to wait with me, to be supportive. Deirdre made a move to stand and serve, but I waved her back down.

"Yeah, Dee-dee, at ease," Ginny told her as she got herself a cup off the shelf. "Hang with us."

"Thank you, Miss Virginia," Deirdre responded, using Ginny's formal name as a quiet commentary on Ginny's Americanizing her own.

If Ginny noticed, she let it slide by. "So what's up?"

I filled her in on what Aya had said, and Evan's speculation that the bullets in San Francisco might have been meant for her. Ginny wanted to know where Aya was now and if she was safe, so I told her that Evan seemed to think she should stay here and that would be a safe enough place to be.

Deirdre cleared her throat. "There was someone enquiring about Miss Aya yesterday, outside the gate," she said, looking as though she thought perhaps she should have told me this before. "He drove up just as I was leaving in the morning."

"What did you tell him?" Ginny asked.

"That I did not know of any such person, and that she was not in residence here, as Detective Paley had instructed us all to say."

"What did he look like?" Ginny persisted.

"Dark, Latino possibly, quite handsome, well dressed in a light suede jacket and a dark blue shirt open at the collar, driving a black Expedition. His hair was longish, wavy, he was in his late thirties, I would say."

Ginny looked to me.

At the risk of a bad pun, I said, "He sounds like a dead ringer."

"For whom?" Deirdre wanted to know.

"The corpse in the garage," I answered. "And he was looking for Aya?"

"Yes," Deirdre exclaimed. "I see now that I should have notified you immediately, but I did not like to interrupt your private time with Detective Paley, and the man thanked me so politely, said that he must have been mistaken, and drove away."

"And then you left, right then." Suddenly something occured to me, and it scared me. "Oh my God, Aya was still in the house?"

Deirdre looked up at me. "Yes, she was."

"He obviously came back later," Ginny filled in the chronology, "after she had left, thank the Lord, and so did someone else. One of them searched Shika's room to look for something, but maybe this guy was sent to kill Aya and *then* get whatever it was they wanted."

I was getting frightened. "And if Gades sent someone to try to kill Aya yesterday, is she safe today?"

"Let's keep her with us." Ginny took a quick sip of her tea, pushing her chair back as she stood. But even as she did I heard the sound of a car driving away from the parking area and down the driveway. I went to the window but could see nothing.

"Was someone running errands?" I asked Deirdre on my way to the garage door. She said she didn't know, but when I peered into the long room, one car space was empty. The blue sedan was gone.

We went quickly through the entrance hall, up the stairs, and to Aya's room. We knocked and waited, but there was no answer. I pushed open the door and called out. But she was gone. On the neatly made bed was a single leaf of paper and the words: "Don't worry about me, I've gone to the temple to pray for Shika and Evan."

"Ginny, when I went to the temple last time, there were two men hanging around, maybe they followed her there, maybe they know she goes there . . ."

"Maybe they're there now," Ginny said, finishing my thought.

We hurried back downstairs, and Ginny gathered up her keys and jacket as she spoke. "And here I thought I was going to have a quiet, incredibly stressful afternoon, but no, I'm going to have a frenetic, incredibly stressful afternoon." She sighed. "Well, at least it's not boring."

I joined her at the garage door. "Deirdre, stay by the phone, if you hear anything, call my cell."

"Of course." She nodded efficiently.

"What about Sabrina?" Ginny punctuated the trouble spot. "She's always so helpful in these situations."

"You know what? You're right. We really need to include her in this." I turned to Deirdre. "Have you got a shopping bag?"

She pulled one out from beneath the sink and handed it over; since we'd be gone a while and Sabrina loves to snack, I filled it with fruit from the bowl on the counter, some cheese and luncheon meats from the fridge, and a small loaf of French bread.

"How about the house keys?" Deirdre pulled at a cord, and a large ring of keys emerged from her apron, varying in size from tiny to the heavy old-fashioned type. "Thanks," I said and went up the back stairs.

Knocking on the door to Sabrina's suite I called out, "Sabrina?" She answered with an invitation to enter, and I stuck my head in.

She was getting dressed. "Hi, is Evan gone already? Is there anything I can do? I feel like I need to help do something," she gushed.

"You can." I advanced into the room, set the bag down, and looked around. The terrace doors were open, and it was a long way down to the garden below. "Do you have a good book?" I inquired seriously.

"Uh, yeah, I started a really good novel about this pirate who's in love with two sisters, but you don't usually like my kind of books . . ." She broke off her explanation of her latest romance novel to ask a confused, "Why?"

"Could you wait here a minute, I'll be right back." Exiting back into the hallway, I closed her door, found the key to her suite, marked with a yellow tag to match the decor, and turned it in the lock. Then I crossed my arms and waited.

As I expected, it was less than ten seconds before I heard her try to open the door. Then she called out loudly, "Callaway! I think I'm locked in!"

I answered in a normal voice, since I was standing just on the other side of the door, "I know, I locked it. Ginny and I have to go out for a while, I left you some snacks in the bag. I'll tell Deirdre to let you out for dinner. Get some studying done."

Turning and walking away I could hear her slamming her palm against the heavy wood and her muffled objections. "You let me out, this isn't fair, I won't do anything, I promise!" And then I was out of earshot.

Ginny and I drove downtown and parked on the main street right in front of the temple, but try as we might we couldn't find Aya, or the blue sedan. No one seemed to have seen her there that day.

Fear was starting to creep up from deep inside my gut.

"Where could she be?" I felt like beating my head against the car window. Frustration and impotence were forcing my stress level up several rungs on a very rickety ladder. Ginny sat staring straight ahead.

"She's been driving one of your cars," she stated.

"Yes, the blue sedan. I told you that," I shot at her. It wasn't her fault, but at this point my temper had a diminutive fuse.

"Teletrac," Ginny said.

"Tell-a-who?" I was already snappy, and incomplete sentences were definitely high-risk.

"Teletrac her. You've got it on all your cars, they'll tell you exactly where she is, or where the car is anyway."

Amazement rinsed all the curt impatience right out of my attitude. "Brilliant! Why didn't I think of that? It's so obvious."

Ginny just cleared her throat and looked at me sarcastically. She didn't speak; she didn't have to.

"Don't push me," I told her. "I'm only temporarily in a better mood."

It took about five minutes for me to reach the company, identify myself, and for them to track the car. It was on the 110, heading south.

"That's the Harbor Freeway," I muttered. "What in the hell could she . . ."

Ginny and I both looked up and said it together: "San Pedro."

"Shit!" Ginny said. "She thinks she's going to go save Shika, doesn't she?" She shook her head forcibly. "She's worse than Sabrina."

"She feels so guilty about this whole thing," I told Ginny, "she keeps saying that everything is her fault. But what does she think she's going to do? Take on an entire Colombian drug ring single-handed?"

"This is one of those damn Japanese 'debt of honor' things isn't it?" Ginny continued, without really answering me. "I bet she thinks she's got to give her life for Shika's or some shit like that."

"When I met her, she said that when you save someone's life, you become responsible for them." I remembered Aya laughing it off, saying that dinner and a massage would do instead. "But she didn't seem to take it *that* seriously."

Strange though, I did feel a certain sense of responsibility for Aya, I felt *invested* in her. Not just because I had saved her life that first day, but also because emotionally she had trusted me.

I tried to reach Evan's cell phone, but his message came on without a ring; he had turned it off.

"Damn, I can't get through," I said.

Ginny looked at me; we were still in the parked car on the side of the street. I was in the driver's seat.

"Get out," Ginny said and opened her car door. She came around to my side and met me as I climbed out.

"What are we doing?" I asked her as she dropped herself in front of the wheel.

"Get in," she told me now. So I went around to the passenger side and got in. "Buckle up for safety." She smiled that slightly wicked smile she gets when she's about to do something incredibly dangerous and enjoy doing it.

"Oh shit," I said and fastened my seat belt, pulling it tight across my chest.

Ginny stunt drives for a living, and I had a feeling we were about to make the one-hour drive to San Pedro in well under half that time.

I kept trying to reach Evan, but no luck; mostly I clutched the armrest with white knuckles and tried not to imagine what would happen to us if Ginny were to make a mistake at 120 miles an hour.

How we managed to get to the port without being arrested or dying in a fiery crash, I'll never know. How Ginny talked us through the security gate remains a mystery to me. She said something about scouting for a movie location, and when the guard was resistant, she told him he had a great look and would be perfect for this small part in the film; he gave her his home phone number, a pass, and a big smile.

We were in. I couldn't believe it. I called Teletrac again, and they gave me a more precise location on the car—it was nowhere near pier twenty-seven. The port is a massive place, and my borrowed car was parked at least a mile from where the action would be going down. That was a relief to us. Although Aya had been sitting next to me when Evan had told us the pier number, she didn't seem to have a very specific idea of where it was. Hopefully that would keep her out of trouble, and out of the way.

"It's almost two-thirty," I told Ginny. "I wonder if the ship is in."

"We could go back and ask Fred," Ginny said. "But he might get a little suspicious."

I supposed Fred was the name of guy in the guard gate; I'd been too wrecked with stress to register his moniker when she'd been conning him. "No, let's just see if we can find Aya and get her out of here."

"Short-term goals. Good, I like that." Ginny drove slowly down the access road where giant cranes loomed up on our left, some of them moving like massive mechanical spiders, easily lifting the containers and placing them onto the bases of eighteen-wheelers.

"This is awesome," Ginny said. "Jeez, how in the hell can any organization keep track of what comes in and out of here?"

"I think that's the point," I speculated. "They can't. I think it's only by sheer luck that they catch the small percentage that they do. Or with inside information, which, let's pray, works for Evan today."

"Amen." Ginny didn't look at me; she was watching for the car. "There it is." She said as she spotted it parked in front of a warehouse.

Aya wasn't in the vehicle. I hadn't really expected that she would be. We parked next to the car and got out.

"Where should we start?" I was looking around.

"I have no idea," Ginny said. "But it looks like we're going for a long walk. She could be anywhere, this place is titanic."

"Nice reference. Let's just ask in here if anyone has seen her." I gestured to the building next to us. We went up to the rusty metal door and peered in through the cracked and cloudy window. It was dark and cluttered by the doorway, but beyond that it was easy to sense that the space was vast. There was light from factory-type windows set high up in the side of the corrugated steel walls.

We snaked our way through crates and boxes until we came to the main area; a concrete floor that stretched in front of us for at least a hundred feet.

I opened my mouth to speak but before anything came out a hand slapped over it and I was yanked backward, stifling a muffled scream before I realized it was Ginny who had silenced me.

She kept her hand over my mouth until I got a good dose of her warning look, and then, releasing me, she pointed across the open floor to the far side of the warehouse.

Two people stood in a cross-hatched shaft of light from the high windows. The dust in the air gave the light a solid shape from its entrance into the building all the way to its rectangular outline on the floor.

They stood rigidly, a man and a woman. When my heart stopped playing percussion in my eardrums I could hear that they were speaking in low angry tones. Ginny and I moved as close as possible to the edge of the open floor, squeezing between the maze of crates until we found a vantage point. The two seemed so intent on their argument that they hadn't noticed us, and we had entered the building wary of what and who was in it.

There was a glow of strangeness about them because of the

distance and the contrasts of dark and light in the building, but even with that, even with the element of disbelief that time-delayed my thought processing, it was quickly apparent who they were. We had found Aya.

And so had Korosu.

Chapter 43

She was facing him defiantly, and he was doing most of the talking. I strained to hear them, cupping a hand behind one ear, but found I could only make out fragments of the conversation.

I thought I heard a bitter laugh from Aya that seemed to cause an angry onslaught from Korosu, which was in Japanese, so I couldn't make out anything.

Glancing at Ginny I turned my hands up in a silent question. What can we do? She shrugged slightly, but her eyes were darting around, looking for a way to move in closer without being seen.

Aya turned her back and made a move to walk away from him. That's when Korosu drew a gun. I cursed under my breath and braced myself to do something, create a distraction, charge out into the open space, anything.

Aya turned back and saw the gun, she screamed at Korosu in Japanese and he retorted quickly, and then a strong male voice rang out from the darkness on the far side of the warehouse directly across from us. Both of their heads snapped in that direction.

"Oh no. I'm afraid I cannot allow you to hurt each other, not yet anyway." Out of the shadows and into the fuzzy light stepped an impeccably dressed Gades, closely followed by two of his men, each of whom held a gun, casually lethal, in their hands at their sides.

Korosu recovered first. "Antonio, I might have known you would show up."

Gades stopped next to a crate, leaned an elbow on it, and spoke as casually as if he were gossiping with friends. "I seem to have misplaced something valuable. At first I thought all the port authority officials swarming around like the busy little worker bees they are had found it, but it became apparent that they couldn't find it either."

He looked back at his men, as if asking them to back up his story. "Could they?" he demanded.

"No, not on the ship," said one of the men with a heavy Spanish accent.

"See?" Gades turned back to the others. "And that started me thinking." He advanced again, toward Korosu. I was mesmerized by the power and confidence of him, walking straight to a man with a pistol in his hand and asking him simply, "Your gun please."

Korosu handed it over. Gades stepped back and set it on top of the crate before propping himself against it again. "Yes, I started to wonder where my cocaine was. And I remembered an associate of mine about whom I entertained doubts." Gades put a hand on the back of his own neck and massaged, as though to relieve the stress that was there, but he didn't look stressed at all, he looked relaxed.

"His name was Leon," Gades continued. "Unfortunately, he died suddenly in an accident involving a certain young lady. And I remember asking myself at the time, What could he have wanted with her?"

I looked at Ginny. What kind of a game was this? Hadn't Gades sent Leon to find out where Shika was?

"But you were very beautiful, and many men wanted something to do with you," Gades said to Aya, "so I let that go. I see now that it was a mistake to do so."

Gades started to move forward again, toward Aya and Korosu, who had not moved or spoken since Gades had begun.

"So, I started to think about where my product went, because I knew that it left Colombia, I was there to see it off. But where did it go?"

"I had some help from you for a while," Gades said to Korosu. "Without your knowledge or permission, it's true. Nonetheless your import business was most eager to take on my 'legitimate' shipments of fixtures just as long as my 'legitimate' associates made the arrangements." Gades put his hands in his pockets and shook his head. "But, when I came to you with a direct proposition, you wouldn't be reasonable." He looked disappointed in Korosu, who for his part did not take his eyes off of Gades; even from my hiding place I could feel the intensity of his look.

Gades shook his head again. "Too bad, it could have been the beginning of a beautiful friendship." He laughed at that, a little criminal humor. "So, now, I find out the reason." Gades's voice took on a harder note. "You have decided to go into business for yourself, but . . ." He paused and let that hang, then said, "You made a mistake. It wasn't hard to figure it out. Leon made all my shipping arrangements, but unfortunately, I couldn't ask a dead man what had happened to it. However, the sailors on my payroll are alive and well. You had the shipment transferred at sea to another boat." Gades chuckled in spite of himself. "Actually, very clever, I congratulate you." He nodded and then grew very still and did not speak for a long minute. Everyone stood, right where they were, Gades and Korosu locked in eye contact, Aya's eyes riveted on the floor between them.

Finally Gades spoke. It was a low growling demand. "Tell me where the shipment is," he ordered. "I want the name of the ship you had it transferred to and the dock number, or . . ." He shifted his gaze to Aya. "I'll kill her."

"No!" came a woman's voice from the same shadows Gades and his men had emerged from. Into the light stepped Shika. "You promised me that you wouldn't hurt them."

Aya's eyes came up for the first time, and her face looked shocked. Gades spun around but recovered quickly. "I asked you to stay in the car." He sounded gently reprimanding, not angry.

"I wanted to be with you," she said to him.

Gades acquiesced after a long look then turned back to Aya and Korosu. "It was quite by coincidence that we spotted you coming in here," he said, "luck. But I suppose the odds were good, since there were so many of my employees on the docks today."

Ginny and I both glanced behind us nervously, as though some of those "employees" might be sneaking up on us, but we seemed to have this side of the building to ourselves. We both turned our attention back to the action on the far side.

"Nevertheless," Gades continued, "I need the name of the ship." He spoke politely and looked from Aya to Korosu. "Please?"

Korosu spoke now for the first time. "You will never find that shipment."

"Ah." Gades nodded more slowly, thoughtfully regarding the two of them. "I was afraid of this." He crossed to Korosu until he was just in front of him. Korosu was a couple of inches shorter than Gades, but the strength of the two of them in full power could have caused spontaneous combustion. "You can't have it," Gades said to Korosu. "It's mine."

"You won't find it," Korosu repeated, and then Gades struck him across the face so fast I never saw him raise his hand. Korosu didn't so much as turn his head, but he didn't block the blow or strike back either. Gades's men brought their guns up but didn't move forward. Shika's hands flew up to her mouth.

"I will find it," Gades said to him. "Make no mistake about that. You can choose how. Easily or painfully, but you will tell me."

A shrill obnoxious electronic musical scale pierced the tense silence of the next moment, followed by a recorded female voice saying, "You have an incoming call, you have an incoming call."

Every head spun in our exact direction. Ginny grabbed me as I fumbled in my bag to find the damn phone, to hit a button, any button that would silence it. Gades's men crossed the space in far less time than it took Ginny to pull me through the maze of boxes toward the door; they beat us there, blocking our exit.

I had silenced the phone by pressing the TALK button, the readout on the tiny screen said BOYFRIEND. It was in my hand. One of the two heavies pushed Ginny and me ahead of them, and we moved out into the open. When the others saw us they each had a distinct and individual reaction. Aya looked frightened, Korosu narrowed his eyes angrily, Shika gasped, and Gades laughed. He *laughed.*

"My, my, Callaway Wilde. You are a woman of many surprises. Thank you for joining us. How did you find us?"

I looked at Aya. "I Teletracked the car," I said, far too loudly. My voice echoed, and I prayed it would carry to the tiny speaker on the phone in my hand.

He crossed to Ginny. "I remember you from the golf course, but I don't believe we've been formally introduced."

"This is my friend Virginia."

"No introduction necessary," said Ginny to Gades. "Your reputation precedes you," she added pleasantly, as though it were a compliment.

"The courageous Virginia. I'm charmed."

"Likewise, I'm sure," Ginny said flatly and turned to Korosu and Aya, "Hi guys, fancy meeting you here." She looked around the whole place and then back to them. "Small world, huh?"

"Very small," Gades agreed, amused by her nonchalance. "And this solves a little problem of mine."

"What would that be?" I asked, adopting Ginny's conversational tone.

"I did promise Shika that I wouldn't hurt Aya." He smiled at Shika, and she returned the expression, before he turned back to us. "But I didn't promise I wouldn't hurt one of you." As he finished the sentence he cut his eyes to Korosu. Now Aya's hand came up to her chest, as though a band had tightened across it and she couldn't breathe. I know all the air had been sucked instantly out of my lungs.

At a nod from Gades, I felt one of his men take my arm and twist it skillfully behind my back, bringing me to my knees. The cell phone clattered to the ground, and the battery was knocked off the back. From the corner of my eye I saw Ginny drop in the same manner. Then I felt the cold barrel of a gun pressed against my temple.

Gades hadn't taken his eyes off of Korosu. "Tell me the name of the ship and everything else you know."

Korosu was watching Gades closely, but his eyes flashed to me quickly; I was stunned at the pain in them. "I can't," he said and then he looked at Aya.

"Let's do this slowly, because I hate to have to kill them both right off." Still without turning he nodded curtly again, and the barrel of the gun was placed against the back of my knee. I closed my eyes, and a wave of nausea threatened to overwhelm me; this was going to hurt like a mother.

At the same time three voices shouted "No." Ginny, Aya, and Shika had called out as one, but it was Aya who continued. "He can't tell you!" she stressed.

"Oh, but he can, and he will," said Gades, beckoning to his hired gun. I shut my eyes and tried to consciously let go of my body, to let the agony of the bullet shattering bone, when it came, belong to someone else.

"No he can't," Aya said quickly, then faltered, paused, and said more slowly, "because he doesn't know." I opened my eyes again and wavered on the edge of collapse.

Very slowly, Gades turned his gaze to Aya. He took two steps forward until he was looking down at her. Her body was quivering, but she held his gaze.

"Could it be?" His voice was filled with amazement, admiration even.

"I moved the shipment," Aya said, in a diminutive but steady voice. "Leon was your supposed legitimate business connection. I met him when he came to conduct the transactions with Korosu. He knew how to move the shipment, and he helped me do it, then he got scared, and wanted to back out."

The pain came, but not in my leg, it landed deep in my heart as I realized that Aya was speaking the truth. Like a cannonball the thought hurled through my brain and exploded on impact: *she came to us, she set Evan on the wrong track, she gave us all the information we had about everyone else.*

"So you had him killed?" Gades asked, as though he was inquiring about the soup of the day.

"No," she said firmly. "He became angry and careless, and he ended up dead."

"Ah, death by police, I think that's called." Gades nodded thoughtfully, as the memory of my bullet entering Leon's forehead smashed up against the other thoughts hurtling through my head. *Aya set that up?* He added, "No good can come from crossing me, that's just not a safe thing to do." The comment was directed at Aya, and I could see from her face that the death threat had landed like an anvil on her heart.

He raised his hand, and she flinched, but instead of striking her, he stroked her face. "My Aya, my beauty, I know you were hurt when it didn't work out between us."

Aya's face went to that cold faraway place as she answered, "You chose Shika, and discarded me." Tears started to run down her face, but she did not blink or so much as flicker a facial muscle; it was disturbing to watch. "She helped me, little fool that she is, by giving me information she didn't understand at all." Aya turned her face to the younger girl, the tears still flowing from a dead face. "Your puppet. I swore that I would never be treated that way again by a man, by anyone; I would have my own money and my own power." She paused for a moment and lifted her shoulders in a vague detached shrug. "Or I would die." She turned back to Gades. "So I am ready, I accept death." She bowed her head, not to him, but to fate.

Gades sighed and shook his head. "Not yet you won't," he said coldly and gestured to the man holding Ginny. "I still need to know where my shipment is." Ginny's assailant leaned over just behind where she was kneeling and pressed the muzzle of his gun to her cheek, lining his face up six inches from the back of her head.

I could have told him that was a mistake.

Ginny snapped her head back hard enough to break through a two-by-four, and I heard an ugly smacking hollow sound as the henchman reeled back and hit the ground, blood pouring from his broken nose. I felt the man holding me twist to see what was happening, and Korosu flew at him, his arm swinging just over me to catch my captor full in the face. Ginny was on the man's gun arm before he had even a second to recover, and she bit down hard on the back of his hand; the man yowled and released his gun. Korosu had knocked the other man unconscious and was leaning to retrieve his weapon when we heard Aya scream.

"Don't touch it!" She had snatched up Korosu's gun, left lying on the crate, and was holding it pointed at Shika. Gades seemed not to have moved at all during the scuffle, and he regarded her calmly as Korosu and Ginny both ceased reaching for the other weapons belonging to the two incapacitated men.

"You're not going to fire that," Gades said serenely. "You've been very clever and you almost got away with stealing from me, although I would have found you eventually, but you are not a killer."

"No?" Aya asked him, equally calm. "Are you sure?"

For the first time, Gades looked doubtful. He pursed his mouth slightly and let his head drop down, as though he was suddenly very sad. "José," he said, heavily. "You killed José."

"Yes. I did. Right there in Callaway's garage." Aya's tone became angry, "He wouldn't take me seriously either. I think he feels differently now." Aya's laugh that followed was teetering on the edge of hysteria, and my heart wrenched at the sound of it. I had heard that laugh before, in my tub when we had talked about my theory of dealing with people who would never understand us. "Fuck them" I had told her, "and learn to enjoy it." I shivered, she had had all this planned and in operation even then, and I had unwittingly encouraged her.

"One thing I would like to know," Gades said, then he smiled and laughed himself. "Several things actually: for instance, does your plan include some kind of backup for this situation? Will we all be joining José?" He let that float, making it sound less like a lurking fear and more like a reminder of how difficult it would be to execute while he nailed Aya with a doubtful look. The barrel of her gun shook almost imperceptibly and then steadied.

It was quiet for a moment while we all considered that question as well as our own mortality. I had landed in an awkward position, and the concrete was digging into my hip and elbow, but I didn't dare move or shift my weight.

"Don't you know?" Gades was challenging now.

Next to me, Ginny muttered something about "the best laid plans."

Shika spoke now, her voice trembling with fear and shock. "Forgive me, I didn't know how much I had hurt you, Aya."

Aya shouted at her two quick words in Japanese. Sounded a lot like "shut up" to me. Whatever it was, it only silenced Shika for a moment. She started speaking again. "Please, let them go."

She was still moving forward and looked utterly devastated. "No more killing. Please, no more. Forgive me."

"You can't have my forgiveness," Aya said through gritted teeth. "I will die today because I failed, and I will not face the dishonor of prison, and he"—she wagged the gun at Gades—"is going with me."

What happened next happened so fast I saw it as several different images simultaneously. Shika's face turned red with anger, and she rushed forward as Aya pointed the gun directly at her and squeezed the trigger. Korosu lunged toward Aya, but the gun flared as he made contact and struck her hand down. At the same moment, Gades stepped to his right, between Shika and the barrel of the gun.

In the ringing silence following the echo of the blast in that resonant space everyone was still. Gades still faced Aya, who stood with her hands locked down by Korosu, Shika was behind Gades, frozen by the gunfire, Ginny and I seemed as unconscious and ineffectual as the two men who lay on the floor.

And then Gades dropped to his knees and looked down at his chest; just inside his right shoulder a dark flow of blood began. Shika screamed and ran forward. He grabbed her arm and looked into her eyes. She took his face in her hands and held it tightly for a moment as she whispered, "Hold on, husband," before she ripped off her shirt and pressed it hard against the wound while encouraging him to lay still. I looked from them to Ginny, who mouthed, "husband?" at me while the thought "they're married?" was ping-ponging against the inside of my skull.

Korosu moved next, twisting the gun easily out of Aya's hand. Too late I heard a movement from the far side of Ginny, the henchman had retrieved his gun while we were all riveted on the drama in front of us, and as he rose he brought the gun up, aiming it at Korosu, who was turned away, his attention on Aya.

"Korosu!" I shouted. He spun around, bringing the gun up, but before it was level, a shot rang out from behind him, and the henchman crumpled to the ground. From the shadows behind Korosu Evan emerged. As the shot from his gun was still reverberating in our ears, he called out sharply.

Suddenly there was noise and movement seemingly from everywhere.

Evan gave quick orders for everyone to be disarmed and handcuffed, told another officer to call an ambulance, and came straight to me.

I was never so glad to see him. "What took you so long?" I asked.

"Well, it took me a minute to figure out your clue and get your car traced." He smiled at me fondly. "That was very smart."

"You told me once that to be really sexy, a woman had to be smart."

"Well I would say leaving your phone on when I called and shouting out the information about Teletrac falls under the you-rock-my-world category."

"How nice of you to say," I managed and then treated myself to a moment of dissolving into relieved tears.

Ginny was not going to be left out of that category herself. "Hey! I'm the one who thought of tracking the car to start out with."

"And I owe you big time for that, Miss Ginny." Evan hugged her with one arm so that he wouldn't have to let go of me. Curtis came up beside us; he was chewing gum and looking completely unruffled, as usual.

"Hey," Ginny said to him casually, not to be outdone.

He looked at the unconscious thug on the ground. "What happened to him?" he asked.

"I gave him a Glasgow kiss," Ginny said with an indifferent shrug.

"Nice work," he said to her, and they high-fived each other. "How's your head?" he asked. She nodded and then looked like she regretted it. "We'll get an ice pack for that." He winked at her, and she smiled as if to say, it's nothing. It was cool competition, but the chemistry between them was so volatile that they were both losing.

One of the port authority officials, somewhat conspicuous because he was wearing a vest with a badge and holding a shotgun, called out to Evan. "Do we book this one?" He was standing next to Korosu.

"No, he's clean." Evan gave one more squeeze, said, "Excuse me ladies, I've got to get back to work," and started to cross the room.

"How do you know?" I asked, trailing after him. "You came too late to hear it all." I was wiping my face dry with my sleeve. Someone extended a hand to me with a scarf in it, a silk scarf with a monogram. Looking up at Korosu, I took it gratefully. Thinking as I did so, that this was probably how Aya got the scarf she left on José. Our eyes met, and though the connection was still strong between us, I hoped my eyes said I was sorry.

Evan explained. "Korosu didn't have anything to do with it. It was Aya who moved the cocaine. I knew that yesterday when I found out Goddess Shipping did business with a certain Leon Samo, and that he had ordered a cargo transfer *after* the ship left Colombia."

That didn't seem conclusive to me, and I opened my mouth to say so when the words froze in transit. Coming toward me, with a shotgun in one hand and a badge on his chest, was the "vagrant" that I had seen twice before.

Evan followed my gaze and chuckled at my amazement. "This is Officer Cage, he's been doing a little research for me."

"I saw you at the temple," I managed to spit out, "and with Korosu. I thought you were working for him."

"Nice to meet you," he said. He had a wonderful smile.

"Get back to work," Evan told him and then said to Ginny and me, "he was tailing Aya, and let me know that she was using the temple to meet her other accomplices. There seem to be more than one of Gades's associates who was willing to make off with his goods. What I wasn't sure of was whether you"—he turned to Korosu—"were involved or not."

Korosu laughed. "I thought he was really homeless. I gave him money to do odd jobs around the hotel."

"That's when he was tailing you, and that's how we found out a few things about you." Evan sounded as though he was disappointed; my head was hurting worse than Ginny's must have been.

"How's he doing?" Evan asked Curtis, jerking his head in Gades's direction, where he lay on the floor with a medic crouching over him.

"He'll live long enough for us to throw his ass in jail." Curtis kept his gruff manner, but he couldn't keep the glint of victory out of his eyes.

Evan looked back to Korosu, and his eyes were cold. "Unfortunately we need evidence to keep him there."

"Well, you've got it now!" I exclaimed, the exhilaration of winning finally coming through to me. "You did it! Aya knows where the shipment is. She can tell you."

Evan's gaze turned to Aya, who sat slumped on the floor, her eyes unseeing. She looked as though she'd unraveled.

"She can't," Evan said. "Because I wasn't the only one who figured out what Aya had done; Korosu did too." He looked at Korosu and shook his head.

Ginny was still a few questions back. "Wait a minute. If you knew the shipment had been transferred, why did you go to pier twenty-seven this morning?"

Evan smiled at her. "I could have been wrong," he said then added, "and if I was right, I needed Aya to think I had bought it so that I could be sure."

"So, where's the cocaine?" I asked, feeling a breeze blow through my brain.

Evan fixed his eyes on Korosu again and said, "Tell me."

Korosu answered with a question. "You already know, don't you?"

A huge sigh came from Evan. "Yes, part of me hoped I was wrong."

Ginny reflected my sentiments exactly as she exclaimed, "Fucking tell us!"

There was a snapping silence for three seconds and then Evan said levelly, "He had it dumped at sea."

This revelation was met with shocked silence, and then a dry laugh from the floor. We all turned and looked at Gades. He was laughing harder and harder, even though it obviously pained him every time it shook his body.

"You know what that means?" He laughed again. "You've got nothing on me." He fell back with an amused but agonized look on his face.

Curtis and Evan looked at each other, looked at Gades, and then looked at each other again, disgusted.

"What about the shooting?" Curtis asked.

"Aya hired the lady sniper," Evan said angrily. "She was never meant to kill anyone, just throw us off. I wondered why a professional with that firepower and a clear shot never hit anything, so I went to some pains to find out. Our informant gave us a perfect description of her."

I could see from the dark look on his face that I didn't want to know how he'd traced that information, and I thought about the blood on his cuff, but I said nothing.

"I wasn't sure at first, but I suspected Aya all along. She was the connection to everything, including us. She needed us to take care of Gades if she was successful, otherwise he would have hunted her down and killed her, that's why she fed me the information about Goddess Shipping, she knew Gades would be there." He looked at the group of people around him, his eyes landing on me. "Didn't you wonder why I let her leave without protection?"

The honest answer was that it had never occurred to me that

she was behind it, but I didn't feel like admitting that. I felt bewildered and out of my league, not a comfortable state of mind for a woman who likes to think she's smart.

Evan crossed over to the two men standing near Aya. "Book her, and let's go down to the station." He turned his attention to the small group around Gades and Shika. "Read them their rights, bring her along, and I'll talk to him at the hospital."

The two men helped Aya get to her feet. I couldn't look directly at her. A kind of sick bile was sticking in my throat when I thought of how I had trusted her, how I'd been drawn in, and I couldn't clear the burning sensation.

Evan walked to Korosu and asked him, "You weren't even responsible for Aya's bruised face were you?"

"No, of course not," Korosu said, affronted, and Evan turned to Aya.

"Did you do it to yourself, or did you ask one of your contacts you met at the temple to do you a favor?" he asked her, but she said nothing. She didn't even look like she'd heard him.

"I'm sorry to have suspected you, but why didn't you come to me?" Evan asked Korosu bitterly. "You've cost me a major arrest that hundreds of law enforcement men and women have spent countless hours on, not to mention endangering their lives." He shook his head disgustedly.

"It's not his fault." Aya's clear voice cut through the background noise of many voices talking in the space.

"What?" Evan turned to her. I still couldn't bring myself to look at her directly.

"It's not his fault." She struggled to a standing position. "He was trying to save me, even after I betrayed him." She looked up at Korosu, and her eyes flickered to life again. "I wanted to blame you. But I was responsible for my own choices, wasn't I?"

Korosu did not speak, but he inclined his head in consent.

She continued boldly. "You always told me I was free to do what I wanted, and you were always kind to me." She dropped her head in the deepest bow she could manage with a man holding her restrained arms behind her.

Korosu spoke to her, and her head raised again. "Forgiveness is freely given. I'm only sorry I couldn't help you sooner."

Tears streaked her face, but the eyes were no longer dead, they were filled with the light of life. "Thank you for trying," she whispered.

Korosu smiled and laid his hand gently on the side of her face, saying, "I haven't stopped trying." He let his hand drop and turned away. The man holding Aya turned her toward the door, and they started to go.

"Wait a minute," I interjected, a light finally going on in my dim gray brain. "Hold on just a minute." Everyone turned to me. "She must have it," I said, the realization infusing my voice with excitement.

"Must have *what?*" Ginny asked, looking confused, but Evan was watching me proudly.

"That's my baby." He smiled broadly and turned to Curtis and the other agents. "I'm with her," he told them.

I'd crossed to Aya, and I looked her in the eye for the first time and asked, "Where is it?"

"Where is what?" Ginny asked insistently.

"The proof," I said simply. "If she killed the man, José, in my garage then she's got it. And you said"—I turned to Evan, who was smiling at me as though I was receiving an Olympic gold medal—"that she needed us to put Gades away if she was successful." It was all crystal clear to me now. "And *if* she was successful, there wouldn't be a shipment to nail on him, so . . ." I moved over in front of her and stood for a moment, then I said quietly, "There must be proof."

Evan beamed. "Yes sir, that's my baby."

Curtis added, "Something that connects him to the shipments and the money, something Shika had, and that's why everybody wanted her."

I looked deep into Aya's eyes. There was no fear there, there was no regret, but deep down a flicker of something spoke back to me, and I saw what it was. Triumph.

"Where is it?" I whispered to her. "I told you once you had to learn to say 'fuck you' and learn to enjoy doing it. Where's the 'fuck you'?"

She smiled ironically and said, "Close to my heart." I reached out and grasped a long black cord that hung around her neck and lifted it off over her head.

From inside her blouse came the single charm that adorned it. Shika let out a suppressed cry, and Gades cursed from the floor. The charm dangled, spinning silver in the glinting sunlight for a moment, before it slowed and revealed itself as the treasure Evan was after, the source of proof that would put Gades away forever.

A safe-deposit box key.

Chapter 44

I only saw Aya once during that interminable afternoon of endless questioning. I was coming out of a small room where I had given a statement to a stenographer and Aya was about to enter. The sight of the lost expression on her face stopped me cold.

She was looking down at the floor, and on her face was a vacuous, disoriented expression. Still graceful and beautiful, she seemed adrift, utterly lost in a sea of law and people who did not understand or care about the defeat she had experienced. I had an idea of the frustration and rage she had experienced in a world where men always regarded her as something less than themselves.

"Aya," I said softly, and she raised her eyes. "All you can do now is tell the truth, help Evan if you can, it will make it easier on you." That was the sum of what I had to say to her.

She looked befuddled, but she nodded once slightly, and then her eyes moved past me, and she was escorted into the room.

I hung my head and let the heaviness weigh on me long enough to experience the searing chill and allow the hurt to begin to pass. Korosu had absolved Aya and offered to continue to pull her back from the dark place to which she had descended. Could I?

"Come on." Ginny was next to me, she'd been waiting for me. "Let's go home."

I didn't see Evan that night or all the next day. He called once, sounding preoccupied and exhausted, to tell me he would probably just go to sleep at his house that night so that he could get some rest.

Feeling ignored and shut out, in spite of my logical deduction that he was being completely reasonable, I hung up the phone and slumped despondently onto my sofa. *Great, the case is over and where is he?*

Sabrina loped into the room and pounced on me.

"I'm gonna get you back for locking me in my room," she said, placing a hand around the top of my knee and squeezing just enough to elicit a ticklish squeal from me.

"Get off!" I laughed, trying to clutch at my morose mood and revel in my own miseries. She'd have none of it.

"Not today, not tomorrow," she drawled, "but one day, when you least expect it: I'll get you!" She smiled devilishly. "And then you'll be sorry you ever messed with Sabrina Valley Wilde."

Now I had to smile; it was the first time I'd heard her use her new name. We'd had it legally changed after discovering we shared a dad. "It's good to see you laughing," I told her.

Cumulous clouds rolled in over the clear blue of her eyes. "I just can't believe what you told me about Shika and Aya. I really liked them."

"Me too," I said gently, seeing moisture form at the base of the clouds in her eyes. "Evan said something about Shika, that she wasn't evil but sort of sad and desperate. I understand that. Between the drug use and being used by a very smart and powerful man, what begins to seem important is very different from what it would be if your influences are good ones."

"But both of them! Is it because of that geisha stuff, you think?" she asked.

"Not necessarily," came a voice from the door. Ginny was on her way into the room. She perched herself on the back of the sofa. "I think it's more the kind of person someone already is going into an experience like that. I mean, supposedly, being a geisha can be very respectable and powerful."

"I think you're right," I added. "I talked to Aya quite a bit, and I was left with the impression that it was her family and their limited expectations of her that hurt her self-esteem far more than anything Korosu or even Gades did to her."

"But what about Shika? I thought she was my friend," Sabrina said sadly.

"I think she was," I said to her truthfully. "She got involved with a bad crowd, but that doesn't mean she didn't really care about you."

"Look," said Ginny, "even in this country women are still struggling to be equal to men, and it's way better here than anywhere else in the world. Hell. In a way, I *admire* Aya for her attempt to take control. It was a fucked-up and utterly wrong way to do it, granted, but she didn't just lay down and get walked over."

As I listened to Ginny I thought of the incredulous looks directed at me by the men I have dealt with in high finance, and I thought of how my blood heated up when they condescended to me. It happened less and less, true, but one good reason for that was how I saw myself. I didn't count on their opinion of me, or their approval, for my self-esteem, not anymore. For Aya, the way she was regarded by others had become everything.

What I said was, "I don't hold being geisha, or in Shika's case training to be geisha, against either one of them. Mostly they dress up very prettily, play an instrument, dance, and act the perfect hostess at parties. So what if they sometimes slept with men and got paid for it? Big fucking deal. I think it's honest."

"It is," Ginny said, knowing what she was talking about, "and it's way better than deceiving a man to get something you want, like these idiot starlets who sleep with producers for parts, to give just one example."

"Or my friend who married that rich old guy for his money and keeps hoping he'll drop dead so she can keep it all," Sabrina contributed.

"Listen," I told them both, "Gades is a very influential man. He played Aya first, and then Shika."

"Aya was sleeping with Gades too?" Sabrina asked, surprised.

"Apparently," I explained. "She said, 'you left me for her' or words to that effect. So obviously they were lovers *before* Shika. That's probably how Shika actually met him, now that I think of it. Aya told me that part of her big-geisha-sister job was to introduce Shika around."

"Oh that sucks," Ginny said.

Sabrina looked scandalized. "So Shika stole her boyfriend?"

I shrugged. "Who knows? The only clear thing is that Gades used both of them to try to get to Korosu, but Gades got his in the end."

"No shit," Ginny pitched in. "If Evan can nail him with the info in the safe-deposit box."

"No, that's not what I mean," I said and smiled at them both. "I mean, *he fell in love with Shika.* He was using her by making her care for him, and he ended up caring for her."

"I still can't believe Shika was married to this bad guy, and she didn't even tell us!" Sabrina was shaking her head.

"Given the situation," I said sagely, "I don't believe I would have told us that either." I laughed, but then my smile faded as I thought of spending another night without Evan.

Sabrina noticed my mood. "What's wrong with you, pickle face?" she asked.

"Do you mean 'sourpuss'?" I corrected.

"Whatever."

"Oh, I'm just feeling sorry for myself," I admitted. "I'm not going to see Evan again tonight."

"Why not?" she wanted to know.

"Because he's tired and he's going to sleep at his house," I pouted. My petulance sounded infantile. I knew it, and I didn't care.

"Well, stupid, go sleep over there with him," she insisted.

"Compromise?" Ginny screamed. "Callaway Wilde, who must be perfect, compromise? Never!"

"Shut up!" I laughed. "And don't call me stupid," I added to Sabrina. "Anyway, what am I supposed to do? I wasn't invited, and it's not like he ever gave me a key." I crossed my arms and sank back into indignant pathos.

"Let's see." Ginny climbed over the back of the sofa and pushed me to one side so she could sit next to me. "What could be a possible solution?" She tapped her forehead twice, then clenched her fists and shook. "Oh, this is so hard."

Sabrina joined in, teaming up with Ginny against me, the little traitor. "I just wonder"—she spoke as if she were on a preschool television series—"*if* she was to call him and tell him she *wanted* to sleep with him if he would say 'no, absolutely not' *or* tell her to come on over? He's always been so mean to her."

"*And* inconsiderate," Ginny nodded, her tone equally Teletubby.

"All right! I get it. But *he* should have asked *me,*" I insisted.

"No." Ginny made a loud buzzer noise. "Wrong. You have to tell him what you need. He told you what he needed, and now you're holding that against him."

"I am not!" I lied. "He's just being thoughtless, and he doesn't care about me."

Ginny and Sabrina looked at each other and then rolled their eyes. Ginny said to her, "She's chicken."

"Okay, all right. Give me the phone."

It rang twice and then Evan picked up. "Paley."

"Hi." I wasn't sure why I felt embarrassed.

"Hi." His voice did the octave change it almost always did when he recognized mine. "What's up?"

"Uh, I was just thinking about our last call and I wondered if you might change your mind." Ginny elbowed me in the ribs. "Ow! Okay, already," I said to her.

"What?" Evan was trying to figure out what I was talking about.

"Not you, me." I took a deep breath. "Actually that's the point of the call: me. I want to see you tonight." I could hear him sigh and came close to nixing the request in favor of the safer emotional retreat, but I forced myself to plunge ahead. "And I know you need to sleep, I understand that, but would it be okay if I, maybe, just came over there and climbed in bed with you? I'll be really quiet."

I could hear the smile in his voice. "That would be great. I'll be there around seven, the gate code is five seven three eight, and I'll tell the housekeeper to leave the front door open when she leaves for the night in case you beat me there."

"Okay. Shall I have Sophie whip up something for us to eat?"

"That would also be wonderful. I'll see you later."

"Great. Okay, bye." I was trying to wipe the crooked toddler smile off my face as I hung up the phone.

Sabrina looked smug, Ginny looked smugger.

"Well, well, well, imagine that," Ginny said to Sabrina as though I weren't in the room, "he didn't hang up on her, and she managed to get what she needed by actually admitting she needed it."

"It's so *weird* how that works," Sabrina chimed in. Magnanimously, I decided not to hate them both. I was feeling too pleased with myself. Rising, I headed toward the entrance hall.

"I'd love to stay and let you gloat," I threw over my shoulder, "but I've got to pack an overnight bag. I'm not allowed to have a drawer at his house, *that* would be too much to hope for."

"Well, don't tell him, for God's sake," Ginny shouted at my back as I kept walking. "You wouldn't want him to be able to work something out with you."

Their peals of laughter followed me into the entrance hall and up the stairs.

Chapter 45

I walked into his house around seven, set the dinner basket down on the kitchen counter, and wandered back out into the entrance hall. There were a few lights left on, for me I supposed, but no sign of Evan or the housekeeper.

Since this was the first time I'd been in his house alone I felt uncomfortable. Where should I wait? I wandered slowly through the living room, the TV den, and the atrium. They were all big and beautifully decorated, but I couldn't get comfortable. I needed to at least give myself the illusion of fitting in, of having a right to be there.

Standing at the bottom of the stairway again I looked up; a light was on down the hall, maybe I would go up and get in the bathtub, or the bed, or make a fire. . . . My shoe heels made a loud clacking sound on the wide marble steps, and I shifted onto my tiptoes to still the invasive noise, asking myself, Why are you trying to be quiet? There's no one here.

The thick carpet in the hallway made me feel less intrusive. I walked slowly down the dimly lit hallway, pausing to admire his framed art along the way, strong charcoal sketches, one Picasso nude. Beautiful. But it was all so separate from me, all so exclusively *his.*

There was only one small lamp on in the master bedroom, but the closet light was lit and the door had been left open. Meditatively, I drifted toward it, drawn to his personal space; that neatly organized piece of his life that didn't hold a space for me.

It was a gorgeous closet—cherry cabinets, suits lined up next to shirts, shoes in rows on shelves; it smelled like him. Taking an armful of shirts I pressed them to my face and inhaled, thinking how much I wanted that smell to be part of my life. I turned away from them, a little despondently. Would I have to ask for entrance into every level of his personal space? Could I?

Turning, I faced the other side of the closet, wood drawers from floor to ceiling, each one labeled neatly with a small, engraved marker. How will he fit me into this? It's already full. I ran my finger over the markers, reading as I went, SOCKS, DRESS SOCKS, UNDERWEAR, HANDKERCHIEFS, CALLAWAY.

What?

I read it again. It still said CALLAWAY.

"Aw." I smiled and felt like crying. He had cleared me a drawer and put my name on it. My pleasure at being thought of was deeply tempered by the size of the gesture. A drawer, just a drawer, it was going to take a long time to inhabit half of his life. I sighed, torn. I know everyone thought of me as the one who had it all, but I was feeling like I was utterly lacking in nerve. To ask for admittance and be refused would take more courage than I possessed. And there was another hard truth revealing itself to me—I wasn't okay with occupying only a tiny place in Evan's life. It wasn't enough. I started to cry, big babyish sobs.

"Callaway?"

I spun around. I must have looked tragically comic, for I could feel the mascara stinging my eyes as it ran down my face.

Evan stood looking at me, perplexed. "Don't you like it?"

"It's just a drawer!" I shouted at him. I couldn't help it, I felt so betrayed, so incapable of dealing with the situation.

He'd grown roots, he didn't move, or sway, his expression was amazement carved in stone.

"I know," I said. "I act like I'm perfect and I couldn't be any further from it, I don't know how to have a relationship, okay, I admit it. I suck at it." I felt desperate, I was making everything worse; I was blowing it. "Well, don't just stand there, say something, tell me how fucked-up I am."

Evan inhaled suddenly, and I realized that he hadn't breathed during my tantrum. He took a second deeper breath and then smiled, his eyes beamed at me, at all my juvenile insanity, at my face streaked with makeup, at my flawed, flailing self. "God, I love you," he said with all his heart.

That snapped me out of it. I was so shocked I stopped crying and feeling pitiful and gazed at him disbelievingly.

"What?" I asked, stunned. "Look at me! How can you love this?"

His laugh rang out in the closet and was absorbed into the fabrics of his clothes and our bodies. I felt it and had to laugh too. I had to laugh at myself.

"Well," I said, smiling but self-conscious now, "I mean, it's just a drawer, and I wanted to feel . . ."

"Open it," he said. And when I looked at him confused, he crossed to me and pulled the drawer himself. It slid silently.

One of the lights from above shone directly into the space, and I screamed.

The drawer wasn't empty. It held a box that sat with the lid flipped up, and the box held a ring. A magnificent yellow heart-shaped diamond, at least seven carats, sparkled up at me like a granted wish.

While I was still gasping for breath, Evan moved beside me and took my shoulders. "Callaway Wilde, I want you, and I want you to know me," he began. "It's not going to be easy, and my world is not always going to be a pretty, safe world. I can't promise you that you won't ever be afraid, or even that I'll always be there."

"I know," I said to him, "I know."

Evan took the ring from the box and got down on one knee. He took my left hand and kissed the back of it before he looked up at me. "How would it feel to you to be my wife?" He held the ring poised just above my finger.

I was speechless. How did I feel? Great, scared, terrified, unworthy, damaged, teenaged, joyous, unattractive, utterly overwhelmed.

But altogether, it felt right, and there was only one answer.

"Perfect," I said. "It feels perfect."

Up Close and Personal with the Author

IF YOU COULD BE ANY ANIMAL YOU WANTED TO, WHAT WOULD IT BE?

Are you kidding?

LETHAL IS THE SECOND BOOK IN THE CALLAWAY WILDE SERIES, FOLLOWING *LOADED.* WAS IT HARD TO WRITE A SECOND NOVEL WITH THE SAME CHARACTERS?

No. It was easier. I know them better and as I write I'm constantly surprised by how the characters develop and what they say. I also had an entirely new set of characters that I loved meeting and developing.

THE RELATIONSHIP WITH EVAN AND CALLAWAY WAS FILLED WITH SEXUAL TENSION IN THE FIRST NOVEL, *LOADED.* HOW CAN YOU SUSTAIN THAT IN *LETHAL?*

Easy, with two sexually charged people like Evan and Callaway, it's tough to keep them off of each other! Also, as in any "real" relationship, there's a new set of challenges and problems for each stage of getting to know each other. And for Callaway and her history of being a loner, becoming truly intimate with anyone is a much more highly charged situation than getting them to sleep with her. She's always wanting what she can't have. In this case, a relationship *and* her total independence.

DO YOUR CHARACTERS COME FROM PEOPLE YOU KNOW?

Yes and no. I can't use people I know directly because it's too limiting. For instance, if I am thinking of a girlfriend I have as being, say, Ginny, I might come to a place where I need Ginny to have a certain response and I would think, "My girlfriend would never say that!" So what I prefer to do is make compilations of people I know. Ginny, for example, is a combination of two women I know. Both of them have quick wits, tons of energy, and are terrific friends, but by combining them, it frees me up to create a unique character who has morphed into something independent of her 'parents.'

YOU WRITE ABOUT LOCATIONS IN LOS ANGELES WHERE YOU LIVE. ARE THEY REAL PLACES?

Yes and no. Like the characters, I find it restricting to have to adhere to actual fact. So I make the places in general factual, i.e. Little Tokyo and Westwood, but I create false addresses, homes, restaurants, etc., within them. This makes it much easier for me to customize my action and atmosphere. Plus, in order to create Callaway's world of incredible wealth, I wanted it to be the way she would like it, not the way it is.

I READ THAT YOU ARE ALSO AN ACTRESS. ARE YOU DOING ANYTHING NOW?

As I write this, I'm just starting to direct Shakespeare's *Twelfth Night* at the Knightsbridge Theater in L.A. I won't be acting in this one, I've played Viola before and I love the play, it's so funny. By the time the book comes out the run will be over and I will probably be acting in something else at the same theater over the summer. I'm hoping to do Noel Coward's *Fallen Angels*. But I've given up acting in film in television for the most part because I much prefer writing in my comfortable home to living in crappy hotel rooms and "hamster cage" trailers on sets. Acting looks glamorous, but it's not the happiest of lifestyles.

WHICH DO YOU PREFER–ACTING OR WRITING?

Writing! I always have. But it can be lonely, I know now why lots of writers have "writer's groups," you need company! Which is why theater is the perfect antidote. I get to work with a fabulously talented group of people to make something better together than we could ever do alone. Don't get me wrong, there's nothing like being on stage and having the audience all breathing together, or laughing, or crying, it's a wonderful feeling! But writing is a much more complete sense of creative control, not a group effort.

IS IT TOUGH BEING A DIVORCED MOM WITH TWO KIDS AND TWO CAREERS?

The only thing that's tough is being away from my children for part of the week. On the other hand it allows me to get so much more done on those days that I can devote myself to my kids when they are with me. I'm fortunate to have a terrific relationship with a man who shares it all with me, and part of that is getting me through the bumpy bits. When I'm in rehearsal for a show, it gets a little nuts, especially during "hell week" which is the week before opening when we do all the technical lighting and stage building set-up for the play. It can be exhausting. I'm always having to remind myself that I have exactly the same number of hours in the day as Einstein, Michelangelo, and every other amazingly productive human had. Of course, lots of them weren't mothers with school library detail.

WILL THERE BE A THIRD CALLAWAY WILDE NOVEL?

Oh yes! I'm really excited about this next book. Something happens in the beginning that really hits Callaway where she lives and I don't want to give it away, but I'm psyched!

ONE LAST QUESTION?

Okay.

IF YOU COULD BE ANY ANIMAL YOU WANTED, WHAT WOULD IT BE?

A flying squirrel.

WHY?

Because just by doing what comes naturally to them, they amaze everyone. Wouldn't that be nice?

They're sexy, smart, and strong . . .

they're the

NAUGHTY GIRLS OF DOWNTOWN *PRESS!*

Turn the page for excerpts of the other Naughty Girls of Downtown Press

THE GIVENCHY CODE

Julie Kenner

DIRTY LITTLE SECRETS

Julie Leto

AWAKEN ME DARKLY

Gena Showalter

The Givenchy Code

JULIE KENNER

I felt fine, and I couldn't quite get my head around the idea that I'd been poisoned and had less than twenty-four hours to find the antidote. If this were a movie—or even an episode of *24*—I'd find the antidote in the last possible second, then I'd turn around and kick the shit out of the bad guy.

Would be nice, but I wasn't going to bank on it.

I shoved Kiefer out of my mind and focused instead on the man who was with me. The man who'd promised to help get me through this. I believed him, too, and already I'd come to rely on his strength, to anticipate his thoughts and suggestions. I'd only known him for a few hours, but my life was running in fast forward now, and Stryker was running right alongside me.

At the moment, though, he wasn't running anywhere. Instead, he'd parked himself back at the computer, and now he pulled up Google and typed in a search.

>>>*New York Prestige Park*<<<

About a million hits came up, all of them raving about the *prestigious* apartments/offices/restaurants on *Park* Avenue. So much for an easy answer.

We were running out of ideas. If we couldn't figure out Prestige Park, we couldn't find the next clue. And if we couldn't find the next clue, I was dead.

"Let me try," I said. I didn't care if there were two thousand pages of hits. We were going to look at every single one of them.

"Hold on," he said, then typed in a new search.

>>>*"New York" "Prestige Park"*<<<

He hit Enter, and *bingo.* A car park. "Well, hello," Stryker said. And I actually almost smiled.

We'd decided to stay in my apartment until we figured out the clue, since moving to some other location would take too much time. But we'd also decided to be quiet, just in case there were other eyes and ears watching us. I'd changed out of Todd's clothes and pulled on my Miss Sixty jeans and a Goretti tank top I'd scored off eBay.

Beside me, Stryker had his cell phone open and was dialing information. "Turn up the radio," he said.

I rushed to the stereo and complied, turning the volume higher and higher until he finally nodded, satisfied. How he'd hear his conversation, I didn't know. Didn't care, either, so long as he got it done. I knew he would, too. The man had it together, that was for sure. He'd told me that his earlier phone call was to a computer geek friend to try and figure out who posted that Web message. Nice to know he was on top of that. And now he'd solved the Prestige Park mystery. And the best part? He was on my side.

Behind me, Stryker muttered into his phone, then snapped it shut. He leaned onto the table, brushing my shoulder as he picked up the pen I'd been using earlier. He scribbled a note, then inched it toward me. *Prestige Car Park—downtown & Bronx.*

"Looks like we're going downtown," he said.

I nodded, trying to remember if the online version of the game extended to the boroughs. I didn't think it did. A plus for me, since, like so many Manhattanites, I was entirely clueless about life outside the island.

He snapped the screen shut on Jenn's laptop, then slid it into the case, balling the cords up and shoving them in, too. I thought about protesting—it was Jenn's computer, after all—but I didn't. Jenn would understand, and we might need the thing. Finally, he grabbed the original message and my notes interpreting it. "Let's go."

I stood up, then took the papers from him. I dumped

them and my pocketbook-sized purse into a tote bag that I regularly schlepped to class with me. "Are we coming back?"

"Not if I can help it."

I nodded, shifting my weight on the balls of my feet, now snugly encased in my Prada sneakers as I stalled in the doorway. What can I say? It was hard to leave. I hated the idea of abandoning all my shoes. Not to mention my handbags, clothes, photo albums, books, and favorite CDs.

"I'll buy you a change of underwear," Stryker said, since my thoughts were apparently transparent. "But we need to get moving. We've already wasted enough time, and—"

"Fine. You're right. Let's go." I told myself that this wasn't good-bye forever—just until we'd won the game.

I tugged the door closed and locked it, my worldly possessions now measured by the width and breadth of the Kate Spade tote I'd snagged last fall in a seventy-five-percent-off sale. "I'll be back soon," I said to the door. I hoped I was telling the truth.

Dirty Little Secrets

JULIE LETO

"I remember when you used to stroke me like that."

Marisela Morales punctuated her pickup line by blowing on the back of Francisco Vega's neck. She watched the soft downy strands on his nape spike and knew her luck had finally turned around.

His fingers, visible as she glanced over his shoulder, drew streaks through the condensation on his beer bottle. Up and down. Slow and straight. Lazy, but precise. He toyed with his *cerveza* the same way he'd once made love to her, and for a split second, a trickle of moist heat curled intimately between Marisela's thighs. For the moment, the part of her Frankie used to oh-so-easily manipulate was safe, encased beneath silky panties and skin-tight, hip-hugging jeans.

Tonight, she'd have him—but on her terms. The hunter had found her prey. Now, she just had to bring him in.

"I don't remember taking time for slow strokes when you and me got busy, *niña.*"

Marisela sighed, teasing his neck with her hot breath one more time before she slid onto the bar stool next to his. She'd been trying to track the man down for nearly a week. Who knew Frankie would turn up at an old haunt? Since they'd parted ways, Club Electric, a white box on the outside, hot joint on the inside, had changed names, hands, and clientele a good dozen times. But a few things remained constant—the music, the raw atmosphere—and the availability of men like Frankie, who defined the word *caliente.*

Like the song said: *Hot, hot, hot.*

"We were young then," Marisela admitted with a shrug, loosening the holster strap that cradled the cherished 9mm Taurus Millennium she wore beneath her slick leather jacket. "Now, I'm all grown up."

Marisela wiggled her crimson fingernails at Theresa, the owner of the club. The way the older woman's face lit up, Marisela figured she was going to get more than a drink. *Damn.* Marisela loved Theresa as if she were her aunt, but now wasn't the time for . . .

"Oh, Marisela! *Mija,* how can I thank you for what you did?"

The sentiment was as loud as it was sincere. So she'd done

a nice thing for Theresa. The world didn't have to know. Good deeds could ruin her reputation.

And a simple thank-you wasn't enough for Theresa. She stepped up onto the shelf on the other side of the bar and practically launched herself into Marisela's arms. Rolling her eyes at Frankie, Marisela gave the owner a genuine squeeze. She deserved as much. She was a good listener, kept great secrets, and mixed the best *Cuba Libre* in town.

"De nada, Theresa," Marisela said, gently disentangling herself. She appreciated the woman's gratitude, but she had work to do.

"Anything for you. Anytime. For you, drinks are on the house from now on, okay? You and . . . your friend."

Even as she tried to be the courteous hostess, Theresa's voice faltered when her eyes met Frankie's. Marisela's ex hadn't been in the neighborhood for years. And in that time, he'd aged. His skin, naturally dark, now sported a rough texture, complete with a scar that traced just below his bottom lip. His jaw seemed sharper and his once perfect nose now shifted slightly to the right—likely the result of an untreated break. Even if he hadn't matured from a devilish boy to a clearly dangerous man, he likely wouldn't be recognized by anyone but Marisela and a few others who'd once known him well—the very "others" Marisela had made sure wouldn't come into Club Electric again, on Theresa's behalf.

"I never say no to free booze," Marisela answered. *"Gracias,* Theresa."

Theresa blew Marisela a kiss, patted her cheek, then

moved aside to work on her drink. To most people, a *Cuba Libre* was just rum and Coke with lime. To Marisela, it was a taste of heaven.

"What did you do for her?" Frankie asked, his voice even, as if he wasn't really curious.

Marisela knew better. She slid her arms on the bar, arching her back, working out the kinks in her spine while giving Frankie an unhampered view of her breasts. She didn't want him to waste his curiosity on what she'd done for Theresa; she wanted to pique his interest another way.

"Last week, *las Reinas* chose this bar as their new hangout. Not quite the clientele Theresa has in mind. Gangs aren't exactly good for business. I politely asked them to pick someplace else."

"Politely?" Frankie asked, his dark eyebrows bowed over his hypnotic eyes. "Last I remember, *las Reinas* didn't respond well to polite."

Marisela shrugged. She'd earned a great deal of respect from her former gang by choosing to bleed out. She'd used every fighting skill she'd ever learned, every survival instinct she'd ever experienced, to escape a lifelong bond to the gang. But she'd survived. Barely.

"They've learned some manners while you've been gone. Lots of things have changed. Like," she said, snagging his beer around the neck and taking a sip, "I don't settle for fast and furious no more."

Awaken Me Darkly

GENA SHOWALTER

First rule of fighting: Stay calm.

Second rule: Never let your emotions overtake you.

I'd broken both rules the moment I began following him.

Kyrin swept out of my way, and I flew past him. The storm had died, but the sun hid behind angry gray clouds, offering hazy visibility. Because of the sheen of ice at my feet, I had trouble stopping and turning.

Definitely not optimal conditions; however, I wouldn't back down.

"You do not want to fight me, Mia."

I whipped around. "Wanna bet on that too?" I sprang forward again, intending to kick out my leg and knock him flat this time, but he reached me first. He grappled me to the ground, pinned my shoulders to the ice, and imprisoned me with his body. Cold at my back, pure heat on top. Neither was acceptable to me.

"Still want to fight?" he asked.

"Fuck yes." I quickly landed a blow to his groin. Yeah, I intended to fight dirty. He doubled over, and I shot to my feet, slipped, then steadied.

Using his prone position to my advantage, I was able to land a blow to his left side and knock the deoxygenated air from his lung. He grunted in pain and sudden breathlessness.

I darted to his right and gave a booted strike. This time, he grabbed my ankle and toppled me to the ground. I lost my satisfaction, felt a moment of desperation. We struggled there, rolling on top of each other, fighting for dominance.

Physically, he had me at a disadvantage, and we both knew it. He could have attempted to smother me, but he didn't.

"It doesn't have to be this way," he panted.

Think, Mia, think.

I still had full use of my legs, and I made total use of them. I gave a scissor-lock squeeze around his midsection, forcing him to release my arms and focus on my legs. That's all I needed. With a four-finger jab to his trachea, his air supply was momentarily cut off in a whoosh, giving me the perfect opportunity to spring free.

My old combat instructor would have been proud.

I took stock of my options. I had to render him unconscious if I hoped to win. He'd defeat me, otherwise. I would have to be merciless, but stop short of killing him. I needed his help, after all. His blood. I didn't want to spill a single drop on this cold, hard ice.

"Concede, damn you," I growled, circling him like a tigress locked on her prey.

"You first," he said, still on his knees.

"I am almost done playing with you," he said.

"Play with this." I launched a flying spin punt into his side.

Quicker than I could blink, he advanced on me. He used his weight to push into me, stumbling me backward. When my body came into contact with his, the strength hidden beneath his clothing jolted me. He was made of solid muscle, easily outweighing me by a hundred pounds, but he didn't once use the power hidden in his fists to strike me down. Why? I wondered, even as I punched him hard in the nose. His head jerked to the side; he made no move to counter. Why didn't he return attack? Why did he go out of his way *not* to hurt me?

I circled him, but he surprised me by grabbing my jacket and tugging. The ice at my feet aided him. Suddenly off balance, I tumbled into him, keeping a viselike grip. His warm breath washed over my face as he leaned close.

"Now you will concede this victory to me," he ground out low in his throat.

"When you haven't hit me once?" I said, a cocky edge to

my tone. I'd fought enough opponents to know Kyrin had had plenty of opportunities, but I wasn't going to admit *that* aloud.

His eyes darkened, revealing a hint of wickedness, and he leaned down until our lips brushed once, twice. Soft kisses, languid kisses. Innocent kisses.

Be the Next Downtown Girl
Contest Rules

NO PURCHASE NECESSARY TO ENTER.

1) ENTRY REQUIREMENTS:

Register to enter the contest on www.simonsaysthespot.com. Enter by submitting your story as specified below.

2) CONTEST ELIGIBILITY:

This contest is open to nonprofessional writers who are legal residents of the United States and Canada (excluding Quebec) over the age of 18 as of December 7, 2004. Entrant must not have published any more than two short stories on a professional basis or in paid professional venues. Employees or relatives of employees living in the same household) of Simon & Schuster, VIACOM, or any of their affiliates are not eligible. This contest is void in Puerto Rico, Quebec, and wherever prohibited or restricted by law.

3) FORMAT:

Entries must not be more than 7,500 words long and must not have been previously published. Entries must be typed or printed by word processor, double spaced, on one side of noncorrasable paper. Do not justify right-side margins. Along with a cover letter, the author's name, address, email address, and phone number must appear on the first page of the entry. The author's name, the story title, and the page number should appear on every page. Electronic submissions will be accepted and must be sent to downtowngirl@simonandschuster.com. All electronic submissions must be sent as an attachment in a Microsoft Word document. All entries must be original and the sole work of the Entrant and the sole property of the Entrant.

All submissions must be in English. Entries are void if they are in whole or in part illegible, incomplete, or damaged or if they do not conform to any of the requirements specified herein. Sponsor reserves the right, in its absolute and sole discretion, to reject any entries for any reason, including but not limited to based on sexual content, vulgarity, and/or promotion of violence.

4) ADDRESS:

Entries submitted by mail must be postmarked by July 31, 2005 and sent to:

Be The Next Downtown Girl
Author Search

Downtown Press Editorial Department
Pocket Books
1230 Sixth Avenue, 13th floor
New York, NY 10020

Or Emailed By July 31, 2005
at 11:59 PM EST as a
Microsoft Word document to:

downtowngirl@simonandschuster.com

Each entry may be submitted only once. Please retain a copy of your submission. You may submit more than one story, but each submission must be mailed or emailed, as applicable, separately. Entries must be received by July 31, 2005. Not responsible for lost, late, stolen, illegible, mutilated, postage due, garbled, or misdirected mail/entries.

5) PRIZES:

One Grand Prize winner will receive:

Simon & Schuster's Downtown Press Publishing Contract for Publication of Winning Entry in a future Downtown Press Anthology, Five Hundred U.S. Dollars ($500.00), and

Downtown Press Library
(20 books valued at $260.00)

Grand Prize winner must sign the Publishing contract which contains additional terms and conditions in order to be published in the anthology.

Ten Second Prize winners will receive:

A Downtown Press Collection
(10 books valued at $130.00)

No contestant can win more than one prize.

6) STORY THEME

We are not restricting stories to any specific topic, however they should embody what all of our Downtown Press authors encompass—they should be smart, savvy, sexy stories that any Downtown Girl can relate to. We all know what uptown girls are like, but girls of the new millennium prefer the Downtown Scene. That's where it happens. The music, the shopping, the sex, the dating, the heartbreak, the family squabbles, the marriage, and the divorce. You name it. Downtown Girls have done it. Twice. We encourage you to register for the contest at www.simonsaysthespot.com in order to receive our monthly emails and updates from our authors and read about our titles on www.downtownpress.com to give you a better idea of what types of books we publish.

7) JUDGING:

Submissions will be judged on the equally weighted criteria of (a) basis of writing ability and (b) the originality of the story (which can be set in any time frame or location). Judging will take place on or about October 1, 2005. The judges will include a freelance editor, the editor of the future Anthology, and 5 employees of Sponsor. The decisions of the judges shall be final.

8) NOTIFICATION:

The winners will be notified by mail or phone on or about October 1, 2005. The Grand Prize Winner must sign the publishing contract in order to be awarded the prize. All federal, local, and state taxes are the responsibility of the winner. A list of the winners will be available after October 20, 2005 on:

http://www.downtownpress.com

http://www.simonsaysthespot.com

The winners' list can also be obtained by sending a stamped self-addressed envelope to:

Be The Next Downtown Girl
Author Search
Downtown Press Editorial Department
Pocket Books
1230 Sixth Avenue, 13th floor
New York, NY 10020

9) PUBLICITY:

Each Winner grants to Sponsor the right to use his or her name, likeness, and entry for any advertising, promotion, and publicity purposes without further compensation to or permission from such winner, except where prohibited by law.

10) INTERNET:

If for any reason this Contest is not capable of running as planned due to an infection by a computer virus, bugs, tampering, unauthorized intervention, fraud, technical failures, or any other causes beyond the control of the Sponsor which corrupt or affect the administration, security, fairness, integrity, or proper conduct of this Contest, the Sponsor reserves the right in its sole discretion, to disqualify any individual who tampers with the entry process, and to cancel, terminate, modify, or suspend the Contest. The Sponsor assumes no responsibility for any error, omission, interruption, deletion, defect, delay in operation or transmission, communications line failure, theft or destruction or unauthorized access to, or alteration of, entries. The Sponsor is not responsible for any problems or technical malfunctions of any telephone network or telephone lines, computer on-line systems, servers, or providers, computer equipment, software, failure of any email or entry to be received by the Sponsor due to technical problems, human error or traffic congestion on the Internet or at any website, or any combination thereof, including any injury or damage to participant's or any other person's computer relating to or resulting from participating in this Contest or downloading any materials in this Contest. CAUTION: ANY ATTEMPT TO DELIBERATELY DAMAGE ANY WEBSITE OR UNDERMINE THE LEGITIMATE OPERATION OF THE CONTEST IS A VIOLATION OF CRIMINAL AND CIVIL LAWS AND SHOULD SUCH AN ATTEMPT BE MADE, THE SPONSOR RESERVES THE RIGHT TO SEEK DAMAGES OR OTHER REMEDIES FROM ANY SUCH PERSON(S) RESPONSIBLE FOR THE ATTEMPT TO THE FULLEST EXTENT PERMITTED BY LAW. In the event of a dispute as to the identity or eligibility of a winner based on an email address, the winning entry will be declared made by the "Authorized Account Holder" of the email address submitted at time of entry. "Authorized Account Holder" is defined as the natural person 18 years of age or older who is assigned to an email address by an Internet access provider, online service provider, or other organization (e.g., business, education institution, etc.) that is responsible for assigning email addresses for the domain associated with the submitted email address. Use of automated devices are not valid for entry.

11) LEGAL Information:

All submissions become sole property of Sponsor and will not be acknowledged or returned. By submitting an entry, all entrants grant Sponsor the absolute and unconditional right and authority to copy, edit, publish, promote, broadcast, or otherwise use, in whole or in part, their entries, in perpetuity, in any manner without further permission, notice or compensation. Entries that contain copyrighted material must include a release from the copyright holder. Prizes are nontransferable. No substitutions or cash redemptions, except by Sponsor in the event of prize unavailability. Sponsor reserves the right at its sole discretion to not publish the winning entry for any reason whatsoever.

In the event that there is an insufficient number of entries received that meet the minimum standards determined by the judges, all prizes will not be awarded. Void in Quebec, Puerto Rico, and wherever prohibited or restricted by law. Winners will be required to complete and return an affidavit of eligibility and a liability/publicity release, within 15 days of winning notification, or an alternate winner will be selected. In the event any winner is considered a minor in his/her state of residence, such winner's parent/legal guardian will be required to sign and return all necessary paperwork.

By entering, entrants release the judges and Sponsor, and its parent company, subsidiaries, affiliates, divisions, advertising, production, and promotion agencies from any and all liability for any loss, harm, damages, costs, or expenses, including without limitation property damages, personal injury, and/or death arising out of participation in this contest, the acceptance, possession, use or misuse of any prize, claims based on publicity rights, defamation or invasion of privacy, merchandise delivery, or the violation of any intellectual property rights, including but not limited to copyright infringement and/or trademark infringement.

Sponsor:
Pocket Books,
an imprint of Simon & Schuster, Inc.
1230 Avenue of the Americas,
New York, NY 10020

Printed in the United States
138529LV00001B/5/P